BLACK SEA AFFAIR

Books by Don Brown

The Navy Justice Series
Treason
Hostage
Defiance

DON BROWN

BLACK SEA AFFAIR

ZONDERVAN.com/
AUTHORTRACKER
follow your favorite authors

Black Sea Affair
Copyright © 2008 by Don Brown

Requests for information should be addressed to:

Zondervan, *Grand Rapids, Michigan 49530*

Library of Congress Cataloging-in-Publication Data

Brown, Don, 1960 –
    The Black Sea affair / Don Brown.
       p. cm.
    Includes bibliographical references and index [if applicable].
    ISBN 978-0-310-27214-4
       1. United States, Navy — Fiction. 2. Russia (Federation). Voenno-Morskoi Flot — Fiction.
3. Terrorists — Fiction. 4. Black Sea — Fiction. 5. Submarines (Ships) — Fiction. 6. Submarine
disasters — Fiction. I. Title.
PS3602.R6947B57 2008
813'.6 — dc220   2007049128

Interior design by Michelle Espinoza

Printed in the United States of America

08 09 10 11 12 • 23 22 21 20 19 18 17 16 15 14 13 12 11 10 9 8 7 6 5 4 3 2 1

This novel is dedicated
to the submarine force of the United States Navy
"Run silent. Run deep."

ACKNOWLEDGMENTS

Special thanks to United States Army veteran Jack Miller of La Mesa, California, and United States Air Force veteran Keith Kinlaw of Charlotte, North Carolina, for their military technical assistance.

And special thanks to Ms. Julie Haack Kral of Charlotte, North Carolina, and United States Army veteran Jack Miller of La Mesa, California, for their superb editorial assistance.

"Any man who may be asked in this century what he did to make his life worthwhile, can respond with a good deal of pride and satisfaction: 'I served in the United States Navy.'"

President John F. Kennedy
Speech to the new plebe class
United States Naval Academy
August 1, 1963

PROLOGUE

Outside the village of Tolstoy-Yurt
The Russian Republic of Chechnya

March 2005

The Russian jeep kicked up a hazy cloud of dust in the afternoon sun, bumping its way along the pothole-riddled gravel road. The bunkered compound at the end of the road, fortified by a high wall of brown sandbags, was classified as top secret, for the survival of the bunker's occupant was crucial to the future of the nation.

And yes, Chechnya was a nation. She had lived for generations, but in reality, had yet to be born. Chechnya would some day be free of the brutal Russian soldiers and their pillaging, rape, and murder. Chechnya would deal a lethal blow to the Russians and become an independent Islamic republic.

This was her manifest destiny.

Even so, Salman Dudayev wondered why he had been summoned here.

True, the highest officials in the liberation movement had sanctioned his work. But he had yet to come face-to-face with leaders of that movement, and certainly not with the great man who had requested his presence.

Was this a trap?

Would he step through the fortified bunker and find himself staring down the gun barrels of Russian FSB special agents?

Two armed guards standing at the entrance of the bunker motioned him forward. He ducked his head, stepping through a dark, open hole and down a dimly lit stairway.

A familiar voice boomed through the dark. "The work that you are doing to bring about the liberation of our country may never be appreciated by the masses, but I thank you from the bottom of my heart."

Squinting in the dim light cast by the gas lantern, Salman looked in the direction of the voice, struggling to study the face of the man who would at last bring freedom to his people.

"It is not the ambition of the scientist to revel in glory, Mr. President —"

"Please." President Maskhadov raised his hand, interrupting him midstream.

In the soft flicker of the candles, the president's grey hair and trim salt-and-pepper beard accentuated his black, piercing eyes.

"Call me Alsan Aliyevich," the president said, speaking as though he had known Salman all his life. "We are brothers in a holy cause, a holy cause for freedom for Chechnya. This makes us friends. Please."

Salman was taken aback. This was a man he revered. This was a man who had served as an officer in the Red Army, and then, after the fall of the old Soviet Union, had become the military leader of his own people.

He inhaled deeply, then exhaled, measuring his words. "Yes, as I was saying" — he took another deep breath and uttered the name — "Alsan Aliyevich. It is not the ambition of the scientist to revel in glory, but to unlock the secrets of the universe to bring about better conditions for all mankind."

"It appears that you were well trained in America."

"Yes. The Massachusetts Institute of Technology is the world's finest scientific research and training institution."

"So tell me, Salman, how is the project coming?"

"My team is gathering the materials we need now, sir. We are still in search of fuel, but —"

President Maskhadov interrupted. "We need this sooner rather than later, you know."

"Yes, I am aware of the urgency."

"They strangle us like an anaconda." He lit a cigarette, inhaled, and blew a puff of smoke. "From all around. Dagestan. Stavropol. North Ossetia-Alania. Ingushetiya."

Another draw from the cigarette. A reflective look on the president's face.

"They will strangle us if we do not act. We must not fail." The president's black eyes pierced Salman. "Do you understand me?"

"Yes, Mr. President."

"You are our best and our brightest. You were selected to study in America because of your exemplary academic record. We depend upon you now, Salman. Is there any ambiguity in what I am asking you to do?"

"None, Mr. President."

"You know they are plotting to kill me. Do you not?"

"I have heard rumors."

"Then move with haste, my friend."

"You have my word, sir." Salman sensed that he was being dismissed. He started to turn when the president touched his shoulder.

"Wait, Salman."

"Yes, sir?"

"I know about your family."

The two words — *your family* — stung like scorpions. Two years had passed, and still he struggled to erase the memories of the massacre, to put the loss of his wife and two children out of his mind.

President Maskhadov's eyes were compassionate. "I am so sorry for your loss."

"Thank you, sir."

"I pray the comfort of your soul, and that your work shall be a medium of vengeance to those infidels responsible for these barbaric crimes."

Salman let the great man's words sink in. "The memory of this barbarism drives my soul, Mr. President. I shall not let you down, and if necessary, I am prepared to enter martyrdom for Chechnya."

President Maskhadov smiled. "Go. Do your duty in haste. For your country, and for Allah."

A guard led him back up the steps, back into the light. He climbed into the jeep. The driver cranked the engine.

They had made it one hundred yards down the road when the explosion rocked the earth from the rear.

The guard hit the brakes. Salman looked over his shoulder. The president's bunker spewed orange flames and black smoke. Armed men in black uniforms swarmed the area.

"FSB!" the driver shouted. He hit the accelerator, kicking up a cloud of rocks and dust, leaving the smoke and fire in the fading distance.

CHAPTER 1

Several years later
Aircraft carrier
The Pacific Ocean

The admiral took a long draw from his cigarette as he scanned the horizon. The ships under his command consisted of an aircraft carrier, a heavy cruiser, and two destroyers. The small armada plowed through rolling blue-green seas, due east into the rising sun. Already steaming in battle formation, the ships' crews stood ready to launch their aircraft.

Based on intelligence being fed into their combat-information center on board the flagship, they had not been spotted yet.

Good. They were about to execute the most devastating attack by a naval force in all human history. Thousands in San Diego would die in the initial nuclear fireballs. Millions more would suffer and eventually die from radioactive fallout. Coming from the sea, this attack would take them all by surprise. A surprise that would never be forgotten.

The commander dropped his binoculars and considered his situation. At the moment, at least, the target was vulnerable and unsuspecting.

A squadron of attacking aircraft could be easily tracked by an opponent's radar long before approaching a nation's coastline, raising an alert. It was not so with ships coming from the sea. Even at the beginning of the twenty-first century, navies were often invisible to an enemy.

The Coast Guard used a radio-based system to follow ships from twelve to twenty miles out. Twelve nautical miles was only about one hour of traveling time. Thus, the Coast Guard wouldn't be able to track an enemy ship until it was too close to respond to the threat.

For all its military strength, America was unprepared for what was about to happen.

Even if the Coast Guard did have satellite technology, trying to use a satellite to spot any given ship on the world's vast oceans was the equivalent of looking for a particular spec in the sand on a beach. The satellite would have to be in the right place at the right time, and the ship would have to sail directly under its cameras. In other words, a satellite would have to be lucky.

Plus, if there were some sort of satellite system up there somewhere, it was unlikely it would spot them. The admiral's warships had gone silent from the beginning of this top-secret voyage. Celestial navigation using the compass, the stars, the charts, and the sun had brought them to the precipice of history. No radio contact was allowed between ships. Only signal lights between ships were used for communication. And there was no active sonar.

There was nothing to alert the target or anyone else of their presence.

His planes would take off, skim the water to avoid radar, and launch their missiles from far offshore. Then, as hundreds of thousands writhed in agony from the devastating fireballs that their missiles would deliver, the planes would return to the carrier for a safe landing.

The admiral checked his watch.

Two hours to launch.

Two hours to history.

The USS Chicago
The Pacific Ocean

Steady as she goes," the captain said. "Continue to maintain silence."

"Steady as she goes, aye, Captain."

The American sub commander flipped a switch overhead, opening the intercom with his sonar room.

"Sonar. Conn. Anything up there?"

"No, Captain. Still nothing."

"Let me know the first time even a blowfish snorts on that sonar. Is that clear?"

"Aye, Captain."

The skipper's lips touched his coffee. The jet-black brew had grown lukewarm and tasted like battery acid.

Fine.

Black, battery-acid coffee. It was the unofficial nonalcoholic brew of the Navy's submarine force. And the ability to drink it without flinching was part of a submariner's rite of passage.

It trickled down his esophagus, stinging a bit, igniting another well-needed caffeine jolt. *Good stuff.* He listened for any unusual noises that would signify the presence of the enemy.

Silence.

Dead air.

These were the sounds of a vast ocean whose underwater spaces were far too grand for the human mind ever to grasp.

Silence.

It was a submariner's best friend.

Hiding under the cover of it, the submariner could attack his prey, and then slip away into the dark waters of the deep before an enemy could drop explosives on him that would crush his skull.

And now, at this moment, the enemy was also silent. One last gulp and his white coffee mug—sporting the inscription "C.O." just over the official emblem of the USS *Chicago* and just under the name *Miranda*—was now empty.

The commander refilled his cup. He gazed up at the steel-grate ceiling of the control room. It was as if he could see through all the steel, through the hundreds of feet of dark water, and spot what may be approaching on the surface.

His sixth sense had taken over beyond the limitations of his eyesight.

They were up there.

Somewhere.

The enemy.

The commander knew it. He knew it from the gut feeling in the stomach. The same feeling he got when he'd hunted whitetail deer back on a friend's ranch in Texas all those years ago. The pit of his stomach twisted whenever a buck moved within firing range. His gut was twisting again.

The intercom in the control room crackled static, followed by the excited voice of the ship's sonar officer booming through it to every corner of the submarine.

"Conn! Sonar! We've got multiple contacts! Multiple ships! Bearing course zero-nine-zero degrees! Sir! Range ... Five thousand yards! Designate contact one Vikrant class carrier with four support ships! Looks like an enemy task force! They're headed this way!"

"I knew it!" the commander said. "Diving officer! Take us to periscope depth."

"Aye, Captain! Making my depth zero-six-zero feet now, sir!"

The bulb nose of the *Los Angeles*–class submarine tilted upward. She began rising through the ocean depths to a targeted depth of sixty feet below the surface. There, her captain would deploy his periscope for a better look at whatever—or whomever—was out there.

Aircraft carrier
The Pacific Ocean

This admiral would not make the mistake that Japanese Admiral Yamamoto made nearly a century ago in Hawaii. Yamamoto set out to smash the American aircraft carriers at Pearl Harbor. He destroyed America's battleships that fateful Sunday morning, but all three American aircraft carriers were out to sea, well beyond the range of the shallow-draft torpedoes of his Japanese Zeros.

A major intelligence snafu had cost Japan the war.

This time, real-time intelligence was better. Three of America's mightiest carriers, USS *Ronald Reagan*, USS *Nimitz*, and USS *John C. Stennis*—half the Pacific carrier fleet—were moored at this very moment like sitting ducks at San Diego's Coronado Naval Air Station, just a quarter mile across the sparkling waters of San Diego Bay and the bustling population of America's seventh largest city.

This powerful armada would strike with nuclear-tipped missiles launched from its planes over a hundred miles offshore.

They would fly in low over the water, the missiles, under radar, barely skimming the tops of the waves on their approach. Reaching the airspace just off Point Loma, their internal guidance system would turn them on a course directly into the heart of San Diego Bay. Seconds later, they would detonate, two hundred yards before reaching the Coronado Bay Bridge.

A nuclear fireball would vaporize the American carriers, then engulf the glistening high rises on Harbor Drive and Broadway. Forty thousand souls attending the Padres-Giants game at nearby PETCO Park would vanish in the air, as the atomic blast wave crumbled fragile buildings in nearby Tijuana, Mexico. Nuclear flashes brighter than the sun would blind onlookers in Los Angeles and points north.

Within hours, northbound Interstate 5 would be jammed with millions of cars driven by panic-stricken Southern Californians, seeking refuge from the nuclear fallout in San Francisco, Portland, and Seattle, escaping the giant mushroom cloud rising in their rearview mirrors over what was left of San Diego.

In the mad scramble, his nation's intelligence operatives would telephone American media outlets, claiming credit for the attack in the name of Islamic fundamentalism. They would claim that nuclear bombs had exploded inside an eighteen-wheeler tractor-trailer truck parked down by the Broadway pier on San Diego's waterfront.

In fact, such a truck had been leased and at this moment parked just for the occasion. Photographs had been taken of it, as recently as yesterday, with the clipper-ship-turned-museum *Star of India* in the background. These photos would be leaked to the international media in conjunction with the cover story. The tractor-trailer, of course, was a ruse. But soon, its image would become the most widely disseminated photograph in the history of the twenty-first century.

Neither the admiral nor his nation were Islamic. But in the horrified chaos of it all, America would fall for it. She would blame the attack on Islamic suicide bombers.

America would never know what hit her.

Nor by whom.

The USS Chicago
The Pacific Ocean

We have periscope depth, Captain," the chief of the boat said.

"Up scope! Now!" the skipper ordered.

Humming and clicking echoed down the stainless steel cylinder hanging in the middle of the control room. The American sub commander grabbed the training handles of the periscope and brought his eyes up to the viewfinder. His jaw tightened at the sight.

One American warship, and only one, had by happenchance discovered the approaching presence of an enemy armada. One U.S. naval vessel stood between the enemy task force and the west coast of the United States of America. She was the nuclear-powered submarine, the USS *Chicago*. Her commander was Pete Miranda, United States Navy, considered to be one of the more aggressive sub captains in the Navy.

Miranda considered his predicament.

He could float a communications buoy and report the armada's presence to the rest of the fleet. But that could alert the enemy that *Chicago* was lurking in the area. Plus, even if he got the signal off, no other ships or planes were close enough to intercept the armada before it was in effective striking distance of the coastline.

Pete was under standing orders to take action against this enemy if its ships and warplanes were observed "engaging in maneuvers that appeared hostile to the West Coast of the United States of America"—General Order 009-001. He was was now faced with the sole responsibility of deciding whether to apply it. If he attacked this armada, he would be the first American commander to execute 009-001.

But what if he was wrong?

His predicament shot through his mind like lightning flashing from east to west.

Down scope! Emergency deep! Six-zero-zero feet! Take her down! Now!"

At Pete's command, the *Chicago* dropped through the water like a roller coaster car on Space Mountain. Clipboards, pencils, anything not bolted down was slung across the control room like the steel orb in a pinball machine.

Pete grabbed the handles on the periscope tube as his men hung on to keep their balances. The diving officer called out depth changes.

"Five hundred feet, Captain ... Passing five-five-zero feet ... Approaching six hundred feet ... Five-seventy-five, five-nine-zero, six hundred feet, Captain."

"Very well," Pete said. "All stop!"

The freefall drop ended. The *Chicago* disengaged her propellers. She was now hovering in the water at six hundred feet below the surface. By diving deep, and by temporarily disengaging his propellers, Pete hoped to make his boat "disappear" into a black hole in the ocean, avoiding the passive sonar on board the aircraft carrier and her support ships, all of which could crush *Chicago*'s hull with powerful torpedo depth charges.

"Nobody flinch."

Sweat beaded on the foreheads of the men in the control room.

"Sonar. Conn. I want to know the moment that carrier passes over us."

"Aye, Captain."

He looked around at his men on the bridge. Their eyes were locked on him, hanging upon his every physical movement, as if his next words would be divinely inspired.

Quickly and silently, he prayed for divine inspiration.

"All right, here's what we're going to do. As soon as that carrier passes over us, we're going to turn the boat around. We're going to raise our depth to one-five-zero feet and get right into her wake. Then we're going to put two MK-48 ADCAP torpedoes right up her can."

Their eyes widened even more.

"I don't have to tell you how dangerous this maneuver will be. We're going to pop up inside her escort screen. We'll depend on the noise from her screws churning water to buffer our presence from their passive sonar. But I can't guarantee we won't be detected by one or more of her escort ships. But by then, hopefully it will be too late. As soon as we release our torps, we'll execute another emergency dive, and get the heck out of Dodge."

"Conn. Sonar. She's passing right over us now, sir."

"Very well. Right full rudder. Set course zero-nine-zero degrees. All ahead one-third."

The *Chicago* swung around, pointing her nose due east, now following the direction of the enemy carrier.

"Prep torps one and four. Make your depth one-five-zero feet."

Chicago's nose pointed upward again, and she began climbing through the water.

"Torps one and four are fully armed and ready, Captain."

"Very well," Pete said. "Depth?"

"Approaching two hundred feet, Captain."

"Good. Continue to climb. Continue to report."

"Approaching one-seven-five feet, sir. Approaching one-six-zero. Depth now one-five-zero, sir. Ship stabilized."

"On my mark, be prepared to fire torp one! Range to target?"

"Range to target, five hundred yards."

"That's too close to detonate," Pete said. "Decrease speed to fifteen knots."

"Aye, Captain."

"Range now?"

"Seven-hundred-fifty yards to target, Skipper."

"Very well, continue to report."

Another minute passed. "Range now one thousand yards to target and expanding, sir."

"Very well—fire torp one!"

"Firing torp one!"

Swoosh.

"Torp one in the water, Captain."

"Fire torp four!"

"Firing torp four!"

Swoosh.

"Torp four is in the water, Captain."

"Dive! Dive! Emergency deep! Take us to eight hundred feet! Let's get out of here! Now!"

CHAPTER 2

United States Naval Base
Pearl Harbor, Hawaii

Accepting the salutes from two United States Marines guarding the sun-baked east entrance of the naval base, Pete Miranda pressed the accelerator with his right foot.

The white Corvette C6 convertible rolled forward two hundred yards to the T-intersection at North Road, where Pete turned right, and then one hundred yards later made a forty-five-degree left on Pierce Street. This was followed by another forty-five-degree, one-hundred-yard left on Nimitz Street, which dead-ended two hundred yards later on Morton Street.

Because of the short streets on the Pearl Harbor Naval Base, he never could get the 'Vette beyond fifteen miles per hour. Slight frustration crawled across his stomach as he sat at the stop sign at Nimitz and Morton.

When he wasn't driving a nine-hundred-million-dollar nuclear submarine through the depths of the world's oceans, Commander Pete Miranda was plagued with one incurable landlubber's disease: an addiction to Corvettes.

His disease was aggravated by the fact that his boat, USS *Chicago*, was home-ported at a naval base that provided little relief for his addiction. After all, Corvettes were born for speed out on the open interstate. Hawaii's scenic beauty surpassed anything on the mainland, but Oahu's compact size made it difficult to find a place to open up the C6 for any period of time. One could make only so many loops around Interstate H1.

Pete waited as two U.S. Navy fuel trucks rolled slowly by, then turned right, creeping behind the second truck for the last hundred-yard trek down to the parking lot at COMSUBPAC headquarters.

Sporting his "ice cream" summer white uniform, with black shoulder boards each bearing the three gold stripes of Navy commander, Pete stepped out of the car, leaving the convertible top down. He grabbed his briefcase from the front seat and walked quickly under the two palm trees flanking the walkway leading to the building's entrance.

Two white-clad Navy shore patrolmen in Dixie-cup hats came to attention. "Good morning, sir." The SPs saluted.

Pete returned the salute and stepped into the building, walking under the blue-and-gold sign proclaiming *Commander Naval Submarine Forces Pacific*, known in the Navy by the acronym COMSUBPAC.

A quick turn down the hallway to the left brought him to the reception area of Rear Admiral Philip Getman, the two-star flag officer in charge of every American submarine operating in the Pacific Theater.

A navy lieutenant commander, also in his summer white uniform, sat at the desk. "Commander Miranda for Admiral Getman," Pete said.

"If you'll have a seat, sir, I'll let the admiral know you're here," the aide said.

Pete sat at the end of the leather sofa farthest from the closed door of the admiral's office. The walls displayed a photographic history of the Navy's submarine force. From a black-and-white photo of the Confederate sub CSS *Hundley*, to color photos of USS *Los Angeles* and USS *Ohio*, for which the Navy's current attack- and boomer-class boats were named, they were all there.

"Coffee, Commander?"

"Please."

When *Chicago* had arrived back at Pearl from her mission off San Diego yesterday, no celebrations or fanfare greeted her upon arrival. Her mission off the California coast had been top-secret.

The only significant officer on hand for the arrival was Pete's immediate boss, Submarine Squadron 3 commodore, Captain Ronald "Rocky" Gaylord, who met Pete as he crossed the catwalk from the submarine to the concrete pier. "Welcome home, Pete," Gaylord had said, slapping him on the back with a knowing nod of approval. "Great job out there."

"We tried, sir," Pete had said.

"Admiral wants you in his office at zero-ten-hundred tomorrow morning."

And with that directive from his boss, Pete was now sitting on the leather sofa outside the big kahuna's office, sipping on a cup of coffee that the admiral's aide had just given him.

Pete expected this meeting. *Chicago* would probably be commended for its performance off San Diego. Probably a Navy Unit Commendation. As commanding officer, he would also be decorated. Under different circumstances, perhaps a Navy Cross. But the nature of this operation would prevent that.

Who cared?

Pete already had a chest full of medals and didn't really care if he got any more. As long as he could drive submarines—and Corvettes—he was a happy camper.

The door opened. "Morning, Pete," Admiral Getman said. "Come on in."

Pete entered the office, greeting the admiral and his boss, Captain Gaylord.

"Have a seat," the admiral said, settling back into his own chair. "Pete, I'll cut to the chase." An unexpected seriousness pervaded the admiral's manner. "AIRPAC is upset that you sunk their aircraft carrier."

Pete suppressed a self-satisfied grin. "I would hope so, sir."

"No, I'm serious, Pete. Admiral Hopkins"—he was referring to Rear Admiral Joe Hopkins, Commander U.S. Naval Air Forces Pacific, known by the acronym AIRPAC—"wants you reprimanded for what you did."

Pete gaped. Was this a joke?

"With all due respect, sir, what's AIRPAC's problem?"

"Like I said, Pete, you sunk their carrier."

Pete locked eyes with Captain Gaylord, who looked down at the floor, and looked back at the admiral.

"Isn't that what submarines are supposed to do, sir? You know our motto. There are two kinds of ships in the Navy. Submarines, and targets."

"Yes, I know our motto. And in real life that's exactly what you're supposed to do. You were supposed to sink the carrier. But, Pete, this was a war game."

Pete glanced at Captain Gaylord again. The gray-haired Navy captain was subtly nodding his head, as if agreeing with Pete. "I understand that it was a war game, sir," Pete said. "And the purpose of the game, as

I understand it, was to practice the implementation of General Order 009-001 under *realistic* conditions. We practiced implementation of the order. We executed the maneuvers that I ordered and frankly, we won. So I ask again, sir, with all due respect, what's AIRPAC's problem?"

"Look, Pete, here's the problem." Getman leaned forward. "As you know, our submarines war-game against our aircraft carriers all the time. It's the same ole story. You know it. The sub versus the carrier. In these war games—which we try to make as *realistic* as possible—sometimes the sub wins. Sometimes the carrier wins.

"Most of our sub commanders bat about .500 in these war games with our carriers. AIRPAC can live with that, because that means that their carrier captains are also winning about half the time. But there's a political problem here. It costs a lot more money to sink an aircraft carrier than to sink a submarine. AIRPAC wants to go to Congress to ask for more money to build these new *Gerald R. Ford*-class supercarriers to replace the current *Nimitz*-class ships.

"Congressional critics say that the carriers are way too expensive. You know the argument—too vulnerable to being sunk by a submarine. Frankly, I agree. I'd rather have a hundred new *Virginia*-class attack subs than one new supercarrier."

Pete nodded his head in agreement.

"But AIRPAC's problem is that these liberal congressmen want to know war-games statistics as ammunition to argue against carrier spending. It's politics, Pete. The problem with you, Commander, is that you don't lose."

Pete shook his head and took a sip of the coffee, which was as disappointing as the direction of this conversation. "What am I supposed to do, sir? Let the carrier win?"

Getman pulled open his drawer and extracted a six-inch, hand-wrapped Dominican cigar. "Gentlemen, care for a smoke?" Though federal regulations prohibited smoking in government buildings, Getman smoked his stogies whenever and wherever he pleased.

"No, thank you, sir," Pete said. Captain Gaylord likewise declined.

"See, Pete, here's the problem," Getman said, lighting the stogie and drawing from it, then releasing a concentric smoke ring which wafted to the ceiling, "AIRPAC says you cheat."

"Sir?"

"Look, I didn't say you cheat. Admiral Hopkins at AIRPAC did." Another smoke ring. "Politics, my boy. You pop up behind USS *Carl*

Vinson, playing the role of an enemy aircraft carrier, launch your torps before they know you're there, and the skipper of the *Vinson*, who just so happens to be under consideration for flag rank, by the way, gets embarrassed.

"If fact, he's double embarrassed because it's not the first time you've done it to him. On top of that, neither he nor his escort ships can find you or sink you as you slither off into the deep. Can't be his fault, can it?" A rhetorical smoke ring followed the question.

Pete watched the smoke ring vaporize into the twirling ceiling fan. "May I ask just how AIRPAC claims I cheated, sir?"

"They claim you violated the rules of engagement by not simulating realistic combat conditions."

"Sir?"

"You popped up on the carrier's tail and chapped his rear with your torps at point-blank range."

"Yes, sir, we did. So what? They neither caught us, nor spotted us, nor sank us."

It appeared for a second that the admiral wanted to grin. Instead, he remained poker-faced. "AIRPAC says in real life it's unrealistic that you'd pop up right in the middle of a carrier battle group for a point-blank shot at a carrier like that. They claim that would be a suicide maneuver that would not be tried if we were using live fire, and that you only took the risk because you wanted to pad your war-game statistics."

Pete wanted to sling his lukewarm coffee across the room. "Sir, that's ridiculous. I'd remind the admiral of the premise of the exercise, of which the carrier and their escort vessels were aware. We were simulating conditions under which I, or any other Navy commander in the area for that matter, would decide how to implement General Order 009-001.

"*Vinson* was playing the role of an enemy carrier with its stated objective *under the rules* to get within range and launch a hypothetical nuclear strike against San Diego using below-the-horizon, smart-guided missiles launched from low-flying planes.

"Under that scenario, sir, I did in fact take a risky maneuver. But before I did, I considered and calculated the danger to my sub and my crew. I also considered the incalculable devastation that would be rained on America if I did not act. If this had been a live-fire exercise against a real enemy, Admiral, I would've done the same thing."

Admiral Getman laid the stogie in an ashtray. "I believe you, Pete. My problem now is that AIRPAC demands I formally reprimand you for violating the rules of engagement."

"Reprimand me? Sir, that would end my career as a naval officer."

"Don't worry, Pete. As much as it might actually *help* your reputation in the sub community if I reprimanded you for chapping a carrier's backside in a war game, I'd only do so if PACCOM or somebody higher up the chain tells me to. I don't think that'll happen." Getman was now chomping on the cigar, which had gone out. "I am, however, going to ask that you consider *voluntarily* stepping down as commanding officer of the *Chicago*."

Pete's stomach sank. "Relinquish my command? Sir, I'd rather you reprimand me."

"Pete, I'm not *telling* you to step down from command of *Chicago*. But we've got something else in mind. It's a mission calling for volunteers. It's highly dangerous, and you're the only sub driver in the Navy that could pull this off. If you say no, that's fine. You can finish your tour as skipper of *Chicago* and your career will not be affected.

"The objective for this mission has been signed off on by the president, but even he doesn't know how we're planning to try and carry out his order. Not yet anyway. If you say no, no one will ever know about this mission, and especially not any future promotion boards when you're up for captain."

Pete sat for a moment. "Sir, I'll do anything my country needs me to do, and anything for the Navy. Whatever it is, I'm in."

Getman smiled. Finally. "Pete, you've got two kids back in Virginia. Why don't you let us brief you on this mission first?" He nodded to Captain Gaylord. "Rockie?"

"Yes, sir, Admiral." Captain Gaylord stood and unrolled a poster-sized color photograph of an ocean-going freighter. Pete noticed that the freighter in the picture was flying a Russian flag off its stern. "This, Commander," Gaylord began, "is the Russian freighter *Alexander Popovich*. I'm showing you this photo because this freighter, and a number of others like it, is becoming an increasing threat to Western security."

"Maritime terrorism threat?" Pete asked.

"Not only a threat, but this particular freighter now has a track record of selling out to terrorists."

"How's that, sir?"

"U.S. intelligence has shown that the skipper of this vessel, a Russian national, has taken a ton of money from the Islamic terrorist organization, the Council of Ishmael, to use his ship for the furtherance of terrorist activities.

"The Russian captain has Caribbean bank accounts where he's parked this money. Most recently, this ship was used to transport a kidnapped hostage through the high seas, where she was eventually transported to a terrorist camp in the Gobi Desert in Mongolia. Remember the name Jeanette L'Enfant?"

Pete raised his eyebrow. The name sounded familiar. "Wasn't she the one who was held hostage with Lieutenant Commander Colcernian?"

"Bingo. One and the same. And we've just tracked another sizable deposit from the Council of Ishmael to this skipper's Caribbean account. Our intelligence believes this is another down payment for a job they're asking him to do. We don't know what, where, or why. But there's no telling what else this skipper might try unless he's stopped."

Pete mulled that for a second. "What can I do to help?"

"The president wants to sink that freighter. He wants him put out of the game permanently."

"That shouldn't be a problem," Pete said. "It's just a freighter. An unarmed freighter against a sub — no contest. Nazi U-boats proved that with their attacks on allied commercial shipping in World War II."

"True, but not so fast," Gaylord said. "It's not a problem sinking her. The problem is getting to her. This freighter operates primarily in the Black Sea. Sure, she comes out once in a while. She was operating in the Med when she worked with terrorists to transport L'Enfant, who had just been kidnapped on the French coast. But she's much harder to find and track once she gets on the high seas."

"That's true," Pete said. "It's almost impossible to find any given ship in the Pacific that doesn't want to be found. That was, as I recall, one of the premises of the war games off San Diego for which AIRPAC now wants my head." Pete raised his eyebrow at the admiral, who shook his head and chuckled.

"Sure I can't interest you in a stogie, Pete?"

"On second thought, I could probably use it, sir."

Admiral Getman slipped an already-cut Montecristo across his desk, along with a silver Zippo. Pete lit the stogie, took a draw, and turned back to Captain Gaylord. "But you can't get a sub into the Black Sea, sir. Not submerged anyway. You'd have to get through the Bosphorus, which is too shallow, too narrow, too treacherous, and which has way too many ships passing through it to risk a submerged passage. And if you went through on the surface, the Turks would know all about it." A draw from the stogie followed. "And so would everyone else."

Gaylord gave a knowing smile. "You've identified the problem, Commander. But we've developed a plan to make it happen. It's a dangerous plan. Once you get in, if you are in fact able to get in without being detected, you may not be able to get out.

"Bear in mind this would be an attack on what is in *theory* a civilian ship flying under a Russian flag. In reality, it's a terrorist ship whose captain is taking money from Islamic terrorists on the side to give them a presence on the high seas, but the Russians, whose intelligence capabilities are not as astute as ours, may not see it that way, and we can't tell them about it lest we expose sensitive information about our intelligence sources. Some enemies of the United States would spin this as an attack on an innocent civilian freighter, which is an act of war. We don't want nuclear war with Russia over this.

"The president wants to sink ships involved with maritime terrorism, but he doesn't want a direct link to the Navy. In this case, secrecy is as important to the success of your mission as actually sinking that ship. If you can't get out, you may have to sink this freighter and scrap the sub. That, of course, could cost you your life, and the life of your crew."

Pete mulled that over. "Where would I get my crew?"

"Just like we're asking you to volunteer, Pete, we're seeking an all-voluntary crew. We recognize that the chances of survival, especially if we have to scrap the sub, will be fifty-fifty at best. So we're being upfront about this, and asking only for volunteers. At the same time, we need the Navy's very best to pull this off."

Pete looked at the admiral, who was leaning back in his chair with his arms crossed.

"I still don't see how we're going to get through the Bosphorus and into the Black Sea."

"Once you accept this assignment, and there's no pressure for you to do so, you'll be flown to your new duty station, where you'll be briefed on the plan. Until then, I'm under orders to reveal nothing else about it. The plan, of course, is top-secret."

"What about the *Chicago*? When would I deploy for this new assignment?"

"As soon as you walk out of this office, we'll put you on a plane back east. That's all I can say."

"I wouldn't have an opportunity to say goodbye to my men?"

"Your men will be told that their skipper has been reassigned to a top-secret mission. A new skipper has already been selected for *Chicago*, if you accept this assignment."

This was all so sudden. Pete wasn't afraid of losing his life. But his men. His crew. They were all the family he had right now. To be unable to even say goodbye ... Still, he was a naval officer, and the needs of the Navy and the call of his country always came first. But what of his two children? He'd not seen them in almost a year. But the call of his country prevailed.

"Okay, gentlemen, I'm in. I'll do this. I'm ready to go."

"Thank you, Pete." Admiral Getman rose and extended his hand, which Pete grasped. "The president thanks you too. And I will miss you."

CHAPTER 3

The Caucasus Mountains
The Russian Republic of North Ossetia

Hidden in the shadows under the crevices of the rocks, their positions were revealed by the red glow of their cigarettes. They had waited for an hour already.

Listening.

Their feet and legs ached. They knew, from surveying this position dozens of times in the daylight, that the mountain steeped down at a forty-five-degree angle. One slip of a boot would plunge them hundreds of feet into a dark abyss.

Sergei checked his watch.

Five minutes till midnight. The time—the nearness to the hour— ignited his heartbeat.

He sucked on his cigarette, flicked it down, and watched the burning tip vanish in the darkness below.

Sergeant Natasha Asimova downshifted, again, and pressed the accelerator to the floor. The engine whined and strained, but kept pulling the KAMAZ 4310 military truck up the incline.

"Are we going to make it, Sergeant?" one of the two guards yelled from the back.

"*Dah, dah,*" she said. "My truck has never failed me on this run." She pressed her boot against the clutch, then downshifted once more.

"Once we make it around the last curve, we will be at the top of the mountain, and then it is all downhill from there."

"Arkady has never made this run before." The other guard laughed. "He's a mamma's boy from the coast at Arkangel. He's afraid of heights!"

"Shut up, Boris Andropovich!" the first guard shot back.

"Comrades! Silence!" Natasha snapped. "I must concentrate, or we will run off the cliff."

"Sorry, Sergeant."

The moon crested over the jagged peaks above their heads, bathing them in a pale radiance, illuminating the shadowy outlines of his comrades, who were also crouched down along the rocky incline below the winding, mountainous road.

Sergei drew the cool, thin Transcaucus air into his lungs. The engine from the distant truck whined and shifted gears, straining to pull its cargo up the incline of the road.

A brief, shrill whistle pierced the chilly night.

Sergei looked to his left. Mikhail, the team leader, signaled thumbs-up.

This is it.

He worked the action on his AK-47. The clank of chinking metal from the other platoon of assault rifles followed, echoing off the rocks and down the steep mountain.

The sound of the truck grew louder … louder …

And then, headlight beams flashed over the crest of the road above their heads.

"*Seachess!*" Mikhail barked in Russian. "Now!"

Sergei and eight other members of the team leaped over the ledge and onto the road.

Dual headlights came out of the night up the hill. The military truck, its engine struggling to make the top of the hill, was slowing under the strain of the climb.

"Stop the truck!" Mikhail shouted.

The truck slowed even more.

Good.

Perhaps this would be easier than anticipated, Mikhail thought, as the freedom fighters approached the truck.

Then the engine revved. Gears shifted. The truck lunged forward. The driver was making a run for it.

"Shoot the tires!"

Multiple gunshots echoed off the canyon walls. The front of the truck thumped down onto the concrete.

"Don't shoot!" The driver, a blonde woman wearing a Russian military uniform, squinted at the high-beam flashlight in her face, then whipped out a pistol.

"Take cover!"

Three sharp bursts rang from the woman's pistol. Sergei immediately fired back in the direction of the driver. "Perimeter positions!" Mikhail ordered. "Out of the truck!"

Sergei and another commando took positions around the rear, training their rifles on the closed doors. The twin back doors flew open. Two silhouettes emerged from the cargo bay.

"Fire!"

The crack of rifle fire, like the sound of a volley fired by an execution squad, echoed against the mountain walls. The two guards who had rushed out the back doors lay bleeding on the road from Sergei's weapon. The driver's head hung out the window, her eyes frozen open in the moonlight. Blood trickled from her gaping mouth.

"Get the cargo," Mikhail ordered. "Now! Move!"

The Alexander Popovich
Sochi, Russia

The telephone rang and Captain Yuri Mikalvich Batsakov pushed up from his rack and rubbed his eyes.

A flip of the lamp switch on the table beside his bed reminded him that he was not alone in the captain's stateroom. The pretty blonde woman—he couldn't remember her name at the moment, perhaps either Elena or Tatiana—grunted and rolled over. Too much vodka was bad for the memory. Not that her name mattered at this time of morning. The clock on the bulkhead showed 3:00 a.m. But still ...

The phone rang again.

"All right. All right." Batsakov cursed as his feet met the cold deck. He reached for the shipboard telephone.

"*Dah.*"

"*Kapitán* Batsakov?"

"*Dah.*"

"This is the guard at the end of Pier Three."

"What is it?"

"Sorry to interrupt, *Kapitán*, but there is a truck here at the end of the pier. They claim to have cargo for your ship. The driver says his name is Mikhail Abramakov. His papers match that, *Kapitán*."

"Oh, *dah*! *Dah*!" Amazing how the prospect of American dollars could cure even a vodka-induced amnesia. "We're expecting that shipment. Wave Abramakov through the checkpoint and send a few stevedores down to the pier. I'll be right down."

"Of course, *Kapitán*."

Batsakov hung up, then picked up the phone again and called the bridge. "Dmitri, this is the captain. Round up three deckhands and meet me at the quarterdeck in five minutes. Yes, of course I know what time it is." He swigged the lukewarm vodka in the clear glass beside the bed. "Get them out of the racks and get them moving! Now!"

He hung up the phone and slapped the now-empty vodka glass back on the table.

"What time is it, Yuri?" The blonde was sitting up, rubbing her eyes and squinting at him.

"Look, Elena, darling, it has been much fun, but something important has come up. I have work to do," he said, putting his arms into a black pea coat. "Go back to sleep. I will send my steward up to help with your things in the morning."

He opened the cabin door and started to step out.

"Tatiana," the blonde snapped.

He looked back in and saw the perturbed-looking blonde helping herself to the bottle of vodka on the side table.

"Excuse me?"

"I'm Tatiana!" Her blue eyes blazed fury as her lips met the opening of the glass bottle. "You called me Elena!" she said, after an angry swig.

"Yes, my apologies. You are so beautiful — that plus the vodka — forgive me — I was not thinking straight. I will call you when I am back in port."

He slammed the door closed just in time to block the airborne vodka bottle. He walked away to the sounds of shattering glass and the fading strains of "call Elena next time you're in port, you fat pig."

Five minutes later, Batsakov approached the quarterdeck of his freighter. The lights along the pier cast an eerie, pinkish glow on the concrete below.

A black panel truck was rolling up the pier. It stopped at the end of the catwalk and switched off its headlights. The doors opened, and four men, dressed in black, stepped into the night. They opened the back of the panel truck and removed a large wooden crate, which took all of them to handle.

As a fifth man started bounding up the catwalk to the ship, Batsakov motioned for his deckhands to head down to the pier to assist in getting the wooden crate out of the truck.

The trio of deckhands passed the figure coming up the catwalk, and less than a minute later, the fifth man reached the quarterdeck. "Permission to come aboard, *Kapitán*?" the man asked.

"You must be Abramakov."

"My papers, *Kapitán*." The black-haired, scruffy-bearded stranger handed a manila envelope to Batsakov. "Mind if I borrow a cigarette while you check me out?"

"No problem." Batsakov glanced at the papers under the quarterdeck lights while holding the cigarette pack in the direction of the stranger. "Looks in order." Batsakov returned the identification papers.

"And my colleagues asked me to give you this." Abramakov handed the captain a second envelope.

"For the love of Lenin!" Batsakov's eyes widened at the envelope full of hundred-dollar bills.

"This is nothing compared to what has been wired to your Bahamian account, *Kapitán*, or what you will receive upon completion of your mission. This is but a small departure bonus of ten thousand dollars cash as a token of our appreciation." Abramakov sucked in on his cigarette and blew his smoke off to the side. "There is one other thing," Abramakov said. "Read this." He handed yet another envelope to Batsakov, who studied the paper.

Dear *Kapitán* Batsakov,

The cargo that you will be carrying is important to the future of the world. You will take it on board at Sochi, and then you will proceed under normal circumstances to set sail in the Black Sea. You will sail to a rendezvous point located at 30 degrees east longitude and 43 degrees north latitude, where you will rendezvous with another civilian vessel of Egyptian registry, whose name is withheld for security reasons.

When you reach the rendezvous point, the cargo will be transferred to the Egyptian ship. Codename for the transfer is "Peter the Great." You will be hailed on international frequencies by the approaching Egyptian vessel, and you will accept transfer instructions from the Egyptian captain.

Upon the safe transfer of the cargo at the coordinates as set forth herein, the remaining half of your fee shall be transferred to the account you have designated, and your duties for this mission shall be discharged.

Thank you for the opportunity to do business with you.

For security reasons, the author of this directive must remain anonymous.

"Well, well." Batsakov folded the directive and stuck it on the inside of his pea coat. "An intervessel transfer on the high seas." A drag from his cigarette. "Brings back fond memories of my days in the Soviet navy."

"We hoped you would view these orders with fondness, comrade." Abramakov flicked his cigarette. "Now then, *Kapitán*, there is this matter of bringing the cargo aboard your vessel."

"Would you like a crane to lift it aboard?"

"No." Abramakov lit another cigarette. "That would cause too much attention. My men can bring it up the catwalk. We will store it below decks wherever you direct us, but we will need a dry compartment."

Batsakov studied Abramakov's beady eyes. Abramakov looked Slavic, unlike the crazy-looking Middle Easterner who worked for the organization that had hired him to transport a woman prisoner from France to Sochi.

This fellow had Russian roots. Perhaps he could strike a rapport here—a rapport that could lead to repeated business. "I suppose, my friend, it does me no good to ask what you are bringing aboard my ship?"

Abramakov laughed. "Think of it as gold, *Kapitán*. The contents of this crate have made you a rich man. Beyond that, there is no need for you to know. Understood?"

Batsakov smiled. Abramakov was right; already the money transferred to his Bahamian bank account had made him rich beyond his wildest dreams. If he could keep dealing with these people—whoever they were—soon he could afford to buy his own fleet of ships.

"Understood, my friend. I will assign somone to find a suitable place for the cargo."

"*Spaceeba, Kapitán.*" Abramakov turned, stepped to the side of the ship, and motioned at the men still standing by the van down below.

Four men dressed in black, like pall bearers carrying an oversized casket, lugged a large, rectangular plywood box across the transom and onto the deck of the *Alexander Popovich*. Captain Batsakov gave a few signals to his deckhands, and the wooden crate disappeared below deck.

Office of the president of the Russian Republic
Staraya Square, Moscow

What do you mean it just disappeared?" The president of the Russian Republic stood, slamming his fist on the large wooden desk. Russia had come so far under his leadership. With America's falling stature around the globe as a result of her military intervention in Iraq, Afghanistan, and other hotspots, the world had become hungry for leadership from another superpower.

And this had been his dream: to restore Russia to her days of unparalleled glory, to the days when she stood as a great world superpower in the wake of the Great War, when she commanded the republics of the great Soviet Union, when her name commanded fear and respect in every corner of the globe. President Vitaly Evtimov was the man for this glorious task. He was the youngest Russian president since Putin. The Western press had called him charismatic, and some had referred to him even as "the Russian JFK."

And now he was at the right place in the right time. Until this. This. The inability to track and contain weapons-grade nuclear fuel could prove to be the type of international embarrassment that would derail his noble and grandiose plans for the motherland.

"Weapons-grade plutonium does not just disappear into the Caucasus mountains!"

Evtimov flung a stack of memoranda out towards the members of the Russian National Security counsel who were present at this hastily called emergency meeting. "I have three dead members of the Russian Federal Army, and more than enough nuclear fuel missing to vaporize the entire city of Moscow!"

"Please, Comrade President," pleaded the minister of defense, a balding, stout man with a ruddy nose. "Please calm down."

"How dare you lecture me about calming down, Giorgy Alexeevich!" Evtimov glared at his defense minister. "How can I remain calm when the army over which I place you in charge cannot muster enough riflemen to guard a shipment of volatile nuclear fuel?"

"Comrade President." The president's chief of staff, Sergey Semyonovich Sobyanin, spoke in a calm voice. "With all due respect, sir, Giorgy Alexeevich's army took security precautions which exceed those often taken by the Americans."

"I do not follow you, Sergey Semyonovich."

"The Americans and the British transport nuclear materials all the time, often on civilian trucks down their interstates or in boxcars on their trains. Often, Comrade President, these materials are not even guarded. In fact, their own Department of Energy has admitted that the Americans sometimes haul not just nuclear fuel, but nuclear weapons in eighteen-wheel trucks up and down their interstates! These weapons are usually accompanied only by specially trained federal agents. At least in this instance our Army had three armed guards."

The president's rage calmed slightly. Vitaly sat down and took a sip of water.

"I should fire the defense minister over this. But for now, we must find this missing plutonium." He studied the faces of the men who formed the most powerful group of men in the Eastern Bloc. "We need to find it before it blows some city off the face of the earth." He eyed the members of the Security Council. There was no response. "Well, don't just sit there. I need answers!"

"Comrade President?" This was the minister of internal affairs.

"Yes, Comrade Minister?"

"Just like the Americans, we depend on anonymity in the transport of these materials, which justifies a light security force. I agree with the chief of staff that a capable security force was traveling with the material. This attack had to have been coordinated by someone who was familiar with our occasional transport of this type of fuel between our nuclear facility in Beslan in North Ossetia and our storage facility in Prokhladnyy in Kabardino-Balkariya."

"Show me where this attack took place," the president said.

"Very well, Comrade President." The internal affairs minister pulled out a map of the region and placed it on an easel.

"As you can see, Comrade President, our truck began its journey at our nuclear facility in Beslan, in the Russian Republic of North Ossetia. That is shown at point one on the map. They were headed to our storage facility at Prokhladnyy, in the Russian Republic of Kabardino-Balkariya, shown here at point three.

"Remember that this area is mountainous. The highest peak in Europe, Mount Elbrus, is located in this republic.

"The ambush occurred at an area along the road at point two. Our vehicle at that time was still in North Ossetia, and after the rebels murdered our driver and two military guards, they rolled our truck down the side of the mountain.

"Point four is the Chechen capital city of Grozny, which as you can see is due east of the ambush point. Considering the proximity of the attack to Grozny, we believe that Chechen rebels are responsible." Mutterings followed nods of heads around the table. "In fact, Comrade President, the ambush point is less than seventy-five miles from Grozny. Witnesses report a military truck going at a high rate of speed in that direction."

"I agree," the minister of civil defense said. "I believe, sir, that the material was transported to the east, toward Grozny, the Chechen capital."

The defense minister spoke up again. "Imagine, Comrade President, if Aslambek Kadyrov and his traitorous separatists in Grozny developed a nuclear weapon with our materials."

"We should've taken out Kadyrov long ago," one of them said.

"It is not too late for that," replied another.

Vitaly Sergeivich Evtimov rotated in his chair and gazed out the window at the bustling sea of humanity on Staraya Square. He folded his arms. What a public relations disaster this would create for Russia if the Western press caught wind.

"Excuse me, Comrade President," the foreign affairs minister said.

"*Dah*," Vitaly said.

"Should we notify the Americans?"

Vitaly faced the foreign affairs minister. "Notify them of what? That we are the first nation to lose track of weapons-grade nuclear fuel to terrorists? We have just started rebuilding our credibility as an alternative superpower to the Americans. If this gets out, we lose face in the international community. We must find this material and punish the thieves before there is mass hysteria."

Vitaly eyed the faces of the most powerful men on the Eurasian continent. They would all obey his commands without hesitation and on a moment's notice. He had selected them all because they had shown unflinching loyalty to him. He would need their loyalty in the midst of this crisis.

This would be a defining moment by which history would judge him.

He would act with sure-fisted power. "You know," he said, "this may present the perfect opportunity for a final solution of the Chechen problem."

That statement brought intense stares.

"What did you have in mind, Vitaly Sergeivich?" Alexander Alexeyvich Kotenkov, the Russian foreign minister, was the only member of the Russian Security Council close enough to the president to refer to him by his patronymic name.

Vitaly declared, "We shall mobilize the Russian Army. We shall descend upon Chechnya from our Volga-Ural and North Caucasian military districts. We shall punish them for stealing this material. We shall crush this opposition once and for all!" He pounded his fist on the desk. "And we must find this fuel before some Chechen lunatic builds a bomb that could vaporize Moscow." He swigged water. "Even if we have to destroy every square inch of Grozny."

CHAPTER 4

The Alexander Popovich
Sochi, Russia

As the sun rose above the deep sparkling waters of the Black Sea, Captain Yuri Mikalvich Batsakov huddled on the bridge of *Alexander Popovich* with the four officers immediately subordinate to him.

Batsakov was still, at heart, a ship's master—although an increasingly wealthy ship's master. And the sea, for all his love of it, was a jealous mistress, capable of swallowing even the greatest of vessels. He must never forget, no matter how many American dollars were funneled into his bank account, that the sea could not be taken for granted—that he was ultimately responsible for evaluating the readiness status of his vessel.

Getting a freighter seaborne was not as simple as cranking an automobile and taking a drive down Moscow's main street, Tverskaya.

A series of performance checks between the bridge and the engine room needed to be performed, and certain actions would need to be logged before *Alexander Popovich* would be declared seaworthy for her return voyage into *Chourney Mara*—the Russian phrase for "Black Sea."

Batsakov instructed the four officers to expedite their respective reports, so that with any luck, *Alexander Popovich* and her twenty-eight crew members would be underway by sunset.

He was about to adjourn the predeparture meeting when a deckhand entered the bridge.

"Excuse me, *Kapitán*. You have two visitors at the quarterdeck, sir."

"Visitors?" Batsakov sipped a glass of vodka. "We are beginning our predeparture checklists, Aleksey. I am busy."

"They are with the Russian government, *Kapitán*."

Batsakov cursed.

If the government suspected what was in the belly of his ship, these men no doubt were FSB officers. Since the old KGB disbanded in 1991 with the fall of the Soviet Union, its domestic successor organization, the FSB, had proven just as ruthless. One of the many things he enjoyed most about being at sea was that the FSB was nowhere to be found.

What would he do if they wanted to search the bowels of the *Alexander Popovich*?

Remain calm.

The ship's manifest showed the cargo to be several cases of Georgian wine. Perhaps that would deter them. If not, he would deny knowledge. Always deny. This would be a truthful response. After all, he did not know with certainty what Abramakov had brought on his ship. He would blame the whole affair on Abramakov and his men.

"Escort them to my stateroom, Aleksey. I will meet them there shortly."

"Yes, *Kapitán*." He left immediately.

Batsakov crossed to a hidden compartment, where he retrieved his GSh-18 semiautomatic pistol. He worked the bolt action of the pistol, stuck it in the holster in the back of his pants, and left the bridge.

Five minutes later, Batsakov arrived at the stateroom. The young deckhand who had approached him on the bridge was standing in the passageway outside the closed door. The captain motioned for the deckhand to step closer and spoke in low tones.

"Are they inside, Aleksey?"

"*Dah, Kapitán*," the young deckhand said.

"Shhh." The captain brought his forefinger across his lips. He patted the young man's shoulder. "Aleksey Anatolyvich, ever since you left the orphanage in St. Petersburg, I have given you a job and treated you as a son, *dah*?"

"*Dah, Kapitán*."

"And I have given you a home, here on the *Alexander Popovich*, *dah*? And you trust me no matter what instruction I give to you?"

"Of course, *Kapitán*. I have seen you in command on the bridge of our ship when she was rolling in twenty-foot swells. I trust you completely. You are the only father I ever knew."

"That's my boy." Batsakov allowed himself a smile. "Listen, Aleksey. Go down to the weapons locker room and get a sidearm. Load it. Then come back and post yourself here outside my stateroom door. Let no one in without my permission. Understand?"

"Of course, *Kapitán*."

National Geospatial-Intelligence Agency
Fort Belvoir, Virginia

Kent Pendleton, a twenty-year veteran intelligence agent, loved working the midnight shift at the National Geospatial-Intelligence Agency's satellite interpretation center.

For one, the traffic wasn't so bad around the Capital Beltway at midnight. And since NGA had moved its headquarters from suburban Bethesda, Maryland, to Fort Belvoir, he could make the trip in less than an hour. The commute time would double during the day. Of course driving back to his home at eight in the morning was another story.

Download time. He typed in a few commands, ordering the computer to download the latest satellite feed from Volgograd. Then he got up from his desk and walked over to the kitchen. Another cup of steaming black coffee was what the doctor ordered to get the squints out of his eyes for seven more hours of staring at computer screens.

When he got back from coffee break, the last satellite photo of Volgograd was still frozen on the screen, and in the upper right of the screen, under the word *Volgograd* were the times the photo was snapped on the satellite's last pass approximately ninety minutes ago. *7:30 Local, 3:30 GMT/UTC, 23:30 EST.*

The aerial photograph began scrambling in front of his eyes, and as the image scrambled, the word *Transmitting* appeared in the screen on red.

A moment later, *Transmitting* vaporized from the screen and was replaced with a new satellite photograph, taken one hundred miles above the area. Under *Volgograd* in the upper right corner, the new times were reflected showing that the image had just been taken and transmitted: *9:00 Local, 05:00 GMT/UTC, 01:00 EST.*

Pendleton clicked each sector of the photograph, giving him enlarged images for closer inspection.

On his fourth click, along the main road leading south out of the city along the Volga River, he spotted something. He rubbed his eyes and squinted again. Was he seeing what he thought he was? He stared at the screen in disbelief. Yes. His eyes were not playing tricks on him.

Armored vehicles.

Hundreds of them.

Tanks.

Personnel carriers.

A massive convoy of the Russian Army was on the move.

"Hey, get a load of this!" The excited voice came from two cubicles over where another intelligence analyst and one of Kent's subordinates, Tommy DiNardo, was reviewing satellite photos shot over the Russian republic of North Ossetia. "I've got military movement — army — headed due east!"

Kent got up and rushed over to Tommy's cubicle. "Will ya look at that?"

"If those aren't armored columns, I don't know what is." Tommy spoke with excitement in his voice.

"I've got the same thing on my screen," Kent said. "The Russian Army's on the move."

"The question is where," Tommy mused.

"Good question," Kent said, glaring at Tommy's screen. "My guess is Chechnya, if we're lucky."

"Why do you say that?"

"The main column from Volgograd is moving down the Caspian Depression, which is very low land between the Caucasus Mountains and the Caspian Sea. We've got to hope they stop at Chechnya, because if they don't, they can easily slip along the Caspian coast into Azerbaijan, and from there, Iran. And from there, it's a straight shot due south to Iranian, Iraqi, and Kuwaiti oil fields." That thought sent a fearful shiver through Kent's body. "And if the Russian Army invades the Middle East, the balloon goes up."

"You mean *kaboom*," Tommy said.

"I mean *kaboom*," Kent said.

"Should we wake the president?" Tommy asked. "I can get the codes for the White House hotline."

"Not our call," Kent said. "But we've gotta move fast."

He reached over and punched in the line to the secretary. "Get G. B. Harrell over at the National Security Agency on the secure line. Yes, now." He replaced the phone.

"Tommy, come see my pics."

They both jogged over to Kent's workstation. Tommy's eyes bulged at the sight before him. "This force looks three times the size of the one on my screen."

"Volgograd is one of the biggest military districts in Russia," Kent told the younger man. "The city was once called Stalingrad. The bloodiest battle in human history took place here in 1942. Over a million people died. This is hallowed ground to the Russian people. They feel that they whipped the Nazis right here, two years before the Normandy invasion. And they well may be right." He set down his coffee cup. "Strategic U.S. doctrine says any major Russian ground invasion of the Middle East would muster in Volgograd and follow this route to the south ... the same route that these forces are following."

"You think this may be it?"

Kent hesitated. "I pray not. We'll know more at our next satellite pass around two-thirty."

The phone rang. "Kent, Mr. Harrell from NSA is on the secure line," the secretary said.

"Thanks." Kent waited for the connection. G. B. Harrell was Kent's counterpart at the National Security Agency at Fort Meade, the duty supervisor for monitoring Northern Caucasus activity. The NSA was the U.S. government agency tasked with intercepting communication signals of potential enemies worldwide.

Harrell's voice came on the line. "Kent, what's up?"

"Our one-thirty satellite pass shows Russian ground forces on the move, south out of Volgograd and east out of North Ossetia."

"What size?"

"Too early to tell, G. B. Maybe two, three divisions. We'll know more when our bird passes over them again."

"Hmm." Harrell paused. "We'd been picking up traffic from that region in the last few hours indicating that a movement of forces was getting underway. But the usual questions—from where to where, and when—have been a puzzle. This helps fill part of the puzzle. Are our birds showing other Russian force movements anywhere in the world?"

"Negative, G. B. Not yet. I'll be meeting with our other Russian action officers here in just a few and I'll call you if that changes. But as of now, Moscow, St. Petersburg, Vladivostok ... all seem quiet."

"Okay," Harrell said. "I'm calling this an urgent matter for top-secret classification that needs immediate attention up the chain-of-command. The national security director and the secretary of defense will need to be roused. They can decide whether to wake the president."

"I concur," Kent said. "I'll notify the NGA director. You can handle NSA and the secretary of defense. I'm sending these photos over now. Let's touch base in thirty to get these reports meshed together. Sounds like we're going to have a busy one."

"Concur."

"Talk to you soon."

The secure line went dead.

The Alexander Popovich
Sochi, Russia

9:05 a.m. local time

Captain Batsakov waited just long enough for Aleksey to return with a loaded pistol before entering his stateroom.

Two men, both appearing to be in their mid to late thirties, sat at his dining table. The men rose as Batsakov closed the door. "Ah, *Kapitán!*" The man on the left spoke in the smug tone of a know-it-all bureaucrat. "I am Agent Fedorov. This is Agent Sidorov." Their identification badges featured the light blue globe surrounded by a gold ring, sitting on a gold pedestal, and back-dropped by the familiar sprawling five-pointed star rising above wreaths of wheat—the terrifying symbol of the FSB.

"Welcome to the *Alexander Popovich.*"

"*Spaceeba, Kapitán,*" Fedorov said. "May we sit?"

"Please." Batsakov motioned the two visitors to resume their places at the table. "Would you gentlemen care for something to drink?"

"Vodka," Fedorov said.

"Vodka for me also," Sidorov added.

Batsakov retrieved two glasses from the cabinet above the sink. "So, gentlemen, how may I be of service to the FSB?" Clear vodka flowed into the glasses. Batsakov handed one to each of the agents.

"*Kapitán.*" Fedorov sipped the vodka. "Rumor has it that you have become, shall we say, a handsomely paid ship's master."

"And why is the FSB concerned about my compensation? I have always paid all of my taxes."

"Yes, of course," Fedorov said. "Well, I suppose as your taxes support the motherland, and you do not use your ship in any way that would embarass the Russian Republic, your compensation *would* be a personal matter, no?"

Batsakov ignored the comment. "So, gentlemen, as I asked a moment ago, how may I be of service to Mother Russia?"

"Hmm." Federov exchanged glances with his partner. "Perhaps, *Kapitán*, the more pertinent question is, how can your ship be of service to Mother Russia?"

Bataskov sipped his vodka and studied the piercing eyes of the two FSB agents. "Agent Federov, undoubtedly you reviewed my governmental file before boarding my ship. Therefore, you know that, despite my fondness for occasionally earning a few extra rubles, my loyalty to the motherland is unflinching."

"Yes, your file indicates, shall we say, a *consistency* in your line of work."

Talking in circles. Batsakov hated this about bureaucrats, and especially FSB bureaucrats. If they wanted to search his ship, why not just say so?

"Gentlemen. As you know we are preparing to get underway later today. I must return to the bridge to oversee all this."

"Why in such a hurry to sail, *Kapitán*? You have a date with some beautiful mermaid in the Black Sea?" Federov chuckled at himself.

His pal Sidorov sneered, then spoke up. "You do realize, do you not, *Kapitán*, that it is a privilege, and not a right, to sail your freighter under the registration of the Motherland, and that your ability to fly the flag of Mother Russia on the high seas affords you certain"—he hesitated and scratched his chin—"shall we say, *privileges* not ordinarily afforded to ships flying the ensigns of other nations?"

"Yes, of course I know it is a privilege not only to fly the flag of our country, but also to be a Russian citizen."

"Hmm." This was Fedorov again. "Then you would undoubtedly volunteer your ship for a diplomatic mission on behalf of the president of the Russian Federation?"

Where were they headed with all this? "Yes, of course. To the extent possible I would do everything I can for our president."

"Good." Federov downed his vodka. "Have some more of this stuff, *Kapitán*?"

"*Dah*, of course." Batsakov refilled the agent's glass to the brim.

"You are aware, are you not, that President Evtimov has been concerned about Western influences undermining stability in a number of the former republics of the former Soviet Union."

"I know what I read in *Pravda*."

"You are aware that over the past few years, beginning with the election of Victor Yushchenko, that Ukraine has drifted closer to the Americans' camp."

"I sail into Ukraine. I hear stories about this debate."

Federov sipped more vodka. "Yes, well, President Evtimov is none too happy about it. And since the Americans lost some of their popularity after the Dome of the Rock attacks, our president has been courting Ukraine very hard."

"Tell me, comrade. How can I help?"

"There is an orphanage near Chernobyl. In fact, the Ukrainian president — Butrin — spent time there as a boy. He visits there often, and holds the place dear to his heart."

"I've heard of it."

"A group of orphans spent summer holiday here in Sochi. President Evtimov has been on the phone with President Butrin of Ukraine. As a gesture of friendship, our president has offered to find a Russian ship sailing for Odessa for the children to ride back on. When the ship arrives in port, President Butrin will be waiting for the children at the docks along with President Evtimov, at which time Russia will offer significant money to Ukraine to upgrade its orphanage facilities. We see that your ship will be sailing for Odessa, and we want you to host these orphans on your voyage."

"How many children wish to ride on my ship?"

"Twelve. Plus their adult counselor. Plenty of room for you to accommodate, *Kapitán*."

"Are you crazy?" Batsakov threw his arms in the air. "What am I? A babysitter? My ship is a dangerous place for children. There is cargo sliding around and there is no one to watch them. They could easily fall overboard. Besides, why not just use a Russian navy vessel?"

"Because President Evtimov wants to deemphasize military ties and emphasize peaceful civilian cooperation. This will only delay your departure twenty-four hours."

Great. Another twenty-four hours for someone to discover the cargo for which I will be paid five million dollars for delivery. But what can I say? "Please tell President Evtimov that *Alexander Popovich* is pleased to be of service to the motherland."

CHAPTER 5

United States Naval Support Activity
La Maddalena, Italy

A JAG officer will be right out, Commander. If you'd like to have a seat here in the lobby, sir, feel free."

"Very well." Commander Pete Miranda looked up at the legalman chief, who had just walked through the double doors leading from the back of the spartan offices that served as the Navy Legal Service Office in La Maddalena.

An updated will was long overdue.

He should've done it when he and Sally divorced five years ago. But the kids were well taken care of back in Norfolk, and there was plenty of life insurance should something go wrong.

Plus, commanding a *Los Angeles*–class nuclear submarine provided no free time. His men, his boat, and the United States Navy were all-consuming.

But the dangerous, top-secret mission ordered by Sixth Fleet had caused him to rethink his will. Certain things should go to his twelve-year-old son, Coley, he had decided: his two Navy Commendation medals; his three Meritorious Service Medals, the bronze "dolphins" worn on his uniform signifying his elite status as a member of the silent service; and his "command" medallion, showing that he was the captain of the USS *Chicago*.

To his thirteen-year-old daughter, Hannah, he would leave his wedding band, which he had saved since the divorce, his watch, his family Bible that his grandparents gave him on his graduation from college, and his officer's sword, which he had carried when he and Sally were married all those years ago.

None of this meant much to the kids right now. But one day—if this mission went south—they just might come to appreciate what their daddy stood for.

Residence of the secretary of defense
Arlington, Virginia

1:08 a.m.

The cacophonous buzz from the telephone on the nightstand brought the bed's only occupant to a stiff, upright position. Unlike the personal telephone on his other nightstand, which rang in softer, more pleasant tones, the tortuous noise from the phone on the left could be from only one of four sources—the White House, the NSA, the Pentagon, or the CIA—and the caller on the other end was calling to discuss an issue of immediate, pressing, national security.

"Secretary Lopez here."

"Mr. Secretary, this is G. B. Harrell, the action officer for Russian affairs at NSA. Sorry to bother you at this time of morning."

"I know you wouldn't call if it wasn't urgent. What's up?"

"Sir, we're picking up significant movement of Russian ground forces."

"Talk to me."

"Several dozen divisions so far. Mostly moving south out of Volgograd. Plus several divisions moving east out of North Ossetia. Most likely destination, Chechnya. But at the strength level we're seeing, at this point we have to be concerned about them moving farther south, sir."

"I'll call the president. Send your report to my office at the Pentagon. I'm headed over there right now."

"Yes, sir, Mr. Secretary."

The White House

9:20 a.m.

Before I order this attack, I need to know that our intelligence is solid."

President Mack Williams folded his arms and turned his back on the small cadre of high-powered advisors gathered around him in the Oval Office. He looked outside. Dew drops on several dozen rose bushes sparkled in the morning sunlight. Out on the South Lawn, lush grass sprawled like a glowing green carpet from the Oval Office, under the black iron gates to the Mall, out to the Washington Monument.

They had told him that the office would impose itself upon him. And in the five years since he had come to the Oval Office, the trim, fifty-five-year old Kansan had seen his hair transformed from pure brown to salt-and-pepper. More salt than otherwise.

Lines of worry had begun to subtly cross his tan forehead, which the First Lady had said gave him a more distinguished look. But Mack Williams knew better. And in a post-9/11 world where the traditional rules of war and peace had become a distant concept of the past, it was inevitable that the weight of the great office would be heavy upon any man.

Still, someone had to bear this weight. For the sake of freedom. For the sake of America. To defend the Constitution against all enemies, foreign and domestic. This was his time and place. He would bear this burden alone.

Mack turned away from the peaceful view of the South Lawn. He folded his arms and gazed at the members of his National Security Council.

"Where are we on all this Russian troop movement?"

"I'll take that one, Mr. President," Secretary of Defense Erwin Lopez spoke up. He extracted multiple copies of reports from his briefcase and handed them out. "Eight hours ago, NGA noticed satellite photos of the first movement of Russian ground forces. We've had four more satellite passes since then. At two-thirty a.m., four o'clock, five-thirty, seven, and eight-thirty. Photos from each of these passes are included in your packets."

Mack began thumbing through the satellite photos as the secretary of defense continued.

"We have massive troop movements from Volgograd, and also some troop and armored vehicle movement from North Ossetia. The divisions driving east from North Ossetia have stopped at the Chechen border.

"The divisions sweeping south from Volgograd are not there yet. At this point we think, sir, that Chechnya is their destination, although there's a danger that they could be headed farther south, into the Middle East. We've intercepted radio traffic which corroborates our theory that this is a massive move into Chechnya, and I'll defer to the director of Central Intelligence for that portion of the briefing."

"Very well." Mack turned to his CIA director, Mitch Winstead. "Mr. Director?"

"Thank you, Mr. President. I'm sorry to say that ground intelligence in the North Caucasus area in the last forty-eight hours has brought about more alarming news, sir."

"Talk to me, Mr. Director."

"Well, sir, from what we've heard on the streets, the Russians seem to have misplaced several pounds of weapons-grade plutonium."

"*What?*" Mack raised his voice slowly. "Repeat that, Mr. Director."

"Sir, the Russian government, like the Soviet government before it, is stone-faced and tight-lipped, but their subordinates on the street don't do a very good job of guarding state secrets."

Lord, please don't let this be true. "Mr. Director, I want to know exactly what you've been hearing."

"Approximately eighteen hours ago, around midnight Caucasus time, rebel forces, probably Chechen, ambushed a Russian military truck in the Russian Republic of North Ossetia. Our sources say the truck was under guard and carried weapons-grade plutonium 239. The driver and the two guards were killed. The plutonium is gone."

"How much is missing?"

The CIA director whipped out a handkerchief and patted his forehead. "Mr. President, bear in mind that we do not know the precise amount, but we believe that at least fifty pounds was taken."

"Fifty pounds?"

"Yes, sir."

"So how much firepower is that?"

The director cleared his throat. "That's more of a military question, Mr. President. I think I should defer that question to the secretary of defense."

The president glared at the secretary of defense. "Well, Mr. Secretary? How much firepower are we talking?"

Secretary Erwin Lopez met the president's eyes. "That's enough to build four or five small thermonuclear devices or ..." SECDEF's voice trailed off.

"Out with it, Mr. Secretary."

"Or, Mr. President, they could package the fuel to build a small hydrogen bomb of approximately five megatons."

"So what would five megatons do, Mr. Secretary?"

The secretary of defense hesitated. His brows furrowed. His eyes shifted around the Oval Office.

"Out with it, Erwin," the president said.

"Five megatons, if they were able to build such a device, would vaporize"—the secretary looked down—"any major city on the entire Eastern seaboard, and then some."

Shudders swept Mack's body. Only the ticks and tocks of the grandfather clock near the entrance of the Oval Office punctuated the respite of silence.

"Lord, help us," the president said.

"We think the Russians believe that Chechen rebels smuggled the plutonium to Chechnya to build a nuclear device. But frankly, sir, we think the Russians are wrong."

"Go on."

"As you know, Mr. President, you directed the CIA and Department of Defense to develop contingency plans to sink the Russian freighter *Alexander Popovich*, the ship used in the kidnapping of Jeanette L'Enfant."

"Yes, I remember that directive. Go on."

"We've recently traced a five-million-dollar transfer from the radical Islamic organization the Council of Ishmael to the captain's Caribbean bank account. Mr. President, that had to be a payment for something—transportation of stolen plutonium would be worth that kind of money."

"Any other reason to suspect the *Alexander Popovich*?"

"Sir, we've maintained surveillance on *Alexander Popovich*. It's home-ported at Sochi, Russia, which is not that far from where we believe the nuclear fuel was heisted. About three o'clock in the morning, just three hours after the attack, a truck showed up with a delivery for *Alexander Popovich*."

Mack mused on that. "Two questions, Mr. Director. First, how did we just *happen* to have someone in place to see this delivery, and second, how do we know that this mysterious truck that showed up in the middle of the night was carrying the plutonium?"

The CIA director and the secretary of defense exchanged glances, and then SECDEF spoke up. "I'll take that one, Mr. President. First, we've been watching *Alexander Popovich* as a result of your directive to devise a secret battle plan to sink it. Since we believe it is connected to terrorist activities, we've had agents on the ground there keeping a close contact on the ship's in-port activities.

"In addition to our CIA operatives on the ground in Sochi, NCIS special agents in Sochi report that *Alexander Popovich* is in port taking on supplies. That report is corroborated by satellite photos. She could be ready to sail in weeks or even days."

SECDEF continued, "Our agents personally watched all this last night from a remote point with binoculars."

Mitch Winstead, the CIA director, spoke up. "In other words, we've already tracked this ship to terrorist activities, and we believe that this ship is being retained for another mission."

Another brief moment of silence followed.

"And I suppose that mission is to take this weapons-grade pluto-nium that nobody has actually seen, then sail off with it so that some terrorist group can blow up the United States?" This was the voice of Secretary of State Robert Mauney, who sat cross-armed to the presi-dent's left.

"Mr. Secretary," Winstead shot back, "in the intelligence world, we can never be one hundred percent sure about anything. What you have said is true. Nobody—at least nobody that we have in our intelligence camp—actually saw what was in that crate hauled on the ship. But mathematically speaking, given the intelligence data we currently have, I'd say that odds favor that, sir."

"Then why are the Russians sending their forces to Chechnya? Do they know something we don't know?" Mauney wrung his hands. "Doesn't that tell us where the plutonium is?"

"With all due respect, Mr. Secretary," Director Winstead replied in deliberate tones, "this is more likely a matter of us knowing something that the Russians don't know."

"Elaborate, Mr. Director," the president said.

"The financial trail, Mr. President." Director Winstead leaned for-ward. "It goes back to the deal that Commander Brewer cut with Com-mander Quasay when we prosecuted those Islamic fighter pilots. Quasay gave us information in exchange for our not seeking the death penalty. That information led us to financial accounts which have allowed us to track cash flow from radical Council of Ishmael accounts to accounts controlled by this Russian captain—Batsakov."

"You don't think the Russians know about this ship's activities?"

"They may have some notion that the skipper is lavishing around in a lot of cash, but I doubt they know about this five-million-dollar infusion of cash into his Caribbean account, or that he even has such an account."

"Mr. President." The secretary of defense fidgeted with his cufflinks.

"Yes, Secretary Lopez."

"Sir, this underscores the need to sink that freighter. We know it has been used by terrorist organizations, that it will be used again by terrorist organizations. It is now most likely carrying enough plutonium to blow up New York City, Los Angeles, or Washington, D.C. The Russians either condone it or have turned a blind eye to it."

"With all due respect, Mr. Secretary," the secretary of state responded, "that idea is too risky." Robert Mauney looked at Mack. "Please, Mr. President, I strongly urge you to give diplomacy a chance."

"Diplomacy?" Secretary of Defense Lopez spoke up. "Our diplomatic relations with the Russians are as low now as they have been since the Cuban Missile crisis. What are we supposed to do? Just say to the Russians, 'Excuse me, but you've got it all wrong on Chechnya, and one of your freighters is carrying the nuclear material you're looking for.'

"Mr. President." Secretary Lopez turned his gaze from the secretary of state and looked at Mack. "The Russians don't know that we're aware of this missing plutonium. If we let them know, that compromises our intelligence on the ground there, and if we let them know that we suspect this freighter of terrorist activities, that ends our opportunity to sink it surreptitiously. If we sink it after we tell the Russians we think it's a terrorist ship"—he shifted his gaze back to the secretary of state—"you've really got a diplomatic challenge, Mr. Secretary."

"All right." Mack waved his hands in the air. "That's enough." Mack let a moment of silence permeate the air. He looked at his secretary of state. "Secretary Mauney, the State Department feels that a military operation against this freighter is too risky?"

"Yes, sir, we do, Mr. President."

"Very well. I'd like you to address that, and after you've finished, Secretary Lopez may respond. Fair enough?" Mack glanced at Lopez, then back at Mauney.

"Yes, sir," both secretaries said at the same time.

"Secretary Mauney, the floor is with the State Department."

"Thank you, Mr. President." The secretary of state rose from his chair, then walked around the conference table to a position just a few feet in front of the president.

"Now, Mr. President, as I understand the Navy's plan, which I have yet to see, by the way"—a halting glance at the secretary of defense, as if insulted that he had not been in on the military planning for the infiltration of the Black Sea—"this freighter would be sunk by a U.S. submarine in the Black Sea.

"Mr. President, the Black Sea is a dangerous place. The Russians consider it their territory. Even today, they protest the presence of warships there. The Russians claim that only the littoral nations surrounding the Black Sea—including Russia, Bulgaria, Ukraine, Georgia, Turkey, and Romania—have a right to have warships there.

"Now if we sink this freighter with a submarine, Mr. President, and sink it in the Black Sea, then the only way to get a sub in there is through the Bosphorus. And as you know, sir, the Bosphorus, which connects the Marmara to the Black Sea, is the narrowest international strait in the world." Mauney stood up. "If I may call on my aide to assist me for a moment, sir?"

"Of course," Mack Williams replied.

Mauney motioned for his aide to approach, and the aide unveiled a large photograph, mounted on foamcore, and set it on an easel. All heads turned toward the photo.

"Mr. President, this is a satellite photograph of the Bosphorus taken from outer space."

"The waterway to the north is the Black Sea. To the south, the Sea of Marmara. Our submarine would have to approach from the south, sail through this narrow and crooked waterway, under the two bridges, and then into the Black Sea in the north. When our mission is complete, we would have to sail out—there's no other way—to reach the safe waters of the Mediterranean.

"This narrow waterway of international strategic importance has been fought over since the fifth century BC, when the Greek city-state Athens depended on grain shipments to be brought in from Scythia on the Black Sea.

"The Roman Emperor Constantine founded the city of Constantinople here. Today, the Turkish city of Istanbul straddles the straits. The entire strait is only about twenty miles long, it is heavily populated on both sides, and it is narrow and shallow. Not only that, Mr. President, but

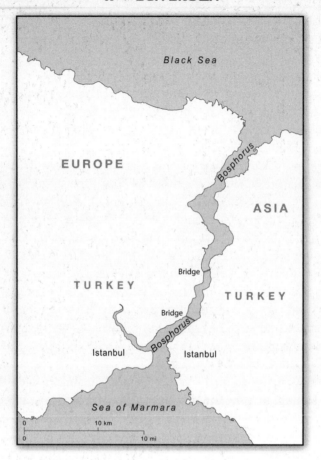

two bridges cross it, which you can see in this map and satellite photo. The bridges connect the eastern and western sectors of Istanbul.

"If we send our sub in on the surface, we're suspect number one when we sink that freighter, which I would remind you, sir, sails under a Russian flag. If the sub transits the Bosphorus submerged, and if we get caught, we run the risk of alienating the Turks. Mr. President, the water in that small bottleneck is shallow. The average depth is about two hundred feet. In some places, I've been told that the water depth is as shallow as a hundred and sixty feet. Plus I've also been told that this waterway is as narrow as fifteen hundred feet through the heart of the city.

"The currents are treacherous. Our sub runs the risk of colliding with commercial shipping or running into rocks. Over fifty thousand ships transit this waterway each year, sir. That's *fifty thousand*. The danger for a collision if we're underwater is grave. A submerged sub running through there would be practically on the bottom, with no room for navigational error.

"We run a grave risk getting the sub in, and then even a greater risk getting it out. What happens if our sub crashes on the rocks and we end up blocking one of the most important waterways in the world?

"Besides, if we sink this ship, the Turks—and the Russians—will be on high alert for the presence of foreign subs passing back through here. I would remind you, sir, that the Turks, with their huge Muslim population, are still furious with us over the Dome of the Rock attack. They could pull out of NATO over this."

Mack mulled that over. He looked at the secretary of defense, Erwin Lopez.

"Mr. President," Secretary Lopez spoke. "Our sub commanders are the world's finest. Not even the Brits hold a candle to us anymore. Besides, we've developed a plan to get our submarine in undetected. Secretary Mauney neglected to mention that. We can get in, perform our mission, and get out. Just say the word."

"Gentlemen!" Mack pivoted around and slammed his hand on the presidential desk. "One at a time!" The president chopped his hand in the air. "Tell me this. Forget about the missing plutonium for a moment. How solid is our intelligence that this ship was linked to the Council of Ishmael?"

"Rock solid, Mr. President," Lopez declared. "When the French lawyer L'Enfant was kidnapped, we're certain she was held on the *Alexander Popovich*. In her briefing to us after our SEAL team rescued her, she talks about being hauled onto a ship, and passing through some sort of international canal which passed through the middle of a city, which we now believe was the Bosphorus.

"They sedated L'Enfant with drugs in one of the lower spaces for most of the voyage, sir. Then they crated her up in a wooden box and slung it through the air, in what we now know was a cargo crane in the Russian port city of Sochi. We have witnesses, Russians in fact, who saw the crate lowered from the ship, Mr. President, and saw them drive off.

"The ship that we're targeting is the Russian freighter *Alexander Popovich*, home-ported in Sochi, Russia, on the eastern coast of the Black Sea. Here's a photo of it." Lopez had an aide place a large black-and-white photo of a long, black ship on another easel. "I remind you, Mr. President, that this ship and its captain have made themselves available for hire as instruments of radical Islamic terrorists."

Mauney spoke up. "So we don't know for a fact that L'Enfant was on board, is that right?"

Winstead said, "L'Enfant described being loaded off a ship in a wooden crate."

"That's still too circumstantial," Mauney said. "Anything could've been in that crate we observed. Eggs. Tools. Anything. Nobody actually saw L'Enfant. All the more reason to hold off on all this. We just don't have enough information."

"Yes, we do," Lopez shot back. "The money trail condemns this captain, sir. We've now gone back and shown payments to this captain coinciding with the L'Enfant kidnapping, and now again, just as this plutonium is disappearing, millions show up in his account. Tell me this is coincidental. These people are enemies of the United States and enemies of the West. Now they've onloaded materials needed to make a nuclear bomb. The secretary of state knows this."

"Gentlemen!" Mack held his palm out like a traffic cop. "So, where is this ship headed, Mr. Director?" the president asked.

"We think Sevastopol, on the Crimean peninsula in Ukraine. Possibly Odessa. From there, who knows?"

"Please, Mr. President," Mauney interjected, pleading with his hands, "if we must attack, and this is only if we *absolutely* must, why not wait until the freighter is out in the open sea?"

"But the Black Sea *is* the open sea," Lopez interjected.

"No, I mean the Mediterranean, or better yet, the Atlantic," Mauney said. "Why sneak one of our subs into what the Russians have considered *their* territory through the Bosphorus? This is the narrowest and most dangerous bottleneck in the world for a sub to pass through. Trying something like this is unheard of. Why not just have one of our subs tail it into the open ocean? That way it becomes difficult for the rest of the world to pin this on us."

Lopez stood, holding his palms upward. "It's much harder to track in the open ocean. Keeping track of freighters with ties to terrorist activities has become increasingly difficult. The ocean is a big space, and if this ship gets out on the high seas with nuclear materials on board, we could lose track of her. And if we lose track of her, and she gets this fuel into the wrong hands, then the blood of the victims is not on my hands!"

Lopez stopped, perhaps realizing how loud his voice had gotten. The secretary spoke again, this time in lower tones. "Look, Mr. President, timing is crucial here. We've vowed to hunt down terrorists expeditiously and anywhere in the world. This rogue Russian skipper and his crew were coconspirators with the Council of Ishmael, and they've proven ready to attack Western interests for hire. This guy may not even be skipper of this ship months from now, *if* we get a shot at his ship anywhere other than the Black Sea. Timing is crucial to the national interest here, sir."

"Timing?" Mauney threw his hands in the air. "The American public doesn't even know that this freighter was used to aid and abet terrorism. What's the point?"

"The point, Mr. Secretary," Lopez retorted, "is that the *terrorists* know full well that it was used. They've paid him again for something. This time for something that could lead to the destruction of an entire American city. And our message must go straight to them, like a clenched fist smashed straight in their mouths."

"Gentlemen!" the president snapped. "I appreciate your passion, but this isn't the back bench of the British parliament." Mack turned to the secretary of defense. "Mr. Secretary, does the Navy have a plan to sneak this sub through the Bosphorus undetected?"

Lopez looked around the room, exchanging sly grins and nods with the chairman of the Joint Chiefs of Staff. "We do have a plan, Mr. President. We call it *Operation Undercover*."

"Interesting code name," the president mused. "So how does it work?"

"Let me put it this way, Mr. President. The terrorists aren't the only ones who can play games with seagoing freighters."

"Explain, Mr. Secretary."

"With pleasure, sir." The secretary stood and motioned for two naval officers, both lieutenant commanders, to approach with an oversized attaché case.

"Mr. President, my friend the secretary of state is right about one thing. Getting a submarine through the Bosphorus is a challenge. Part of the problem is the shallow depth. With an average depth of a hundred-sixty feet, if our sub goes in too deep, she risks grounding or colliding with rocks along the bottom. If she comes up to periscope depth, she risks being spotted from the air.

"Mr. President, here's a photo of one of our *Los Angeles*–class boats, the USS *Chicago* at periscope depth just off the coast of Malaysia. In this photo *Chicago* is under sixty feet of water, yet in the daytime, she's clearly visible from any aircraft passing over, and there are hundreds of aircraft over Istanbul.

"Our challenge, clearly, is finding a way to block the sub from view from the air. We took the problem to Newport News Shipbuilding. They mulled it over, and the solution they came up with is this. Commander?"

The lieutenant commander assisting the secretary of defense removed the photo of the *Chicago* and replaced it with a schematic diagram that looked like a blueprint.

"This," Secretary Lopez said, "is the blueprint for *Operation Undercover*, which is the code name for the portion of the mission to get our sub in the Black Sea.

"As you know, Mr. President," Secretary Lopez began, "six months ago you authorized the Defense Department to come up with a plan for submarine infiltration of the Bosphorus and other strategic waterways to deal with rogue freighters like the *Alexander Popovich* and for other strategic reasons."

The president nodded his head.

"We've carried out your orders, sir. And the concept here," the secretary said, pointing at the diagram, "is brilliant. Under this plan, which we have been working on for months, naval engineers cut a watertight compartment in the bottom of an existing freighter.

"Ladies and gentlemen, this has already been accomplished. Naval engineers at Newport News cut a compartment into the lower hull of the Russian freighter *Volga River*, which has been in port at Norfolk."

"What happened to her crew?" the vice president asked.

"Let's just say that her crew is enjoying an unexpected but extended visit to the United States."

"I don't even want to hear it," the president said.

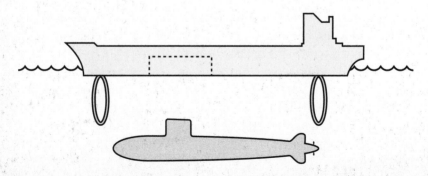

That comment brought chuckles from the group.

"Anyway," the secretary of defense continued, "the ship is being manned by a U.S. Navy crew, posing as civilians. They all speak Russian. The *Volga River* is now in the Mediterranean, awaiting orders to rendezvous with the U.S. submarine.

"A *Los Angeles*–class submarine, the USS *Honolulu*, manned by a volunteer crew of submarine veterans, is on standby in La Maddalena, Italy, awaiting your orders, Mr. President. That crew understands that if they are called upon to carry out this mission, they may never return."

Silence again, except for the grandfather clock ticking and tocking. The secretaries of state and defense seemed to have run out of gas. All eyes returned to the president.

"Okay, here's what I'm ordering," the president declared. "Deploy the *Honolulu* out of La Maddalena. Send her out to the rendezvous point to link up with the *Volga River*. I've not made a final decision on this attack. Not yet anyway. But I want our sub ready to go if and when I give the order."

"Yes, sir, Mr. President."

"We are adjourned."

CHAPTER 6

3 p.m. local time

The Alfa Romeo coupe jolted along the narrow cobblestone streets, headed to the main gate of the U.S. submarine base.

From the passenger's seat of the sports car, Commander Pete Miranda took in the vibrant colors of the picturesque Mediterranean-style buildings in the center of town. A few minutes later, the car cleared the last small building, opening a spacious view of the blue waters of the Straits of Bonifacio. Sparkling wavelets glistened in the afternoon sun, creating the illusion of a crystal-blue carpet separating the Italian island of La Maddalena from the French island of Corsica, just a few miles to the north.

The pristine beauty of the sight masked the reality that these were some of the rockiest and thus most dangerous waters anywhere in the world for navigating a submarine in close quarters around a sub base.

La Maddalena had been home to a small U.S. nuclear submarine base since 1973. Pete had grown to love this, his favorite Mediterranean port-of-call. Unfortunately, the Sardinians and the Greenpeace activists had carped about the presence of U.S. nuclear boats at La Maddalena ever since USS *Hartford* scraped bottom and ran aground in 2003.

As a result of all that, the gorgeous base at the northern tip of this tiny island would soon be closed. How fitting that one of the last missions launched from this place would be the most dangerous, and most significant to the defense of the America he so loved.

Stogie clamped between his molars, Pete exchanged salutes with the petty officer at the main gate of the U.S. submarine base.

Change was happening all too fast, Pete Miranda thought, as the car rolled through the gate and onto the base. There was the unwelcome change in his personal life—separation and divorce, alienation from his family. And in the wider world, the years following the end of the Cold War had brought closure to many of the great U.S. naval bases around the world: Charleston, Long Beach, Treasure Island, Subic Bay.

And now ... this.

The closing of these great ports-of-call was disturbing to him. Was the Navy losing its significance around the world? Which begged the question, was he losing his own? After all, the Navy was in him, wasn't it?

That thought led him often to the thought of retirement. But his love of the Navy, his love of the sea, his love for submarines would not let him retire. Not yet, anyway. Not voluntarily.

Somewhere, it was still out there. He knew it in his gut. The mission that would define his significance as a naval officer. This was why he couldn't retire. Not yet. The mission that would define his legacy might cost him his life. So be it. He would face the mission bravely, and perform it to the best of his abilities.

Pete looked over to his left. The chief petty officer in the driver's seat pulled the Alfa Romeo into a parking space. Across the street a *Los Angeles*–class submarine was moored alongside the pier. A group of naval officers and enlisted men milled about on the pier.

"Let me check on things, Skipper," the chief said. "I'll come get you just as soon as the crew is ready."

"Sure thing, Chief." Pete puffed his stogie as the chief got out of the car.

The chief returned from across the street and opened the passenger door of the Alfa Romeo.

"Ready, Chief?"

"Aye, aye, Skipper."

"Very well," Pete said. "Let's do it."

Pete stepped out of the car, crossed the street to the end of the pier where the submarine was moored to his right. A crew of one hundred officers and enlisted men were lined on the pier in four rows to his left.

"Attention on deck!" a lieutenant commander called from atop the aluminum platform erected just in front of the four rows of men.

The crew came to sharp attention as Pete, followed by the chief, stepped up four aluminum steps and joined the lieutenant commander on the platform. He dropped the stogie on the platform and stamped it out.

"Afternoon, Frank," Pete said to the lieutenant commander, accepting and returning the salute of his new executive officer.

"Afternoon, sir." The executive officer sharply held his salute. "Sir, I present to you the officers and crew of the USS *Honolulu*."

"Very well." Pete dropped his salute, and the XO crisply followed. Pete stepped to the podium, turned, and faced the brand-new crew.

"Gentlemen, at ease!"

Pete looked out and saw one hundred of the Navy's finest kick from strict attention to parade rest. Beyond them in the background, the adjoining concrete piers were empty of ships and empty of men. Other than circling seagulls, not another soul, beyond Pete and these men, was anywhere within earshot. The Navy had cordoned off a five-hun-dred-yard guarded perimeter around the ship to maintain secrecy.

"Good afternoon, gentlemen. I'm Commander Pete Miranda. Up until one hour ago, I was commanding officer of the USS *Chicago*.

"Some of you I know. Many of you I don't. Here's what I know about all of you. You have been in the Navy at least twenty years. You're all within one year of retirement or have retired within the last year.

"You've all volunteered for this mission. And although a hundred others also volunteered, you were screened, selected, and flown here because your records as submariners are exemplary. And you've all been apprised of the danger in what we may be called on to do.

"I want you to take this moment to look at the man on each side of you."

Men looked to their left and their right.

"If the president of the United States gives the order that is being contemplated in Washington even as we speak, there's a better than even chance, that thirty days from now, either you, or the man next to you, or both of you ... will be dead."

Pete's words reverberated off the concrete pier.

Wind whipped off the water, and the chorus of wheeling gulls provided the only background to the moment of icy silence.

"You may, even at this hour, gentlemen, step away from this mission. And if you step away, there will be no shame, no disgrace, and your naval personnel records, which will never confirm your participation in this mission should you go, will in no way be adversely affected.

"Not that your naval records mean a heck of a difference at this point, since most of you—like me—are old geezers in the Navy and about to go to the beach permanently anyway."

That comment brought a few chuckles, a brief respite to the deadly seriousness of the moment.

"In a moment, I will give you an opportunity to step away from this with honor. But before I do that, you deserve to know what you're getting into.

"Just over forty-eight hours ago, a sizable amount of weapons-grade plutonium-239 was stolen by terrorists in the Caucasus Mountains of Russia."

That comment brought murmuring and looks of grave concern in many of the men's faces.

"The Russians, who haven't publicly acknowledged the problem, think the plutonium was captured and has been transported east to Chechnya. They've mobilized their army, and they appear prepared to wipe Chechnya off the face of the earth to try and find the plutonium.

"We, on the other hand, believe the plutonium has been smuggled to the Russian city of Sochi, on the Black Sea, where it has been stored on a rogue Russian freighter with terrorist ties. We believe that freighter may be about to sail, and if she does, the president may call upon us to slip into the Black Sea, through the Bosphorus, submerged, and sink her."

More murmuring.

"It is imperative, for the national security of the United States, that this mission remain top secret. There will be no glory, no triumphant victory parade, no public honor for what you are about to do.

"As you know, United States relations with Russia and most of the Islamic states have soured since two Islamic terrorists posing as U.S. Navy pilots attacked the Dome of the Rock in Jerusalem. So the Russians have cozied up with the Islamic states in the Persian Gulf. They have not been able, ironically, to deal with radical Islamic elements in their own backyard in Chechnya.

"By sinking this freighter, if we are able to get that far, we will in fact be doing the Russians a favor. Remember, that plutonium could just as well be used in a bomb against a Russian city as an American city, since the Chechens hate the Russians so much. Or, the plutonium could be split up and used in multiple bombs to advance the cause of Islam against both American and Russian citizens.

"Therefore if called on, we must"—Pete chopped his hand in the air. The eyes of each man froze on him—"I repeat we *must*, find her and sink her before she gets out of the Black Sea. If we fail in our mission, we will have failed America. We will have failed millions who will never know that we are here … millions of innocent men, women, and children … who if not incinerated by a nuclear blast, would be subjected to the indiscriminate path of burns, blindness, boils, and cancer from flash, heat, and radioactive fallout."

The gong of ship's bells filled the silent void.

"Gentlemen, to underscore the gravity of this situation, our intelligence believes that enough weapons-grade plutonium is missing to build a bomb ten times as powerful as the bomb that fell on Hiroshima.

"I said a moment ago that we will be doing the Russians a favor by sinking the freighter. But the Russians, in their ignorance, won't even realize we are doing them a favor. All Russia will know is that we've sunk a freighter flying their flag.

"Ordinarily, an attack on a civilian freighter of one nation by the naval vessel of another nation is an act of war. That's the way the Russians will see it if we are discovered. And that's why the Russians must never know what hit this freighter."

He eyed every man before him.

"Listen to what I have to say, because this is where the rubber meets the road." Pete stopped again. "We cannot risk the capture of the *Honolulu*." His voice resonated over the chopping wavelets lapping against the hull of the submarine. "We cannot link this freighter's sinking to a U.S. submarine. Gentlemen, once we attack this freighter, if we can find her, the chances of getting back out of the Black Sea through the Bosphorus undetected are slim. Not impossible, but I want you to understand the danger.

"So after the attack, gentlemen, we are going to make an effort to link back up with the freighter and slip back through the Bosphorus the way we came in. But remember that the Black Sea is not the Pacific Ocean. There are fewer places to hide.

"If we are able to attack this terrorist freighter, we'll have to get out of there fast. Otherwise, we may have to scuttle the *Honolulu*." The men looked to each side, with looks of bewilderment on their faces. "That's right. We may have to abandon ship, and then send her to the bottom of the Black Sea. That's the potential sacrifice your country is asking you to make. Any questions?"

A senior chief torpedoman's mate raised his hand.

"Senior chief."

"Sir, I know it's not the Pacific, but still, the Black Sea is a big place. Assuming we can pull off this maneuver and get through the Bosphorus without getting spotted by the Turks, just how does Washington expect us to find this freighter once she's underway?" The seasoned senior chief spoke in a drawl that made him sound like he was from Arkansas. "I think we all know that tracking the location of freighters at sea is a problem that is hard even for the U.S. Navy. There are just too many of them, and the oceans and seas of the world are just too big. I mean, no disrespect intended, sir, but ain't this like looking for a needle in a haystack? Sir?"

A number of the prospective crewmembers nodded in agreement at the senior chief's question.

Pete looked the senior chief in the eye, and eyed every crew member standing before him. "Gentlemen, the senior chief asks a great question. Frankly, I should've covered this. But then again, that's why God created chiefs and senior chiefs and master chiefs—to make sure the old man's backside stays out of a sling. Right?"

A wave of laughter followed that comment. *Old man* was an endearing term used in the Navy to refer to a commanding officer of a ship, submarine, or shore station, and had nothing to do with an officer's chronological age.

"Thank you, Senior, for keeping this old man's rear out of the tar pit, even before we set sail." More laughter.

"No problem, Captain," the senior chief torpedoman said.

"I want you all to understand that we may never find the *Alexander Popovich*. This *is*, in a sense, like looking for a needle in a haystack. Even in this smaller section of the Black Sea, we are still dealing with thousands of square miles of water. We may be trying this dangerous docking maneuver for nothing. We are risking our lives on a lark that our satellites are good enough to track her down, to feed us her coordinates, and let us hunt her down and kill her.

"But here's how we're gonna try to find her. Our intelligence has picked up rumblings that the ship will be sailing from the Russian port of Sochi to Odessa in Ukraine. And from there, probably out of the Black Sea and who knows where.

"So here's what we're gonna do. We're gonna sneak through the Bosphorus under the freighter *Volga River*, and when we make it into the Black Sea, we will disengage from the *Volga River*. From there, we will sail to the entrance of the shipping lanes leading to Odessa. We will stay there, submerged, waiting. We will set an underwater steel trap. If *Alexander Popovich* shows up, we will spring that trap with two MK-48 torpedoes under the midsection of her hull. That should do the trick.

"And as she sinks to the bottom of the sea, we will engage in full power and get the heck out of there." There were multiple instances of head nodding. The answer seemed to have done the trick. "Any other questions?"

There was no response. "Gentlemen, you've given your lives to the Navy, and you've volunteered for this mission. You're the best that this country has to offer. You have a *right* to ask questions."

A chief petty officer raised his hand.

"Chief?"

"Well, sir. I think we're all either divorced or never married. The Navy is our lives, but we do have families back in the States. Many of them depend on our Navy salaries. If those salaries were gone ..." The chief hesitated, searching for his words. "We all know that this business may bring death at any time. We knew that the day we enlisted. But I guess what I'm asking is ... are we going down with the sub, sir?"

A large cloud cast a shadow over the sub and her prospective crew. "Fair question," Pete began. "No, chief, we won't ask you to go down with the sub. We will abandon her, if possible, and the crew will board life rafts. Before abandoning ship, we'll arm all sensitive equipment with plastic explosives. We will trigger automatic timers that will flood the ballasts. All computers, data storage, et cetera, will be destroyed. We'll have thirty minutes at most to paddle away from the sub before she sinks."

Another hand shot up. "Yes, petty officer?"

"Skipper, are we going to try and transit the Bosphorus submerged?"

"A freighter has been retrofitted and is somewhere out there right now." Pete nodded his head to the south, toward the open waters of the Mediterranean. "The plan is to come up under the bottom of the freighter and surface, partially. We'll bring the sub's sail into a water-tight compartment under the bottom of the freighter, where large O-Rings attached to the hull of the freighter will retract around the bow and stern of the sub.

"We'll have the element of surprise going in. Hopefully, no one will suspect what we're doing. Coming back out, that won't be the case. When the freighter goes down, every ship in the Russian Black Sea fleet will be hunting every inch of water looking for the vessel that attacked it. If we stop under the *Volga River* to reattach, every Russian and Turkish chopper in their respective air forces will be on the freighter like white on rice. We'll try to get out, but we may have to scrap the sub.

"A moment ago, I said that this crew will be moved to rubber lifeboats as the sub sinks. Speedboats will be deployed from obscure ports in Turkey, Bulgaria, and Romania to search for our crew. If we are found, we will be taken back to the shorelines of those respective countries, where the plan is to smuggle us ashore, circumventing customs, and then we will be transported to the United States embassies in those respective countries.

"If we are fortunate enough to make it that far, we could be in for a long stay within the sanctuary of those embassies. We would be evacuated under diplomatic immunity, in very small numbers to avoid suspicion, over a long period of time. In other words, by bringing only two or three of us out per month, it could take up to three years before they can get us all home.

"Now all that is true *if* they find us out there in our floating rafts before our food and water supply runs out."

Pete ran his hand through his hairline. "Of course if they don't find us ..." He let that sentence trail off. "Well, as you know, it is a pretty big body of water out there. And with the currents and the weather ..."

He let that comment hang. A cloud floated across the sun.

He pulled the Garrison cap from his belt, adjusted it on his head, donned a pair of shades, and spoke with the sharpest military bearing he could muster.

"Gentlemen, with no pressure, and no obligation, and no dishonor if you say no, I say to you this day that your country needs you. If you're prepared to go with me on your last voyage, understanding that there will be no glory, and finally, understanding that the price for saving thousands and perhaps even millions may be your own lives—then signify your acceptance of your responsibility by taking one step forward."

There was a pause. For a frozen moment in eternity the wind swirled in the silence. There was no movement in the line.

And then, on the far left, a step forward.

Two steps forward in the left center.

At the right end, and right center, the clicking steps of leather soles echoed against the concrete.

Wind whipped into the American flag at the end of the pier, energizing it with a fury. Then the Italian flag flying beside it came to life. Perhaps even the wind recognized that Old Glory was still the leader of the world.

They stepped forward, one by one, in the front and back lines. And when the wind had subsided, the movement of the four human lines was finished.

Every single man, now standing at crisp attention, had stepped forward.

Pete struggled for his words, but choked on the lump welling in his throat. He gripped the podium, squeezing it. A sub commander must not show tears to his crew.

"Never have I witnessed such bravery as is displayed in the sight before me." He inhaled deeply, then exhaled. "I thank each one of you for what you have done."

"Thank you, Skipper!" one of them shouted.

"We're with you to the end, sir," another called.

He held his hands out, palms down, signaling that no more public comments were necessary.

"We'll get underway at sixteen hundred hours. That's two hours before sundown, gentlemen. Our orders are to sail, to submerge, and then to await orders from the president."

Each man stood at attention, eyes forward.

"Any questions?"

There were none.

"You are dismissed."

The White House

11:00 a.m. local time

Douglas MacArthur Williams, having been raised at Fort Leavenworth, Kansas, and named for one of the greatest generals in American history, was the son of a career Army officer.

From the anteroom just beside the Oval Office, that same Douglas MacArthur Williams, now president of the United States, let memories of his father wash across his mind.

The lifelong dream of Colonel Manchester Elliot Williams was to see his son follow three generations of Williams men in the long grey line at West Point. The old tank driver had called his boy "Douglas" since his early days to remind both father and son of the great general who had proclaimed that "in war there is no substitute for victory, that if you lose, the Nation will be destroyed."

The old man's dream would not be realized. Mack attended the University of Kansas, where he had gone to law school, and then took a commission in the U.S. Navy as a JAG officer.

This Navy compromise seemed to assuage the colonel's disappointment in Mack's shirking West Point and the Army. The colonel did, at least, drive from Leavenworth to Lawrence to watch "Douglas" sworn in as an ensign, United States Naval Reserve.

Still, Mack never saw the pride return to the old man's eyes until that cold Tuesday in January, three years ago.

The old warrior donned his Army dress uniform and stood just ten feet away on the inaugural platform at the Capitol overlooking the National Mall, as his son was sworn in as commander-in-chief of the Army that the colonel loved so much.

"Son." There had been a pause as the two locked eyes. "I'm proud of you." And the old officer, standing on the sidewalk in front of the United States Capitol, did what officers do in the presence of their commander-in-chief. Colonel Manchester Elliot Williams stood as erect as any boot camp recruit, and with as sharp a precision as his eighty-two years could muster, shot the smartest, crispest salute that the young president would ever see.

Three weeks later, in the family's living room in Fort Leavenworth, Colonel Williams' cold body was found faceup in the middle of the floor. His eyes were open, his face frozen in a beatific smile, and in his hand they found a small green New Testament published by the Gideons. Inside the New Testament, at the third chapter of Romans, a wallet-sized photo of Ensign Douglas MacArthur Williams, JAGC, USNR, served as the old man's bookmark.

Three days later, across the river from the Lincoln Memorial, they buried the old warrior in the frosty ground of Arlington National Cemetery with full military honors. The president, who had never known his father to crack open a Bible, prayed that the colonel's eyes had finally been opened to the truth. By presidential directive, both the Bible and the photograph were buried with the old soldier.

Three sharp rifle volleys were followed by the slow, melodic rendition of taps. His father's resting place joined the graves of thousands and thousands of others, all marked by white crosses.

That day, over protests by the Secret Service, the president had insisted on taking a solitary stroll among the grave markers. The names all blurred together now, but the places ... the places still stood in his mind. The markers did not always reveal where they had died, but the president knew the places well.

Verdun. North Africa. Sicily. Belgium. Normandy. The Solomon Islands. The Phillippines. Inchon. Vietnam. Grenada. Panama. Afghanistan. Iraq.

At least these men died with honor, recognized by their country, and were buried on hallowed ground where hundreds of thousands would pay tribute to their immortal sacrifices.

But now, the men that he was about to send on this dangerous mission would never be so honored. Their mission would be unknown outside of a small circle of Americans with a need to know. And if they died, which they probably would, their bodies would never be honored as his father's had. They would be swallowed forever in the black abyss of the sea.

Death was a risk every American sailor understood.

But how could he explain this to their families? At least he knew where his father was buried.

But what of the children of the officers and crew of USS *Honolulu*?

Would they wonder all their lives what happened to their fathers? To disappear on a clandestine mission. To be lost at sea and never seen again. To have no answers for them. To have no tombstone in a national cemetery on which to rest their hands.

Perhaps diplomacy could solve this impasse. Perhaps the secretary of state was right.

What would Colonel Williams say?

Never had the commander-in-chief felt so alone.

The Al Alamein
Entrance to the Aegean Sea

4 p.m. local time

Over the sea to the east, pillars of gray clouds danced on black streaks of rain. To the west, toward the jagged Greek coastline, the sun had started its downward trek, bathing the great ship in a luminescent orangish hue. But with the wind blowing hard across the flybridge from the east, Salman Dudayev did not have to be a man of the sea to know that soon the massive ship would sail through a torrential downpour.

"The islands are beautiful, aren't they?" Salman directed this question to the captain of the *Al Alamein*.

"Ever seen the Greek Isles before?" Captain Hosni Sadir asked.

"In photographs." Salman removed his sunglasses. "This is my first time at sea."

"The Island of Kalymnos is twenty-five miles to our east. To our north, twenty-five miles off our bow, is the Island of Patmos."

"Ah ... the home of the apostate renegade, John," Salman said.

"The author of that infidel propaganda they call Revelation."

Wind gusted hard across the bow. The freighter rolled from the pitching seas.

"We will pass Patmos in an hour." Sadir cupped his hand around a fresh cigarette and fired up a Zippo lighter.

Salman ignored the comment. "How far to the Bosphorus from here?"

The captain cursed when the wind blew out the tip of his cigarette. He fired up the lighter again, sucked in, and caught a burning ember at the end of the cigarette. "A little more than a day."

Wind whipped harder across the spacious open deck. Whitecaps rushed alongside the ship. Her bow plowed into the swells. The captain turned to Salman. "So what's in this for you?"

Rage welled within Salman. "The Russians stormed my house. They were looking for me. They raped my wife and daughter, then murdered them with their bloody bayonettes. When I reached them, the murderous Russians were gone." His lips froze. He squinted in the wind.

"And you, Captain? Why would you commit yourself and your ship to this mission?"

Raindrops splattered across the bridge. "Stalin deported my grandfather to Siberia with the entire Chechen population during the Great War. He never returned. The rest of my immediate family moved to Egypt. There, I fell in love with the sea. But we always kept in touch with our cousins, who returned to Chechnya in the fifties."

The captain stopped. He seemed caught up in his thoughts.

Salman studied the deep lines in his face. "And for that you would sacrifice your ship?"

Rain-darted wind stung their faces. The captain stared at the sea as he spoke. "When Maskhadov became president, we felt that there was hope for our homeland. When he introduced Islamic Law in 1997, we began the process of leaving Egypt to return to our homeland and families. I would retire from my role as a ship master. But they raided a mosque near Grozny and killed all of my aunts and uncles and cousins. And then they killed Maskhadov."

The rain was driving now, but the captain stood like a rock. "The Russians let all the other states go. Belarus. Ukraine. Moldovia. Georgia. But not Chechnya. They will never allow an Islamic state to exist on their borders." Rainwater drenched his black beret and his all-weather jacket.

"I was there when they killed him," Salman said.

This brought the captain's eyes off the raging sea. Sadir raised his eyebrow.

"Maskhadov," Salman said. "I was there when they killed the president."

"So we understand one another."

"Yes," Salman said. "You sacrifice your ship for your family, and I help you sacrifice it for our martyred president and my beautiful wife and daughter."

The captain turned from the rain, ducked under the eaves of the flybridge, and fired up another cigarette. "I am prepared to sacrifice all for my martyred family, for our martyred president, and for our bleeding nation." He blew a cloud of smoke, but the wind carried it back into Salman's face. "Are you and your men ready to do the same?"

"All my men have stories similar to ours, *Kapitán*. They are the brightest sons of Chechnya. They are at work below even now. Get us the fuel, and we will deliver."

The captain dropped his cigarette on the deck and stamped it out. "Out there. Somewhere. We will find what you need. And when this is over, though we will never see it, there will be a new day for Chechnya and a new day for Islam."

CHAPTER 7

The USS Honolulu
Five miles east of La Maddalena

4:30 p.m. local time

A thick overcast hung over the aqua blue waters of the Tyrrhenian Sea, and the air was heavy with the smell of rain.

From the open bridge atop the sail of the USS *Honolulu*, Commander Pete Miranda surveyed the open waters through his binoculars. The horizon out toward the Mediterranean was open, except for the northeast-bound ferry that ran from Sardinia to the Italian port of Civitavecchia.

Lieutenant Commander Frank Pippen, Pete's executive officer, along with the officer of the deck and two lookouts joined Pete on the small open bridge area. All five men wore orange weather jackets and blue ball caps with USS *Honolulu* stenciled in gold.

Pete handed the binoculars to one of the lookouts standing behind him, then extracted two Montecristo cigars from his khaki shirt pocket under the weather jacket. He handed a cigar to his XO.

"Thank you, sir," the XO said.

"My pleasure, Frank." Pete flicked a lighter and lit the end of Frank's cigar. Pete allowed himself a few drags, taking in the view for a few minutes without saying a word.

"Tell me about your family, Frank."

"Emily and I divorced several years ago. Never had kids."

"Anybody special since?"

"You know how it is. You meet women in bars." The XO took another puff, coughing as if he were choking on the smoke.

"You okay?"

"Yes, sir." Regaining his equilibrium, Frank continued. "Here today. Gone tomorrow. The Navy's a jealous mistress." Another puff on the Montecristo. More coughing. "How about you, sir?"

"How about me ... what?"

"Family, sir?"

"I was born in Chile. My family immigrated to Texas. I met Sally at North Texas State." His voice cracked. A long puff helped him check his emotions. "She and I got married my senior year, and then I went off to OCS. I think they were hot on Latin American officers. I applied for subs, got picked up for the program."

He looked away from his XO. "Anyway, Sally and I divorced five years ago after having two kids. Haven't seen 'em in almost a year."

Three seagulls danced in the air in front of the submarine, just out over the partially submerged bow. The thought struck Pete that he may never see his ex-wife or two children again. Another lump swelled in his throat.

"Too bad, sir."

"My daughter Hannah is thirteen now. She's got the sweetest Cinderella face you'll ever see. She's kind of standoffish, though. Doesn't wanna be hugged. And my boy Coley." Another drag from his cigar. "Well, he's my boy."

"And your wife?"

"What about her?"

"She ever remarry?"

"Nope." Another puff. "I tried getting back together. She wanted none of that."

Honolulu rolled slightly through the swells on top of the water. Pete squinted and exhaled a cloud of blue smoke.

"Anybody special since?" The XO looked at him.

"Like you said, XO. The Navy's a jealous mistress."

"Yes, sir."

Cool wind whipped up from the east, from the direction of the Italian mainland. The great city of Rome lay 225 miles across the open water of the Tyrrhenian Sea—off to their left. Pete had taken submarines along this southeasterly course toward the Mediterranean many times, and always felt reverential awe for the great seas of biblical times. These ancient waters had been sailed by the Greek and Roman navies of antiquity.

Other than the sound of the sub's engines churning through the water, silence reigned. Pete wanted to savor these last moments of communion with the salt air and the sea breeze.

"Do you think he will do it, sir?"

"Do I think who will do what?"

"The president. Do you think he will order us in?"

"I hope and pray that he won't, Frank. But given our current relations with Russia and given the president's big push to curtail terrorist activities, I think he will. But we'll see."

Another pause.

"I'm praying too, Skipper," Frank said. "I'll be honest with you. In all my years in the Navy, I've never felt like I've started a mission where death was a real possibility. Lately, the Navy has gone unchallenged by all the other navies of the world. But this is different."

Their eyes locked. "Yes, Frank, it is."

"I'm ready to go if I have to, Captain. I'm ready." The XO's voice was sure and steady.

Pete slapped Lieutenant Commander Frank Pippen on the shoulders.

He checked his watch. It was time.

"XO, take her down," Pete ordered.

The XO picked up the microphone on the bridge. "Control bridge." A brief pause. "Sounding."

"Bridge. Control. Sounding one-two-zero fathoms."

"Lookouts, clear the bridge!" Frank ordered.

Three orange-jacketed lookouts scrambled down the aluminum ladder leading to the control room.

"Officer of the deck, prepare to dive!" the XO ordered.

Pete descended the ladder from the open-air bridge leading to the control room. A rumble on the aluminum ladders followed him. Pete hopped from the last step to the control room floor, then announced, "Captain is down."

"Captain is down!" the officer of the deck parroted.

Clanking and rumbling on the steel-grated floors echoed throughout the sub. Men jogged down metal ladders. Some slid down the handrails like batman descending the batpole. Red lights flashed on and off. Cacophonous sirens sounded.

"XO down." Frank hopped from the ladder to the deck of the control room.

"XO is down!" the officer of the deck parroted.

"Submerge the ship!" Pete ordered.

"Diving officer submerge the ship!" the XO parroted. "Make your depth one-five-zero feet."

"Make my depth one-five-zero feet! Aye, sir!" the diving officer repeated, then said, "Chief of the watch. On the 1MC!" The diving officer's order opened up every loudspeaker on the sub for every crew member to hear the next commands.

"Dive!"

"Dive!"

"Dive!"

Over flashing lights and warning alarms, the words that electrified the soul of every submariner—*dive, dive, dive*—echoed throughout the ship.

"Make your depth one-five-zero feet," the diving officer told the planesman, the petty officer in the blue jumpsuit who sat at the control of the submarine. "Five degrees down bubble."

Sweat beaded on the planesman's forehead. He pushed the steering wheel down ever so slightly.

Honolulu's nose angled down under the surface. Her ballasts began flooding with salt water. Geysers of water shot into the air from the forward section of the sub as rushing water gushed into the forward ballasts.

She continued angling down, down under the surface. Time was of the essence. Pete had to get *Honolulu* on station, in a position to perform this mission if President Williams ordered it.

"Approaching one-five-zero feet," the diving officer said.

"Very well," Pete said. "Set course for one-three-five degrees. All ahead two-thirds."

"One-three-five degrees," the OOD parroted—*Honolulu* was on a course due southeast. "All ahead two-thirds."

"Maneuvering. Conn. All ahead two-thirds."

"Conn. Maneuvering. All ahead two-thirds."

Honolulu's engines revved. She sliced through the depths, a silent hunter-killer on a life-or-death mission.

The **Alexander Popovich**
Sochi, Russia

9:00 a.m. local time

Captain Batsakov checked his watch. From the bridge of *Alexander Popovich*, he looked over at the concrete pier and cursed. The unexpected and unwelcome visitors from FSB had delayed his sailing for twenty-four hours. The holdup was that group of kids from the blasted orphanage.

Politicians.

They were all the same.

They all had their agendas, strutting about like proud peacocks with their chests puffed out and their thumbs hooked under their suspenders. These bloodsuckers would cost him millions if he did not untie his ship from the concrete pier and find that Egyptian freighter. Not to mention loss of possible future business. The blasted Islamic terrorists had more American money than the Americans themselves.

He was tempted to thumb his nose at the FSB and sail without the little terrors if they didn't show up soon. But if he did that, the authorities could send a Russian submarine to sink him, if they could find one in the Black Sea fleet that was still seaworthy. Even in the best-case scenario, he would never be able to sail into a Russian port again.

Batsakov cursed.

The problem, it seemed, was that the orphans had gone on a camping trip up in the Caucasus Mountains and had not returned in time to travel yesterday.

The phone rang on the bridge.

"For you, *Kapitán*," one of the bridge hands said. "It is the pierside telephone."

Batsakov reached for the phone. "*Dah!*"

"*Kapitán* Batsakov?"

"*Dah.*"

"This is Radimov at the pier shack."

"What is it, Radimov? I am busy."

"My apologies, *Kapitán*. It is the children. They are here."

Finally. Batsakov checked his watch again. If he could get them boarded in the next thirty minutes ...

"You are sure they are all here, Radimov?"

"They rolled up in an old bus, *Kapitán*. They are all hanging out the windows like monkeys."

"I'll be right down." Batsakov cursed again, then slammed down the phone.

uiet! Quiet children!" Twenty-five-year-old Masha Katovich stood at the front of the bus, barking instructions at the group of twelve orphans who were crawling all over themselves, giggling and talking and pointing at the object outside the right side of the dirty old bus.

That object was a large black ship, a freighter, to be precise. She understood their exhilaration. She too became excited when they told her that the group that she had been chaperoning here in Sochi would sail home to Ukraine on board a ship!

She had never even seen a ship. Neither had the children. And now they were here, exhilarated, and she had to get them under control.

"Children! Quiet!"

Nothing.

"Children. No quiet, no ship ride!" Their volume decreased. "No quiet, no ship ride!"

This tactic worked. She could hear herself think. Twenty-four sparkling eyes latched upon her.

"Stay here with the driver and remain quiet. I am going to meet the people from the ship, and then we will go on board!"

Cheering followed that announcement. Masha shook her head. "Don't let anyone out," she ordered the driver, who nodded his head as she stepped out of the bus.

aptain Batsakov's skull was about to explode.

He would get his ship off the pier, if he had to go horsewhip the little devils up onto the deck. And if the FSB tried to board, he would take them out to sea, shoot them in the back of the head, throw them to the sharks, and tell the authorities that they fell overboard when they had overdone it on vodka.

He checked his watch, snorted, and stormed across the deck to the gangway. From there, he looked down and saw the white bus that Radimov was talking about. In fact, he saw Radimov milling about down in front of the bus. Why wasn't he herding the blasted urchins out?

Batsakov bounded down the gangway. He reached the concrete pier, accepted and returned a sloppy salute from the half-drunk sailor at the bottom, and met eyes with Radimov, who still stood in front of the parked bus.

"Radimov! Get these … these …" He held his hands in the air, searching for something more diplomatic to call them than devils. "These *young individuals* off the bus!"

A young woman stepped around the front of the bus. Her black curly hair bounced on her shoulders. Her slim waistline complemented casual jeans and an unkempt green shirt. She smiled.

"These *young individuals*, as you call them, are mine." Her blue eyes blinked at him. "And who, may I ask, are *you*?"

He was about to announce "I am the captain of this ship" when a sporty-looking black Volga 3111 automobile pulled toward them. Batsakov winced at the faces of the two FSB agents who had invited themselves on board his ship less than forty-eight hours ago and announced that he would be forced to host a floating kindergarten.

The two FSB agents, in black suits and black sunglasses, stepped out.

"Ah, *Kapitán*," said the first one, whose name Batsakov remembered as Federov. "I see you and Miss Katovich are becoming acquainted." The agents walked toward the captain and the woman.

"We were getting off to a good start." The young woman locked her eyes on Batsakov again. "I'm Masha Katovich. I work for the relief organization that sponsors summer trips for these orphans." She extended her hand, as if expecting him to kiss it.

He obliged. "You aren't FSB like your friends here?" That brought laughter from her, but no reaction from the stone-faced agents.

She flicked her head toward them. "I envy their salaries and their car. I am but a mere social worker, *Kapitán*."

"I wouldn't describe you as a *mere* anything, my dear." She had mollified his anger about the late sailing, he realized. "I shall gladly transport your orphans to wherever you wish to sail."

"*Kapitán*," spoke the second one, whose name he had forgotten in the immediate glow of Masha Katovich. "Unfortunately, my colleague and I cannot sail with you. Developments in Chechnya have us occupied. You will be met by other FSB agents at the pier in Odessa. They will come onboard and bring the children off. There will be no need for you to disembark. If you choose to disembark, wait until after the ceremonies at the dockside. Meantime, Miss Katovich will assist you during the course of your journey."

"Miss Katovich is coming with us?"

"If that is okay with you, *Kapitán*." She smiled at him.

"But of course. My ship is your ship."

"Then with your permission, I will round up my *young individuals* and get them on board. I am sure you are anxious to set sail, and apologize if we have held your ship up in any way."

"Please, bring your children aboard. And no apologies are necessary, Miss Katovich. Radimov here will assist you in finding your berthing spaces."

She smiled, nodded, stepped into the bus, then barked a command. A minute later, they emerged, like baby geese following their mother goose. One by one, in single file, holding a single linen bag with whatever possessions they owned, they marched up the gangplank and onto the deck.

Batsakov followed them up to the deck and ordered the gangplank removed.

It was time to sail.

The USS Honolulu
The Straits of Sicily

10:40 a.m. local time

Pete and Frank had just finished their inspection of Torpedo One when the 1MC began blaring. "Alert one! Alert one! Incoming emergency action message! Alert one! Alert one! Incoming EAM!"

"Weps, report to your duty station!" Pete ordered the weapons officer. "XO? Come with me!"

"Aye, Captain."

They rushed back through the narrow passageways. Sailors wearing dark blue ball caps stepped back and shouted, "Make way! Make way for the captain!"

Pete stepped into the radio room. "Attention on deck!" the radio officer called.

"At ease," Pete barked. "Where is it?"

"Here, sir."

Pete ripped the message from the radio officer's hands and spread it out on the table. Frank looked over Pete's shoulder.

EMERGENCY ACTION MESSAGE

FROM: NATIONAL MILITARY COMMAND CENTER — WASHINGTON, D.C.
TO: THE USS *HONOLULU* , THE USS *CHARLOTTE*

SUBJECT: ACTION MESSAGE

REMARKS:

Russian weapons-grade nuclear fuel confirmed missing.

Russian freighter *Alexander Popovich* reportedly underway from Sochi 0700 hours Zulu time this day.

Russian high command apparently unaware of presence of fuel on board *Alexander Popovich*.

Russian forces amassing on Chechen border.

The USS *Honolulu* rendezvous with Russian freighter *Volga River* for execution of *Operation Undercover*.

Proceed through Bosphorus, then seek out and destroy *Alexander Popovich* in Black Sea.

The USS *Charlotte* establish patrol area Sea of Marmara. Stand by for updated coordinates and orders.

Set DEFCON 4 by order of National Command Authority.

Pete looked at Frank. "XO, All department heads report to the galley in thirty minutes for an officers meeting at"—he glanced at his watch—"ten hundred hours Zulu time."

"Aye, Captain." Frank picked up the microphone, switching to the 1MC. "Now hear this. This is the XO." Frank's voice echoed throughout the passageways of the submarine. "All officers report to the galley at ten hundred hours Zulu time. This is the XO."

"Give me that." Pete reached for the microphone. He flipped a switch opening a direct line to the control room. "Radio. Conn. This is the captain. Notify engineering. I need full power. Now! That is all." Pete slammed the microphone back in its holster. "May God protect our souls."

CHAPTER 8

The Alexander Popovich
Forty miles east of Sochi, Russia

12:45 p.m. local time

Captain Batsakov peered out through his binoculars, pretending to scan the deep blue horizon of the Black Sea. The key now would be finding this freighter.

At his current speed of 15 knots, or 17.3 miles per hour, it would take at least thirty hours for *Alexander Popovich* to reach the rendezvous in the western sector of the Black Sea. That, of course, meant that they would arrive in the rendezvous sector as the sun was setting, complicating matters even more.

Locating civilian freighters on the open seas was problematic. Not even the great navies of the world were efficient at tracking freighter traffic. Trying to find the Egyptian freighter in the dark would be next to impossible. So they would probably have to steam in circles and wait for the sun to come up, and hope that the freighter was in the area.

Of course, sunlight was not a problem at the moment. This fact was apparent in his binocular-assisted view provided of the lovely Masha, who was currently waving her hands like a traffic policeman down on the deck. How was she able to stand there so calmly, smiling while keeping track of those twelve little devils who were running around on the deck like monkeys released from a zoo?

"*Kapitán?*"

"Yes, what is it, Petrov?" Batsakov did not put aside his binoculars.

"The galley, sir. They wish to know if you would like some food brought to the bridge."

"*Dah, dah.*" Batsakov waived his hand. "Vodka and a sandwich would be fine."

"Right away."

After a moment, another voice materialized over the captain's shoulder. "Stunning, isn't she?"

Batsakov dropped the glasses and locked eyes with his first officer, Joseph Radin. "Are they prettier than in our day, Joseph? Or do our old minds play tricks on us?" He handed the binoculars to the first officer, who took a grinning turn. "Or perhaps our luck is getting better on this voyage."

"You know, *Kapitán*, sometimes our old minds can cloud our better judgment." Radin set the binoculars on a ledge as a steward brought a silver tray with a bottle of vodka, two clear glasses, and an assortment of finger sandwiches.

"*Spaceeba.*" Batsakov took the vodka. "That will be all." He nodded at the young mess steward, dismissing him. Then, taking a sip, he lowered his voice. "Do I hear a cautionary tone in your last comment, Joseph?"

The first officer put his hand on Batsakov's shoulder, lowering his voice as well. "*Kapitán*, you and I have sailed together for a long time. *Dah?*"

"*Dah.*"

Radin nodded his head once down toward their beautiful visitor. "What if she is FSB?"

The suggestion was like a wet blanket. Batsakov felt his eyes widen. "I asked her. She denied it and laughed."

"Of course she denied it. But can we take this risk?"

The first officer's point was well taken. Batsakov filled Joseph Radin's glass.

Radin continued. "Even if she is not FSB, can we afford to have her witness the transfer of our cargo to the Egyptian freighter? Suppose someone asks her? Suppose she is interrogated by FSB? Or worse, what if she *is* FSB?"

"What are you saying, Joseph?"

Their eyes locked. "We cannot afford a slipup, *Kapitán*. This mission is worth more money than either of us have ever made in our lives. We all know, unfortunately, that accidents sometimes happen at sea."

Captain Batsakov let his eyes wander down to the deck again. "Perhaps you are right, friend. But what a waste. Let's keep an eye on her before making a final decision on this."

Their glasses clanked and they drank.

She had been sitting for no more than five minutes when she heard their excited voices.

"Masha! Masha!"

Masha Katovich removed her sunglasses and looked up from her deck chair. Two skinny blonde boys, their ribcages visible as they panted excitedly, stood over her. They made excited gestures with their hands.

"Anatoly, Sasha, what is it? I'm trying to catch a nap."

"Masha! Masha!" Their voices ran together. They pointed to something out over the side of the ship. "Get up and come look!"

A gust of cool breeze refreshened her face. "Why not?"

She dropped her novel on the deck, then pushed herself up. The children stood near the side of the ship. "Get back away from the railing!" she shouted. They ignored her, and instead laughed and pointed out to the sea.

"Dolphins!" Ten-year-old Natalia smiled from ear to ear.

A hundred yards or so off to the side, fifteen or twenty bulb-nosed dolphins danced and played in the water. The chorus of laughter and chattering from the children warmed Masha's heart.

But the cold hand on her shoulder from behind startled her.

"Miss Katovich." A bearded deckhand, smiling with two missing front teeth, was standing so close to her that she could smell the liquor on his breath. "You like dolphins?"

The voice. The twisted smile. His presence seemed sinister. She felt the urge to pray. "Yes, they are beautiful, are they not? The children are enjoying them so much."

"How you like to swim with dolphins?"

"Well, I don't swim all that well."

He reached forward.

She stepped back.

"What's the matter? You no like sailors?"

"No. That's not it. You ..."

"Come with me, miss. The *kapitán* wants to see you."

She looked down. Her orphans, all twelve of them, stood around her in a semicircle. Their concerned eyes were as wide as the full moon. She flashed a reassuring smile at them. "It is all right, children. I will return to you in just a few minutes."

Captain Batsakov sat behind his desk in his stateroom, pouring the clear liquid from the bottle with the red, white, and yellow sticker wrapped around it.

Stolichnaya, the famous Russian brand, was Batsakov's vodka of choice. His lips caressed the glass. Alcohol seeped down his throat, warming the internal cavities of his body.

Vodka was the drink of angels, and Stolichnaya was the vodka of God.

Only the weak believed in God.

No matter. Stolichnaya numbed his soul. That mattered.

Besides. The soul did not exist. The soul was a fairy tale. Just like these beliefs in Allah and God and Jesus or whomever.

Only the here and now mattered. Only the money that he was about to make mattered.

He reached into the drawer and extracted the black Makarov PM 9 millimeter pistol. He brought the gun to his nose and sniffed the smell of burned powder from the last time he had shot at sea lions off the port side of the *Alexander Popovich*.

Three knocks came at the door.

"*Dah!*"

"*Kapitán!*" Aleksey Anatolyvich called from outside in the passageway.

"What is it, Aleksey?"

"Miss Katovich is with me."

Batsakov disengaged the safety of the pistol, worked the slide, loading a live round into the chamber. The silencer was in place. Good.

What a waste this would be. Would he shoot her in the cabin now? He could keep the body in the closet and dump it overboard at dark. Or perhaps he would simply use the gun to scare her into keeping the children in line. The problem with that tactic was that she might tell someone. He took another swig of vodka.

"Send her in."

Batsakov placed the pistol in his lap. The door opened. The beautiful brunette stood in the entryway of his cabin.

Aleksey pushed her in the back of her shoulder. She stepped forward into the cabin, almost stumbling.

The door slammed closed. The sight before him caught him unexpectedly off guard. The white sweater drew attention to her sun-kissed complexion and seemed to accentuate the radiance of her blue eyes.

Obviously, Aleksey had escorted her to her stateroom to change before her important meeting with the captain. He imagined her fussing about her appearance and her wardrobe, as women often do, and insisting that she be allowed to change and freshen up before being brought into his presence.

That thought brought him a smile.

His eyes drank in the sight of her long legs, her trim waistline, and her curly brunette locks. At that point, Batsakov realized that he was staring like a salivating dog.

"Please be seated, Miss Katovich." He hid the pistol in his lap and out of her view.

"Thank you, *Kapitán*." Her eyes danced nervously around the cabin. She sat upright in the aluminum chair just in front of his desk. She crossed her legs, exhibiting a perfect, statuesque posture.

"Are you enjoying your cruise?"

"I enjoy seeing all my children so happy. We were watching the dolphins just before you called me up here."

"Hmm." His eyes fixed on hers. "Care for vodka?"

"No. Thank you, *Kapitán*."

Captain Batsakov knew what he had to do. Just bring the pistol above the desk and shoot her between the eyes. He took another sip. *Just get it over with, Yuri Mikalvich*. He refilled his glass with another round of Stolichnaya. *Think of the security risks. Think of the riches that will await upon success of this mission ... No, we will not kill her yet.*

"Why would a beautiful, intelligent young woman like you be doing work with orphans? The pay must be pathetic. Why not work for the government?"

She mustered an uneasy smile. "I was an orphan, *Kapitán*. God took care of me, and he called me to give my life to take care of the fatherless."

"Hah." Batsakov nearly choked on his vodka. "You believe in God, do you?" Her face seemed to change from a nervous contortedness to a confident peacefulness. What was it about these God-believers that triggered this sort of idiotic trance whenever they talked about their religion?

She folded her hands across her perfectly crossed legs and leaned forward, her nervous smile now looking something less than nervous. "Yes, *Kapitán*. I believe in God. And I believe in the living Son of God."

He sneered. "And just who would that be? This so-called *living Son of God* of whom you speak?"

She leaned back, still smiling, obviously ready to talk some more about her religion. He used the opportunity to unobtrusively slip the pistol under his belt in the middle of his back. He would lead her from the outer office area of his cabin back into the bedroom, where he would do what needed to be done.

"That would be Jesus, *Kapitán*."

Batsakov snorted. "Well, just make sure that you and this Jesus of yours keep these children out of my way, and out of my crew's way, and that they wander nowhere other than the main deck and their cabins unless escorted by a crewmember. Am I clear on this?"

"Perfectly clear, *Kapitán*."

"*Kapitán* Batsakov!" The excited voice of the first officer blared over the intercom.

"What is it?"

"*Kapitán*, we have found the Egyptian freighter."

"This soon? Impossible."

"We are not sure, sir. We need you on the bridge."

"Be right there." Batsakov looked at Miss Katovich. "Wait here. Help yourself to my vodka or anything else you would like. I will be back later. There is more that we must discuss. I wish to make sure that we have no misunderstandings concerning our expectations of you." He threw on his pea coat and stormed out of the cabin.

Office of the president of the Russian Republic
Staraya Square, Moscow

President Evtimov paced across the red carpet just in front of the large executive desk.

"Read that communiqué again, Foreign Minister."

"*Dah*, of course, Mr. President." The Russian foreign minister cleared his throat and again read the short communiqué that was delivered only thirty minutes ago by the ambassador from the United States of America.

Dear Mr. President,

    These are difficult times in which we live. We know that sometimes it becomes necessary for nations to employ military force by legitimate means for the purposes of self-preservation and the advancement of democracy.

    Both of our great nations have been in recent years the victims of terrorism, and as a consequence, have often found it necessary to resort to military force to ensure peace and stability within our national boundaries.

    While we recognize the right of the Russian government to act in this manner, we have concerns about the size and might of the Russian ground forces currently deploying in the Caucasus region.

    Our allies in the region have expressed concern that armed conflict may spill over and beyond the southern borders of your great nation.

    We hope and trust that your intentions do not go beyond the borders of your country. Part of our concern about the size of your force is that the firepower that you are mobilizing appears to be disproportionate to the strength of any rebel forces concentrated in Chechnya. The United States remains committed to human rights violations of innocent civilians caught up in military action. We support basic human rights of citizens all over the world, including the human rights of innocent citizens in Chechnya.

    To the extent that you could provide words of reassurance that we may pass on to our allies, I would be most appreciative.

                   Very respectfully,
                   Mack Williams
                   President of the United States

"Prepare this response to the president of the United States, and deliver it to the American ambassador." President Evtimov looked at his foreign minister.

"Dear Mr. President,

"Thank you for your cable of this day in which you expressed your country's concern about human rights within the Russian Republic.

"Russian ground forces have been mobilized in what is a purely peacekeeping mission. Our forces are currently operating to foster a common goal of our two countries, namely to preserve democracy within the Russian Republic.

"To the extent that military action may be required in the preservation of our democratic goals, rest assured that our forces will not attack civilian targets. Thank you for your concern about the future of democracy and human rights in the Russian Republic.

"Very respectfully, Vitaly Evtimov, president of the Russian Republic."

The USS Honolulu
The Mediterranean sea depths

2040 local time

They sat around the small table in the middle of the galley. Their faded wash khaki uniforms took on an electric-looking hue under the fluorescent tube lights mounted just overhead. All bore faces of stone. This was the second officers' meeting called in the last ten hours.

They rose, all twelve of them, as the commanding officer of the USS *Honolulu* stepped through the hatch from the outside passageway.

"Attention on deck!"

"At ease." Commander Pete Miranda motioned the men back to their seats.

"Gentlemen, we're close to showtime," Pete announced. He quickly studied their faces. Eyes were bloodshot from lack of sleep. Some showed signs of fear. Pete felt fear himself. A little fear was a good thing. Beneath the fear, beneath the bloody veins, their eyes showed a steely determination like none he had ever seen in a submarine wardroom.

"Let's get down to business. I'll start by asking the XO to brief us on our current position." Pete looked at Frank Pippen, who was seated immediately to his right. "XO?"

"Cap'n." Frank stood, took one step back to a mounted easel board, and rolled down a navigational chart showing the waters around the Greek peninsula. "Gentlemen, as of our last sounding, we were here." He pointed to a spot in the Mediterranean south of the Peloponnisos Peninsula and northwest of the Island of Crete. "Our current position puts us approximately fifty miles southwest of the Greek Island of Kythira.

"Within the next couple of hours, we will cross into the next time zone, UTC plus 2, and soon after that, we reach the entrance of the Aegean Sea. From there, we turn northeast and move under the waters surrounding the Cyclades Islands. We will clear the islands approximately one-hundred-fifty miles east of Athens, and from there we head due north to the waters just off the Island of Limnos. That's where we dock with the freighter and proceed through the Dardanelles.

"We'll piggyback under the freighter through the Sea of Marmara to the entrance of the Bosphorus. If we slip though, they cut us loose about twenty miles into the Black Sea, and we go hunting." Frank looked at Pete. "Skipper?"

Pete rose as Frank returned to his seat. "Gentlemen, we have several complicating factors. First, we're in a race against time. *Alexander Popovich* could get out of the Black Sea before we get in. Now one advantage we have is speed. We're three times faster than the freighter.

"Also, intel now believes that this freighter is scheduled to make a port visit to Odessa in Ukraine before leaving the Black Sea. If that's true, that could be our lucky break. This means that if we clear the Bosphorus, we'll sail due north and set our patrol area off the Ukrainian coast, in the waters off Odessa. Hopefully, we'll spot her and sink her before she ever makes that port visit.

"Now if we miss her, then the USS *Charlotte* is on submerged patrol in the northeastern sector of the Aegean Sea. *Charlotte* is *Honolulu's* backup, just in case. If she gets that plutonium past both subs, we've lost this game."

A new round of concerned glances.

"Any questions?"

There were none.

"Be ready. Be on your toes. And pray that God's will be done. I'll be in my stateroom for about thirty minutes. Until then, the XO has the conn."

Vandenberg Air Force Base
Near Lompoc, California

Kent Pendleton brought the binoculars to his eyes and adjusted the focus into full view. The vertical tower sitting atop the launch pad was two miles downrange from the observation platform, but the powerful binoculars brought the sight into full focus.

White steam spewed from the base and sides of the illuminated Delta II rocket, as the countdown echoed from loudspeakers blaring in the observation area and flight control rooms.

"Ten ... nine ... eight ... seven ... six ... Ignition sequence started ..."

The rocket shook on the pad under the igniting combustion of its boosters.

"... four ... three ... two.... one ... We have ignition!"

Orange fire and white smoke mushroomed from the base of the launch tower.

"We have liftoff!"

The Delta II lifted into the sky ... first slowly, as if a giant, invisible hand was gently raising it off the ground, and then rapidly gaining speed, shooting through the sky like a blazing rock shot from a slingshot.

Streaking a ghastly white mark across the heavenly twilight, it turned on a trajectory headed into the southern sky, growing smaller, smaller, and finally disappearing behind its wispy jet stream.

Five minutes later, a second Delta II burst into the sky, blazing across the heavens to the south, seemingly in pursuit of its predecessor.

Kent checked his watch. *Good. Ahead of schedule.*

His job here was done. Sure, it was a long shot, but a long shot was better than no shot. Barring computer or mechanical malfunctions, Redwoods I and II, the satellites sitting atop the Delta rockets, would reach their destinations before he got back to Washington. Now, if the cameras on board those satellites could just get a lucky shot at the *Alexander Popovich.*

The USS Honolulu
The Aegean Sea

The captain's stateroom on board a *Los Angeles* – class nuclear submarine was not much larger than a walk-in closet. Even so, considering the sardine-can berthing arrangements available to the rest of the crew, the captain's quarters was a haven of luxury.

Once the *Honolulu* rendezvoused with the freighter *Volga River*, there would be no time for sleep. From that point on, the skipper would need to be as well rested as possible.

In drill after drill throughout the years, Pete had learned the importance of sleeping when one could. Clarity of thinking would be required for dozens of decisions with dangerous implications that could mean the difference between success and failure or life and death. Of course, in the Cold War and the uneasy peace that followed, Pete's naval career was a series of drills and high-stakes war games.

But this mission was no game. Torpedoes would be fired in defense from a larger threat. Real people would die. His boat would become the most hunted warship in the world.

For the benefit of his crew, to insure that their captain was fresh, Pete Miranda positioned the pillow under his head, flipped off the small lamp, and lay faceup on his rack.

Darkness was never complete on a submarine. Light streamed under the hatch separating his stateroom from the passageway. Sounds of sailors passing by outside, though muffled, constantly reminded him of his surroundings.

Pete flipped the lamp back on, then reached down into the locker under his rack and felt the blue photo album that he always kept there. Other than his U.S. Navy uniforms, the album was about the only thing he'd gotten to keep following the divorce.

His daughter Hannah had taken gold, glittery paint and written the word *Memories* on the outside. Inside, she had arranged a panorama of photographs that told the colorful story of his life with Sally and the kids in the years before the divorce.

The first photo, an eight-by-ten image of Pete as a slim, young lieutenant j.g., in his summer dress whites, showed him holding Hannah in his arms in front of the pink and green bougainvillea vine in their front yard at their home in California. She first came home from the hospital that day, and the photo taken on that August morning revealed the head of black hair.

The commander drank in the sight of his baby girl. She was the most beautiful little baby ever born. And she was *his* little girl.

Until the divorce.

The blare of the 1MC shocked him out of his daydream.

"Alert one! Alert one! Incoming emergency action message! Alert one! Alert one! Incoming EAM!"

Pete dropped the album on the rack and swung his feet onto the deck.

"Captain Miranda, report to the conn, please!"

Pete picked up the phone line connecting to the control room. "CO here. On my way."

He scrambled out the hatch, turned right, and sprinted along the steel grated floors. Sailors stood back, clearing a pathway for their commander.

Pete stomped up a short aluminum stairway to the second deck, and then stormed into the control room, where Frank Pippen stood in the middle of the room, under the periscope mount. He was holding a white sheet of paper and barking orders to the officers and enlisted men.

"Attention on deck!" the chief of the boat shouted.

"At ease! I have the conn!" Pete said. "What is it, Frank?"

"New EAM, Captain." The XO handed the message to Pete. "Looks like Turkey's heating up, sir."

Pete whipped his reading glasses out of his front shirt pocket, then looked down.

EMERGENCY ACTION MESSAGE

FROM: NATIONAL MILITARY COMMAND CENTER—WASHINGTON, D.C.
TO: ALL U.S. SHIPS AT SEA AND U.S. NAVAL SHORE FACILITIES
SUBJECT: ACTION MESSAGE—TURKISH—GEORGIAN MILITARY
         SITUATION

REMARKS:

President of Turkish Republic has requested NATO ground and air forces reinforcement in NW Turkey in response to massive Russian military buildup in Caucasus region.

President of Republic of Georgia has requested NATO military aircraft overflights in response to same.

U.S. National Command Authority has endorsed Turkish and Georgian request to NATO Secretary General under codename *Operation Fortify.*

British government has concurred in endorsement.

Elements of 82nd and 101st Airborne Divs ordered deployed effective immediately to NW Turkey.

Set DEFCON 3 by order of National Command Authority.

Pete crumbled the message in his hands. "Great. Just great."

"What do you make of it, Skipper?"

Pete held his hand out, signifying *later.* "Mr. COB," he said to the chief of the boat. "On the 1MC."

"The 1MC, aye, Captain." The COB flipped a switch on an overhead control panel and passed the microphone to Pete.

"This is the captain speaking." Pete's words echoed into every section of the submarine. "We've just received another emergency action message from Washington. Due to the Russian military buildup in the Caucasus region, the Turkish and the Georgian governments have requested NATO support.

"Turkey, gentlemen, is a member of NATO. Georgia is a former Soviet republic with strained ties to Russia. Georgia has applied for NATO membership. Our government has endorsed that application, and the Russians don't like it because they want to keep Georgia in their sphere of influence.

"Our commander-in-chief has also endorsed the request for NATO buildup in northwestern Turkey and for military flights over Georgia. The 82nd and 101st Airbornes are on their way to Turkey.

"Gentlemen, United States military forces have been elevated to DEFCON 3."

Pete paused and looked around the control room. The eyes of every man were glued on him.

"The last time U.S. forces were at DEFCON 3 was during the Cuban Missile Crisis in 1962.

"Needless to say, all this complicates our mission. Not only is this dangerous enough, but now we may be sailing into a war zone. There's a powderkeg burning in the region, gentlemen. And they've called on us to go there. One slipup and NATO's in a shooting war with Russia. None of this makes our job any easier. With Turkey on eggshells, you can bet they'll be watching everything moving through the Bosphorus with an eagle eye.

"Be on your toes. The safety of your shipmates and the security of the free world depends on us.

"Be alert. Be professional. You are Americans. That is all."

CHAPTER 9

The Alexander Popovich
The Black Sea

Captain Batsakov stormed up the outside ladder on the portside of his ship and into his bridge. His first officer, Joseph Radin, was standing on the starboard wing side of the bridge with several officers and deck-hands. They were taking turns squinting through a telescope and were pointing out to the horizon and chatting excitedly.

"What is it, Joseph?" Batsakov's voice boomed across the tile floor of the bridge, pulling the officers' attention away from whatever they were looking at.

"An Egyptian freighter, *Kapitán!*" He turned and pointed off to the starboard. "Out there. He seems to have stopped in the water!"

Batsakov rushed across the bridge and squinted into the tele-scope. The freighter was about five hundred yards off the starboard, and appeared to be dead still in the water. He adjusted the scope to the ship's stern and zeroed in. The sea breeze blowing from the west was stretching the ship's ensign out over the water behind the stern.

The three horizontal stripes of the flag, from bottom to top, were black, white, and red. In the very center of the flag, a small gold war eagle could be seen.

The flag of the Arab Egyptian Republic!

"Right full rudder. Steady course zero-two-zero!" Captain Batsakov ordered.

Masha felt the ship tilting to the right. The aluminum chair that she was sitting in slid across the floor. Her heart pounded as she grabbed the captain's desk to stop the slide. "Lord, protect my children. Do not let any of them fall into the sea!"

Talk poured out of the intercom into Batsakov's cabin.

"Have we achieved radio contact?" Batsakov's voice asked.

"Negative, Captain."

"Open VHF-FM channels 13 and 16," Batsakov said.

"Opening channels 13 and 16," a voice said. "You have the microphone, *Kapitán*."

"This is the captain of the Russian freighter *Alexander Popovich*. To the captain of the Egyptian freighter. Please identify yourselves."

There was nothing.

"Maybe they are waiting for us to give them the call signal, *Kapitán*."

"No, they were supposed to send us the call signal," Batsakov said. "I have Abramakov's letter right here spelling it out."

"Perhaps they have their signals mixed up," another voice said.

"Perhaps we should go ahead and bring the cargo up to the deck just in case."

"But what about all those runt children playing hide-and-seek down on the deck?" someone said.

"Throw the runts overboard!" another voice suggested.

What? Masha's hands went to her mouth in disbelief.

"Silence!" Batsakov barked. "Joseph, what do you think?"

There was a pause.

"*Kapitán*, we have an Egyptian freighter out here in the sea lanes near our certain course from Sochi to Odessa. We are not yet at the rendezvous point. That is true. But this is a perfect interception point in the sea. It is as if they have stopped in the water and are waiting for us. My guess is that they are waiting for us to signal first. I think we should. There is too much money on the line to pass this opportunity. If we are wrong, the signal will be unintelligible gibberish. Leave the crates below until later.

"But kill the girl now. We cannot afford to have her as a witness. *Kapitán*, there is too much money on the line."

Dear Jesus! Masha prayed. *What is happening?*

"I've decided to kill the girl later. We will need her to contain the little piglets roaming on the deck until just before we turn them over to the president of Ukraine. It doesn't matter what she witnesses. She can't tell anybody right now about it anyway."

"But, *Kapitán* ..."

"The decision is made. I will kill her later. But I agree with you on the rest. I will send the code now and we shall see what happens."

Masha wanted to run.

But where?

Was the outside of Batsakov's stateroom guarded? He had left in a hurry. Maybe he had not posted a guard outside or bothered to give any instructions. Could she hide with her children somewhere in the bowels of the ship and escape when they reached land?

Batsakov's voice over the intercom interrupted her thoughts. "This is the captain of the *Alexander Popovich*. Now hear this. Peter the Great! Again I say, Peter the Great!"

Office of the president of the Russian Republic
Staraya Square, Moscow

Comrade President, the defense minister is here, sir. He says it is urgent that he see you."

President Evtimov leaned back in his chair, crossed his arms, and exchanged irritated glances with his foreign minister and his chief of staff.

Despite the words of support that each had given him in favor of the defense minister, Evtimov wanted to strangle Giorgy Alexeevich Popkov. Popkov's excuse-making was pathetic. The Army lost the nuclear fuel, and Popkov was in charge of the Army. Procedures and safeguards should have been in place to prevent this, especially near Chechnya. The fact that the Americans were also sloppy wasn't good enough.

"Send him in," Evtimov growled at his secretary.

The defense minister, a short man in his late fifties, in a charcoal-grey suit with silver hair and jet-black eyebrows, stormed into the president's office flailing his hands. "I am afraid I have disturbing news."

"What, Giorgy Alexeevich? The Chechens have already made a bomb with our plutonium?"

"NATO is deploying forces to northeastern Turkey, Comrade President."

"What?" Evtimov felt as if he had been punched in the face. "What's behind all this?"

"The Turkish president has made this request. He apparently believes that our buildup in Chechnya is not defensive in nature, and that we may be planning to cross into Georgia and then Turkey."

"Americans," Evtimov snorted.

"You think the Americans are behind this request?" the foreign affairs minister asked.

"Of course," the president retorted. "Who else would engineer such paranoia for the sake of finding an excuse for a military buildup? Just like Vietnam, Korea, Panama, Grenada, and Iraq, and every other country where they've tried to station their military ever since the Great War. Mack Williams is like all American presidents—a power-hungry cowboy."

The defense minister nodded, as if relieved to find a topic of common ground with the president. "As a matter of fact, Comrade President, the Americans did endorse the Turkish request to NATO."

"Of course they *endorsed* it." Evtimov made quotation marks with his fingers. "They endorsed it after they concocted the idea behind the scenes. Typical Yankee foreign policy. I know the Americans well, Giorgy Alexeevich."

"And the British have signed onto it as well," Defense Minister Popkov added this almost as an insignificant afterthought.

"Obsequious sycophants," Evtimov said.

The defense minister sat up a bit straighter, smirking with a tad more satisfaction. "The president of Georgia has also contacted NATO to request air support."

"Air support?" Evtimov unleashed a profanity-laced tirade. Nothing infuriated the Russian president more than the West flirting with nations of the former Soviet Union. "And I suppose the Americans have *endorsed* this request also."

"Comrade President, American F-16s and British Tornados are already flying close air support over northern Georgia. They are twenty miles from our forces, even as we speak. Our tanks are within range of their Sidewinder missiles."

"Bloodthirsty capitalists," Evtimov fumed.

"Not only that," the defense minister added, "but two Delta II rockets were launched from their base in California. Probably satellites for additional command-and-control of military operations."

Vitaly Evtimov's Slavic blood expanded the veins in his neck and temples.

"Comrade President," the foreign affairs minister spoke up.

"Not now, Alexander Alexeyvich!" Evtimov waved his foreign affairs minister off, stood again, and, turning from the small group of advisors, gazed out through the windows behind his desk overlooking 4 Staraya Square.

Pedestrians crossed the streets and sidewalks; businessmen carried suitcases. Some women were in business suits and others carried children on their backs like papooses.

From this vantage point, Moscow gave the appearance of vibrancy. And if one didn't know better, the grand city in many ways resembled the way she looked when she was the capital of the greatest nation on earth.

What had become of the great Soviet nation?

What had gone wrong?

The disintegration of the Soviet Union was the greatest blow to the once-proud Russian bear.

Ukraine had left, although now, with the election of President Butrin and the declining popularity of the Americans, Evtimov saw an opening for reconciliation at the upcoming summit in Odessa on orphanages. Russia would offer Ukraine considerable money for its orphanages, against a perfect political backdrop of the twelve Ukrainian orphans arriving on the Russian freighter.

But now, just as progress was possible with Ukraine, the Americans and their cronies were after Georgia!

Would Vitaly Sergeivich Evtimov go down as the Russian president that finally lost Georgia to NATO and the west? Never over the grave of Lenin would he watch this happen!

He turned to his advisors. "Gentlemen, the Slavic blood of the Russian people make us the strongest people on the earth!" He slammed his palm on his desk. "The most militant dictators in human history could not conquer us. Napoleon and Hitler tried and failed. And we will *not* be intimidated by, nor will we ignore this American buildup on our doorsteps!" He eyed every man in the room. "I am ordering full mobilization of our forces!"

"But, Comrade President," the foreign affairs minister spoke up again.

This time, Evtimov decided to let the minister speak. "What is it, Alexander Alexeyvich?"

"This buildup of opposing forces on the Georgin-Chechen border exacerbates the great risk that an accidental shot might be fired, which could lead to all-out war."

"Your point?"

"All this goes back to that stolen plutonium. Why not tell the Americans and the Turks what happened, and explain to them that we have stepped up our forces to locate the plutonium *and* to destroy the Chechen rebels' capacity to build a nuclear bomb?"

"And admit that our military forces are incompetent?" Evtimov glared at his defense minister. "Chechnya is *our* territory. Chechnya is none of their business. Do you really believe that the Americans would not mobilize if we sent our most elite airborne divisions to the northern Mexican border, across the river from Texas?"

No answer.

The moment called for decisive leadership.

"My order stands. Call up all reserves. Order the full mobilization of all Russian forces. Bring three more divisions to the Chechen-Georgian border to counter the American threat."

The White House

President Mack Williams had long since doffed the navy blue pinstripe jacket and was now crossing his arms, rocking back in his chair behind the huge cherry desk. The verbal salvos between his secretaries of state and defense were escalating.

"This whole idea of moving the 82nd and 101st Airborne Divisions so close to the Russian buildup is too risky, Mr. President," the secretary of state pleaded. "The region is a powder keg. We've already got this secret plan to sneak our sub into the Black Sea and sink their freighter. Now this." The secretary of state chopped his hand in the air. "Now the Russians are mobilizing more forces. That's thousands of troops staring down gun barrels at point-blank range.

"One spark and you've got war. Please, call them back, Mr. President, or at least position them in southern Turkey, sir. And there's no legitimate reason for U.S. Air Force jets to fly over Georgia, sir. Georgia's *not* a NATO member yet."

Mack looked at his secretary of defense.

"But they've *applied* for membership," Secretary of Defense Lopez shot back. "And we should allow overflights because Turkey *is* a NATO member and they've requested our presence. Either NATO means something or it doesn't. Plus, with the public relations beating we've taken over the Dome of the Rock fiasco, we need all the goodwill we can muster." Seretary Lopez wagged his finger, but pointed it at no one in particular. "Not only that, but both the Bush Administration and this administration have endorsed the request from Georgia to join NATO. Plus, I remind my friend the secretary of state that the 82nd and 101st are being deployed to Turkey, not Georgia. The Russians are in Chechnya, not Georgia. So it isn't like our troops are on the Russian border."

"Oh, come on," Secretary Mauney said. "Georgia's such a tiny nation that there's no significant geographic barrier. What? Fifty to a hundred miles at the most?" Mauney looked at Mack. "Mr. President, rather than risk war, why not just tell the Turks that the Russians are looking for plutonium, that they don't have to worry about a border incursion, and that our buildup is unnecessary?"

A smooth feminine voice joined the fray. "But what if we're wrong in our assumptions, Mr. Secretary?" Cynthia Hewitt, Mack's national security advisor, asked. "Suppose this buildup has more than one purpose?"

"Explain, Cyndi," Mack said.

"Suppose the buildup has a *dual* purpose—to find the plutonium *and* to invade Georgia to bring it back in the Russian fold?"

"Ridiculous," Mauney quipped.

"Is it?" the sandy-haired Hewitt retorted. "We know Evtimov's staunch opposition against Georgian NATO membership. Their intelligence is notoriously shoddy. Maybe they believe the plutonium is in Georgia and use that as a *pretext* for an invasion."

"Impossible," Mauney said. "We've concluded that the plutonium is somewhere on the high seas."

"We know that. The Russians don't know it," Secretary Lopez retorted.

"Well, then why not just tell the Russians what we think, Mr. President? Why not just tell them we think the plutonium is on this freighter somewhere in the Black Sea? Let me open a dialogue with Foreign Minister Kotenkov. We can seek a *joint* solution on finding this plutonium. Give diplomacy a chance, sir. Just tell them that the plutonium is on the *Alexander Popovich* and perhaps they can board it, find the plutonium, and all sides can stand down before someone sets off a thermonuclear device."

"The reason we can't just do that, Mr. Secretary"—the secretary of defense responded in a slow cadence—"is this. What if the Russians don't buy it? What if they claim that their intelligence is better than ours? Suppose they refuse to board or inspect the freighter? If they take that position, then if and when we sink that freighter, the whole world, *including* the Russians, will know who did it. And if you want a war, Mr. Secretary"—the secretary of defense turned and looked directly at the secretary of state—"just let it get out that we torpedoed one of their unarmed civilian freighters. Remember the *Lusitania*?"

The British liner *Lusitania* was torpedoed by German U-Boats in 1915, helping bring the U.S. into World War I.

"And don't forget this. The skipper of the *Alexander Popovich* has sold his ship's services to terrorists. It must be sunk, even if it isn't carrying that plutonium."

"But—," Mauney interjected.

"Let me finish, please." Lopez erected his index finger from a balled fist, as if lecturing a classroom full of high school students. "If we tell the Russians what we are thinking, they will demand to know *how* we know. And whether we reveal our sources or not, we risk exposing our intelligence sources on the ground. We have undercover operatives whose lives would be at risk in the entire country."

Secretary of Defense Lopez stopped talking. Mack looked over at Secretary of State Mauney, expecting a response. None came. Cynthia Hewitt, her gaze sweeping between the president and the secretaries of state and defense, did not speak either. The three spirited participants in this debate had run out of gas. All eyes turned to Mack.

"All right," Mack said. "The secretary of state makes valid points." Mauney nodded a small smile of appreciation. "However, in the end, getting that plutonium out of terrorists' hands is the very best thing we can do to avoid a nuclear holocaust. The United States is in the best position to do that." He looked at the secretary of defense and the national security adviser. "Alone. Mixing the Russians into the fray only complicates matters. Given their history of institutional paranoia and bureaucratic incompetence, and the grave uncertainty as to how they would respond if we opened a dialogue with them, I'm concerned that we would lose valuable time. Ladies and gentlemen, we don't have time to lose. What we *do* have is terrorists with plutonium.

"Having said that, the secretary of state's well-founded concerns are valid." He turned to the secretary of defense. "Secretary Lopez, issue an order that no U.S. *ground* forces are to be positioned anywhere within one hundred miles of the Georgian border without my approval."

Then turning to the secretary of state, he said, "Secretary Mauney, prepare a communiqué to the Turkish ambassador reaffirming our support for them and explaining my decision to them."

"Yes, Mr. President."

"Also, prepare formal requests to the British government, and all other NATO governments sending forces that all NATO ground forces observe a one-hundred-mile barrier for the time being."

"Yes, Mr. President." The secretary of defense scribbled notes on a legal pad. "What about overflights, sir?"

"The United States Air Force shall patrol the skies of Georgia as requested by the Georgian president, but shall not approach closer than twenty-five miles of the Chechen border."

This brought a wince to the secretary of state's face.

"Rules of engagement, Mr. President?" This was the secretary of defense.

"Use of force is *unauthorized* by United States aircraft *except* in self-defense. That means no firing by our planes unless we are fired upon first or otherwise threatened. At that point, U.S. pilots have weapons-free authority to the extent necessary to defend themselves. Anything else?"

No one spoke.

"That is all. For now."

CHAPTER 10

The USS Honolulu
The Aegean Sea

onn. Sonar. We have contact! Three thousand yards dead ahead! Contact appears to be a ship of the class of Russian freighter *Volga River*. Bearing zero-two-zero degrees."

"Mr. Smith," Pete was speaking with Chief Warrant Officer William Smith, who was standing in the control room at the sub's fire control console. "What's your screen showing?"

"Sir, my screen verifies one contact, sir. Mark as Sierra twelve."

"Very well," Pete said. "Dead slow ahead."

"Dead slow, aye, Captain."

"Coordinates?"

"Twenty-five degrees east, forty degrees north."

"Right on the money," Pete mused, checking his watch. "Chief of the Boat, make periscope depth."

"Making periscope depth, aye, Captain."

"What do you think, Skipper?" Frank Pippen asked.

"I think we've found our ride, Frank."

"I have periscope depth, Captain," the chief of the boat said.

"Up scope," Pete ordered.

The stainless-steel vertical cylinder in the middle of the control room hummed and clicked. Pete stepped behind the periscope, grabbed the training handles, and brought his eyes up to the viewfinder. Bright daylight shone above the dark green ripple of breaking waves. In the center of the screen, a long, low-lying ship sat on the water, a dark silhouette against the bright blue behind it.

"She's a freighter, all right," Pete mused. "Open a hailing channel, Frank."

"Aye, sir," the XO said. "Conn. Radio. Open a frequency. Channel fourteen."

"Radio. Conn. Hailing frequency open."

"Very well." Pete kept eyeing the ship through the periscope. "Mr. Pippen, please broadcast the code and let's see what we've got."

"Aye, Captain." The XO accepted the microphone from the chief of the boat. "Would you like to do the honors, Captain?"

"Why not?" Pete stepped away from the periscope and took the microphone from Frank.

"Hailing frequency is open, sir."

Pete held the microphone to his mouth, then pressed the switch opening the broadcast band. To ensure the mission's secrecy, both the submarine and the freighter were under orders from Washington to communicate only with a series of predetermined cryptic radio exchanges that would make no sense to anyone listening.

He spoke slowly. "Polar bear. Polar bear. Zero-Six-Zero-Six."

Nothing.

Men on the bridge looked around nervously.

Pete repeated the code. "Polar bear. Polar bear. Zero-Six-Zero-Six."

Thirty seconds passed. Crackling erupted over the PA system. "Piggyback. Piggyback. Zero-Six-Zero-Three."

Cheering erupted in the control room.

"Initiate docking sequence, Captain?" the XO asked.

"Very well," Pete said. "Initiate docking sequence. Take the mike, XO." Pete handed the microphone back to Frank. "Broadcast next sequence."

"Aye, sir." Frank took the mike and pressed the broadcast switch. "Yankee-one. Yankee-one."

A short silence. Static over the speakers, then, "Red Sox-two. Red Sox-two."

"Same choir. Same songbook," Pete said. He looked back through the periscope, switching to high-powered magnification. Men in dark wetsuits were scrambling over the gunwales, down netted ladders, and into the water.

"We've got SEALs in the water. They're waiting for us, gentlemen. All ahead one-third."

"Ahead one-third."

"Let's take this slow and easy. Last thing we need is a collision that sends us to the bottom before we get to fire a torpedo."

The Alexander Popovich
The Black Sea

The captain had not yet returned to his stateroom. He was still on the bridge. Masha knew this because his voice was still mixed with the squeaks and chatter blaring over the loudspeaker.

How could this be happening? Forty-eight hours ago, Masha and her children were filled with excitement at the thought of taking a cruise on a ship across the Black Sea.

And now this.

Was she living a nightmare?

She had replayed it in her mind a hundred times in the last five minutes.

Kill the girl now. We cannot afford to have her as a witness.

I've decided to kill the girl later.

At least she knew their motives. They wanted her dead. And it had something to do with the cargo and the money they were making for transporting it to an Egyptian freighter. What could this cargo be?

Probably drugs. Perhaps heroin. What else could command so much money? This would explain why they wanted her gone.

She had to get out of the stateroom and find her children.

Perhaps she should make a run for it. But what if a guard was posted outside the stateroom? She wandered from the outer office into the captain's living area. A small galley area was located just past the head of the single bed.

A sink. Some drawers. Maybe ... She opened one of the drawers. Several stainless steel steak knives glistened under the fluorescent light.

She picked one and held it up against the light. This one would do. Long enough to plunge into a man's heart.

At least the captain did not want her killed immediately. But what if he discovered that she had overheard everything that was said on the bridge? Would he kill her now instead of later?

Cold sweat beaded on her forehead.

She had to do something. A small volume control knob was attached to the loudspeaker. She reached for it, turning it counterclockwise. The chatting and static diminished. Voices on the bridge were gone.

Good.

Perhaps he wouldn't know that she had heard everything. But what if he discovered that she'd tampered with the volume control? No time to worry about that now. For now, she had to get out of the captain's stateroom and find her children.

She slipped the knife in her sweater, then prayed quickly.

Lord, protect my children and protect me. Somehow, keep us from harm. I pray that I will not be forced to use this weapon in my pocket. But if I have to use this knife, then give me strength and the courage to use it quickly and effectively. Make my hand swift and deadly in the defense of your children.

She opened the door.

A man stood in the passageway. Their eyes locked.

Masha shuddered, thinking of the knife hidden under her sweater. Should she use it now?

This was not the sailor who had brought her to the cabin. This sailor's boyish face and soft, innocent eyes paralyzed her.

"Hello, miss," he greeted her politely.

"Hello to you," she said. "I am Masha. I am in charge of the orphans running around the ship."

"Yes, I know who you are." His voice was as soft as his eyes, and his smile was even softer. "You are also the *kapitán*'s guest."

"I'm sorry, but what is your name?" She knew this look. The look of a shy boy around a pretty girl for the first time.

He gazed at his weather-worn boots. "I am Aleksey Anatolyvich. I am a deckhand and the *kapitán*'s assistant."

She flashed him a soft smile. "The *kapitán* has a handsome personal assistant, I should say."

His face flushed crimson. He looked back up. "Thank you, ma'am."

"Well, Aleksey Anatolyvich, I am a guest of the *kapitán*, as you can see, but he has been detained with important business." She touched his arm, ensuring that the blood did not leave his face. "Perhaps you could accompany me to my cabin."

"But the *kapitán* ..."

"Aleksey." Her hand caressed his arm up to his shoulder. "The *kapitán* is detained. He told you to keep an eye on me. *Dah*?"

"*Dah.*"

"Come keep an eye on me." She studied his face. "I must gather my children from the deck before dinner with the *kapitán* tonight. Besides, I need you nearby so I do not fall overboard. *Dah?*"

"*Dah.*"

He nodded. She took him by the arm and led him down the passageway.

The Al Alamein
Sea of Marmara

Thank you for having me on the bridge at this moment, *Kapitán*," Salman said. "It is a beautiful sight, is it not?"

Captain Sadir smiled at the view outside the bridge of his ship. Before him lay the glorious sight of the twenty-mile, narrow strait of water that split the great city of Istanbul in half and connected the Marmara and Black Seas. Sailing through the Bosphorus was like floating through an Islamic paradise. Colorful mosques and minarets sparkled in the Turkish sun on both sides, lining Istanbul's busy shores like precious jewels in a necklace.

Ever since they left Port Said, the young scientist who would lead them to glorious martyrdom had captured the attention of Captain Sadir.

"Yes, it is beautiful indeed," Sadir replied. "I fear that you might be too occupied on our return voyage to come topside and enjoy the sights."

"Thank you, *Kapitán*," Salman said. "If we are able to rendezvous with the Russian freighter and obtain the fuel, then most of my time left on this earth shall indeed be in the bowels of this ship."

A moment of silence followed between the two men. "All ahead five knots," the captain ordered.

"Ahead five knots," the helmsman repeated.

Sadir turned to the young man. "Yes, Salman, you will build a floating hydrogen bomb within the bowels of my ship. But remember this. The place we are headed will be far more beautiful even than this great city of mosques rising above the waters."

"I will do my job, *Kapitán*, if given the opportunity."

Sadir brought a cigarette to his lips as two other ships—a freighter flying the horizontally striped azure and gold ensign of the Ukraine, and a cargo ship flying the French flag—moved in front of *Al Alamein.* Both ships sputtered black smoke into a bright blue Turkish sky.

The Ukrainian ship was just now inching its way into the Bosphorus.

Another moment passed. A string of three channel tugs were chugging in a line out of the mouth of the Bosphorus. Off to the side was a Turkish Navy patrol boat headed in the direction of the *Al Alamein.*

"*Kapitán.*" The radio operator was over on the right side of the bridge, with a telephone cradled under his neck. He was waving his hand in the air, making agitated gestures.

"What is it?" Sadir asked.

"It is the Turks." He was out of breath. "They are boarding ships entering the Bosphorus. They wish to board the *Al Alamein.*"

CHAPTER 11

The Alexander Popovich
The Black Sea

Bring her alongside," Captain Batsakov ordered from the bridge. "Steady as she goes."

Alexander Popovich inched up behind the stern of the Egyptian freighter. The inscription identifying the ship was painted across the black stern in white Arabic lettering. But the flag, now in full view as it furled and unfurled in the Black Sea breeze, was clearly Egyptian.

The seas were calm. Good. The last thing Batsakov needed was for rolling swells to pitch his five-million-dollar prize overboard during the transfer to the Egyptian.

"Steer five degrees port."

"Five degrees port, aye, Captain."

The helmsman turned the ship's massive wooden wheel an eighth of a rotation to the left. *Alexander Popovich* angled slightly to the left, giving the slow-moving Russian freighter plenty of time and maneuvering room to avoid ramming the Egyptian freighter from the rear.

"Perhaps their radio isn't working," Joseph Radin, the *Popovich*'s first officer, said.

Dark-skinned sailors could now be seen milling about on the deck of the Egyptian freighter. Some waved at the Russian freighter.

"Call them again," Batsakov said.

"Peter the Great! Peter the Great!" Joseph Radin barked into the radio.

Still nothing.

Then static.

Then a burst into the *Popovich*'s radio from the Egyptian. "Engines down!"

Batsakov slung a full glass of vodka across the bridge. Shattering glass was followed by a string of profanity. "We should've known better. We aren't even close to the coordinates Abramakov gave us. We have wasted valuable time!"

"*Kapitán*, I urge you, remain calm," Joseph said. "We are but two hours off schedule. We had to investigate. They were Egyptian. It appeared that they had come looking for us."

Batsakov grabbed the open bottle of vodka on the charting table. He brought the bottle to his lips, turning it bottoms up.

"We will sail to the original rendezvous area, Yuri Mikalvich," Joseph said. "You will lead us there, my *kapitán*. We will deliver our cargo. Then we will be rich men!"

Batsakov was unsure if the hot vodka was mollifying his anger or fueling it.

"Think about it, Yuri Mikalvich," the first officer said, patting him on the back. "Two-and-a-half million American dollars in your pocket!" A greedy tone permeated Joseph's voice. "A full million for me and the crew divides the rest! Our lives will never be the same at the end of this voyage, *Kapitán*."

Batsakov finished the vodka. His first officer was right. Their lives would never be the same. This was no time for temper tantrums. He had to focus. A fortune was on the line. He was a good sea captain. He would find this freighter, deliver the cargo, eliminate the Masha Katovich problem, and drop these bratty orphans off in Ukraine to satisfy the politicians. Then he would sail the *Alexander Popovich* to the Bahamas, where he would collect his fortune and wait for another assignment. Or perhaps collect his fortune and simply retire.

Batsakov's eyes met his first officer's. "You are right, Joseph. Let us go find the Egyptian!"

"To the Egyptian!" Now Joseph was raising his own glass of vodka. Batsakov held up his bottle and clanked it against Joseph's glass.

"To the Egyptian!" Batsakov repeated the comment, pretending to drink from his now-empty bottle.

"Allah would be pleased!" The first officer laughed, swilling his own vodka.

That comment ignited a volcanic guffaw from within Batsakov's belly, bending him over double. "Yes, Allah would be pleased," he said, cackling at the notion. The captain regained his composure, stood erect, and issued his next order.

"Resume course two-seven-zero. All engines ahead full!"

The Al Alamein
The Sea of Marmara

Captain Hosni Sadir watched the armed boarding party from the Turkish Navy walk across the main deck of his ship for what seemed like the hundredth time.

The Turks were an inexplicable oddity, Sadir thought. They were 98 percent Muslim. But since the 1940s, they had been allied with the Americans. Many Arab Muslims could not understand this unholy alliance.

But his Muslim brothers in Chechnya understood it.

Fear of the bloodthirsty Russians drove this alliance. The more than a quarter of a million Chechen martyrs who had gone to paradise since 1994 would approve of their Turkish Muslim brothers doing whatever was necessary to halt the expansion of Russia, even if that meant sleeping with the infidel Americans.

Sadir watched as the party, consisting of two officers and three Turkish marines, looked in crates, opened hatches, and poked around in areas where there was nothing significant. It would take weeks for such a small group to search every inch of this ship, and if they stopped every ship trying to get through the Bosphorus, they would effectively shut down one of the world's busiest shipping arteries. The economic superpowers would not let that happen.

As long as the Turks did not go below and discover the lead-walled laboratory and the silver radioactive suits waiting for Salman Dudayev's team, he had no worries. And even if they did, he still had no worries. This was Allah's mission, and he was Allah's servant.

One of the inspectors approached. "I am Lieutenant Baghadur of the Turkish Navy. Our party has completed its inspection. You are free to pass, Captain."

"A pleasure having you on board the *Al Alamein*." Captain Sadir accepted the Turk's salute, then watched the boarding party climb down the ladders into their patrol boats. When they were safely away at a distance of two hundred yards, he headed down the main deck to the ladder leading back up into the bridge. Thirty minutes later, *Al Alamein* passed north, steaming at eight knots under the first bridge spanning the Bosphorus.

The USS Honolulu
The Aegean Sea

The officer of the deck, Lieutenant Darwin McCaffity, had just completed a final sweep on the scope. It confirmed a dark image of the freighter's hull against the lighter water through the periscope head window. A quick check of the side-scan sonar to confirm the ship's position showed all was ready.

"Captain, the ship is ready to vertically surface." McCaffity's voice came from just a few feet away in the dimly lit control room.

"Very well, Mr. McCaffity," Pete said. He stood in the center of the darkened control room, watching the ship's control party maintain the seven-thousand-ton submarine completely motionless at 160 feet under the surface of the Aegean Sea.

"Commence ascent."

"Aye, sir, commence ascent."

Good plans were often as good as the paper they were written on, Pete thought, as his crew began blowing air into his sub's ballast tanks to raise her up toward the giant freighter floating just above them.

Good plans often got people killed. Especially during military operations.

Commander Pete Miranda knew of good plans gone awry. He'd attended a dozen military funerals over the years. Most involved accidents from high-risk plans that had never been tried before.

Pete wiped sweat from his forehead as his chief of the boat, Master Chief Jack Sideman, called out changes in the submarine's depth during its ascent. Sideman was serving as the *Honolulu*'s diving officer.

"Passing one hundred feet, Captain.

"Passing ninety-five.

"Passing ninety feet."

Honolulu was executing a stealth procedure never tried or even practiced by another submarine in the history of naval warfare. This was a potential recipe for disaster.

Pete would prefer to have drilled this procedure with his crew. The efficiency and precision of a submarine in a deadly environment—and every dive into the depths of the ocean could turn deadly with one mistake by one of the hundred crewmen—was crucial. The Navy's response: *Practice. Practice. Practice.* The urgency of this crisis would not allow for that.

"Easy. Easy. Bring her up slow and easy, Mr. COB," Pete said.

The procedure that they were attempting was delicate and dangerous.

Hovering underneath the Aegean Sea at a depth of ninety feet, just below the freighter *Volga River*, *Honolulu* was blowing incremental amounts of compressed air from her air flasks into her ballast tanks. This tedious process was making the sub just slightly lighter and bringing the top of her sail closer to the bottom of the drifting freighter.

The *Honolulu* was 360 feet long. The *Volga River* at 1065 feet long and weighing over sixty tons was a giant in comparison. Because of *Volga River*'s size, an ascent that got out of control had the potential to reek havoc on the submarine, like facing the punch of a heavyweight boxer.

A mistake could sink the submarine.

Pete glanced at the docking schematic devised by Naval engineers back at Newport News. It was mounted on a table next to his position.

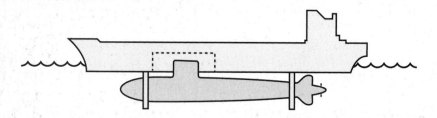

The plan was to raise the sub gently through the water, inch by inch, until finally, the top of the submarine's sail surfaced into the mammoth watertight compartment that had been cut into the ship's hull.

One problem was movement by the freighter. The *Volga River* had disengaged her propellers, but she was not entirely still in the water. All ships, even the mightiest aircraft carriers and the largest oil tankers, were prone to drift in the sea.

The process of docking a 6100-ton submarine with a 40,000-ton surface ship left no room for error.

If the ascent through the water was off even just a few feet, the submarine's sail could collide with the keel of the freighter. If the ascent was too rapid, a collision could threaten the watertight integrity of his sub. But the danger that Pete feared the most were the huge titanium O-rings that were mounted by Naval engineers under the bow and stern of *Volga River*.

In theory, if *Honolulu* could surface into the open space in the bottom of the freighter, the O-rings would then slowly collapse inwardly along a mechanized track until they gently caressed the bow and stern sections of the submarine. Once in place, they would serve as a giant cradle in which the sub would rest on its transit under the freighter through the Bosphorus.

Should the sub miss and strike one of those O rings at too fast of a rate ... Well, no skipper wanted a giant underwater hatchet taking a hack at his boat. Such a disaster might just send *Honolulu* to the bottom.

This was all compounded by the problem of murky visibility. Submarines do not have windows so that captains can look out and simply drive the ship to some point under the water. And even if they did have windows, the darkness in the depths of the sea would leave a submarine skipper like Pete Miranda staring into a black abyss.

Like an airplane flying through thick cloud cover in the middle of the night, submarines operating under the sea rely totally on instruments for navigation. For her eyes, *Honolulu* used active and passive sonar to determine what objects might be in the water around her. GPS was used to determine the sub's exact latitudinal and longitudinal coordinates on the earth. Active sonar shot a very loud *ping* through the sea that could be heard for miles away and could be heard by warships operating in the area.

Detection could not be risked.

Therefore, Pete had ordered that *Honolulu* turn off her active sonar. The entire ascent operation was being driven by a GPS homing device positioned inside the *Volga River* that was feeding data to computers in the *Honolulu's* control room. The idea was to bring the submarine up just under the bottom of that GPS device.

As a human backup to the GPS, a team of Navy SEALS, decked in black scuba gear and oxygen tanks, swarmed outside the submarine. They swam with powerful underwater lights and underwater transmitters. These transmitters provided contact directly to the bridge of the freighter and the control room of the submarine.

If the ascent was off target, the SEALs could press a transmitter on their watches, which would alert the sub to implement an emergency dive through the water to avoid the collision.

That was the plan anyway.

"Eighty-five feet."

"Slow and easy," Pete said. "Easy does it."

"Eighty feet."

Something felt wrong. The sub seemed to be ascending too fast.

"Seventy-five feet."

"Easy. Reduce the blow a bit." A lower air-rate blown into the ballast should slow things down.

"Seventy feet."

An alarm buzzer sounded on the control panel. One of the Navy SEALs swimming outside the submarine had pressed his emergency transmission button. The SEALs had spotted trouble in the ascent.

"Sound collision alarm!"

The alarm siren blared throughout the submarine. The siren started with a very low pitch and continued to a high shrill, then repeated itself.

"Collision alarm! Collision alarm! Rig ship for impact!" Alarms rang all over the ship. Like firemen rushing into action at the news of a blazing structure, men's feet trampled all over the steel grated decks, rushing to their stations for a collision.

"Execute emergency deep!" Pete's order rung over the 1MC, over the sound of the claxons, trampling feet, and ringing bells.

"Emergency deep. Aye, Captain."

"Sixty-five feet."

"Wrong way!" Pete snapped. "We're continuing to rise. Emergency deep! Flood ballast tanks! Now!"

"Sixty feet."

"Execute emergency deep! Now!" Pete slammed his fist against the railing in the control room. Like a fast-moving elevator, the boat kept rising. This was taking too long. Time was running out.

"Fifty-five feet."

"Emergency deep!" The chief-of-the-watch's voice rang throughout the ship over the 1MC.

"Ahead full!" Pete ordered. The cavitation bell rang three times, alerting the throttle man in the aft of the engine room to bring the ship to full power.

"Fifty feet!"

"Rig for impact!"

Water flooded the main ballast tanks. In an instant *Honolulu*'s nose dipped dramatically. Clipboards, coffee mugs, and anything else not buckled down slung across the control room. The sub dropped, angled nose-first, like a cart on a roller coaster. Pete grabbed the mast in the center of the control room, hanging on and praying as his boat plunged to a depth of four hundred feet.

Incirlik Air Base
Adana, Turkey

aptain A. J. Riddle, United States Air Force, throttled the F-15E Eagle slightly forward, to the number one waiting position at the end of the three-thousand-meter runway.

Riddle had just reported for duty last week from Seymour Johnson AFB in North Carolina. His transfer to the U.S. Air Base at Incirlik, strategically located less than fifty miles from the aqua-blue waters of the Mediterranean and less than one hundred miles from the northeastern border of Syria, provided the best opportunity for aerial combat, he had figured.

Captain Riddle was itching for some action. He had expected to tangle with the Syrians or the Iranians. He had not expected this.

Riddle unrolled his navigational chart for a last glance at his flight plan.

This flight plan would take him on a northeasterly route, directly into Georgian airspace.

Georgia was a tiny border country. Barely one hundred miles of it separated the Turkish and Chechen borders — the distance of a millisecond, or so it seemed to a supersonic jet fighter.

Riddle knew what loomed on the northern side of the Georgian border. Formidable Russian MiG-29 jets, all intent on defending what they considered their territory, filled the Chechen airspace. This would be like lighting a sparkler while pumping your gas.

A sparkle against a fume — and *poof*.

If the president wanted U.S. warplanes patrolling Georgian airspace, and if those orders included a "weapons free" to fire if fired upon, then so be it. Captain Riddle was trained to take on and defeat any fighter pilot from any air force in the world. But the Russians? The Cold War was supposed to be over. Wasn't it?

A. J. Riddle had supreme confidence in his abilities to engage and defeat a MiG-29. But if he shot one down, then what?

If he shot down an Iranian jet, what were the Iranians going to do about it? Invade San Francisco? Shoot down a Russian jet, and the problem was escalation. What if one of his Sidewinders ignited World War III?

From the ready position at the end of the runway, Riddle looked up. Another giant C-17 Loadstar from the States glided in for a landing. The 82nd Airborne Division was staging at Incirlik. Within the next few days, the division would be ferried by helicopter to points in northeastern Turkey.

"Eagle One. Incirlik Tower. You are clear for takeoff. Runway five-nine. Eagle One, you may proceed."

"Incirlik Tower. Eagle One, roger that."

Captain Riddle pushed full throttle. The Eagle's engines screamed, pushing him down the runway in a great roar, gathering tremendous speed. The F-15 rocketed skyward.

A few minutes later, Riddle banked the plane to the northeast, then prayed that he would see no Russians.

The USS Honolulu
The Aegean Sea

This time, the ascent had gone more smoothly. At least so far, they were on target. No abort signals from the SEAL team.

Yet.

"Ten feet," the diving officer was saying. "Still ascending. Five feet. Three feet."

A scraping, thuddish sound reverberated throughout his boat. Pete grasped the periscope tube in the center of the control room. The men at their watch stations anxiously listened for further sounds that would indicate the submarine was being torn apart by the heavy freighter.

"Contact. Skipper, we have contact!"

In the dim light of the control room, their eyes danced upward, nervously.

Another scraping thud shook the boat. Men wiped their foreheads. Some breathed heavily. None said a word.

The silence was deafening.

Static from the radio crackled the silence.

"The eagle has landed. Repeat, the eagle has landed."

Cheering broke out in the control room. Pete allowed a smile to cross his face. The first dangerous stage of the mission was over. Pete uttered a silent prayer of thanks, then raised his hands, palms down, signaling for quiet in the control room.

"Magnificent job, gentlemen. Now let's enjoy the ride—and hope that we make it through the Bosphorus."

The Alexander Popovich
Somewhere in the Black Sea

Masha sat on the small single bed in her wardroom. Her hands shook uncontrollably and her knees were knocking.

Her Black Sea cruise with her orphans, something that they had looked forward to with uncontrolled anticipation, had become a sur-realistic nightmare. Would she become a victim like in those American horror movies? Would they toss her body to the sharks?

How could this be? What about the twelve precious young souls that she was responsible for? What if they killed her? Would her children then disappear over the side of the ship?

The young man standing outside seemed nice enough. But Aleksey Anatolyvich worked for the enemy. Should she kill him or befriend him? Or should she kill the captain or the first officer or whomever on the bridge that was advocating her immediate death?

But even if she killed all these men, what good would it do? She could not sail the ship to America or some place where she might be welcomed. Wherever she ended up, she would be arrested for murder.

What if she could somehow get onto the bridge and radio for help? But who would she call? Russia was run by the mafia, and there were no Americans in the Black Sea. And even if there were, how would she get on the bridge undetected? Plus she had no idea how to use the radio.

"Miss Katovich, is everything okay in there?"

"Yes, Aleksey," she lied. "It takes a little while for a girl to get ready."

She buried her face in her hands. *Lord, help me*, she prayed.

She had to think of something. Then she remembered it.

The little black Bible that was a present from the American missionaries who visited the orphanage last year was stashed somewhere in the bottom of her bag.

She reached through the shirts and underwear, fumbling for it. When the tips of her fingers felt that black leather, she pulled it out, opened it, and read the message on the first page. The message was penned by the missionaries who gave it to her.

Presented to Masha Katovich,
    In this book you will find all the answers to life's problems.
    If you are ever in doubt, ask him to show you the way!

                    Given in Christian love,
                    Eugene and Carol Allison,
                    Charlotte, NC, USA.

She remembered the looks in their eyes.

They seemed so sincere, as if they really believed what they had told her and written to her. They had led her in something they called "the sinner's prayer," and she asked Jesus into her heart when they did. That had gotten her into the habit of occasionally praying to God. And even though she had intended to learn more about this new faith, she had not read much of the Bible they gave her. She had carried it around like some kind of good luck charm.

Now desperation overwhelmed her. She could not explain it, but she wished that the kind couple from America could be with her right now.

Lord, if the Allisons are right that this book has answers, then show me what to do. Show me now. Time is running out.

She opened the Bible. Its pages showed a book called Esther.

"Miss Katovich?"

"Please. Give me five minutes?"

"Very well."

Before her eyes was the seventh chapter of Esther.

So the king and Haman went to dine with Queen Esther, and as they were drinking wine on that second day, the king again asked, "Queen Esther, what is your petition? It will be given you. What is your request? Even up to half the kingdom, it will be granted."

Then Queen Esther answered, "If I have found favor with you, O king, and if it pleases your majesty, grant me my life—this is my petition. And spare my people—this is my request."

Masha whispered, "Spare my children, Lord. This is my request!"

CHAPTER 12

The National Geospatial-Intelligence Agency
Fort Belvoir, Virginia

The black-and-white photographs were shot several days ago by a KH-12 "keyhole" satellite whose orbit had been altered to two hundred miles directly over the Russian port city of Sochi.

How fortuitous, Kent Pendleton thought.

Kent extracted the photos from the large manila photograph and studied them.

The pictures could be of any freighter in the world docked alongside a pier, Kent thought. To his eyes, they all looked alike. But like a man's fingerprints, no two ships were exactly alike.

And though many were very similar in outward appearance, there was no other ship in the world exactly like the *Alexander Popovich*. Studying the satellite photo shot over the port of Sochi, Russia, Kent could not tell one freighter from the next. But the supercomputers stored on the two White Cloud ocean surveillance satellites just launched atop the Delta rockets from Vandenberg could tell the difference. At least, if the satellites got a clear shot of the ship again, they could.

At an orbit of two hundred miles, the birds would circle the earth every ninety minutes. Their orbit was staggered so that every forty-five minutes, one or the other would pass over the sea lanes in the Black Sea leading to the Ukrainian port of Odessa.

If the *Popovich* happened to pass under one of the birds, and if the cloud cover cooperated, and if the *Honolulu* made it through the Bosphorus and happened to be in the vicinity, then maybe, just maybe . . .

Finding a freighter on the open seas was like looking for a needle in a haystack.

It would all depend on a lucky shot.

The Alexander Popovich
The Black Sea

Captain Batsakov sat at his desk in his stateroom, studying the navigational charts of the Black Sea. *Alexander Popovich* was still more than two hundred miles from the rendezvous point.

He took a drag from his cigarette and cursed. He'd wasted two hours by pulling alongside that Egyptian freighter. Hopefully, by this time tomorrow his ship would be near the rendezvous point. Tossing his reading glasses on the table, he pushed back from the desk and stood up.

A knock came on the cabin door.

"Who is it?"

"It is Aleksey."

"Enter."

The stateroom door opened. Aleksey stood in the entranceway. "Captain, I have Miss Katovich here with me."

With all the commotion about the false alarm, Yuri had nearly forgotten about his beautiful but soon-to-be-dead passenger.

"Bring her back in, Aleksey."

"Yes, *Kapitán*." Aleksey motioned. She stepped in.

Yuri's chest thumped.

She wore a black sleeveless dress, cropped just above the knees. A string of elegant pearls were draped around her perfect neck. What a terrible waste this would be.

"Beautiful dress, Miss Katovich."

"I bought it in Sochi when I found out we would meet the president." Her blue eyes sparkled at him. "It cost me a month's wages, and some help from other sources too. Do you think it was worth it?"

He inhaled. "Every ruble was well spent, my dear."

She flashed a flirtatious smile. "I'm told that the *kapitán* often dines alone." She nodded at Aleksey. Her eyes twinkled. "What a shame."

"Yes, well ..."

"My children wish to meet you, *Kapitán*. You are a busy and important man as a ship's master, but perhaps you could spare a few short moments to come meet them?"

"Well ..."

"They have many questions of such a great man of the sea."

"Well, I suppose ..."

"And afterwards, *Kapitán*, not to be intrusive or presumptuous, but I was thinking ..."

"Perhaps dinner, Miss Katovich? In my stateroom?"

"I would be honored, *Kapitán*. And afterwards, I would be equally honored by a personal tour of your ship."

Batsakov felt himself smiling. But why do all this if he was going to kill her? Was he looking for a reason to change his mind? Then again, what was the harm? They were hours from the rendezvous point. His crew could drive the ship. Perhaps this would be a nice respite and a bit of fun. Even condemned prisoners got sumptuous last meals.

"With pleasure, Miss Katovich. My chef will prepare a dinner in the galley fit for a king." He extended his arm. "Lead me to these poor little orphans of yours."

Erebuni Air Base
Outside Yerevan, Republic of Armenia

Captain Alexander Giorsky, Air Force of the Russian Republic, sat at the small desk in the briefing room and gazed out the window, across the runway, and into the distance. The purple, snow-capped mountain just across the border to the south majestically dominated the horizon in a powerful, almost godlike manner.

The mountain was in another nation now, in enemy territory. On it were two radar and monitoring stations for tracking the flight patterns of Russian warplanes, including his own sophisticated and powerful MiG-29.

Even so, ever since his prestigious assignment to the Erebuni Air Base in Armenia six months ago, Alexander had had a difficult time shaking his fascination with Mount Ararat. The world's most storied mountain remained a symbol of Armenian pride, even though it fell into Turkish hands in 1915. According to the Bible, Noah landed his ark there after the great flood of antiquity. Some even claimed to have seen the ark frozen up somewhere in the icecaps. Alexander often found himself squinting up at the icecaps, and had even studied the mountain with binoculars, as if perhaps he might even see the ancient boat himself!

Although the Republic of Armenia was the first nation to officially recognize Christianity, and although the Russian Orthodox Church had officially replaced atheism as the religion of the motherland after the breakup of the USSR, Alexander knew that the whole story of the great flood and Noah's ark was a myth.

It had to be.

What man could have done such a thing so long ago? To have built an ark and put all those animals on it?

Still, why his obsessive fascination with the story? Was it all this Armenian folklore talk that Noah's great-great-grandson Haik had built the Tower of Babel at the foot of the mountain and became the father of all Armenians?

Alexander brought his binoculars to his eyes and scanned the base of the mountain, as if part of the tower—if there ever were such a tower—would still be there.

Get a grip of yourself, Giorsky! You are a fighter pilot in the Russian Air Force! You fly the most sophisticated fighter plane in the world. You have a job to do!

"Attention!" An Air Force sergeant stepped through the doorway of the briefing room just in front of Colonel Stratsovich, the wing commander, who clicked into the room holding a clipboard and a pointer. A pale-looking man wearing a black suit trailed the colonel and the sergeant.

"At ease, comrades!" the colonel said. "Be seated."

Alexander and the other pilots shuffled into their desks and focused their attention on the front of the room.

"Comrades, as you know, throughout the years, the base here at Erebuni has been a major force in our aerial bombardment of rebel operations in Chechnya. Recently, we have enjoyed a ceasefire from hostilities. But now Moscow calls upon us once again. But this time, the circumstances have changed. The stakes are altered. The danger is higher."

He turned to the pale-looking man. "Comrades, I present to you Special Agent Andrei Federov. Russian FSB."

The pale man, a typical-looking FSB bureaucrat who looked to be in his early thirties, stepped to the podium. His black eyes swept across the pilots. A cold arrogance exuded from his silent expressions—the typical look of aggrandized self-importance worn by many young FSB officers who bought into the agency's garbage about being the most elite intelligence force in the entire world.

"Pilots of the 426th Russian Air Force, I greet you in the name of the president of the Russian Republic, Vitaly Evtimov."

The pompous toad spoke as if he personally knew Evtimov, as if he had just come from a lunch at 4 Staraya Square. His bulging eyes surveyed the room, as if his claim to have come in the name of the president would impress a room full of seasoned MiG-29 pilots.

"After the breakup of the Soviet Union, and ever since the first bloody Chechen war in 1994, the 426th Air Force has heroically ruled the skies over the traitorous rebels in Chechnya. Were it not for your supremacy in the skies, it is possible that this conflict would have been lost already and that a radical Muslim nation would have been set up on the soft underbelly of Mother Russia."

Tell us something we do not know.

"This time, you are being called upon again for your bravery."

What a political suck-up.

"But this time, the stakes are higher." He paused. "This time, Chechen rebels have stolen plutonium, and they have brought it to Chechnya. We believe they are about to build a bomb that could vaporize all of Moscow!"

The FSB bureaucrat had succeeded in riveting the pilots' attention. "I am no pilot, so I cannot tell you how to do your jobs. The colonel here will do that for you." Federov nodded at Colonel Stratsovich, who nodded back. "I can tell you this, however. By order of the president, we will bomb Chechnya into submission, and we shall keep bombing until the rebel leaders return our plutonium!" That brought cheers and whistling from the action-hungry pilots. "They shall return the plutonium or they will all die!"

More cheers and applause. Perhaps this Federov bureaucrat had a political future.

"Our mission is complicated and more dangerous than ever. This time NATO planes—many of them armed—will be flying within a short missile's shot of the battleground."

The pilots looked at one another.

"The president of Georgia has requested that NATO warplanes patrol Georgian skies, to ensure that no Russian planes enter their airspace.

And the president of Turkey has requested NATO ground support. The elite American 82nd Airborne Division is at this hour arriving at the NATO Air Base in Incirlik."

"Bring them on!" one of the pilots shouted.

"We are ready!" shouted another.

"Comrades." Federov held his palms down to calm the pilots. "President Evtimov does not want a war with the Americans or NATO. But the president views these actions as provocative by the Americans, whose aim is world domination, *and* he is most displeased about NATO's flirtation with Georgia, which as you know was a longstanding Socialist Republic of the former Soviet Union."

"Send us through the skies of Georgia, and we shall teach the Americans a lesson!" Alexander shouted.

"Yes, that would be nice," Special Agent Federov said. "But unfortunately—or fortunately, depending on your perspective—those are not the president's orders." He paused. "The President's orders are to fly to Chechnya through Azerbaijan, to avoid Georgia if at all possible, but to defend yourselves if fired on."

"We will defend ourselves!"

"I am sure you will," the FSB agent said. "This concludes the political portion of this briefing. I return the podium to Colonel Stratsovich, who will brief you on the military aspects of this operation."

The tall, lean, and weather-worn Russian Air Force colonel stepped back to the podium. "Comrade Federov has stated our objective—to bomb Chechnya into submission while avoiding the airspace of Georgia."

The colonel's strong eyes swept the room. "I realize that many of you, comrades, wish to tangle with the United States Air Force, to show the world that the Persian Gulf wars were not a real representation of what would happen if the Americans were to fight with our best pilots and our best planes."

"*Dah*! *Dah*!"

"But these are not our orders. So here is how we shall accomplish our mission." The colonel nodded. The sergeant unfurled an aerial map of Armenia and the surrounding countryside. The colonel's pointer tapped the center of the map. "Here, comrades, is our current position at the Erebuni Air Base.

"The Georgian border is sixty-five miles to our north, and the most direct route to Chechnya would be to fly due north, through Georgia, just to the west of the capital city of Tbilisi and directly into Chechnya, which is one-hundred-sixty miles from where I am standing.

"In the old days, when Georgia was a Soviet state, we would fly this route." The colonel winced and shook his head. "Now, to avoid Georgia, we will take off and fly to the northeast, across Lake Sevan to the Kura River in Azerbaijan. Fortunately, Azerbaijan is still our ally. That is a distance of one hundred nautical miles. From there we turn southeast for sixty miles to avoid the easternmost section of Georgia, then due north into Dagestan, and then we turn to the northwest, where we will deliver our munitions on targets of opportunity in Chechnya, and in particular, around the capital city of Grozny. We will return by the same route." The colonel stopped and eyed them all. "Any questions?"

Alexander raised his hand.

"Yes, *Kapitán* Giorsky."

"Colonel, as I understand our flight pattern, in order to avoid Georgian airspace, as the Americans say, we are essentially going around our elbows to get to our thumb?"

That brought a few chuckles.

"I know it is frustrating, comrades. But we are professional officers of the Russian Air Force. And let us focus on our goal. We are not seeking a fight with the Americans. Our goal is to drop our ordnance so that that a nuclear bomb is not built by the radical Islamic forces in Chechnya."

The colonel's comments resonated. "Be prepared. Be ready. Be vigilant. Go now and do your duties." The colonel nodded at the sergeant.

"Attention!"

Alexander and the other pilots rose from their chairs.

"You are dismissed."

The USS Honolulu
The Sea of Marmara

Other than the hum of the freighter's engines overhead, eerie silence pervaded every sector of the submarine.

Honolulu had shut her engines to avoid any possible sonar detection, and the sub was being carried through the water in the giant O-rings under the *Volga River*'s hull.

Other than coordinates on the control panel, the control room lighting was subdued.

The GPS showed them at 41.10 degrees north latitude and 29.10 degrees east longitude. Speed indicator showed the sub moving under the water at five knots. They were headed on a course of three-five-six degrees, just slightly to the west of due north.

Pete had served aboard United States submarines all over the world. The Pacific. The Atlantic. The Med. The Indian Ocean. But 41.10 degrees north latitude and 29.10 degrees east longitude was a location under the seas that he had never sailed.

Pete eyed the amber screen showing the electronic map of the shoreline above their location. Two land masses were split into by a long, narrow waterway. His executive officer, Frank Pippen, stood at his side. Their eyes met, and there was a silent look of amazement. All around the control room, men looked up in bewildered silence.

Their position—41.10 degrees north latitude and 29.10 degrees east longitude—was the entrance to the Bosphorus Strait. *Honolulu*'s crew could do nothing, except depend on the the *Volga River* to carry them through these dangerous waters. If the *Volga River* could stay in the middle of the channel where the water was deep enough, if the Turks did not stop her, if the sub didn't scrape the rocks in the treacherous channel, if they could make it just another nineteen miles ...

"Ever watch *Star Trek*, Mr. Pippen?" Pete asked his executive officer.

"Watched all the reruns, Skipper."

"Remember the beginning of the show when the *Enterprise* would swoosh through the stars with the theme song and Captain Kirk's voice came on with that line about 'Space ... the final frontier'?"

"Gives me goosebumps just thinking about it."

"Know what other line I'm thinking about if we can hang on about three more hours and make it through to the Black Sea?"

Frank smiled. "Let's see if I can remember it. Hmm. 'These are the voyages of the *Starship Enterprise*'?"

Pete's eyes stayed on the black and amber GPS monitor. The monitor now showed the submarine and the ship in the southern channel of the Bosphorus Straits, headed north, toward the first bridge spanning the European and Asian sectors of Istanbul. All around them, millions of Turks were undoubtedly carrying on their affairs in the daily bustle of one of the world's most historic and exciting cities, oblivious that a United States nuclear submarine was at this moment transiting the waters just a stone's throw from their work and play.

"Good guess, but not exactly."

Master Chief Sideman wore a sly grin on his face.

"Anybody else? Chief of the Boat? You've got that cheese-eating grin on your face."

"Would the skipper be referring to Captain Kirk's immortal and timeless declaration that the *Starship Enterprise* would 'boldly go where no man has gone before'?"

Pete felt himself smiling. "Gentlemen, your chief of the boat is a learned and articulate man of the world, having embarrassed your distinguished executive officer by reciting such valuable information — information that is of vital importance to the United States Navy and to the security of the United States of America."

That brought a roar of laughter from the control room crew, and a "thank you, sir," from the COB, as the electronic image of the ship and sub could be seen on the monitor turning to the northeast in the middle of the channel, and making a slow approach toward the First Bosphorus Bridge.

The laughter subsided.

"Enjoy this moment, gentlemen," Pete said. "No matter what happens from this moment on—whether we live or die—at this moment you are doing something that no submariner in the world has ever done before. You are transiting the Bosphorus underwater. And if we make it another seventeen miles or so, you will be the first American submarine crew ever to go on a combat mission in the Black Sea."

Pete let that thought seep in.

"In the next few days, I expect things to get hot for us. But no matter what, gentlemen, always remember that you were here. Now." He looked at every one of them, fighting back tears. "And always remember, I am very proud of you—each and every one of you."

"We're proud of you, Skipper," one of them said. "We're in this together."

The control room fell silent again, except for the faint hum of the freighter's engines above. That seemed appropriate, given the gravity of the moment. All eyes went back to the black and amber screen. They were now passing under the First Bosphorus Bridge.

Pete contemplated it all.

If the Turks were going to stop them, they probably would have by now. His sub was making history. But this history would never be recorded in the books or studied at the Naval War College.

They passed under the First Bosphorus Bridge, beginning a slight turn to the left, now on a course due north and headed toward the second bridge.

If this would be his last mission, if he would soon die, if he would sacrifice all for country and was about to lead his men to their watery graves with him, why not let his mind linger a little longer on the eternal memories he had left behind. Coley crossing home base after his first home run. Hannah beaming from getting superior scores at "Miss Michelle's" dance competitions. The children's first communion. Making sandcastles and sandsharks during summer vacations at Hilton Head. Their giddy laughter when playing "tickle monster." Their first steps. He was there for it all before the divorce.

In the silence of the moment, he envisioned the last time he saw them. For in three hours, God willing, there would be no time for daydreaming. Twenty miles into the Black Sea, *Volga River* would retract her giant O-rings, and *Honolulu* would be set free to become again what she was meant to be: a deadly hunter-killer of the depths.

He would find and destroy the *Alexander Popovich*.

The rest would be in God's hands.

CHAPTER 13

Erebuni Air Base
Outside Yerevan, Armenia

Captain Alexander Giorsky sat in the cockpit of his MiG-29 Fulcrum at the end of the runway at Erebuni Air Base. The Fulcrum was armed with the latest laser-guided air-to-surface missiles, soon to be delivered courtesy of the Russian Air Force to targets around Grozny.

But Giorsky wasn't concerned about the ground munitions at the moment. Rather, his focus was on the R-73 Archer air-to-air missiles that he would fire at an American fighter.

The MiG-29 had defeated the American-built F-16 on many occasions in war games conducted by the German Luftwaffe. But the F-15 Eagle was another question. The twin-engined Eagle was not as good as the U.S. Navy's now-retired F-14 Tomcat, nor was it as nimble as the smaller F-16 Falcon. But the Eagle was much faster than the Falcon, carried more Sidewinder missiles, and had a better long-range attack capability. Still, the Eagle would have its hands full againt the MiG.

The final check on the R-73 Archers showed them ready to go. The R-27 Alamo medium-range air-to-air missiles were mounted and ready.

Giorsky signalled thumbs-up to his wing man, Junior Lieutenant Staas Budarin, who sat in the cockpit of the Fulcrum at the end of the runway just behind him.

Captain Alexander Giorsky could not suppress his adrenalin at the prospect of tangling with an American F-15 Eagle. If so, he would show the Americans that the MiG-29 Fulcrum was the best jet fighter in the world, and that Russian pilots were the best in the history of air warfare.

The Alexander Popovich
The Black Sea

She weaved her hand through his outstretched elbow, plastering a smile on her face. When his bloodshot eyes and lecherous grin turned her way, she brought her other hand to his elbow also, for added spice. They stepped onto the main deck of the freighter. Cool breezes from the blue waters of the Black Sea chilled her all over.

The children were playing and laughing over in the center of the main deck. One of them spotted her, followed by shouts of "Masha! Masha!" They charged her with arms outstretched—all twelve of them—like a stampede of wild horses.

She released the man who would have her dead and kneeled down, holding her arms wide open. Little Dima was the first to embrace her. Blonde and scrawny, his slightly crossed blue eyes radiated like the full moon through the thick glasses that the Allisons had bought for him.

But his smile! Oh, how his smile could light up a room. Or a house. Or a city block for that matter!

She would have never admitted it, but Dima was her favorite. She would adopt him if she were married and could afford it.

Her arms wrapped around him tightly, and her hands felt the leathery third-degree scars all over his back. Scalding water poured on him by an abusive parent had nearly killed him. When a relative called the police, they snatched him out of the hellhole where he was living and brought him to the orphanage.

"I love you, Masha!" He smiled and planted a huge kiss on her cheek.

She kissed his forehead. "I love you too, Dima."

Sasha, Katya, Svyetlana, Staas, and the others rushed her like little ducklings swarming their mother. They hugged and kissed and kissed and hugged. She let all twelve of them get into the act before she said anything.

"Children, this is *Kapitán* Batsikov. He is the captain of the *Alexander Popovich*. He came down to meet you! Would any of you like to ask questions to a real sea captain?"

"*Kapitán*! *Kapitán*! Can I drive the ship?"

"*Kapitán*! I want to see them making the food!"

"*Dah*! Me too."

"Children! One at a time!"

They hushed but kept raising their hands and standing on their tiptoes.

"Let me handle this!" Batsakov said in a grandfatherly voice. He went down on one knee. They surrounded him. Masha wanted to vomit.

The knife was tied to her thigh with a scarf. She considered driving it into the man's back.

She glanced down at Dima, whose eyes were glued on the captain. She would rather go to prison than let him die.

"Miss Katovich!" Masha realized that the captain was calling her name. "They want to know if they can go swim with the dolphins. What do you say?"

"Oh, I think the water is too deep and we are too far from shore!" she said.

"Besides," Batsakov added with a sinister laugh, "you might get eaten by the sharks! Ha, ha, ha!"

"You mean there are really sharks out here?" Sasha's eyes were bug-eyed.

"*Dah! Dah*," the captain said. "These waters are filled with sharks. If you ever fall overboard, better to let yourself drown, because soon the sharks will come and bite off your feet, and then bite off your legs, and then ..."

"Really?"

"*Dah! Dah!*" the captain continued. "And then they will eat your arms and your head and save the rest of your body for the crabs! Ha! Ha!"

Their eyes widened. Masha wanted to plunge the knife in his back.

"And now, children, I must go. Miss Katovich and I have a dinner date. But do not fear," the captain said. "My friend Aleksey here will take good care of you while we are gone. He is a *real* sailor and he will show you the ship. He will answer any more questions you have. And when the time comes, he will put you all to bed!" He turned to Masha, extending his elbow again. "Shall we?"

"Of course, *Kapitán*, with pleasure." She took his elbow. "Have fun with Aleksey, children!" Her eyes caught Dima's. He looked bewildered, probably because she was with a man. "I will see you all soon!"

They ascended a steel stairway leading back up toward the captain's stateroom. He turned to her. "What did you think of my child psychology?"

"Child psychology?"

"Telling them the sharks will eat them! Now they will not get too close to the side of the ship, and will not fall overboard! Ha! Ha! Ha!"

How will I make it through this? "Ah, you have talent as a child psychologist also."

"I have many talents, as you will see."

A moment later, they reached the captain's stateroom. He opened the door. They stepped inside. He closed the door behind them.

The USS Honolulu
The Black Sea

Easy, gentlemen, we're almost home free," Pete said.

Volga River had cut her engines, just according to plan, at a point twenty nautical miles north of the Bosphorus. The giant retractable arms holding the O-rings that had cradled the submarine were inching their way apart in opposite directions. Soon, the sub would be free from the mother ship. It was showtime, and they all had their game faces on.

"Diving Officer."

"Aye, Captain."

"When those O-rings clear our bow and stern, on my command, initiate an emergency deep procedure."

"Aye, Captain, on your command."

"I want you to take her to six hundred feet and hold."

"Six hundred feet and hold, aye, sir."

"Officer of the Deck."

"Yes, Captain."

"When we level at six hundred, I want all ahead one-third, and then bring depth back to one-five-zero. Pass those commands along to the engine room and diving officer."

"Aye, sir."

"From there, I will give my coordinates for setting a new course."

"Aye, Captain."

The Alexander Popovich

Thank you, Boris. Unless Miss Katovich would like something else, that will be all."

Yuri Batsakov looked at his guest sitting across the table. She nodded at the ship's chief chef, who wore a white chef's apron and hat. "Thank you, Boris," she said. "It is all so lovely, and smells so delicious."

She even spoke with grace, unlike the bimbos that he was accustomed to. Perhaps she could be trained to make a good pirate's wife, he thought, and then dismissed that thought when he remembered the money that was at stake for completing this mission.

"If you need anything, *Kapitán*, I will be waiting in the mess galley for your ring," Boris said.

"I will call you if we need you."

The ship's chief chef nodded and stepped out of the captain's stateroom, leaving the captain alone with his guest.

Finally.

It was about time.

"Tell me, my dear, do you like wine?"

"I love it." She seemed uncomfortable. Probably their age difference.

"And what is your preference, white or red?"

She smiled. "Red, please."

"Ahh! You are in luck." He stood and walked to the cabinet in the small galley in the captain's suite. "I have saved this for a special occasion. This pinot noir is over twenty-five years old. From the finest vineyard in Georgia!"

"I *love* Georgian red wine." Her tone relaxed. "It is a shame it has gotten so expensive."

He grunted. "Yes. Things are different with Georgia from my early days in the Soviet Navy, when Russians and Georgians served proudly alongside one another." He filled her glass with the dark red liquid, then did the same with his. "Perhaps we should propose a toast?"

She displayed a grin that again seemed forced. A sip or ten was definitely in order. "I am not a very good toaster or even a very good public speaker. I should consider it a privilege if you would do the honors. After all, it is your ship, *Kapitán*."

He reached across the table and touched her hand. She did not recoil. This was a good sign. "Very well, then I shall do the honors. And I would like to propose a toast" — what words would make her most relaxed and at ease in enjoying the evening? — "to your children, the twelve delightful and adorable orphans hand-selected to meet the president of Ukraine!"

That brought about a smile. She raised her glass and touched his. "And do not forget," she said. "It is rumored that the president of Russia will be at the dockside as well. And I believe that to be true. After all, why else would Russian FSB agents help me with money for a dress for a special occasion?" She brought her lips to the glass and he followed her lead.

"Perhaps"—he took another sip—"because they are red-blooded Russian males, whose blood, at the sight of you, turns darker and redder than the wine from which you sip."

She smiled and looked down. "Oh, *Kapitán*, you make me blush."

"That is my objective."

The telephone rang from the bridge. This had better be good or someone would walk the plank.

"Excuse me for a moment, my dear." He stood and walked over and picked up the telephone receiver. "*Kapitán* here. What is it?"

The voice on the line was his first officer, Joseph Radin. "Sorry to disturb you, *Kapitán*, but it is urgent."

"What is urgent at the dinner hour?"

"It is the Egyptian freighter. It has made contact with us."

"I am busy, Joseph. We are not even in the sector yet. You told me before that we had found the freighter and we wasted half a day."

"But, *Kapitán*, this is no false alarm. The freighter is eight miles off our bow, and it is broadcasting the signal."

"Do you mean to tell me that we have an Egyptian freighter off our bow, but this one is specifically broadcasting the signal *Peter the Great*?"

"*Dah*, *Kapitán*. The freighter has broadcast this signal five times already."

Batsakov looked over at Masha. She was sipping her wine.

"Very well, Joseph," Batsakov said. "I will be up to the bridge in just a few minutes." He hung up the phone and walked back to the table. "Miss Katovich, it seems that each time you are a guest in my cabin, I am being called to the bridge by my crew. They always seem to have something urgent at hand, which more often than not, turns out not to be so urgent. The matter for which I am now being called, unfortunately, may take several hours, during which time, unfortunately, the delicious meal that Boris has prepared for us may become too cold to enjoy."

"I understand, *Kapitán*. The captain of a great ship like the *Alexander Popovich* has heavy responsibilities for his ship and the lives of his crew and passengers." She touched his hand.

It must have been the effects of the wine, Batsakov thought.

"Please, do not feel bad. You have great responsibilities as a sea captain. Perhaps I will stay here and finish my wine and my meal, if that is all right with you, and then I will see myself out."

"Yes, I insist. And I also insist that you give me the privilege of seeing you again under different circumstances."

She smiled, and touched his other hand. "I am certain that our paths will cross again."

"Of that I am certain also." He stood and walked out of the stateroom and into the passageway.

He would see Masha Katovich again, all right.

He would see her when he blew her brains out and tossed her to the sharks.

What a waste.

MiG-29
Codename Fulcrum Three
Northwest of Grozny, Chechnya

Alexander Giorsky banked the supersonic Fulcrum in a large, swooping turn to the left, pointing the nose back to the southeast. Their target destination: the city of Grozny, the Chechen capital, which sat in the foothills of the Caucasus Mountains, just at the edge of the Caspian Depression.

Giorsky's targets on this run included a warehouse on the northeast side of Grozny, a railroad depot, and a second warehouse.

"Sniper Two, are you there?" Giorsky was calling to his wingman, Junior Lieutenant Staas Budarin, who was piloting the other MiG-29 in this attack tandem. This was Staas's first combat mission, which Giorsky knew would bring out the jitters in a man's stomach no matter how thorough the training.

"Sniper One. Still here, sir. Looping on your right wing. Awaiting instruction."

"Sniper Two. Descend to one-five-zero-zero. Lock on targets. Watch for incoming SAMS."

Unfortunately, the two powerful S-24B surface-to-ground rockets that each plane was carrying were unguided weapons. Thus, the MiGs had to swoop down low, get visuals on their targets, and then release their weapons in visual conditions.

"Descending to one-five-zero-zero. Following you, *Kapitán*."

Giorsky watched the altimeter spin in counterclockwise loops. 5000. 4500. 4000. 3500. 3000. 2500. 2000.

"Approaching one-five-zero-zero."

"Roger that, *Kapitán*, approaching one-five-zero-zero."

The altimeter leveled at fifteen hundred. "Sniper two. Hold at one-five-zero-zero. Follow me in."

"Holding at one-five-zero-zero," Staas Budarin said. "Following you, *Kapitán*." The junior lieutenant's voice reflected a tinge of nervousness.

Giorsky focused on the ground, searching for the target identified as Warehouse Number 24.

He knew that the Sunzha River snaked through the city from the southwest to the northeast. Warehouse 24 and Train Depot 3 were located at the vortex where the railroad crossed the river just to the northeast of the city. According to the preflight intelligence briefing, Lieutenant Budarin's targets, Warehouses 25 and 26, were located adjacent to Giorsky's. That was a good thing. The less Staas had to think for himself, the better.

Giorsky's eyes followed the river through the city, out to the northeast. The railroad bridge came into view. And right beside the bridge, all four targets appeared! Adrenaline shot through his chest.

"Sniper Two! I have visual on our targets. Let us do one more loop, and approach targets from the northeast. Follow me."

"Sniper One. I am behind you, *Kapitán*!"

They did another wide, circling loop, this time heading back toward the southwest.

"Sniper Two, go to one thousand feet and prepare to release."

"Sniper One, I'm going to one thousand now."

The ground rushed below them now, and approaching rapidly in the distance, Giorsky saw Warehouse 23.

"Sniper Two. Release weapons. Now!"

"Releasing weapons!"

Giorsky pushed the firing button, freeing the powerful S-24B rockets from his plane. "Five—four—three—two." He looked down to his left and saw three warehouses and a railroad depot in smoke and flames.

"Good shooting, Staas!"

"Thank you, *Kapitán*!"

Giorsky glanced down for another look at their kill. This time, multiple flashes and bursts were coming from the ground. "Sniper Two! SAMs inbound! Climb! Again I say climb!"

Giorsky pulled back on the stick and hit the jet's afterburners. The MiG shot toward the heavens. Explosions rocked the skies all around the aircraft.

"Sniper One, this is Sniper Two! I'm hit! I'm hit. Repeat, I'm hit."

"Okay, Staas! Okay! Hang in there!"

"I'm bailing out!"

"No! Do not bail. Repeat. Do not bail!"

Giorsky knew that bailing into the hands of Islamic Chechen rebels was instant suicide. He had to think fast ... for both of them.

"Okay, Staas. Can you hear me?"

"*Dah, Kapitán*, I can hear you."

"Staas. Are you injured?"

"Stand by."

Static.

"Staas? Do you have control of your aircraft?""

"*Kapitán*, I can climb and descend, but I cannot turn the plane! Tell me what to do! I think I should bail."

"No! No! Do not bail. Repeat. Do not bail! Not yet. Listen, Staas, if you can continue your climb, follow me up. We must get above SAM range."

"Continuing my climb, *Kapitán*!"

"Relax, Staas. Everything will be fine."

Giorsky eyed the jet's altimeter. 2500. 3000. 3500. He looked around in the sky behind and below him, but saw only blue. "Are you still with me, Staas?"

"I am here, *Kapitán*. Still climbing."

"Do you have a visual on me?"

"*Dah, dah*. I see you."

"Good. Staas, you are doing well. Keep your eyes on me and follow me to ten thousand."

"My eyes are on you."

Captain Alexander Giorsky was not a praying man. But if he were, this would be the time to throw out a prayer for his wingman. The plane kept climbing. 8500, 9000, 9500, 10,000.

They leveled off. Giorsky looked out to his right, just above him at eight o'clock. The MiG-29 was there, just off his left wing.

But the compass showed a bearing of one-eight-zero degrees.

Due south.

In a matter of minutes, Staas's plane would be over the airspace of the nation that the president of the Russian Republic had ordered all Russian warplanes to avoid at all costs. And since Staas could turn neither to the left nor the right, nothing could be done about it.

What to do? Giorsky considered ordering Staas back down to treetop level when they reach the Georgian border. But now, NATO radar on Mount Ararat and at other listening posts in Turkey had already spotted them headed toward the border.

"Sniper One. Have you checked our compass heading?"

"I see it, Staas."

Should he fly into the forbidden airspace with his wingman, which would involve disobeying the president's order? Or should he let Staas go it alone, crossing through a beehive of NATO fighter jets?

If Staas could make it just another fifteen minutes, even on this course, he would be back over Armenian airspace, where he could bail out to a far more friendly reception than Chechnya or Georgia.

"What do you want me to do?"

"Hold course. When you reach the Armenian border, bail out."

"What about crossing into Georgia? Are you coming with me, Alexander?"

What to do?

While Giorsky would welcome a scrap with an F-15, poor Staas, as green as he was, stood no chance against the more experienced American pilots even if his plane were fully operational. Without maneuverability, Sniper Two was a sitting duck.

The Georgian border was less than a minute away.

Giorsky pushed the stick down and to the left, banking his plane around in a big circle, back towards Grozny.

"Sniper One. Where are you going?" Staas's voice shook. "Are you leaving me?"

"*Nyet*, Staas. I am not leaving you. I am only looping around to come in behind you. That way, I can better keep an eye on things. I will stay with you all the way to Armenia."

"*Spaceeba, Kapitán.*"

"Think nothing of it. You would do the same for me."

A few seconds later, the planes crossed the northern border of Georgia.

CHAPTER 14

EC-2 Hawkeye
Codename Papa Bear
28 miles southwest of Kars, Turkey

The U.S. Navy EC-2 Hawkeye, with its twin propellers and dome on the top that looked like a giant flying saucer affixed to the aircraft, had taken off from the aircraft carrier USS *Nimitz*, operating off the northwestern tip of Cyprus.

The revolving dome atop the aircraft gave the Hawkeye the unique ability to watch all air traffic, military and civilian, for a range of five hundred miles each way. For the next four hours, the Hawkeye would quarterback all of NATO air activity for military missions over northeastern Turkey and Georgia.

From inside the plane, Navy Master Chief Rick Cantor monitored air activity over Georgia, Chechnya, and Armenia all afternoon. The screen showed that dozens of Russian sorties had been taking off from Erebuni Air Base in Armenia, flown to Chechnya through Azerbaijan, dropped their bombs, and returned along the same route.

No sign, however, of any Russian planes threatening Georgian airspace. Not until fifteen hundred hours.

Master Chief Cantor was sipping his last mug of coffee when radar showed two blips representing hostile aircraft heading straight for the Georgian border. Cantor squinted his eyes to make sure he wasn't seeing things. The blips were crossing into Georgian airspace from Chechnya!

Russian MiGs.

If not intercepted, their flight path would take them straight over of the Georgian capital city of Tbilisi.

F-15 Eagle
Codename Eagle Three
35 miles east of Tbilisi, Georgia

Eagle Three! Papa Bear! Be advised two hostile aircraft penetrating Georgian airspace in your sector! Course one-eight-zero degrees. Range twenty-five miles. Bandits flying south roughly along forty-five-degree east longitudinal line on course for Tbilisi. Intercept! I repeat, intercept!"

"Papa Bear! Eagle Three! We're on it. Plotting course for intercept!" A. J. Riddle made a wide, looping circle, bringing his Strike Eagle back on a course to the west. His wingman, Air Force First Lieutenant Travis Martin, followed suit.

"Eagle Four! Eagle Three!"

"Eagle Three," Lieutenant Martin said.

"Travis, on my mark, hit afterburners. We've gotta cut these suckers off."

"Roger that, sir."

"Stand by, Travis. Three, two, one, now!"

Captain Riddle pushed his throttle to the floor. The F-15 rocketed to the west on an intercept course for the Russian planes. First Lieutenant Martin followed suit.

MiG-29
Codename Fulcrum Four
80 miles east of Tbilisi, Georgia

Junior Lieutenant Staas Budarin was watching the plethora of activity on his radar screen.

Most of the white blips against the green background represented military flights by NATO aircraft crisscrossing the airspace around Tbilisi. So far, none of the NATO flights in the area had responded to the intrusion by MiGs into Georgian airspace.

Staas looked down at the mountainous terrain passing seven thousand feet below. At least there were no bursts of white smoke in sight. Of course, they were well above the range of most surface-to-air missiles. But the air-to-air variety caused concern, particularly the short-range

Sidewinders and medium-ranged Phoenix missiles armed on most of the American interceptors.

Staas felt totally alone. Captain Giorsky, who was tailing him about two miles to his rear, had ordered radio silence until they were over Armenia.

F-15 Eagle
Codename Eagle Three
45 miles north of Tbilisi, Georgia

Captain A. J. Riddle looked out from the canopy of his F-15 Eagle at three o'clock. Adrenaline shot through his body.

"Papa Bear! Eagle Three! I've got two MiGs in sight! Bearing one-eight-zero. Headed straight toward Tbilisi. Awaiting your instructions."

"Eagle Three! Papa Bear. Orders from National Command Authority are as follows. Intercept. Intercept. Attempt to divert. If bandits enter Tbilisi airspace, attack. Repeat, if bandits enter Tbilisi airspace, attack."

A command relayed from National Command Authority meant that the president himself was involved in the order being relayed. That thought brought chills to A. J. as he repeated the order back to the airborne command post on board the Hawkeye. "Roger that, Papa Bear. Intercept. Intercept. Attempt diversion. Attack if Bandits enter Tbilisi airspace."

"Eagle Three, Papa Bear! Copy that, Eagle Three."

A. J. flipped the switch opening a direct channel to his wingman, Lieutenant Travis Martin. "Eagle Four, Eagle Three. I've got the lead guy, you take the rear. Our orders are to intercept, attempt diversion, but attack if bandits enter Tbilisi airspace. Got it?"

"Got it. Roger that, Eagle Three. I'm following your lead."

MiG-29
Codename Fulcrum Four
40 miles north of Tbilisi, Georgia

Staas looked out the cockpit to his left. The F-15 Strike Eagle had swooped in from out of nowhere, and was matching speed about forty yards or so out to his left. Staas recognized the insignia of the United States Air Force painted on the side of the war bird. The American pilot was making all kinds of motions with his hand and was pointing to his left.

This hand signal needed no translation from English to Russian. The American was ordering Staas to "peel off."

Junior Lieutenant Staas Budarin had to somehow let the American know that turning was impossible, that they simply needed a harmless passage of overflight through Georgia for a few more minutes before reaching Armenia.

He held his palms up, and began pointing straight ahead, over and over again.

This seemed to make the American angrier. The pilot gave the "peel off" signal with a renewed vengeance. He was pointing to his left faster, and with staccatolike chops.

Captain Giorsky had ordered radio silence. But that was academic now. He must somehow tell the American that his intentions were harmless. He switched on an international hailing frequency on his radio and prayed that the Yank understood Russian. *"Ya nee magu perverneetzyah! Ya nee magu perverneetzyah!"*

F-15 Eagle
Codename Eagle Three
35 miles north of Tbilisi, Georgia

Eagle Three. Papa Bear. What is your status?"

"Papa Bear. Eagle Three. Visual contact made. I'm getting angry hand gestures and transmission in Russian. Bandit refuses breakoff. Repeat, bandit refuses breakoff."

"Eagle Three. Papa Bear. Bandit entering Tbilisi airspace. Execute shoot-down order. Repeat, execute shoot down."

"Papa Bear. Eagle Three. Roger that. I'm breaking off to acquire firing position."

MiG-29
Codename Fulcrum Three
35 miles north of Tbilisi, Georgia

Captain Alexander Giorsky had been watching this strange game of cat and mouse between the F-15 and his junior partner. Now the

American seemed to be breaking off the pursuit. The Strike Eagle looped away from the Fulcrum, making a wide turn far out to the left.

Perhaps this was a good thing. Perhaps the American had understood the broadcast on the international frequency when Staas had said, "*Ya nee magu perverneetzyah!*" *I cannot turn left.*

Perhaps not!

The American was now looping in behind the Fulcrum, as if to acquire a firing position.

Giorsky decided to break radio silence.

"Fulcrum Four, Fulcrum Three. Bandit on your tail! I'm locking onto him. Hit afterburners! Now!"

F-15 Eagle
Codename Eagle Three
35 miles north of Tbilisi, Georgia

Captain A. J. Riddle had trained for this all of his professional career. Now the moment was at hand.

This was a moment that most American fighter pilots never encountered. Still, for this moment, most American fighter pilots would give their right arms.

The opportunity to engage a hostile enemy aircraft.

But reality was not what he had expected. Instead of the high adrenaline that he imagined would come at this moment, sobering reality chilled his body.

He was about to shoot down an enemy aircraft, if that aircraft did not shoot him down first. Someone would die. His adversary could be a family man, like him, with a wife and small children at home.

And even if the other pilot survived, women and children on the ground could be killed by falling wreckage from the aircraft.

Captain Riddle swung the Strike Eagle around to the rear of the Fulcrum, which was still on a course for the dead center of Tbilisi. He mentally reminded himself that the Russian had refused to peel off, and was engaged in a military sortie for the center of the capital of a nation that was a United States ally.

The S-24 surface-to-ground rockets that the MiGs typically carried could be targeted for any place in the capital, including the parliament building or the presidential residence. Its Alamo missiles and its cannons were a threat to NATO planes, including his own. The Russians had been ordered to stay out of Georgia. This pilot was taking hostile action by violating that order. The rules of engagement left only one option.

Riddle settled the Eagle into a chase position about a mile behind the Fulcrum, and five hundred feet above it.

Riddle armed missile number one, then fed the tracking data from the plane's radar into the fire launch computer.

Three seconds later, a red flashing light appeared on the console.

Target acquired. Target acquired. Target acquired.

Riddle felt that surge of adrenaline. His thumb pressed the *fire* button.

The AIM-9L Sidewinder missile dropped from the right wing about ten feet through the air, then ignited in a burst of flame and white smoke, streaking out in front of the F-15.

"Papa Bear. Eagle Three. Missile in the air!"

MiG-29
Codename Fulcrum Four
30 miles north of Tbilisi, Georgia

*B*eep. *Beep. Beep. Beep. Beep. Beep. Beep. Beep.*

The strident alarm brought Staas's eyes to the flashing red monitor on the cockpit control panel. Next to the *Engine Failure* alarm, this was the one alarm most dreaded by fighter pilots.

Missile lock! Missile lock! Missile lock!

Staas felt cold sweat all over his body. *Kapitán* Giorsky had tried radioing him, but he could not hear because of the alarm. His hands trembled as he hit the transmit button.

"*Kapitán*! He has locked onto me! Help me!"

There was no answer.

"*Kapitán*! Missile in the air!"

MiG-29
Codename Fulcrum Three
28 miles north of Tbilisi, Georgia

The petrified voice came squeaking over the air-to-air frequency and into Giorsky's headset.

"Help me, *Kapitán*! Please, help me!"

Giorsky saw the Eagle downrange, but Staas's Fulcrum was out of sight.

"*Kapitán*! Missile in the air!"

"Staas, pull up! Pull up now! Pull up and hit afterburners!"

Giorsky armed the R-73 Archer missile and pushed the launch button.

F-15 Eagle
Codename Eagle Three
30 miles north of Tbilisi, Georgia

A. J. Riddle could do nothing but wait. The seconds seemed like an eternity as he watched the Sidewinder close in on its target.

Time to impact. *Five seconds. Four. Three. Two. One.*

A burst of smoke in the sky five miles downrange.

Smoke and debris fell in multiple plumes, streaking down, down toward the ground.

Captain Riddle checked his radar screen. The target had vanished.

Riddle looked for signs of a parachute. Nothing on the horizon.

Beep. Beep. Beep. Beep. Beep. Beep. Beep. Beep.

The warning indicator light located directly above the radar sceen was flashing. A fast-moving heat-seeking missile was closing in!

A. J. pulled up on the stick and shot the Eagle up, up directly into the sun, which at this altitude was a blazing ball. He tried looking away, but the G-forces pushing him back in his seat made it difficult to turn his face away.

The missile came fast, like a bloodhound sniffing a deer, homing on the exhaust from the Eagle's turbofan engines. Cockpit monitors showed the missile closing distance.

2000 yards.

1500 yards.

1000 yards.

A. J.'s life flashed in a lightning bolt in front of him. Memories of Christmases and Thanksgivings past, with his cousins and grandparents around the dining room table for holiday meals. His graduation from USC. His marriage to Mary Frances. The birth of their son Michael and daughter Holly.

500 yards.

400 yards.

A. J. gripped the joystick with his right hand.

300 yards.

200 yards.

He punched the button, firing five decoy flares into the blue sky. The flares popped out like fireworks on the Fourth of July.

As the flares exploded, he jerked the stick a hard left.

The plane twirled and tumbled out of its ascent. The horizon spun like a gyroscope. The altimeter dropped like a rock. A. J. was on a roller coaster ride. His stomach was still at twenty thousand feet. The rest of his body was somewhere well below that. He thought about ejecting, but an upside-down ejection could be fatal.

He fought, desperately, to regain control of his aircraft. At six thousand feet, the horizon leveled out again, and his stomach caught up with the rest of his body.

A. J. looked up. The Russian missile had flown through the decoys and locked onto the sun's rays, exploding harmlessly in the sky. He scanned the sky above him, looking for the Russian.

"Eagle Three. Eagle Four. You okay?"

"Eagle Four. Eagle Three. Piece of cake."

"Great flying, boss."

"No time for that. Where's our bandit?"

"Got him on my scope," Lieutenant Travis Martin said. "Still at course one-eight-zero at ten thousand. He's over the outskirts of Tbilisi."

A. J. looked down at his radar scope and spotted the MiG. "It's payback time, Travis. Let's go get him!"

Captain A. J. Riddle set the Eagle for a course of 180 degrees and hit the afterburners.

MiG-29
Codename Fulcrum Three
Over the northern outskirts of Tbilisi, Georgia

Another fifteen minutes or so, and the danger would have passed, Giorsky thought. He had continued monitoring his radar scope for signs of the two F-15s. Perhaps the R-73 Archer missile had done its job.

Nothing like a heat-seeking missile up another plane's rear to jar the enemy's confidence a bit.

If he had only fired the Archer before the American launched the Stinger that hit Staas. Giorsky had scanned the skies for parachutes, but saw nothing. Under the circumstances, he couldn't circle the area looking for signs of life.

Poor Staas. Shot down on his first combat mission only three months before his first child was to be born. The ultrasounds showed that it would be a boy. Staas was building a plastic model of the Fulcrum that was to be his boy's first present. What pride he had taken in building that model. He had spent hours painting the tiny red star on the plane's tailfin.

Giorsky would write to Staas's widow. He would tell Irina that Staas spoke of his unfailing love for her. Then he would finish building the model for Staas's son. He would write to the boy. He would remind the son that Staas died the death of a combat hero in defense of the Motherland.

Giorsky wondered about the pilot who shot Staas from the skies. Was he still alive? Did he have a wife or children? If so, who would write his family and tell of their father's death? But was the American really dead? Had he even been shot down?

Surely he had killed the American. True, he had wanted to tangle with an F-15. But not this way. Not by firing a missile up the American's jet stream without first a test to see who was the better pilot.

It seemed so unchivalrous. To let a missile fight for a warrior. Whatever happened to gladiator against gladiator? Or ace against ace?

He felt like he had shot a man in the back. Then again, that is exactly what the American had done to Staas. But this was part of the age of high-tech warfare.

Even still, he admired the American's tactics against the missile attack. The evasive maneuver was just what Giorsky would've done against a fast-moving infrared missile: climb for the sun, then at the last second before impact, release decoy flares and roll out.

In theory, the missile would be fooled by the decoy flares, and come out on the other side sniffing the heat from the sun. At least that was the theory.

In reality, this was a desperate do-or-die maneuver that could work, but only if the roll-out was not premature.

Roll away too early, and the missile would recover, catch up, and not be fooled again.

Roll too late, and the warhead was up your tailpipe.

All this was a nerve-wracking game of Russian roulette. And nobody played Russian roulette like the Russians. Not even the mighty Americans.

Giorsky checked his radar screen again.

Still nothing. Only forty miles to the Armenian border. Just a few more minutes and he would be home-free.

Perhaps this was his lucky day.

F-15 Eagle
Codename Eagle Four
Over Tbilisi, Georgia

First Lieutenant Travis Martin was piloting his F-15 Eagle a quarter of a mile ahead of Captain A. J. Riddle's plane.

"Eagle Three, Eagle Four."

"Eagle Three," Captain Riddle said.

"Sir, he's within range of my Sidewinders. Shall I do the honors?"

"By all means, Lieutenant. He's all yours."

Martin armed missile number two, then fed the tracking data from the plane's radar into the fire launch computer.

A red flashing light appeared on the console.

Target acquired. Target acquired. Target acquired.

Travis Martin hit the *fire* button. The Sidewinder dropped from the wing of the Eagle and fell through the air. A second later, the missile burst forward like lightning, painting a white streak through the blue skies above Tbilisi.

MiG-29
Codename Fulcrum Three
Over southern outskirts of Tbilisi, Georgia

Beep. *Beep. Beep. Beep. Beep. Beep. Beep. Beep.*

The alarm riveted Giorsky's eyes to his radar screen. Two enemy jets were converging on him from behind, almost at forty-five-degree angles. One was slightly closer than the other. A missile, probably a Sidewinder, was streaking toward him from the closer jet.

Giorsky pulled back on his stick, aimed the Fulcrum at the blazing sun, and hit the afterburners. G-forces plastered him back into his seat. The missile was closing fast.

400 yards.

300 yards.

200 yards.

100 yards.

Giorsky fired eight decoy flares from the belly of the Fulcrum and pushed the stick hard left.

F-15 Eagle
Codename Eagle Four
Over Tbilisi, Georgia

Lieutenant Travis Martin had followed the MiG on its rapid ascent and was craning his neck, scanning the dark heavens above him when an exploding cloud of smoke and fire appeared at two o'clock, about two thousand yards from his position.

"Yeah! Captain, we've got missile detonation."

"Eagle Four. Eagle Three. I see that too. Any signs of the MiG?"

"Don't see him, sir. I think I got him!"

"Don't count your chickens before they hatch."

"Eagle Three, Eagle Four. Nothing could've survived that, sir."

"Let's hope you're right. Swing back around on my wing. We'll sweep the area, call in our report, then head back to Incirlik. Our relief should be on station in ten minutes."

"Roger that, Captain. Making my loop now."

MiG-29
Codename Fulcrum Three
Somewhere over Tbilisi, Georgia

The missile had smashed into one of the decoy flares, setting off an explosion that had rocked the Fulcrum, sending it into a tailspin. The plane had dropped several thousand feet, but Giorsky had regained control.

He had gotten lucky again.

No, not luck.

Skill.

He thought about quitting while his luck was still good.

The two F-15s that had tried shooting him down streaked over his plane, about a thousand feet above him, headed southwest—in the direction of Incirlik.

Alexander did a quick check of his instrument panel to make sure that no damage had been sustained by the explosion.

A quick decision was at hand. Head for Armenia, or . . .

Alexander turned the Fulcrum in a southwesterly direction, pulled back on the stick, and hit the afterburners.

F-15 Eagle
Codename Eagle Three
Somewhere over Tbilisi, Georgia

Eagle Three. Papa Bear. Be advised your relief is on patrol over Tbilisi. Set course for two-two-two degrees and return to base."

"Papa Bear. Eagle Three. Acknowledge," Captain Riddle said. "Set course two-two-two and return to base. We're on our way home." A. J. reached down and hit the frequency switch for direct contact with Travis Martin in Eagle Four.

"Eagle Four. Eagle Three. You copy that, Travis?"

"Copy that, Captain, I'm on your wing."

A. J. looked out to his right and saw the familiar sight of Travis's F-15 floating in the sky.

"Got you in sight, Eagle Four. Let's go home."

"Roger that, boss. There's no place like home."

For the first time since takeoff from Incirlik earlier in the day, A. J. Riddle breathed a relieved sigh. He wasn't certain that Travis Martin's missile had brought down the Fulcrum. But of this he was certain. Captain Adam Silverstein in Eagle Five, and his wingman, First Lieutenant Jim Blanchard in Eagle Six, were now on duty over the skies of Tbilisi.

If the MiG had escaped, or if more MiGs crossed the border from Chechnya, Silverstein and Blanchard would have to deal with them. At least for now.

A. J. sat back in his cockpit. Despite all the emotions of actually having killed a man, all the years of training had paid off. He had scored his first combat victory. He had taken evasive action in a tension-filled life-or-death situation to evade an enemy air-to-air missile. He would give briefings up the chain-of-command about his encounters with the two MiG-29s. He would be summoned to discuss the evasive maneuvers with other pilots who would be flying into the theater. Articles would be written in Air War College journals about the first encounter between an F-15 and a MiG-29.

But all that could wait. For now, this would be a ride home that he would enjoy. The first item on the agenda when he landed would be to call his bride Mary Frances and tell her how much he loved her.

Then he would ask to speak to his boy Michael and his girl Holly and he would tell him that he loved them too. Life was too short and too fragile, Captain A. J. Riddle had decided in the last fifteen minutes, not to pass up any opportunity to tell a loved one how much they are loved.

There may never be another chance.

With the hum of the wind rushing around his windshield at more than six hundred miles an hour, A. J. closed his eyes for just a few seconds of relaxation.

EC-2 Hawkeye
Codename Papa Bear
50 miles south of Kars, Turkey

The Navy Hawkeye flew in broad circles around the city of Kars, Turkey, where Navy Master Chief Rick Cantor kept his eyes glued to the radar scope showing air activity over the entire nation of Georgia, plus parts of Turkey, Armenia, and Chechnya.

From his duty station ten thousand feet above the Turkish landscape, Cantor's attention had been riveted on the missile exchange between the two Russian MiG-29s and the two United States Air Force F-15s.

Cantor was tracking the Eagles beginning their return flight to Incirlik when a blip reappeared on the radar screen that moments ago had disappeared.

The blip showed that one of the MiGs was alive and well. Apparently it had disappeared behind the turbulent explosion of the Stinger missile and somehow had momentarily dropped off the screen. Now the MiG was back and was making a run at the departing F-15s!

"Eagle Three! Threat. Two-two-zero. Eight o'clock. Ten thousand!"

F-15 Eagle
Codename Eagle Three

Master Chief Cantor's warning shot an electrical jolt through Captain Riddle. He looked down at his radar screen. The bandit had returned from the dead! The MiG-29 was chasing the two F-15s, and did not seem intent on stopping at the Turkish border!

"Eagle Four, Eagle Three! On my word, split!"

"Roger that!"

The splitting maneuver would force the bandit to commit to one Eagle or the other.

"On my mark ... Now! Split!"

A. J. Riddle jerked his joystick to the left. Travis Martin jerked right. The F-15s cut away from each other, almost at forty-five-degree angles, as if splitting at the vortex of the letter Y.

The Eagles rolled and fired more popping flares from their bellies, streaking past like fireworks on the Fourth of July.

"Eagle Three. Papa Bear. Bandit broke left. He's on your tail."

"Roger that, Papa Bear."

Captain Riddle had a few more flares to fire, but after that, his ability to evade would depend on pure piloting skills.

The Eagles split in opposite arches, dropping several dozen smoking flares through the blue sky. The flares popped, each a fizzling fire streaking a trail of smoke across the sky to confuse enemy heat-seeking missiles.

"Eagle Three, what's your status?" A. J. heard Papa Bear's inquiry, but could not free himself to respond.

"Papa Bear. Eagle Four. Eagle Three has shifted. Off my nose."

A. J. heard Travis Martin's voice, but again could not respond. He had to focus on keeping his aircraft at such an angle that it would be difficult for an infrared missile launch.

"Eagle Four to Eagle Three. Bandit six o'clock. Eagle Three, break left!"

A. J. responded to his wing man's instruction by again jerking the stick hard left. The horizon spun like a spinning gyroscope. Shooting through the sky at six hundred miles per hour, in a belly-up position, he fired one more round of flares, and then peeled harder left.

"Papa Bear, he's giving me a good fight," A. J. said, managing to get off a quick radio burst in the midst of the hard bank.

"Eagle Four. Papa Bear. What is Eagle Three's status?"

"Negative roll. Five thousand. Eagle Three is defending. Firing flares."

A. J. craned his neck around. The Fulcrum was behind him still, maybe within five hundred yards. Too close for a missile shot. This guy was going for machine guns!

"Eagle Three, Eagle Four!" Lieutenant Travis Martin's voice sounded in again. "Keep that turn going! Bandit! Six o'clock."

"Roger that," A. J. said, pushing harder on the stick to the left. He battled the G-forces to look around again. The Red Baron was still at an angle, but was closing closer to a straight line. He remembered the intelligence reports that for close-in combat, the Fulcrum was rumored to be more agile than both the F-16 and F-15. No wonder this guy was trying to get in close. Plus the close distance made it too risky for Travis Martin to launch a missile at the Fulcrum for fear of taking out A. J. as well.

This guy was a shrewd fighter pilot, and had a bucketful of Russian testosterone.

"Eagle Three! Eagle Four! I've got shots in the air! Repeat, shots in the air!"

A. J. looked out to his right. White tracers flew through the air just past his right wing! This cat was already firing his thirty-millimeter cannon.

If the Russian straightened out that angle just a bit more, this party would be over. He had to try an evasive maneuver to get in behind the Russian and become the pursuer, rather than the pursued.

One thousand three, one thousand two, one thousand one. A. J. yanked back on the stick and hit his afterburners. The Eagle stalled for a split second, and then shot toward the heavens. He put the Eagle in a reverse vertical loop, like riding the inside loop of a roller coaster. The horizon was rightside up, then standing on its end, then upside down, then standing on its end again.

The plane emerged from the loop and the horizon was in its proper place. The Eagle was now behind the Fulcrum.

"Yeah! Take that, Igor!" A. J. pushed down on the throttle. The Fulcrum might be more maneuverable, but the Eagle had the speed. The Fulcrum's jet engines were growing larger as the Eagle closed the distance.

The Fulcrum tried a quick left-turn belly roll. The Eagle matched the turn and the acrobatic roll. "Good try, but not good enough!"

Now the Fulcrum tried banking hard to the right. A. J. pushed his stick to the right, and the Eagle followed suit.

"Eagle Three. Papa Bear. What's your status?"

"Papa Bear. I've got him in my gunsights. He's pretty good, but I'm moving in for the kill." The horizon was at a forty-five-degree angle now, as the planes continued their hard bank to the right. The Eagle was inching closer. The Fulcrum was within a hair of A. J.'s gun sights.

A. J. flipped a switch and armed the Eagle's twenty-millimeter cannon with exploding shells.

"Papa Bear, I'm moving in for guns." A. J. gave his jet slightly more throttle. The angle closed some more. The Fulcrum was almost in the crosshairs ... almost ... getting closer ...

A. J. squeezed the trigger of the six-barrel Gatling-style cannon. "I got shots in the air!" Tracers flew at the twin tailpipes of the Russian jet with twenty-millimeter exploding shells. Fire erupted in the Fulcrum's tailpipe and black smoke spewed forth immediately.

"Bull's-eye!" A. J. shouted, as the MiG started a downward streak. "Bull's-eye!" He repeated. "I got him!"

"Great work, boss!" Lieutenant Travis Martin said.

"Keep an eye on that plane," A. J. said. This kill would be legitimate, if he had to keep shooting bullets into the falling wreckage all the way to the ground. *No more ghost planes resurfacing on radar. Not this time, baby.*

"Eagle Three, Eagle Four. Bandit's dropping like a rock. I've got a parachute in the sky at two o'clock."

A. J. looked out and saw a white chute with a man dangling at the end.

"Mark position," he said, then radioed the control plan. "Papa Bear, Eagle Three. We've got a downed Russian MiG and parachute at ..." A. J. was shocked that the dogfight that had erupted over Tbilisi had spilled over the Turkish border. The Russian pilot, if he was still alive, would parachute into NATO territory. "Fifty miles east of the Turkish border."

"Eagle Three, Papa Bear. Copy that. We've got choppers in the area. Eagle Three, be advised the area is now free of bandits. Proceed as ordered, return to Incirlik."

"Papa Bear. Eagle Three. Roger that. We're coming home."

U.S. Army Apache helicopter
Fifty miles east of Arivan, Turkey

CWO4 Adam Jackson, United States Army, sat in the cockpit at the controls of his Apache attack helicopter. He was hovering at five hundred feet over the snaky, mountainous road between the Turkish towns of Kars and Arivan.

Chief Warrant Officer Jackson had heard the radio traffic between the Navy EC-2 Hawkeye and the U.S. Air Force F-15 about the downed Russian jet. As soon as the transmission was complete, he spotted a white parachute, about two miles downrange, floating down toward the road just to his east.

Jackson pivoted the chopper on a stationary rotating axis in the air, dipped the nose, and flew toward the descending parachute.

"Papa Bear. Apache One. I have a visual on that parachute. Repeat, I have a visual on the parachute. He's coming down fifty miles east of Arivan. Looks like he may land on the main road."

"Apache One. Papa Bear. Proceed to landing site. Rescue downed pilot."

"Papa Bear. Roger that. Proceeding now."

Jackson pressed the aircraft's internal intercom system to the Apache's cargo bay.

"Ranger leader, be on alert. We've spotted the Russian pilot. He's coming down two miles downrange."

A voice came back through Jackson's headset. "Roger that, Apache One. Just get us into position and we'll take care of the rest."

"Roger that, Ranger leader. Stand by."

Jackson hovered for a moment. When the pilot hit the ground, Jackson nudged forward on the throttle. In a moment, he was hovering directly over the downed pilot, who was looking up, shielding his face from the chopper's downdraft. His clothes, hair, and downed parachute were blowing wildly in the wind.

"Ranger leader, we're at one hundred feet."

"Okay, Apache, we're good to go!"

Four one-hundred-foot ropes dropped from the chopper's cargo bay. A squad of U.S. Army Rangers, wearing camouflaged combat fatigues, shimmied down the ropes in groups of fours.

Jackson looked down. Six Rangers were already on the ground. They surrounded the Russian and pointed their M-16s at him from every direction. The Russian's hands were in the air. Jackson looked for a spot on the road, about a hundred yards downrange. He steered the Apache to just above the spot, and then set the chopper down on the road.

CHAPTER 15

Office of the Russian minister of defense
Red Square, Moscow

Three hours later

Giorgy Alexeevich Popkov, the Russian minister of defense, sat at his desk, alone, organizing papers for his meeting with President Evtimov. He knew what Evtimov would be looking for:

Bomb assessments.

Damage reports inflicted on Chechnya.

An update on NATO flights over Georgia and NATO troop movements in Turkey.

But mostly, the president's mind would be on one subject: plutonium.

He imagined Evtimov's grueling cross-examination in front of the rest of the cabinet: "What is the status of the plutonium? Do we have any leads on the plutonium? Have we found where they are trying to build the nuclear device? You are my defense minister, Giorgy Alexeevich. I hold you responsible for the success or failure of this mission."

How he dreaded it all.

Hot rumors floated around the political circles of Moscow that the defense minister's head would soon roll, that the president still seethed about the loss of the plutonium, that Popkov's head had not yet rolled only because of the influence of his old hunting and vodka-drinking friend, Sergey Semyonovich Sobyanin, who just happened to be the president's chief of staff.

But how much longer would Sergey Semyonovich stick his neck on the chopping block?

Giorgy Alexeevich needed positive news to carry to the president. Something. Anything. Perhaps an intelligence leak of sorts. Something that would suggest that the Russian Army was closing in on the stolen bounty.

The truth, however, was this. Russian ground and air forces were pounding Chechnya with unprecedented strength, but they were no closer to finding the plutonium than when this all started.

Why?

What could have gone wrong?

There was a knock on the door.

"Open."

Olga, his secretary of five years, stood in the doorway.

"Pardon me, Minister," she said, "but General Ivanov is here to see you, sir."

General Alexander Ivanov was the military chief of the Russian Air Force. "I do not remember an appointment with Ivanov."

"You did not have an appointment, Minister. The general says it is an emergency."

Fabulous. Another emergency. That's all Giorgy Alexeevich Popkov needed before meeting with an angry president. "Send him in, Olga."

The general, tall and lean with high cheekbones and white hair, wearing his crisp green Air Force uniform with a multitude of medals, stepped into the spacious office.

"Ah, General Ivanov. To what do I owe the pleasure of this surprise?"

"I am afraid there is bad news."

Popkov stood and ripped off his glasses. "Spit it out, General."

"We have lost two of our Fulcrums. One of our pilots is presumed dead. The other has been captured by the Americans."

"The Americans!" Popkov slammed his fist on his desk. "Explain this!"

"Two of our jets delivered their rockets against ground targets in Chechnya. They wound up in Georgian airspace. American F-15s engaged them. One was shot down over Tbilisi. The other was shot down over the Turkish border."

"Do our pilots not know the president's orders? Our instructions were specific. No planes over Georgia. And now you are telling me that our planes are not only over Georgia, but also over Turkey?"

"Yes, our radar tapes are showing that, Comrade Minister." The general spoke in a stoic voice.

"You are aware, are you not, that Turkey is a member of NATO?"

"Of course, Comrade Minister."

"And you are aware, are you not, that the motto of NATO is that an attack against one is an attack against all? And that a Russian jet over Turkey is at least, in theory, the equivalent of a Russian jet over Britain or America?"

"Of course, Comrade Minister, I am aware of this. But our jet was not attacking Turkey. And reviewing the radar tapes, I am convinced that the incursion of Turkish airspace was inadvertent."

"*Inadvertent?*" Popkov wanted to fire his air boss on the spot. "And are our pilots so incompetent that one of them would *inadvertently* violate Turkish airspace, General?"

"Minister, in reviewing the tapes, three things are clear. First, our jets were over Georgia, but they were on a direct course for Armenia. We do not understand why. We did not attack anyone or anything in Georgia. Our incursion of Georgian airspace appears to have been accidental.

"Second, the American F-15s fired on our planes first. Not the other way around. The Americans were the aggressors here. Our planes fired back in an attempt to defend themselves.

"Third, our MiG was engaged in a dogfight with an American F-15 when it crossed over into Turkish airspace. When you are engaged in a dogfight for your life, you pay no attention to the borders below you. I believe that our pilot did not intentionally fly across the Turkish border."

"General, I remind you that our objective here is to recover plutonium, not to start World War Three with the Americans!"

"And I would remind the minister that the *Army*, and not the Air Force, lost our plutonium to begin with."

"You're out of line, General!" Popkov slammed his fist on the desk again. "You expect me to tell the president that both our Army and our Air Force are incompetent?"

"My apologies, Minister."

"I should fire both you and your Army counterpart on the spot right now!"

"Please, Minister."

Popkov ran his hand through his hair. "Sit down, General. I must think."

The general complied.

"Listen, General. This plutonium ordeal has caused great consternation in Moscow in the highest levels of the Russian government. There are those who would, shall we say, replace the upper leadership in the Defense Ministry." The general did not respond. "And if upper level leadership in the ministry is replaced, that would ordinarily not only include the minister of defense, but also the chief of the Russian Army, and the chief of the Russian Air Force, the position which you currently occupy. Do you understand me, General?"

The air general sat erect with his cover in his lap, an unemotional rock. "Yes, Minister. I believe that I understand you."

Popkov tapped a pen on his desk. "Well, if there is any ambiguity about what I mean, then what I mean is this. This incident did not happen as you say it did. Now you understand me?"

Enlightened recognition crossed the general's face. His steely eyes lit up, at least to the extent that such cold black eyes were capable of lighting up. "I understand perfectly, Minister."

"This means, of course, that whatever happened up there will need to be supported by the paperwork."

"Of course, Minister."

"Radar tapes, transmission recordings, whatever—will need to back the report I give the president. Will that be a problem?"

"No problem whatsoever, Minister."

"Good. I meet with the president in one hour. To the extent that you can provide supporting information for my report, that would be very helpful. You do understand the importance of all this, no?"

"Consider it done, sir!"

"Very well, General. You are dismissed."

Office of the president of the Russian Republic
Staraya Square, Moscow

Three hours later

President Vitaly Sergeivich Evtimov sat behind his large desk, discussing the Chechen and Georgian situations with Foreign Minister Kotenkov.

"I believe the solution, Vitaly Sergeivich, is oil."

"And just like that, you believe Georgia will return to her native Soviet roots?"

"Ukraine seems to be leaning that way."

"Ukraine is different, Alexander Alexeyvich," Evtimov said. "Ukraine is stronger than Georgia. And whether Ukraine breaks its fascination with America will depend upon President Butrin. Ukraine's size and independence gives it the luxury of playing footsie with both east and west." He walked over to the wet bar to pour a glass of imported Georgian red wine. "Care for a drink?"

"Please, Comrade President." The president handed his defense minister a glass of vodka. The defense minister took a sip and spoke again. "Your point about Ukraine is valid. Their economic independence lets them play both sides of the fence. Just the opposite is true of Georgia."

"I do not follow you," the president said.

"The Georgians, like so many other nations, are cash-strapped. Unlike Ukraine, they are totally dependent on outside resources to survive. That's where we have an opportunity with Georgia."

"Go on," the president said.

"Our petroleum resources in Siberia, Comrade President, could change the entire economy of that tiny country. Perhaps we offer to open a pipeline."

The president pondered that. "But does that break this insatiable desire for all things Western that we have been fighting with in so many of our former republics?"

"I think it gives us an opportunity, yes."

"I hope you are right. But if we do not find this plutonium, it may not matter. Besides, I am bothered much by this NATO overflight request. Do you know what that means, Alexander Alexeyvich?" Vitaly Evtimov glared at his foreign minister as he swilled down vodka. "That means that we have United States warplanes buzzing the skies on our southern border!" The president drained his glass. "How would Mack Williams like it if we had armed MiG-29s buzzing along the Rio Grande River or making armed flights over Tijuana?"

The president's intercom sounded.

"*Dah.* What is it?"

The voice of the president's chief of staff, Sergey Semyonovich Sobyanin, boomed through the box. "Comrade President. The defense minister is here for you, sir. He knows that he is early, but he says that the matter is urgent."

The president exchanged glances with his foreign minister. "Very well. Send him in."

The double doors to the presidential office swung open. In a charcoal grey suit, the defense minister walked in. Giorgy Alexeevich Popkov always had an ashen look about him, but this time, his face signaled disaster.

"What is it, Giorgy Alexeevich?"

"Comrade President, I am afraid there is disturbing news from the front."

"Let me guess, Giorgy Alexeevich. The Chechens have already made a thermonuclear device with our plutonium."

"It is not the Chechens. It is the Americans."

"The Americans?"

"They have shot down two of our planes."

"How ... what planes?"

"Two MiG-29 Fulcrums, sir."

The president looked at his foreign affairs minister, whose mouth was agape at this point. He looked back at Popkov. "Comrade Minister, the MiG-29 is the most maneuverable fighter in the world. At least that is what *your* office has told us. I demand an explanation!"

The defense minister brushed his hand through his hair, shifting his beady eyes between the president and the foreign minister.

"You are right, Comrade President, that the MiG-29 is the world's finest fighter plane. But even the greatest fighter plane in the history of mankind is vulnerable when ambushed."

"Ambushed? Are you saying that our planes were bombed by the Americans while they were sitting on the ground?"

"No, sir. Not bombed."

"Then what?"

"Our planes were operating over Chechnya, as you instructed, sir. They had dropped their bombs successfully on targets in Grozny. On their way back to Erebuni Air Base outside Yerevan in Armenia, they were flying near the Georgian border.

"Two United States Air Force F-15s were operating just inside the Georgian border, flying roughly parallel to our planes. The American planes were less than five miles from our planes.

"For whatever reason, the American planes launched a missile attack on our planes at point-blank range. We do not know if the American pilots panicked or what. But because they attacked at point-blank range, even the Fulcrums had a difficult time escaping."

"Our MiGs got off no shots in defense? I gave our pilots instructions to defend themselves, did I not?" the Russian president said.

"Yes, you did, sir. The problem here is the rules of engagement."

"What is wrong with the rules of engagement?"

"Our pilots may fire at the Americans only if fired upon. This leaves them with little option in a point-blank attack. Our pilots had no reason to believe that the Americans would fire their missiles across the borders into Chechnya at close range. Had the rules of engagement been different, the Fulcrums would have prevailed."

The Russian president let that sink in. "Are you telling me that the American planes fired their missiles from Georgian airspace into our airspace?"

"*Dah.* Their Sidewinder missiles do not understand international boundaries, Comrade President."

"But that makes no sense," the foreign minister interjected. "If they attacked our planes in Chechnya, how do they have one of our pilots? Did they send their 82nd Airborne across the border to capture our flyer?"

"A good question, Minister," the defense minister said. "Their missile exploded near one of our planes. Our pilot heroically ejected before his MiG went down. But because he was so close to the border, and because of strong wind currents, he was blown across the border into Turkey. Naturally, I would expect the Americans to concoct some other version of the events to save face."

"Naturally," the foreign minister said.

The Russian president detected skepticism in the foreign minister's voice. "It is amazing," Evtimov said, "that our pilot could bail out of a plane struck by a Sidewinder missile, is it not, Giorgy Alexeevich?"

The defense minister squirmed. But then again, Giorgy Alexeevich Popkov always squirmed.

"Yes, it is amazing that our pilot survived. But that is a testament to the strength of the MiG-29, that it could withstand a direct missile attack, and yet, our pilot could survive!"

President Evtimov's eyes locked with his foreign minister's. An awkward moment of silence ensued. "Sit down, Giorgy Alexeevich." Evitmov was still fuming about the fact that American warplanes were over Georgia. Had they kept their planes away, this would have never happened.

Yet something about the defense minister's version of the events was tempering his anger. He looked at his trusted friend and advisor, the foreign minister.

"What is your take on all this, Alexander Alexeyvich?"

The foreign minister pondered for a moment. "If what we are hearing from the battlefield is accurate, then technically, the Americans have committed an act of war. Great wars started over lesser things. The assassination of the Archduke of Serbia, as you will recall, plunged the world into the First World War.

"While this is technically an act of war, at this point, there is at least a plausible explanation. Perhaps their pilots panicked, believing that our planes were about to enter Georgian airspace.

"Comrade President, I would urge measured restraint. Two planes are not worth a possible nuclear exchange."

"Then what are your recommendations, Alexander Alexeyvich?"

"That we take four steps. First, that we call for an emergency meeting of the UN Security Council, seeking to condemn the Americans for their hostile acts. Second, we demand the immediate release of our pilot. Third, we demand monetary reparations from the Americans for the family of the dead pilot. And finally, we issue a stern warning that any further attacks against Russia or its interests will result in war."

President Evtimov thought for a moment. "Your recommendations are accepted. Contact our ambassador to the United Nations and call for an emergency meeting immediately."

CHAPTER 16

The White House Situation Room
Emergency meeting of the National Security Council

Four hours later

I'm asking you … I'm pleading with you, Mr. President. Call this thing off and do it right now." Secretary of State Robert Mauney extended his hands toward the president, almost as if he were a starving man begging for bread.

"That would be a mistake, Mr. President." Secretary of Defense Erwin Lopez retorted. "Our sub is in the Black Sea. The plan is being executed to precision. Remember what's at stake if we don't find and stop this freighter. Nuclear material in the hands of terrorists!"

Secretary Mauney shot back. "But that was *before* the U.S. Air Force took out two of their fighters." Mauney glared at the secretary of defense. "Now terrorist nukes may be the *least* of our worries. We may be facing *Russian* nukes if this freighter attack backfires."

"Oh, *please.*" Lopez's voice dripped with sarcasm.

"All right. All right." President Williams held his palms out. He'd refereed enough arguments between these two. If the Democrat press knew what really went on behind the scenes, rioting would erupt in the streets of Washington.

Still, Secretary Mauney had a point. "Let's hear Secretary Mauney"—he nodded at the secretary of state—"and then we'll hear from Secretary Lopez." Another nod at the secretary of defense. "Secretary Mauney?"

"Thank you, Mr. President. As you know, the State Department has always opposed *Operation Undercover* as being too risky to our security interests. The idea of slipping an American submarine into the Black Sea to attack an unarmed Russian freighter seems preposterous. If the attack were exposed to the world, we'd look like the Germans sinking the *Lusitania*. Who would suspect plutonium was on that freighter?

"The State Department has also opposed *Operation Fortify*, our combined air and ground operations in Turkey and Georgia.

"As you know, my concern with *Operation Fortify* was the very close and dangerous proximity of armed American and Russian forces.

"Now we have American planes and Russian planes shooting at each other. One Russian pilot is dead. Another is in our custody."

The Secretary of State held up a document. "One hour ago, Mr. President, our ambassador to the United Nations received this from the Russian ambassador. The Russians plan to introduce this resolution to the Security Council in New York for debate later today. They are requesting that the Council adopt it."

> Resolved: The Government of the Russian Republic calls upon the Security Council to adopt this resolution condemning the United States of America for its unwarranted and unprovoked attack on aircraft of the Russian Air Force, who were operating peacefully within the borders of the Russian Republic at the time of the attack.
>
> The Security Council demands the immediate release of the innocent and captured Russian pilot, namely Captain Alexander Giorsky, who was piloting his aircraft in Russian airspace, over the Russian Republic of Chechnya at the time of this unwarranted and unprovoked attack.
>
> The Security Council further condemns the United States for the death of Junior Lieutenant Staas Budarin and calls upon the United States to immediately pay reparations in the amount of ten million American dollars to Lieutenant Budarin's widow and to establish a trust fund endowed with ten million American dollars for the benefit of Lieutenant Budarin's unborn child.
>
> Furthermore, the government of the Russian Republic considers the firing of missiles into its territory by any foreign power to be an aggressive and unsubstantiated act of aggression. Any further attacks by the United States of America on Russian territory will be considered to be an act of war under international law.

Stunned silence swept the room. The secretary of state had gotten the group's attention. Only the secretary of defense looked unimpressed.

"Consider our predicament, Mr. President. We shoot down two of their planes, capture one of their pilots, and we are darn lucky, frankly, that we are not already at war.

"Think how bad this gets if we sink a civilian freighter and are discovered." There were no comments. "It's not too late to stop this, Mr. President. Please, sir, I urge you to do just that." The secretary of state had finished his plea.

"Anybody?"

"Secretary Mauney makes some good points, Mr. President," Vice President Douglas Surber said.

"Maybe we should rethink this, sir." This was National Security Adviser Cynthia Hewitt.

Others nodded their heads.

Mack eyed his chairman of the Joint Chiefs, Admiral John F. Ayers, who sat across the table, resplendent in his Navy service dress blue uniform, complete with rows of red, green, pink, and blue service ribbons.

"Admiral Ayers, what's your take on all this?"

Ayers looked at the secretary of defense, then back at the president. "Mr. President, I'm no politician. I'm just an ole sea dog who's done his best to serve his country. I will say now what I've said before. If we can locate that freighter, we can send her to the bottom of the sea. And if she's got plutonium on board, we'll send that to the bottom of the ocean too. But if you're asking me to comment on a political strategy, sir, I'd have to defer to the secretary of defense on that one."

"Fair enough." Mack nodded at Secretary Erwin Lopez. "Mr. Secretary, do you concede that the secretary of state makes some good points? Should we rethink this?"

The secretary of defense inhaled deeply. "Mr. President, with all due respect to my friend the secretary of state, his points might be well-taken if"—Secretary Lopez held up his right index finger—"and I mean *if* the underlying facts were based on accurate information."

Lopez's black eyes scoured the room with a delightful satisfaction. Other Security Council members exchanged glances.

"But that declaration is based on bogus information. Our planes were defending the airspace of a United States ally, Georgia. Russian planes had invaded Georgian territory when we shot.

"This notion that we fired our missiles into Russian airspace is Soviet propaganda. These Russian planes were practically over Tbilisi, the capital city of Georgia, when this dogfight broke out." Secretary

Lopez was now chopping his hand in the air, like a karate master about to smash a cinderblock.

"If anybody committed an act of war, it was the Russians. *They* sent armed military aircraft into a foreign nation without permission, and our radar tapes will prove that unequivocally!" A dramatic pause followed that statement. Lopez lowered his voice. "Mr. President, I say we welcome this debate before the Security Council. Our radar tapes will reveal the truth, that the Russians invaded Georgian airspace, when they clearly did not have overflight rights. This is a violation of one of the most basic principles of international law.

"We should draft a counter-resolution condemning the Russians, take the debate to the Security Council, display the radar tapes, and expose the truth for the world to see." The secretary sipped bottled water. "We cannot, and we should not, let the lies that the Russians are propagating deter us from this mission, which is crucial to the security of America and the free world. I urge you, Mr. President, stay the course. Do not be dissuaded. Do not be deterred."

Lopez's speech had been dramatic. Mack waited for a moment before turning back to the chairman of the Joint Chiefs of Staff. "Admiral, where's the *Honolulu* at this time?"

"Mr. President, she's in the Black Sea positioned along the forty-fifth latitude. This is the northwestern sector of the Black Sea — one of the narrowest sections. If you trace a line along the forty-fifth parallel, it's approximately one hundred eighty miles from the Romanian coast in the west, to the Crimean Peninsula in the east. *Honolulu* is submerged right out there in the middle of this sector, about ninety miles from Romania and ninety miles from Sevastopol in Ukraine. Simply put, she's sitting right dab in the middle of the shipping lanes headed northeast to Odessa, where we think the freighter is headed."

"Thank you, Admiral." The president looked at the secretary of state.

"Secretary Mauney, Secretary Lopez disputes the truth of the Russian contentions, and suggests that we debate them about the merits of this, *and* that we move the Council for our own resolution condemning them. What are your thoughts on the secretary's proposal?"

The secretary of state poured a glass of ice water from one of the silver pitchers along the mahogany table. He took a long gulp, stalling long enough to collect his thoughts. He put the glass back down on the table, and then began speaking in soft tones.

"Mr. President, I don't doubt Secretary Lopez's sincerity. If the United States military has concluded that our planes never fired their missiles into Chechnya, and that the Russian planes were over Tbilisi when we shot them down, then I believe that the Russians are lying. They have a long history of misinformation, going all the way back to before the Bolshevik Revolution.

"Therefore, I agree that we should challenge them in front of the Council and in front of the world on this point. And if you instruct me to do so, I will give Ambassador Ward her marching orders to challenge them at the Security Council, or if necessary, I will go to New York myself to debate the matter." Mauney closed his eyes for a moment, then opened them. "Oh, and there's one other thing. I do recommend that we release the Russian pilot as a measure of good faith."

"Thank you, Mr. Secretary. I noticed you did not comment on the condemnation proposal," the president said.

"That's where I may differ with the secretary of defense."

"You don't think we should condemn the Russians?" The president looked at him curiously.

"Mr. President, the Russians deserve condemnation for their actions. But the issue is whether we want to fan the flames by pushing for a resolution of condemnation. We should take the high road by exposing the truth without getting down in the sewer with them by arguing over condemnation resolutions.

"But whether we seek a condemnation resolution or not, I stand by my previous recommendation, sir, that we abort *Operation Undercover* as being too risky under the circumstances. Sir, if this goes afoul, it could trigger all-out war." The secretary took another drink from the glass as if it were all hard to swallow. He set the glass down and said nothing else.

"Anything else, Secretary Mauney?"

"No, sir, Mr. President. The decision is in your hands."

The National Geospatial-Intelligence Agency
Fort Belvoir, Virginia

Kent Pendleton was taking a coffee break when the piercing staccato rang through the work areas.

Beep. Beep. Beep. Beep. Beep. Beep. Beep. Beep.

"Boss, you've gotta get in here!" Tommy Dinardo was yelling from the computer room.

The strident alarm meant that the computer on board one of the two satellites orbiting the earth over the western sector of the Black Sea had spotted a match.

"It's Redwood Two!" Dinardo was saying. "Check this out." Dinardo handed Kent a black-and-white photo that had been printed from the real-time feed from the satellite. "Computer's saying we've got a match."

Kent took the photo and compared it to one of the satellite photos taken of *Alexander Popovich* while she was in Sochi. The image of the ship at Sochi looked identical to the image of the ship plowing through the Black Sea.

"We've got a match!" Kent said. "Tommy, get the Pentagon on the line. Prepare to broadcast coordinates to the *Honolulu*."

"You've got it, boss!"

The White House Situation Room
Emergency meeting of the National Security Council

Mack pondered the words of his secretary of state, spoken just moments ago.

"Mr. President. The decision is in your hands."

The secretary was right. The decision *was* in his hands, and his hands only. If the Russians discovered that an American submarine attacked a civilian Russian freighter in the Black Sea, nuclear war could follow—especially on the heels of the two MiGs being shot down.

On the other hand, the plutonium on that ship could wind up in a nuclear bomb in Washington, or New York, or San Diego, or any other major American city.

This was a no-win situation. War now, or nuclear holocaust later, one or the other guaranteed.

He thought of his father, Colonel Manchester Elliot Williams, the man he had respected most in life. What would the colonel do?

The colonel would quote his favorite line from Douglas MacArthur. "In war there is no substitute for victory, that if you lose, the nation will be destroyed."

With all eyes boring on him, Mack silently prayed for wisdom. The more he prayed, the more MacArthur's words kept ringing in his ears.

If you lose, the nation will be destroyed.

"Ladies and gentlemen, I am reminded at this moment of the words of President Harry Truman, who said *the buck stops here*, and I also am reminded of the words of President Teddy Roosevelt, our youngest president, who spoke so eloquently of *The Man in the Arena*.

"Today, I feel like that man in the arena. It is a lonely feeling which carries awesome responsibility. But as President Truman said, the buck stops here.

"Our predicament is no easy one. Either way, we face the consequences of war and destruction. If we scrap *Operation Undercover*, as the secretary of state has suggested, millions could die from the weapons-grade plutonium that is now on the high seas and that is destined for the hands of terrorists.

"If we sink the *Alexander Popovich* and we are discovered, we face a dicey situation with Russia. As the secretary of state has pointed out, this is an explosive predicament that could lead to war.

"Some would call this a no-win situation.

"A number of years ago, I received some wise counsel by a Christian pastor who was a dear personal friend. It was a tough time in my life, and my friend was there for me every day.

"I don't remember everything that he told me during those dark days, but one thing that I'll never forget is this: He told me that our mantra for the day, for each and every day that we are given on this earth is to *do the right thing*.

"Do the right thing." His eyes swept the room. "And so I apply that mantra to the situation at hand. The first right thing to do is to expose the truth. So we will go to the UN Security Council with our radar tapes in hand, and we will expose the truth about what happened over the skies of Georgia. I will not allow Russian threats, based upon lies about this incident, to govern the course of my conduct as president.

"And then, there is a verse from the book of Proverbs that comes to mind. It goes something like this. 'You are a poor specimen if you cannot stand up to adversity.'

"This nation faces great adversity at this hour, even though most Americans outside the upper levels of Congress and the executive branch don't realize it. But I can tell you this. We will stand up to it. We will stand up to adversity and we will defeat it.

"The secretary of state shall have our ambassador to the United Nations challenge the Russians vigorously at the Security Council. The secretary of defense will provide the State Department with all radar tapes, and with all technical support necessary for presentations not only before the United Nations, but for purposes of immediate release to the press as well.

"Any questions so far?" Mack looked at the secretary of defense.

"Understood clearly, Mr. President. Secretary Mauney and his staff have our full cooperation."

"Good." Mack looked at his secretary of state. "Secretary Mauney, I've considered your recommendations on how to handle this matter before the UN and I value your input."

"Thank you, sir."

"Here's what we are going to do. First, I agree that seeking reciprocal sanctions against the Russians is not necessary."

Mack saw a relieved look on Robert Mauney's face.

"As far as the missing pilot goes," the president continued, "I think we should return him."

Mauney exhaled.

"But not yet."

Mauney raised his eyebrow.

"The problem with an immediate release of that pilot is twofold. First, if we release that pilot, we appear to authenticate to the rest of the world the Russians' version that we shot into their territory."

"Good point, Mr. President," the secretary of state conceded.

"Secondly, Russians flew warplanes over Georgia. There must be some consequences. If we simply turn the pilot over, what deters them from doing it again?"

"Agreed, Mr. President," the secretary of defense chimed in.

Secretary Mauney grimaced.

"Therefore, Secretary Mauney, I want you to open talks with the Russians on the release of that pilot, but as a condition, there must be some acknowledgment on their part that our pilots did not fire into their territory and that their pilots were over Georgian territory."

"They won't like it, sir."

"I don't care if they like it or not. Put some face-saving language in there if you want, but that's the way it's going to be."

"Yes, sir," the secretary of state said.

"Now, Secretary Lopez."

"Yes, Mr. President."

"I have three directives I want to underscore. First, all activities in Turkey and Georgia will continue as previously directed, until otherwise ordered by me."

"Yes, sir."

"Second, I want you to organize a press conference at the Pentagon this afternoon to get the facts out about what happened in that dogfight over Georgia."

"Will do, sir."

"Finally, there is to be no change—repeat no change—in the operational orders for *Operation Undercover*. We've come this far. We've gotten our sub into the Black Sea. We're going to find that freighter, sink her, and keep that plutonium out of the hands of terrorists. We're going to do this because it's the right thing to do."

Mack surveyed the room. Stone silence and electric tension dominated the atmosphere.

"Any questions?"

There were none.

"Very well, let's all get to work. This meeting is adjourned."

CHAPTER 17

The USS Honolulu
The Black Sea

Commander Pete Miranda walked around the control room, sipping black coffee and checking his watch. Now they were in a waiting game.

But submariners were good at that. Just waiting.

All the training, all the drills, all the practices, the repetitions, the checklists, etc. It all came down to this.

Running silent, running deep.

Waiting.

"What's our position, Chief of the Boat?"

"Forty-five degrees north latitude; thirty degrees, thirty minutes east longitude. Depth one-five-zero. Hovering at ground zero, Skipper."

"Very well, Mr. COB, thank you."

"Aye, sir."

To be a hunter. A predator. To kill from the depths of the sea and return silently back to ports unknown. This was the duty of the submariner.

Even still, in the serene silence of it all, Pete hoped they would never have to launch a torpedo.

Pete was unafraid of dying. Nor was he afraid of the naval dragnet that would sweep the area soon after the freighter's sinking.

None of that drove this feeling. There was just a hope that somehow, some way, the crisis could resolve itself in another way.

They'd already made history by entering the Black Sea. But beyond a tiny handful of Americans in the Navy and at the very upper echelons of the United States government, this moment would never be known. It would never exist in the history books. Not that Pete cared about making the history books. He did not.

But his children, Hannah and Coley, the son and daughter he had not seen for a year, were weighing on his heart.

All his life's regrets flashed through his mind. His marriage to the Navy. Christmases gone by when he was alone, without his children to open presents under the Christmas tree.

He closed his eyes and saw thirteen-year-old Hannah. Her hair was wavy and black as coal. Her skin was fair and her eyes were a deep, haunting blue. She was his Snow White, a princess always in his heart. And her smile when she sat on his knee and put her arms around him made every part of his soul melt.

Coley was born a year after Hannah. He too had inherited Sally's wavy, jet-black hair. While Hannah was sugar and spice and everything nice, Coley was all boy.

The kid got into everything, and Pete thought he was going to burn the house down from one of the many "chemistry experiments" Coley conducted in his room. To keep Coley's mischievous streak in check, Pete insisted that the boy play sports. Coley experimented with baseball and basketball, before settling on soccer, in which he excelled as the fastest, most agile and lithe forward on the team.

That thought brought a proud smile to the captain's face.

The history books could fall off a cliff as far as Pete was concerned. Most of them were revisionist anyway. But his heart's desire was for Hannah and Coley to know what their ole pop sacrificed here, in the Black Sea, and to know that he had done it for America—that he had done it for them.

If only some way they could know.

But his death, should it come, would kill a last chance to hug his little girl or play catch with his boy. *God forgive me for my poor choices. Forgive me for letting this time slip away.*

How surreal it all was. To be here, yet in the eyes of millions and the eyes of his children, to vanish into oblivion ... never to be heard from again.

The cacophonous static of the ship's communication speaker broke the serenity of the moment.

"Conn. Radio! Receiving emergency action message!... Recommend alert one. Recommend alert one!"

Pete barked at the officer of the deck. "Officer of the deck, on the 1MC, sound alert one!"

"Aye, Skipper! Sounding alert one!" The OOD picked up the microphone and switched the frequency to the 1MC, broadcasting the alert all over the ship.

"Alert one! Alert one! Incoming emergency action message! Alert one! Alert one! Incoming EAM!"

Pete looked at Frank Pippen, who was now wearing his battle-ready game face. "XO, follow me."

"Aye, Skipper."

"Mr. McCaffity, you have the conn!"

"Aye, Skipper, I have the conn," replied Lieutenant Darwin McCaffity, the officer of the deck.

In the midst of warning buzzers sounding off and on, like a buzzing alarm clock without the snooze button, Pete bounded down the steel, grated decks to the radio room, which was on the same deck as the control room. The radio officer, Lieutenant Walt Brown, had already printed a hard copy of the EAM and was holding it out for the captain.

"Looks like we've got a target, Skipper," the radio officer announced. Pete snatched the message from his hand. He spread the sheet on the charting table.

EMERGENCY ACTION MESSAGE

FROM: NATIONAL MILITARY COMMAND CENTER — WASHINGTON, D.C.
TO: USS *HONOLULU*
SUBJECT: ACTION MESSAGE

REMARKS:

Be advised U.S. reconnaissance satellites have spotted Russian freighter *Alexander Popovich* operating in vicinity of USS *Honolulu* current patrol area.

Alexander Popovich last spotted 1030 hours Zulu time at 44 degrees north latitude, 33 degrees east longitude on course bearing 340 degrees.

Carry out battle plan. Seek and destroy.

Pete handed the message to Frank. "Lieutenant Brown, pass me the microphone."

"Aye, Skipper." The radio officer complied.

"On the 1MC."

Lieutenant Brown punched a button. "You've got the 1MC now, sir."

"Thank you, Lieutenant." Pete pressed the broadcast switch and spoke into the microphone. "All hands, now hear this. This is the captain." He paused for a moment as his voice echoed in all the passageways and compartments of the three-hundred-sixty-foot submarine. "We've just received an updated EAM from Washington. *Alexander Popovich* is in our area, and she's coming our way. When we find her, we're going to sink her.

"Torpedo Room, be prepared. All departments and all personnel, be prepared. Be alert. Be ready to go to battle stations at a moment's notice.

"When we sink her, I expect that within an hour, we will face a naval dragnet covering the entire western sector of the Black Sea from the Russian, the Ukrainian, the Romanian, and the Bulgarian navies." He looked at Frank Pippen, who slowly nodded his head. "This is dangerous business, people. But you know that. Stay on your toes.

"Just remember, we do not carry out this mission for glory, nor for recognition, nor for the history books—for no one will ever remember, or even know that we were here.

"We carry out this mission to save the lives of millions—to save the lives even of your loved ones"—images of Hannah and Coley rushed into his mind—"and of mine." He paused for a second. A crew should never sense that their captain is losing control of his emotions. "This is the captain. That is all."

Pete handed the microphone back to the radio officer. He turned to Frank. "XO, where's Lieutenant Jamison?" He was referring to Lieutenant Phil Jamison, the ship's intelligence officer who had been requested to volunteer for this mission because of his proficiency in Russian.

"In his stateroom, sir," the XO said.

"Summon him to the control room. It's time to put his skills to work."

"Aye, Captain."

Office of the president of the Russian Republic
Staraya Square, Moscow

The audacity of these Americans!" The Russian defense minister, Giorgy Alexeevich Popkov, paced to and fro in front of the president's desk, waving his hands in the air. "To claim that *our* planes violated Georgian airspace. Typical Yankee lies!"

"This would not be the first time that the Americans have twisted things to their liking for propaganda purposes," President Evitimov said, exchanging curious glances with his foreign minister.

"We shall expose their lies!" Popkov flailed his hands in the air. "We shall produce our radar tapes and show the world direct evidence of their aggressive and belligerent behavior."

"Sit down, Giorgy Alexeevich!"

The defense minister complied.

"I would rather expose our stolen plutonium!" Evtimov said.

That comment brought a tension-filled silence. Popkov squirmed in his chair like a writhing snake.

"Well, Comrade Defense Minister, what have you to say about this?"

Popkov looked around the room, exchanging glances with his friend the chief of staff, as if Sergey Semyonovich Sobyanin would tell him what to say.

But Sergey Semyonovich looked away from his old friend. Good. Sergey was smart enough to know where his loyalties should lie.

"We shall find the plutonium, Comrade President," Popkov stuttered. "We have reason to believe it is in Grozny."

"We do, do we? Based on what?"

"Based on our intelligence on the streets, which is highly reliable."

"And if we do not have the plutonium yet, how do you propose that we go about getting it?"

The weasel pulled himself up a bit. "By following the course that you have so boldly set forth when we began this operation, Comrade President. By pouring more forces in against the rebels. By pummeling them, and by sticking to our commitment to do so until Chechnya is a literal wasteland."

"And what if all this does not work, Giorgy Alexeevich? What if that Chechen rebel Aslambek Kadyrov is at this moment building his bomb in some town other than Grozny, and we are bombing the wrong place?"

Popkov crossed his right knee over his left, then switched back and crossed his left knee over his right. "Please, I remind us all"—his eyes swept the room again—"patience is in order. Only a few days have passed since we discovered all this. Besides"—he folded his arms and leaned back in his chair with a satisfied smile—"we always have the option of withdrawing our forces and executing General Order 46."

That comment brought stunned silence. General Order 46, named such because the forty-sixth longitude ran just east of Grozny, was a highly classified plan thought of and presented by Popkov in his first act as defense minister two years ago. General Order 46 had created heated controversy in the upper levels of the Russian command.

The plan called for the total withdrawal of all Russian forces in Chechnya, followed by the dropping of a neutron bomb over the Chechen capital city by Russian aircraft.

Unlike a thermonuclear device, which would vaporize and obliterate everything within a multi-mile radius, a neutron device, at least in theory, would leave all structures intact. Buildings, bridges, and roads would all be left standing after the attack for subsequent repopulation by Slavic Russians.

But the presence of lethal neutrons would destroy all human and animal life in the city and in the countryside for miles around.

There were too many questions about the plan. How would they assure that deadly neutron radiation would not drift into Russia? What about the reaction of the international community? Was there a way to execute this without Russia's fingerprints being on it?

President Evtimov had shelved the plan for the time being. Privately, Evtimov worried that Popkov may try something without his permission.

"Let me make it perfectly clear, Giorgy Alexeevich, that General Order 46 is not an option at this time, and certainly will never be an option without my express approval. Are we clear on this point?"

"Extremely clear, Comrade President."

"You may continue our conventional buildup and pummel Grozny to the stones, but I want no mention of General Order 46 anymore unless I bring it up. Are there any questions?"

The weasel slumped back into his chair. "No. There are no questions, Comrade President."

Evtimov turned to his foreign minister. "I have been thinking, Alexander Alexeyvich, that in light of the worsening crisis in Chechnya, and because of the timing of our upcoming resolution in the United Nations condemning America, perhaps we should postpone my meeting with President Butrin?"

The foreign minister leaned forward. "No sir, I do not believe it advisable to cancel that meeting."

President Evtimov raised his eyebrow. "Really? Why do you say this, Alexander Alexeyvich?"

The foreign minister leaned forward in his chair. "We have a unique opportunity to bring Ukraine back into the eastern camp. And there are several reasons for this."

"What are your reasons?"

"First"—the foreign minister brought the tips of his index fingers together—"cancelling the summit will signal to the world that we consider Chechnya to be a serious international crisis. The more we signal business as usual, the better."

"Good point," President Evtimov said.

The foreign minister continued. "Also, I know Vlaçlav Butrin well. He is bighearted. Orphans are his passion. I remind you, Comrade President, that the orphans aboard the Russian freighter live in the very same orphanage where President Butrin himself was raised. Trust me, Vitaly Sergeivich, your offer to spend millions of rubles on Ukrainian orphanages will strike close to his heart. Your presence there at the dock will be meaningful to him.

"I suggest that the theme of your visit be on humanitarian cooperation, with Russia committing to become a major partner with Ukraine on the issue of orphans.

"I can have our staff prepare a major speech for you, Comrade President, on Russia's determination to take care of displaced Ukrainian orphans who continue to suffer residual radiation as a result of the Chernobyl nuclear disaster."

The president thought about that for a moment. "Ah, yes. Excellent points, Alexander Alexeyvich. Think of the photo opportunities for the Western media with all those orphans hugging me and Butrin!"

The foreign minister nodded his head in agreement. "Not only that, Comrade President, but if your speech is good enough and we throw enough Siberian oil money behind this orphans project, you, my dear friend, might even win the Nobel Prize for Peace."

"The Nobel Peace Prize?" Nods of agreement came from other cabinet ministers. "How about that?" The idea resonated in his head and grew more appealing. He let the words roll slowly off his tongue. "President Vitaly Sergeivich Evtimov. Winner of the Nobel Peace Prize for his work in helping the poor Ukrainian orphans!"

"That sounds very nice, Comrade President." This was Sergey Semyonovich Sobyanin, the president's chief of staff.

"Yes, indeed it does, Sergey. Thank you very much."

"*Dah. Dah,*" the men of the cabinet were saying.

"In fact it sounds so good," the president continued, "that I'll drink to that." That brought cackles and laughter from the cabinet members present.

"Sergey!" the president said through laughter.

"Yes, sir."

"Have the waiter bring rounds of vodka for everyone. We shall celebrate my upcoming summit with President Butrin, and more importantly, my soon-to-be-awarded Nobel Prize for Peace."

More nods of approval. A round of cheering from the members of the cabinet. Then, four uniformed waiters marched into the president's office with silver trays full of glasses, ice, vodka, caviar, cheese, and crackers.

They drank and toasted and laughed and cackled about the Nobel Prize.

After a few minutes of gaiety, Evtimov checked his watch. "Gentlemen, it has been a productive meeting, but we must get to work. You are all excused, except Sergey Semyonovich." He nodded at his chief of staff. "I need a few words with you."

"Of course, Comrade President."

The ministers filed out of the president's office, and when they did, only the president, the chief of staff, and three members of the president's personal security detail remained.

The president nodded at one of his bodyguards to close the door.

"Sit back down, Sergey Semyonovich."

The chief of staff complied.

"Tell me, Sergey, what do you think of our defense minister?"

Sergey Semyonovich hesitated. "What do you mean, Comrade President?"

"You and he are longtime friends, as I understand it?"

"For years, we drank vodka, hunted deer in the forest, and went to banya together."

"And now, Sergey, where do your loyalties lie?"

The chief of staff spoke without hesitation. "My allegiance is with you, Vitaly Sergeivich. You are my president, and you are my friend. I have no other allegiances."

"Then I can trust you, even in matters concerning the defense minister?"

"Totally."

"Then tell me. What do you think of the defense minister's ... stability?"

"I have my concerns."

"Is this true?"

"Yes, sir."

"How so?"

"I thought the reference to General Order 46 was, under these circumstances, wholly inappropriate."

"Hmm." The president studied the face of his chief of staff. "And what of the circumstances surrounding the shooting down of our planes?"

"I am suspicious of Popkov's accounting."

"Why do you say this?"

"First, it is unlikely that the Americans would fire into our airspace. Possible? Yes. Likely? No. It is also unlikely that our pilot would float by the wind from Russian territory to Georgian territory. Both these events are possible, of course. But with two unlikely events in the same story, combined with the fact that Giorgy Alexeevich feels that you are blaming him for the loss of plutonium ..."

"Do you feel he should remain as defense minister?"

"That is your call alone, Comrade President."

"You did not answer my question, Sergey Semyonovich. Do you feel he should remain as defense minister?"

The chief of staff looked down at the floor, then looked back up at the president. "I believe that Giorgy Alexeevich has become unstable. That makes him dangerous, especially since he is in command of the most powerful army in the world."

"No, *I* am in command of the most powerful army in the world."

"Of course you are, Comrade President. But should Giorgy Alexeevich become more deranged, how can we be assured that he will remember who is in charge? Unless they know that he is contradicting your orders, our generals will obey him." A pause. "What if he ordered execution of General Order 46?"

Sergey Semyonovich's point was well-taken. "Are you willing to help me take care of the problem?"

The chief of staff shot the president a suspicious look. "Take care of the problem, sir?"

"Again I ask you, Sergey Semyonovich, are you willing to help me take care of the problem?"

Their eyes locked. "Yes, my president, I will take care of the problem."

The Alexander Popovich
The Black Sea

The next day

Masha stood in the passageway leading out to the main deck of the ship. She looked around to see if anyone was watching. No one was in sight. She had decided to move the knife from her thigh to her back, thinking that repositioning it would give her quicker access when she needed it. But the sharp knife had slipped down a bit down her back, and she needed to position it higher under her bra strap.

She would need to use the knife soon, she had resolved. She did not know when, or how.

But soon.

Donning her sunglasses, she stepped out into the bright afternoon sun on the main deck of *Alexander Popovich*.

She glanced toward the center of the deck, where the Captain Batsakov's loyal sidekick, Aleksey Anatolyvich, had erected a net across the deck. The orphans were patting a ball back and forth across the net with their hands. They laughed and cackled as they played.

Aleksey seemed good with children. She prayed that she would not have to hurt him, and that somehow, he would become her ally.

"Dima, come over here!"

The skinny little boy with the bug-eyed glasses bounded across the deck with a wide grin on his face. The brisk sea breeze blew through his blonde hair, disheveling it as he wrapped his arms around her. She held onto him for a bit longer than usual.

"Are you having fun, Dima?"

"*Dah*! Aleksey teach us how to play volleyball on ship!"

"Yes, I see that!"

She glanced at the children again. Aleksey's eyes caught hers, and he threw her a big wave. She waved back. He turned back to the other eleven. Good.

"I have heard of this game, volleyball. They play it in America."

"You play volleyball, Masha?"

"No, I have never played."

"You want to learn?"

"No, not right now."

"Why not, Masha?" Those long-lashed, pleading eyes melted her. These eyes would melt an iceberg in the Arctic Sea. What was she to tell the boy? That she could not play because if she walked out into the middle of the deck she might become a target for someone with a sniper rifle?

"I cannot play because right now we need to put more lotion on your back so you do not burn, that is why."

"Aw, Masha. Again?"

"Yes, Dima. Again. Turn around."

The boy complied.

She squirted the white sunblock into her hands, then rubbed his rough, leathery shoulders. The boy recoiled from the coolness of the lotion. Her hands moved from his shoulders down to the awful skin grafting that covered his entire back.

The skin, or what was left of it, was twisted and contorted and scarred hideously from the scalding water that was poured on him. To her fingers, his skin in the center of his back felt like a miniature mountain range.

She thanked God that he felt no pain from it anymore. She also thanked God that Dima was oblivious to it all, even though strangers who saw his back for the first time often grimaced.

"Okay, Dima, that's good. Go back out and play now."

"You come too, Masha?" He tugged at her hand and flashed those puppy dog eyes again.

"Maybe next time, Dima." She shooed him back out to the center of the deck and prayed that there would be a next time. Masha considered her predicament. There was no real possibility for escape. She couldn't swim to safety. They were planning to kill her, and if they did, what would become of the children? The question now was whether she should kill first or wait to be killed.

God, give me wisdom.

She remembered the words of the Allisons, that God would help her in all things. *God, please get me and my children off this ship alive. Amen.*

CHAPTER 18

Commander Pete Miranda stepped back into the control room of the USS *Honolulu.*

"I have the conn," Pete said.

"The captain has the conn." Lieutenant McCaffity stepped aside for his commanding officer.

Pete took his position in the center of the room. His XO, Lieutenant Commander Frank Pippen, who had followed him back into the control room, stood at his side.

"Mr. COB, any sign of Lieutenant Jamison?"

"Not yet, Captain. I'm sure Mr. Jamison will be right here," the chief of the boat said.

Pete checked his watch. At that moment, Lieutenant Phil Jamison, the ship's intelligence officer, walked into the control room.

"You called, Captain?"

"Ah, Mr. Jamison. How nice of you to join us."

"My apologies, Captain. I was in the head, sir."

"Ah," Pete said. "The proverbial call of nature."

"Yes, sir. No excuses, sir."

Snickering arose around the control room.

"No time for that," Pete said. "As you know, Lieutenant, satellites have spotted our target in the area."

"I heard the broadcast on the 1MC."

"That ship could pop up any minute on our sonar."

"Yes, sir."

"If and when it shows, we are going to sink it. And at that point, we will float our antenna to the surface, and will be monitoring local radio traffic, probably from Russian ships. We won't have time for EAMs. I will need you here, immediately translating any Russian radio traffic that we might intercept."

"I can do that, sir."

"Until further notice, your duty station is here in the control room, with me and the XO."

"Aye, Captain. With pleasure."

The Alexander Popovich
The Black Sea

Captain Batsakov thought about assigning the task to Joseph Radin.

After all, the first officer was the leading proponent of killing her. Perhaps Joseph could find some satisfaction in it all.

If not Joseph, the other option was Aleksey Anatolyvich.

Aleksey could lead her to an isolated spot on the ship, shoot her in the head, and then toss her to the sharks after sundown. Nobody would notice. Aleksey would do whatever he was told. But then again, perhaps Aleksey did not have the stomach for the job.

Regardless of who did the job, Masha Katovich's death would be on the head of the bloodthirsty Russian government for forcing this idotic babysitting mission upon the *Alexander Popovich*.

The telephone rang in the captain's stateroom.

Batsakov picked up the receiver. *"Dah."*

"Kapitán, this is the first officer on the bridge."

"What is it, Joseph?"

"Sir, we have been trying to raise you on the ship's intercom system. Did you not hear us?"

"I haven't heard a thing."

"My apologies, *Kapitán*, but we have tried a dozen times or so. Would you like for me to send an electrician to your stateroom to see if it needs repairing?"

"Hold on, Joseph. Let me have a look at it before you do that."

Batsakov laid the phone down on a table and walked over to the intercom. Something looked odd. *The volume knob!* It was turned all the way over to the *off* position.

This was odd. In all the years he had been the skipper of *Alexander Popovich*, he had never touched that volume control, not even when he had women in the cabin, because the crew knew not to bother him unless it was an emergency.

Who did this? Perhaps Aleksey? That made no sense. The boy had never touched it in all these years.

What about one of the porters? Again, never in the ten years that he had commanded *Alexander Popovich* had anyone ever touched that knob that he could remember. Why would they? His crew members understood that their own safety could depend on the captain's ability to communicate with the bridge in times of emergency.

Batsakov scratched his head.

He thought back.

He had left Masha in the stateroom alone during the false alarm with the first Egyptian freighter. Perhaps in the frenzy of the moment, the bridge had neglected to turn off the microphone. What if she had heard something when he left her alone and did not want him to know that she heard it? What if she had overheard all the talk on the bridge about the Egyptian freighter and their precious cargo?

He turned the volume back up and returned to the telephone.

"Joseph, I think I have solved the problem," Batsakov reached into his desk drawer and extracted the GSh-18 semiautomatic pistol. "Try the intercom now."

"Can you hear me, *Kapitán*?" Joseph's voice boomed over the intercom.

"*Dah*, I hear you clearly."

"*Kapitán*, I am sorry to interrupt, but we received a radio transmission from the Russian consulate in Sevastopol."

"What do they want?" Batsakov worked the bolt action on the pistol, then turned off the safety lock.

"They are requesting that all crewmen of *Alexander Popovich* wear dress uniforms upon arrival in Odessa. They also want to make sure all orphans are dressed in their best clothes."

"How far are we from Odessa?"

"Stand by, *Kapitán*."

If he had any doubts about Joseph Radin's recommendation to kill Masha Katovich, this little knob incident had erased those doubts.

"*Kapitán*, we are maintaining a course of three-four-zero degrees and are now approximately one hundred fifty nautical miles from Odessa."

At that distance and speed, they would sail into port in the morning, just about eight hundred hours.

"Very well, Mr. Radin. Radio Sevastopol. Tell them we will all be dressed nice and spiffy. Tell them I will pass the request about the children along to Miss Katovich."

Batsakov jammed the pistol under his belt. He donned a windbreaker to conceal the gun from her view. He knew what had to be done.

The USS Honolulu
The Black Sea

They called him "the Bloodhound."

At least that was his nickname in the Navy's elite sonar community. But it wasn't his nose that had earned him the reputation.

It was his ears.

The legend started when they gave him those hearing tests right after he enlisted. He remembered them vividly even thirty years later — those blasted *diminishing beep* audio tests that so many recruits wound up going batty on.

They claimed he scored the highest ever on the initial screen. He was penciled in for the sonar school immediately. And when he had twice tried getting out of the Navy, the recruiters pulled some strings to double his enlistment bonus.

The money was too good.

He stayed.

Still, the Bloodhound understood perhaps better than anyone in the Navy that sound carried for miles under water. That was the whole idea behind passive sonar — to simply listen, carefully and intently, to the sounds of the deep.

The problem for the average ear, however, was to distinguish the natural sounds of the sea — the sounds of fish and mammals and currents and underwater volcanic activity — from manmade sounds. This was challenging when the manmade sounds were off at a great distance, perhaps at a distance of several miles.

Master Chief King discovered long ago that the best way to listen to the sea was like listening to classical music. To sit back, close one's eyes, and drink in the washing harmony of notes and block out all else.

In the back of his mind, he knew that a Russian freighter was somewhere in the area. But to hear it, he would have to meditate on the symphonic orchestration of sounds that God had created for the largest kingdom on planet earth—the kingdom under the sea.

He closed his eyes and slumped back, ever so slightly, making himself forget even the important fact that he was on board a United States nuclear submarine.

A faint gurgling in the water came from a distance.

The wake of propellers or natural whirlpools? Now the gurgling was gone. A minute later, the gurgling was back.

Master Chief King opened his eyes, and then closed them again. A faint whine came through the water. The whine was gone.

Perhaps whales mating.

Perhaps not. The gurgling got louder; then louder.

The Bloodhound opened his eyes again. The faint whine returned over the sound of the gurgling. The whine got louder. And then louder!

This was no whale. This was the screw of a ship!

"Soup!" the Bloodhound called out the name colloquially used for the sonar supervisor. "Check this out!"

Master Chief King gave headphones to Lieutenant Daniel Boers, the *Honolulu*'s sonar officer.

"Hear that?"

The sonar officer strapped on the headsets.

The other sonar tech blurted out, "I've got broadband contact! Bearing three-four-zero. Citing tracker sierra and ATF!"

King and Boers looked over the sonar tech's shoulder at the broadband screen, on the spherical array, known as a waterfall. The waterfall showed streaks of long, green fluorescent rain falling down across the black screen. But at the number 347, a bright white streak was flowing down.

Lieutenant Boers picked up the mike.

The sonar officer's voice boomed into the tension-filled control room.

"Conn! Sonar! We have a possible freighter, single screw. Bearing three-four-zero. Speed ten knots. Designate contact master two-eight!"

Pete looked at his XO, then took the microphone.

"Sonar. Conn. Aye! On the 1MC. Man battle stations!"

"Man battle stations! Aye," the OOD said, then picked up the 1MC. "General quarters! General quarters! Man battle stations! Man battle stations!"

All over the ship, men in blue jump suits ran to their positions as the general quarters alarm sounded throughout the submarine. "Battle stations! Battle stations! Man battle stations!"

"Mr. McCaffity. Report."

"One moment, Captain," the officer of the deck said. "Departments still reporting in, sir." Five seconds passed. "Captain, all departments have reported in. All personnel are at battle stations awaiting your orders, sir."

"Very well," Pete said. "Torpoedo room! Rig for ultra quiet! Rig tubes one and four, fully ready."

"Rig tubes one and four, fully ready. Aye, sir," the officer of the deck parroted.

"Conn! Sonar! Contact maintaining course three-four-zero degrees. Range two thousand yards."

"Captain, torpedo room reporting tubes one and four are rigged and fully ready."

"Very well. Let's have a look at the target. Diving officer, take us to periscope depth."

"Aye, Captain, take us to periscope depth."

The depth meter, a black screen with a red light, showed 150. As the diving officer blew compressed air into the hull, the number got progressively smaller. *140, 130, 120.*

The numbers began slowing in their descent. *90, 80, 70, 60.*

When the number stabilized at 60, the diving officer spoke. "The ship is at periscope depth, Captain."

"Very well. Up scope."

"Up scope."

The OOD hit the button on the Type 18 search periscope on the starboard side of the sail. There was a *click, click, click* noise as the electric motor within the tubing extended the scope above the surface.

"Scope's up, Skipper," Lieutenant McCaffity said.

"Very well." Pete brought his eyes to the ocular sockets, rested his hands on the grips, and began a slow, three-hundred-sixty-degree sweep of the horizon above.

Green water lapped the bottom of the lens, and clear blue sky dominated the top. Pete stepped another quarter to his left, carefully sweeping the horizon in a counterclockwise direction.

The view in the scope showed a panoramic display of blue and green water against sky. As the scope swept the horizon, a wedge rushed by in the water. Pete stopped the scope and slowly turned it back to his right. *Bingo.* The grey wedge was a ship headed this way.

"Target's in sight!" Pete said. "She's heading this way. Let's get to her broadside for a better shot. Ahead one quarter."

"Ahead one quarter."

"Right full rudder."

"Right full rudder."

Through the periscope, Pete watched his submarine close the distance to the freighter. His only problem—the freighter was headed north and *Honolulu* was going south.

Pete waited until the sub had passed alongside the freighter, then ordered a full turning maneuver to bring *Honolulu* alongside headed in the same direction.

"Left full rudder. Make course three-four-zero degrees."

"Left full rudder. Making my course three-four-zero degrees," the helmsman said.

The submarine closed the distance with the freighter and was soon off to her side.

"Make your speed ten knots."

"Making my speed ten knots, aye, Captain."

The underwater turn and speed adjustment now had *Honolulu* running parallel with the freighter, out to her port side, at a distance of about 1800 yards. Through the scope, Pete saw the freighter from bow to stern. She was low in the water, which Pete found a bit odd. But was she *Alexander Popovich*? He wanted a better view.

"Raise the attack scope."

"Raising attack scope, aye, Skipper." The OOD hit the button raising the second periscope on the submarine, the Type 2 attack periscope, giving the captain ultra-high magnification power for viewing the target.

"Mr. Jamison."

"Aye, Captain."

"Did you bring those intel photos of *Alexander Popovich*?"

"Got 'em right here, Captain."

Pete swung the attack scope around in the same direction as the search scope. When the moving freighter was in sight again, he hit the magnification trigger, producing an up-close, full-screen view of the ship, churning water and moving from right to left.

"Mr. Jamison, let me see those photos, please."

"Aye, Captain." The intelligence officer handed the captain three glossy, eight-by-ten, black-and-white photos of *Alexander Popovich* taken from broadsides. Pete studied the photos, then looked through the scope at the ship again, then at the photos.

"XO, take a look."

"Yes, sir." Lieutenant Commander Frank Pippen looked in the attack scope, then looked at the photos. "We've found our target, Captain. Exact same contour lines."

"I concur," Pete said. "Right full rudder. Turn into her broadsides. Close to within one thousand yards. Prepare to attack."

CHAPTER 19

The Alexander Popovich
The Black Sea

Captain Batsakov stepped out from the superstructure in the rear of _Alexander Popovich_ onto the main deck of his ship. He saw Masha Katovich, in white shorts, a light green sweater, and wearing sunglasses. She stood near the starboard gunwale about one hundred yards away with her arms crossed, watching those children of hers play a stupid game of volleyball with Aleksey.

He could shoot her from here, but he would have twelve little talking witnesses. And he could not toss the little rats overboard with her, not with the presidents of Russia and Ukraine waiting for them.

Batsakov needed to think this through.

He looked at his watch. It was just past two o'clock.

He would distract the little rats by throwing them a big ice cream party tonight. Perhaps Aleksey could dress as a clown or something. They would be told that Masha was sick, that she would join them back at the orphanage.

He would instruct the ship's chef to fill their ice cream with powder from sleeping pills taken from sick bay. Because the powder had no taste, they would not know they were being drugged. They would be told that if they finished the first bowl, the second bowl would have chocolate on top!

The first bowl would make them drowsy. The second would knock them out like sleeping dogs.

They should be completely groggy in the morning from their ice-cream induced hangovers. So groggy, hopefully, that no one would mention the absence of Masha Katovich.

His only worry was the little rat they called Dima. The hideous-looking scarback seemed to cling to her like she was his mother or something.

He would shoot Katovich and toss her overboard. And then, he would have Aleksey bring Dima to the back of the ship where no one could see. They would toss the little rat overboard too, and then tell the others that Dima was seasick and Masha was taking care of him.

Yes, that would most certainly work, especially since Masha and Dima were always together. Then they would report this tragedy to the authorities. Poor Dima, who was at play on the deck, was running, got too close to the edge, and fell into the sea. Masha, a wonderful and heroic woman who would give her life for her children, dived into the sea after him. They circled the area looking for survivors, but found no one.

Yes, that would be the perfect alibi. That would work.

Now was the time.

"Miss Katovich!"

She looked up at him and waved.

He motioned her toward him. "Come over here! I need to see you for a moment."

She started walking toward him. Something was odd about her walk. She seemed to be scratching her back.

She approached to within a few feet of him. "I was watching the children play the American game called volleyball."

"Yes, I can see." He nodded toward Akelsey, who still had the rats occupied. "Listen, Masha, something important has come up."

"*Dah*?" She kept scratching her back.

"We have received a radio transmission from Sebastopol about the children."

"About the children?"

"*Dah*. Walk with me, please." He led her back onto the small deck-way surrounding the superstructure in the rear of the ship. They kept walking. They were almost near the stern now.

Batsakov looked around.

They were out of sight of anyone else on board.

He reached inside his coat and felt for the pistol.

The USS Honolulu
The Black Sea

Torpedo tubes one and four are flooded, sir," the OOD said. "Awaiting your orders!"

"Range?"

"Range to target—twelve hundred yards, sir."

"Easy," Pete said. "Just a little closer."

"Are you going to fire both torps, Captain?" the XO asked.

"One torpedo should do the job, don't you think, XO?"

"On a Russian freighter, I should think so, Skipper."

"I say we save torp four." He glanced at Frank. "We may need it."

Frank did not respond for a couple of seconds. "You got that right, Skipper."

"Range to target?"

"Range now eleven hundred yards."

Pete raised his finger. "On my mark, prepare to fire torpedo one."

"Range now one thousand yards."

"Fire torp one!"

"Fire torp one!"

A powerful *swoosh* rocked the *Honolulu.*

"Torp's in the water!"

Tension filled the control room. There was no turning back now.

"Range to target?"

"Torpedo is at eight hundred yards and closing, Captain."

Pete checked his watch.

"Now seven hundred yards."

"Six hundred yards to target and still closing."

"Time to impact?"

"Time to impact fifty seconds, Captain. Now five hundred yards."

Pete checked his watch again.

"Range four hundred yards. Time to impact forty seconds."

The Alexander Popovich
The Black Sea

The wind whipped hard around the stern of the ship. A sudden surge of cool air in her face and hair emboldened her to the task at hand.

She knew this was the time.

It was either him or her.

She held her hand in place behind her back to avoid revealing the knife until the last second.

"Something wrong with your back, Miss Katovich?"

"I think I pulled a muscle, that is all. What did you want to see me about?"

"It is about the children." He pulled a black pistol from his jacket. "I am sorry to have to do this to such a beautiful woman."

"Emergency! Emergency!" A voice boomed over the ship's loudspeakers. "Torpedo in the water! Torpedo in the water! Brace for impact!"

The captain looked up. She dived at his midsection, lunging at him with the knife. A deafening explosion rocked the ship, spraying columns of seawater high into the air. The explosion knocked Masha off her feet. The ship rolled and listed in the water.

Masha pushed herself up and saw the captain writhing on the back deck, just in front of the Russian flag that flew off the stern. The knife was plunged deep into his midsection just below his sternum. Blood gushed around the knife. The captain moaned. "My ship! Oh, my ship!"

The gun had fallen on the deck near his outstretched hand. Adrenaline shot Masha's hand toward the gun. When she grabbed it, the thought hit her.

Dima!

The USS Honolulu
The Black Sea

Contact! Contact! We got 'em, Captain!" Cheers erupted in the *Honolulu*'s control room. Officers and enlisted men high-fived each other.

"Quiet! Quiet in the conn!" Pete held his palms down. His men responded to his call for silence. "I understand your exuberance, gentlemen, but we've still got work to do."

"Conn. Sonar."

"Go ahead, Sonar!"

"Captain, we're picking up sounds of explosions coming through the water."

"Any other contacts in the area?"

"That's a negative, Captain. Not yet, anyway!"

"Notify me when we make first sonar contact." Pete looked at his OOD. "Lieutenant McCaffity. Up scope."

"Up scope, aye, sir." McCaffity pushed the button to raise the Type 2 attack periscope. A few seconds later, Pete brought his eyes to the scope again. The powerful blast of the Mark 48 torpedo had broken the freighter into two sections. The torp had exploded under the keel, just as it was designed to do, essentially breaking the ship's back.

Thick black smoke billowed from the forward section, which was listing badly, and had floated about one hundred yards from the aft section. As bad as it was listing, the bow section might have another five minutes before slipping under the surface.

Pete hit the magnification button. This brought the whole wreckage into a close-up view.

The back section was also floating, but listing. Pete could see people scrambling around on the deck of the back section. They looked like ... *Children?*

No. His eyes were playing tricks on him. Pete squinted and looked again. Whoever he saw running on the deck of the sinking freighter was gone.

It was time to get out of here.

"Down scope."

"Down scope, aye, Captain."

"Five degrees down bubble, make depth one-five-zero feet."

The submarine dropped another ninety feet in the water from a depth of sixty feet to a depth of one hundred fifty feet.

"Float VLF buoy," Pete said. "I want to monitor any low frequency radio waves for a while."

The submarine released its very low frequency buoy, designed to float to the surface to monitor for radio signals emanating from sources on the surface.

"Chief of the Boat, how far to our rendezvous point with the *Volga River*?"

"Approximately two hundred miles, south-southeast, Captain."

"Set course for one-seven-zero degrees. All ahead one-half. Let's get out of here."

The Alexander Popovich
The Black Sea

We need the captain! We must find the captain!" the helmsman shouted in a panic.

"I am in charge on the bridge!" First Officer Joseph Radin snapped. "The captain may be dead! We have no time. Get our radio up and running or we will all go down and never be found."

"I have a connection, Mr. Radin!" the communications officer announced. "We have a broadcast frequency!"

"Give me that microphone!" Radin took the microphone in hand. "Mayday! Mayday! This is the Russian freighter *Alexander Popovich*. We have been struck by torpedo! Location: Black Sea. Ninety miles west of Sevastopol. We have children on board. We are sinking!

"Mayday! Mayday! This is the *Alexander Popovich*. We have children on board and we are sinking!"

"Mr. Radin!" the helmsman screamed. "We must leave now! We are sinking!"

Masha pulled herself up off the deck, trying to keep her balance. The ship was tilting to the left, forcing her to toss the gun back down to the deck and hang onto a rope that was strung between the walkway. She grasped the rope tightly as she walked back around the deck toward the ship's midsection.

The smoke and flames resembled the special effects in an American science fiction movie. The bow section of the ship had broken off and was standing on its end in the sea, perhaps a hundred yards away from the rest of the ship.

Masha froze in her tracks, paralyzed by the sight of it all. A great creaking sound, then twising metal, then almost a moaning came from the bow section.

The bow section stood up higher in the water, then higher. Now about a hundred feet off the surface of the water, the tip of the bow pointed up toward the sun, like a skyscraper standing erect in the water.

For a few seconds more twisting sounds followed. The sea grew strangely calm, and then the bow of the ship began slipping down into the water, disappearing into a huge whirlpool.

A loud explosion rocked the back of the stern section. Masha looked back. Flames lapped into the sky from behind. The heat intensified. The air was warming, almost like an oven.

The front of the stern section was angling down, slightly at this point, into the water. Waves lapped onto the deck in front of her. Behind her, the flaming rear section was rising into the sky, as if the floating hulk was turning into a flaming seesaw.

Masha had seen clips on the internet of the World Trade Center Towers falling. The sinking bow died in the same surrealistic manner. Now the stern section would soon do the same.

"Masha! Masha!" Sasha's voice screamed across the tilting deck. Crouching to avoid falling from the tilt, she walked across and embraced him. Katya was crying beside him. "We are going to die! We are going to die!"

"No! No! We are not going to die!" Masha looked around for her children. They lay all over the deck. Screaming. Wailing. Crying. "We're sinking! We're sinking!"

"We are going to be okay!" She frantically tried to comfort them all. Some were bruised and bleeding. Many had black smut on their faces.

"Dima! Dima!" She looked around everywhere for him. *Please God, let him be alive.*

"Masha! Get over here!" Aleksey was behind her, leaning over the side of the ship.

Masha pried the children's arms from around her and ran to the side of the ship. Aleksey was slowly uncoiling the rope from a winch. She looked over the side. A wooden lifeboat was slowly descending down to the water.

"Masha! Look in the box just to your right. There is a rope ladder. Get it out. We need to get the children off the ship!"

"Where are the rest of my children?"

"Some are in the water already! I threw them flotation devices! Hurry!"

Masha ran for the rope ladder, and together they unrolled it over the side.

"You must go now!" Aleksey Anatolyvich screamed at Masha.

She looked over the side of the ship, down into the water at the empty lifeboat. "I am not going without my children!"

"Masha, I will send your children down one by one! I need you at the bottom to help them into the boat! Do what I say, or all of them will die!" She looked down at the boat, then back up at Aleksey. "Okay."

She reached for his hand, then stepped her foot over the side of the sinking ship.

"Now put your foot on the rope."

The rope was wobbly. Shaking, she stepped down one step. Then another. Then another. Finally her foot reached for the side of the lifeboat. It bobbed in the water. She felt for it, and then dropped into the bottom of the lifeboat.

She looked up. The kids were climbing down the ladder. The first one to reach the bottom was Katya. After Katya came Anatoly. Marina and Ekaterina climbed down. And then, Masha looked up. Sasha was hanging onto the rope ladder about halfway down the side of the ship.

"I am afraid. I no want to go," he was saying.

"Sasha, come down, we must hurry!"

"Go, Sasha," Aleksey yelled from above.

"I am afraid." His little legs were trembling. "I want to go back up."

"No, Sasha!" Masha yelled.

"Sasha, go down!" Aleksey yelled even louder.

The boy took his foot, stepped out of the rung, and then reached for the next rung. The rope ladder began wobbling. A look of stricken panic crossed his face. The ladder swayed from the left to the right.

The world shifted to slow motion.

The boy lost control of his grip. He fell through the air.

"Sasha!"

He splashed into the water about twenty feet from the boat.

He did not come up.

The USS Honolulu
The Black Sea

Conn. Radio."

"Go ahead, Radio."

"Captain we're receiving a VLF radio transmission in Russian. Most likely a distress signal from *Alexander Popovich*."

Pete looked at Lieutenant Jamison. "Ready to go to work, Mr. Jamison?"

"Aye, Captain."

"Radio. Conn. Patch that message over the loudspeaker."

"Yes, sir, Captain."

A few seconds later, the sound of someone speaking Russian was broadcast into the sub's control room. Lieutenant Jamison made notes on a legal pad. A curious look crossed his face. The message ended.

"Well, Lieutenant."

Jamison looked at his captain. "Sir, it was a mayday. They say they were hit by a torpedo, they are sinking, and that they have *children* on board."

"Talk about lowlife Russian propaganda," the chief of the boat said. "I've heard that the Russians are the world's worst for this sort of thing."

"Lying slimeballs," came another voice.

A cramping beset Pete's stomach. "Mr. Jamison, read the message verbatim."

"Aye, sir." Jamison held up the legal pad.

"Mayday! Mayday! Mayday! This is the Russian freighter *Alexander Popovich*. We have been struck by torpedo! Location: Black Sea. Ninety miles west of Sevastopol. We have children on board. We are sinking! Mayday! Mayday! This is the *Alexander Popovich*. We have children on board. We are sinking!"

"That's odd," Frank Pippen said. "Why would they include a reference to children?"

"To try to get rescuers out here faster, that's why," the OOD said.

"Or maybe they really did have children on board," Pete mumbled.

"Sir?" This was the chief of the boat.

"When I viewed the wreckage on the attack scope, I saw people running around on the deck. At first I thought I saw a bunch of kids. I looked again and they were gone. I thought my eyes were playing tricks on me."

Dead silence pervaded the control room. Pete felt tormented. To have a chance to survive, which was a slim chance, he needed to get the *Honolulu* out of the area as fast as possible. Besides, even if children were on board, what could he do?

Should he further jeopardize the lives of his brave men for a happenchance rescue of some children who might already be dead?

But these were children.

Deep in his gut, he now knew it was true. Somehow, some way, children wound up on that freighter. What a colossal intelligence failure. But that wasn't the point.

He thought of Hannah and Coley. Suppose his own children had been on board that ship. Who would reach out a hand to save them? But even if he disobeyed orders and surfaced, the chances of a rescue at this point had to be slim-to-none.

He wiped cold sweat from his forehead. Never had the weight of command felt so burdensome. He had not been paralyzed by the decision to volunteer for this mission. He had never had qualms about sacrificing his own life.

He prayed silently. *God give me wisdom. Give it to me fast.* He remembered a verse from the Bible. Jesus said, "Bring all the little ones to me." Then another verse flashed into his mind. "And whoever welcomes a little child like this in my name welcomes me. But if anyone causes one of these little ones who believe in me to sin, it would be better for him to have a large millstone hung around his neck and to be drowned in the depths of the sea."

"Make course three-four-zero degrees. Alert SEAL team. Be on standby for rescue effort. Prepare to surface."

CHAPTER 20

Bilbek International Airport
The Crimean Peninsula, Ukraine

Captain Pavel Zalevskiy sat at the end of the runway with his hand on the throttle. The stewardess had just handed his co-captain the passenger manifest. Zalevskiy studied the manifest.

Another light flight. Only eighteen passengers were on board for the short hop over the northwestern quadrant of Black Sea to Constanta, Romania, a flight that would take them on a course of almost due west.

Probably the typical midweek mix of businessmen and a handful of tourists, he surmised. Fortunately, the State was heavily subsidizing the airlines. Eighteen passengers would not pay for the fuel one way. Hopefully, the plane would be at least halfway full on the return trip.

He handed the manisfest back to the stewardess. "Strap in, Natasha."

"Yes, *Kapitán*," the blonde said.

"Crimean Flight Eighteen, Bilbek Tower. You are clear for takeoff."

"Bilbek, Crimean Eighteen. Roger that. Proceeding now."

Zalevskiy pushed on the throttle, and the Russian-built Tu-134 aircraft began rolling, then picking up speed as it raced down the runway. A moment later, the jet had lifted off the Crimean Peninsula. A moment after that, the jet was over the waters of the Black Sea.

Other than strands of wispy cirrus clouds miles above, the skies were a clear, pristine blue. The first ten minutes of the flight were refreshingly clear of turbulence. Pavel settled into the cockpit for what looked like a routine, velvety-smooth flight over to Romania. And then, the peaceful hum in the cockpit was suddenly punctuated by distressed calls of "Mayday!"

Pavel sat up, listening intently to the words crackling over the speakers. As soon as he understood the situation, he contacted the control tower. "Sevastopol Control, Crimean 18."

"Go ahead, Crimean 18."

"Sevastopol, I've got a mayday on VLF from the freighter *Alexander Popovich*. The mayday claims the ship is sinking. Repeat, the mayday claims the ship is sinking. Request permission to go to one thousand for a visual."

"Crimean 18, Sevastopol. Permission granted. Go to one thousand. Monitor for as long as fuel permits. Advise."

"Sevastopol. Crimean. Descending to one thousand now."

The Al Alamein
Mediterranean Sea

Course and position?" Captain Hosni Sadir was asking.

"Twenty miles north of Crete, sir," the Egyptian helmsman replied. "We must make a course correction soon, or we will run into the island."

"Very well." Captain Sadir sipped a cup of hot tea and glanced at the navigational charts spread out on the table. "Upon my mark, make your course ninety degrees. Chart new course for Gibraltar."

"Yes, *Kapitán*."

Sadir checked his watch. Salman Dudayev stepped onto the bridge. "Ah, Salman," Sadir said. "How is the world's most brilliant physicist?"

A sly grin came from the Chechen. "Thank you for the compliment, *Kapitán*. If our plan works, perhaps I will allow you to call me that on the other side of paradise."

"Care for tea?"

"No, thank you. There is still much work to do."

Another sip of tea. "And how is your work coming?"

"The plutonium was stored in two large, radioactive-proof barrels," Salman said. "It took a while to open it, but now my assistants are molding it into special metal bowls that we have on board. After that, we will start on the explosives and detonators."

Hearing Salman describe his work brought a tranquil peace over the captain's body. Surely this peace was from Allah the munificent. "Perhaps you can soon give me a tour of this hydrogen bomb facility you have constructed in my ship."

"With pleasure, *Kapitán*. But remember that you must wear a radioactive suit. I am sure we have some your size."

Sadir chuckled. "Perhaps when we leave the Mediterranean I will accept your offer to go on that tour."

"Of course, sir."

Sadir checked his watch again. "Helmsman, make your course zero-nine-zero degrees. Plot new course for the Rock of Gibraltar."

Lifeboat
The Black Sea

"Sasha!" Masha was standing in the boat, screaming. Sasha had not come up from the spot that he had fallen into the water. The children leaned over the side of the boat, staring into the water and screaming his name. "Sasha! Sasha!"

"Get back, children!" she yelled. Sasha could not swim. Neither could she.

A huge splash threw a wave of water into the boat. Masha glanced up, realizing that Aleksey had jumped in the sea.

All the children were wailing now.

"Jesus, help us!" she blurted.

There was a stirring in the water. Aleksey popped up, blowing air out of his mouth. Sasha was cradled under his arm.

"Help me get him into the boat," he called up at Masha.

She reached over and yanked the little boy under his arms. He slid into the boat, his face pale and his body limp.

"Sasha! Sasha, wake up!" Masha shook him. "Please wake up!"

Aleksey swam around to the back of the boat and pulled himself into the boat. He took Sasha into his arms, locked arms around the boy's waist, and then squeezed his abdomen.

"Sasha!" Aleksey slapped his face.

The boy coughed and spat water from his mouth and nose.

"Sasha!" Masha pleaded. Sasha's blue eyes blue opened, then rolled towards her. He was coughing, but a weak smile crossed his face. "Oh, thank God!"

Aleksey ripped a knife from his pocket. He sliced one of the ropes tying the lifeboat to the ship. "We must go!"

"No!" Masha grabbed Aleksey's hand. "Not without Dima!"

"Move!" He shoved her away. "Dima is fine. He is in one of the other lifeboats."

"What other lifeboats? I do not see any other lifeboats!"

"There are lifeboats on the other side of the ship. Now we must get away or we will all be sucked down when she sinks." He pushed her away, then shoved a paddle against the ship. The boat drifted away from the sinking freighter.

"Look! It is sinking! It is sinking!" The children screamed and pointed over the back of the lifeboat.

Masha looked over her shoulder and saw the floating hulk slipping down into the sea.

"Don't look!" Aleksey was screaming. "Keep paddling. We must get away or we will be sucked under with her!"

Masha turned her head, attacking the sea with her paddle with all her might. Aleksey sat beside her, paddling off the right side. The boat slipped forward through the Black Sea.

"It is gone!" The children were yelling and pointing.

"Do not stop, Masha! We must get far away! There will be a great suction!"

Masha kept paddling. The bow of the boat began turning. "Why are we turning?" In a moment they had spun all the way around the sinking ship. The boat kept turning, bringing them around another full rotation. This time the ship had disappeared.

A rushing current pulled them back, back toward the spot in the water where the ship had gone under.

"Paddle!" Aleksey yelled. Masha tried, but to no avail. The boat was now spinning in a whirlpool. Other whirlpools spun all around them. The current grew faster. The sea sucked floating debris into the vacuum left by the sinking ship.

"Jesus, save my children!"

The USS Honolulu
The Black Sea

Boat's on the surface, Skipper!"

"Very well. Deploy SEAL team for rescue ops."

"SEAL teams already in the water, Skipper."

"XO, follow me! Mr. McCaffity, you have the conn!"

Pete donned his orange all-weather jacket, then stormed out of the control room, up the ladder, toward the bridge. Enlisted men had already opened the hatch, and sunlight streamed into the open space as Pete climbed quickly up the ladder.

Two lookouts were already posted in the open air bridge as Pete stepped under the blue skies and the late-afternoon sun.

"Your binoculars, Skipper."

"Thanks, Chief."

"The wreckage was off in that direction, sir."

The chief petty officer pointed in an easterly direction, and Pete brought his binoculars to his eyes. Pete swept the horizon. Black smoke billowed into the sky. At least one small lifeboat was in the water. And it was in serious trouble.

Lifeboat
The Black Sea

The lifeboat was spinning rapidly now, almost like one of those rides at the amusement park in Kiev. Masha had abandoned her paddling and was now wrapping her arms around as many orphans as she could reach.

The water was getting choppy and was splashing into the boat. Waves breaking over the side drenched their clothes. The orphans screamed and cried.

"Do not panic! Do not panic!" Aleksey was yelling, as he fought the current and the whirlpools with his paddle.

Masha closed her eyes. The words that the Allisons had written in her Bible came to mind.

If you are ever in doubt, ask him to show you the way!

"Jesus! Jesus! Save us! Please! Save us!"

The wooden lifeboat was half full of water now. The children huddled in the middle of the boat, shivering and crying. Masha spread her arms across their shoulders, like a mother hen protecting her flock. Aleksey sat in the back of the boat, his legs spread, his mouth agape.

She closed her eyes and prayed again. Something felt different. The motion. Or lack of it. She opened her eyes. The boat had stopped spinning! Debris floated on the top of the water, but nothing was being sucked down. In fact, pieces of wood, plastic, and Styrofoam that had been sucked under were now floating back to the surface.

She bowed her head, cried some more, and thanked God that they had not been swallowed by the sea. At least not yet.

The boat tilted to the left. A shrill scream pierced the air.

"Monster!"

Crimean Airlines Flight 18
Over the Black Sea

Captain Pavel Zalevskiy looked down over his right shoulder at the long, black, cigar-shaped object floating in the water.

Odd, Zalevskiy thought. He had flown an old Tu-124 antisubmarine warfare aircraft for the Ukrainian Navy. He had experience spotting submarines in the Black Sea. But this did not look like anything put out by the Russians or any of the other littoral nations surrounding the sea.

He lowered his altitude to one thousand and banked around for another look. This boat almost had the shape of one of those *Los Angeles*–class boats used by the Americans. But that would be impossible. There was no way that even the Americans could get an *LA*–class boat through the Bosphorus submerged. Everyone in the world would know if they had sailed through on the surface.

Zalevskiy trained on the sub with his binoculars. Orange-jacketed men were on the bridge, looking out over open sea. With the movement of the plane, however, he could not keep his eyes trained on the sub for more than a couple of seconds.

He pushed the button opening up a line to Sevastopol.

"Sevastopol Tower. Crimean Eighteen. I have an unidentified submarine on the surface. Resembles United States *Los Angeles*–class design. Coordinates forty-five degrees north latitude; thirty degrees, thirty minutes east longitude."

"Crimean Eighteen. Sevastopol Tower. Did you say *Los Angeles* class?"

Pavel took another look over his shoulders. "Definitely not *Kilo* and not *Tango* either." He was referring to the two classes of Russian subs now in the naval base at Sevastopol, which the Russians now leased from Ukraine.

"Thank you for your work, Crimean Eighteen. We will notify the Ukrainian Navy. Crimean Eighteen, go to ten thousand and resume course for Constanta."

"Crimean Eighteen, roger that. Resuming ten thousand. Good luck to the Navy."

Lifeboat
The Black Sea

The scream and the tilting boat brought Masha's eyes off to the left. A black creature with goggles and a hose in his mouth was pulling up on the side of the boat.

"Lieutenant John L. Smith, United States Navy," the creature said. Having studied some English at university, Masha realized that the man had just spoken to her in English.

The children stopped screaming, but most still cried. They huddled on the other side of the boat, staring at the strange man in the black rubber suit.

"Is everyone okay?" the man said.

"I Masha. This Aleksey," Masha tried her broken English. She gestured at the children. "We okay."

"Great, great." The diver put the hose back into his mouth and disappeared under the water again.

In a second, others were swimming in the water around the lifeboat. An inflatable rubber raft appeared on the surface. Some of the divers climbed into the rubber boat. Some swam with a rope from the back of the raft to the lifeboat. Others attached some sort of small outboard motor to the rubber raft.

They pulled a cord, and the motor started. The others disappeared underwater. In a moment, the rope tightened, and the lifeboat was moving through the water. The men in black driving the rubber boat made a wide turn in the water, and Masha saw the long, sleek outline of a submarine off in the distance.

CHAPTER 21

Ilyushin Il-96 jetliner
150 miles northeast of Odessa, Ukraine

President Vitaly Evtimov looked out the window of the presidential cabin and saw the MiG-29 Fulcrums that accompanied all flights made by the president of the Republic.

If this summit were successful, perhaps he could pull President Butrin out of the American orbit.

The plan was to have the orphans step off the freighter, then climb Odessa's most famous landmark, the Potemkin Stairs, the long staircase of over two hundred steps that started at the waterside and went straight up the hill to Primorskaya Street, where they would be ceremoniously greeted by the two presidents.

He looked over the speech that had been written for him for the joint ceremony by the pier in Odessa.

> To my dear friend President Butrin, and to the warm, peace-loving people of Ukraine, I bring heartfelt greetings and open arms from the people of Russia.
>
> We are bonded by a history forged by war, tempered by peace, and destined for prosperity.
>
> Today, we enter into a new era of cooperation that will bring good will to all peoples of our region.
>
> But justice for all will never be realized until there is justice even for the weakest of the earth.
>
> For the orphans of the Ukraine, for the orphans of the East, we share your compassion ... and we share your passion.

Evtimov could read no more. He folded the speech and put it back in his briefcase. The events in Georgia still had him fuming. How had his Fulcrums been gunned down by American F-15s? Although the most serious international crisis still loomed around the missing plutonium, Evtimov found it difficult to contain his temper about America's meddling with what was essentially a Russian problem.

He had swallowed Russian pride by using diplomatic rather than military force in reponse, and supposed that the proposed UN condemnation proposal was the best solution. But if the Americans fired on any other Russian targets, he may not be so apt to respond diplomatically.

Next time, he would respond with the hammer and the sickle. That thought brought some degree of satisfaction.

"Pardon me, Comrade President."

Evtimov looked up and saw his chief of staff, Sergey Semyonovich Sobyanin, standing in the entrance to the presidential cabin. He wore a grave look on his face.

"What is it, Sergey Semyonovich?"

"It is the orphans, sir. We believe that the freighter they were on has sunk."

"Sunk?"

"A distress call came on a VLF frequency from *Alexander Popovich*, the freighter carrying the orphans. The distress call claimed that the freighter had been hit by a torpedo and was sinking."

"A torpedo? Who? How?"

"We don't know. A Ukrainian airliner that heard the signal is reported to have flown over the area and seen a submarine on the surface near where the freighter was last believed to have transmitted."

"What submarine? One of ours?"

"The pilot believes that the submarine could be of the U.S. *Los Angeles* class."

"Impossible!"

"I would think so also, Vitaly Sergeivich. But the airline pilot is a former ASW pilot in the Ukrainian Navy. He could be mistaken, of course. But something is not right."

The president stood, crossed his arms, and walked back and forth down the aisle.

"Does President Butrin know?"

"Yes, sir. Butrin knows."

"And?"

"He wants an emergency meeting with you at the airport as soon as you land."

Evtimov let that sit for a minute. "I have a feeling the Americans will help us get Ukraine back despite ourselves."

"Perhaps," the chief of staff mused.

"Notify the commander of our Sevastopol naval base. I want every ship and plane we have scouring that sector of the sea. If the Americans are responsible, we will find that sub and sink her. And then we will kick them out of Georgia, and kick them wherever else we need to kick them! Every ship and plane. Do you hear me?"

"Yes, sir, Comrade President."

Lifeboat
The Black Sea

The rubber boat churned through the water, towing the lifeboat in its wake. It approached the stern of the submarine.

Men stood on the top of the submarine, in orange jackets, waving directions at the rubber boat. A small, floating ramp extended from the back of the submarine into the water.

The children's fear had transformed into a fixated fascination, at least for now. For that, Masha was grateful. At least they had calmed down a bit. Aleksey, however, still sitting in the front of the boat, was strangely subdued, as if he had turned into a ragdoll. Perhaps he was exhausted from getting them off the ship and fighting the whirlpool.

One sailor tossed a rope into the lifeboat from the submarine while another crouched down the ramp and stepped into the boat. He tied the rope to the boat. Others on the submarine pulled the bow of the boat up onto the floating ramp.

The man spoke in perfect Russian. "I am Lieutenant Phil Jamison, United States Navy. Welcome aboard the USS *Honolulu*. But we must hurry. Come, children!"

Inside, Masha cheered. *Americans!*

Aleksey went up the ramp first. The children scampered up the ramp in a single-file line, and the men were lifting them up and passing them to other men who were inside the hatch of the submarine. Finally when Sasha headed up the ramp, Masha left the boat.

"This way, ma'am." The Russian-speaking lieutenant directed her to another orange-jacketed sailor, who stood beside the open hatch. The sailor took her hand and helped her climb down a ladder.

An officer stood at the bottom of the ladder. At least, she assumed he was an officer. He wore a dark blue jump suit and had gold oak leaves on his collars. The name *Pippen* was written across his chest.

This officer spoke no Russian. He put his hand on her shoulder and led her down a very dark, narrow hallway in the submarine. He directed her into a room off to the left, where the children were congregated. It looked like some sort of a dining room and had fluorescent lights hanging overhead.

He pointed to a seat at the end of one of the long metal benches at the table.

She sat and exhaled.

And then, it hit her.

Dima!

"Dima! Dima! Where is Dima?" She stood, screaming. "Dima! Dima! Dima!"

"Settle down, ma'am! Settle down!" some of the Americans were saying.

"Masha, calm down!" Aleksey said. "I am sure he is fine. We did what we had to do!"

"No! You said there were other lifeboats!"

"Get a corpsman in here! Now!" one of the Americans said.

"Prepare to dive! Prepare to dive!" Alarms sounded all over the submarine.

"No! We cannot leave Dima! No! No!"

"Dive! Dive!" the loudspeaker was saying.

One of the American sailors, a big man with muscular arms, pinned her to the table now. She felt the submarine begin to sink under the water.

"Nooooo!"

Another sailor wearing a blue jumpsuit walked in, carrying a syringe with a long, silver needle that sparkled under the lights.

"Jesus! You said you would help me! Please help Dima!"

The sailor stuck the needle into her arm.

"No!"

Fluorescent lights overhead started spinning. Sleep overpowered her.

The White House

President Williams was sipping tea with the Honorable Jack W. Davis, the Irish ambassador to the United States. They were accompanied by Robert Mauney, the United States secretary of state.

Mack liked the Irish, liked their temperament, and had even joked with Ambassador Davis that he was a Notre Dame fan, at least when Notre Dame was not playing Kansas.

This was good small talk, Mack thought, especially since he was not comfortable discussing the ambassador's true agenda. The Irish wanted America to press Britain on the issue of independence for Northern Ireland.

Personally, Mack did not care whether Northern Ireland was part of Ireland or Great Britain. And while he liked the Irish, America needed Britain's power, influence, and prestige, especially at a time when anti-American sentiment was at its highest point in history.

"I know it is a very delicate situation, Mr. Ambassador, and I will voice your concerns to Prime Minister Anthony." He was referring to his close personal friend British Prime Minister Anthony McMillan.

"My government appreciates your consideration, Mr. President."

"I cannot promise anything, except that I will speak to him."

"That is all we can ask."

The phone buzzed on the president's desk as the ambassador took another sip of tea. Thank goodness.

"Excuse me, Mr. Ambassador."

"But of course."

The president picked up the phone for his appointments secretary, Gale Staff. "Yes, Gale?"

"Mr. President. I'm sorry to interrupt, but the secretary of defense and chairman of the Joint Chiefs are on the line. They say it's urgent, sir."

"Patch it through to the ante room."

"Yes, sir."

The president hung up. "Mr. Ambassador, my apologies, but the secretary of state and I are needed for an urgent phone call."

"By all means, sir. I was just leaving."

"No, we can take it in the next room."

The Irish ambassador smiled. "No reason to displace the most powerful man in the world. Please take your call here in the Oval Office. I will show myself out. Perhaps we can speak later, Mr. President."

"You are a friend and a gentleman, Mr. Ambassador." Mack shook the ambassador's hand, and Secretary Mauney walked him to the door.

"Gale, we'll take that call in the Oval Office. Put 'em on speaker."

"Yes, sir."

Secretary Mauney closed the door to the Oval Office, then sat in a Queen Anne's chair just in front of the presidential desk.

"Mr. President, you have Secretary Lopez and Admiral Ayers on the line," Gale Staff said.

"Erwin. John. What's up?" the president said.

"Good news and potentially disastrous news," Secretary Erwin Lopez said.

Mack looked at the secretary of state. "Good news first."

"We've confirmed on solid intelligence that the *Honolulu* has sunk the *Alexander Popovich*, Mr. President."

"Excellent," Mack said. "When and where?"

"Best we can tell, between thirty minutes to one hour ago. In the Black Sea. About one hundred miles west of Sevastopol."

"Now what's the potential disaster? Have the Russians discovered us?"

"Mr. President, this is Admiral Ayers."

"Yes, Admiral. Go ahead."

"Sir, we've intercepted some radio traffic. The *Popovich* sent out a distress signal before she sank, claiming that children were on board."

Mack locked eyes with Secretary Mauney. "Admiral, did you say children?"

"Yes, Mr. President."

"I mean, can that be confirmed?"

"Frankly, I'm worried about it, sir," the admiral said.

Mack's pulse raced to about two hundred beats per minute. "Why do you say that, John?"

"President Evtimov is on his way to Odessa. He and President Butrin of Ukraine were going to welcome a group of orphans sailing from Sochi, to announce some sort of Russian-Ukrainian humanitarian initiative for displaced orphans. While we can't be absolutely sure that the orphans were on the *Alexander Popovich*, the pieces are starting to fit together, Mr. President."

"Dear God, help us." Mack buried his face in his hands. "How did our intelligence miss that?"

"Can't answer that, Mr. President," Secretary Lopez said. "I guess we could ask the CIA about that."

"That's not good enough!" Mack snapped, looking up at his defense secretary. "If this is true, the Navy is just as culpable as the CIA. And ultimately, if this is true, these children's lives are on my shoulders."

"You did what you had to do, Mr. President," Admiral Ayers chimed in. "We had no way of knowing, sir. Besides, at least we got the plutonium."

Mack buried his head back in his hands. "Dear God, what have I done?"

Ilyushin 11-96 jetliner
50 miles northeast of Odessa, Ukraine

Comrade President. As you requested, Admiral Voynavich is on the line."

"*Spaceeba*, Sergey Semyonovich." The president took the secure air phone from his chief of staff and spoke to his Black Sea fleet commander. "Admiral, you are familiar with the distress call from our freighter off Sevastopol."

"Yes, sir."

"And you know my orders?"

"Yes, Comrade President."

"Well, as you know, I am about to meet with President Butrin in just a few minutes when we land. This meeting is an opportunity to shore up our relations with Ukraine. This whole orphans issue is killing him on the inside. Are you aware of this?"

"Yes, sir. It is my understanding that Butrin once lived in an orphanage."

"I want to assure President Butrin that we will find and sink that submarine. Understood?"

"Yes, sir."

"Drop every sonobuoy we have into the Black Sea, if we have to. Find that sub. I hold you personally responsible for this, Admiral. Do you understand me?"

"Comrade President, our Bear bombers are already dropping sonobuoys in the water even as we speak. We will cover that area with so many sonobuoys that no one could ever escape. This is one sub against the entire Black Sea fleet. Not even the Americans are that good. You have my word as an officer, sir. We will find and destroy this submarine."

The USS Honolulu
The Black Sea

Miss Katovich! Miss Katovich!"

The faint sound of her name spoken in Russian slipped softly through the ringing in her ears.

"Masha. Masha. Wake up."

The voice had changed its tone. Now it seemed more familiar. Somehow sweeter.

Yet despite the sound of her name, the world was still black.

But in the midst of it, something small and white flickered far away. Like a single flickering star on a cold wintry night. The small white object was coming at her, floating through space. It grew larger and larger. It came into vision now, this bright, white object in the midst of her black universe.

It was a cross! Floating through space, coming at her, bringing chills to her spine. Did this have anything to do with what the Allisons had told her about? Was she hallucinating? Had she drowned and gone to heaven?

"Miss Katovich!" The cross grew closer, larger. Its pure angelic whiteness obliterated the dark.

And then fluorescent lights hung over her head.

The officer, the American officer who had spoken in Russian, was standing over her. She squinted her eyes for a better view.

"Miss Katovich," he said again in Russian. "Does this little fellow belong to you?"

She rolled her head and saw the smile of an angel.

"Dima!" The boy rushed to the table and threw his arms around her. "I must be in heaven!" Tears of joy streamed down her face.

When her hands felt the scars on his back, she knew she was not in heaven. She knew he was real and still on earth. In heaven, his back would be healed. But God had answered her prayer from heaven.

"Don't cry, Masha," the boy was saying. "I love you."

"I love you too, Dima." But she could not contain her tears.

"Our Navy SEALs found him hanging onto a flotation ring and brought him on board just a few seconds before we submerged."

"Oh, thank you, thank you!" She reached out to touch the officer's hand.

"We took him to sick bay to check him out. He is okay!"

"I am so grateful! All my children are alive."

"I am grateful too, Miss Katovich."

CHAPTER 22

Tu-142 Squadron 118
Over the northwest quadrant of the Black Sea

They crisscrossed the skies in a series of triangular patterns south of the coordinates where the Crimean airlines jet had spotted the mysterious submarine on the surface of the water. They were long-range Russian "Bear bombers" of Black Sea Squadron 118.

Each was long and sleek, with two propellers on each wing and enough fuel to fly hundreds of miles before returning to base.

They filled the skies over the Black Sea with hundreds of parachutes. At the bottom of each parachute, long, floatable cylinders dangled in the skies, falling, falling, and finally splashing down in the waters below.

The cylinders were sonobuoys. When they hit the water, they began transmitting active and passive sonar signals through the water to seek out the presence of anything large and metal moving under the sea. Their signals would then be transmitted to aircraft in the air, and ships in the sea. Using a technique known as "triangulation," like a hunter tracking a wounded animal in the woods, they would close in on their prey, then call the bloodhounds in for the kill.

Russian attack submarine Alrosa
Black Sea

Kapitán. We just received this message."
Captain Yuri Gagarigan put on his reading glasses and studied the message.

From: Commander, Naval District Sevastopol
To: All Russian Submarines Patrolling Black Sea, Northwest Sector
Subj: Unidentified Hostile Submarine in Sector

Be advised unidentified submarine, possibly U.S. *Los Angeles*–class boat reported operating in sector.

Unidentified submarine last spotted on surface approximately ninety nautical miles west of Sevastopol forty-five minutes prior to transmission of this message.

Unidentified submarine believed to be hostile, and is believed to have attacked and destroyed civilian Russian freighter *Alexander Popovich.*

Alexander Popovich was transporting women and children to Port of Odessa for joint ceremony with presidents of Russia and Ukraine.

Bear bombers currently dropping sonobuoys in the area.

By orders of the president of the Russian Republic, you are to seek out and destroy.

"Impossible." Gagarigan folded the message and handed it back to his XO. "A *Los Angeles* – class submarine in the Black Sea. How could it be?"

"I do not know," the XO said.

"What is our current position?"

"One hundred miles southwest of Sevastopol, *Kapitán.*"

"Bring me the navigational chart for the sector."

"Yes, *Kapitán.*"

A moment later, the executive officer spread the navigational chart on the navigation table in the control room.

"Let us plot the sub's last postion and plot our current position."

After quickly scanning the charts, the Russian sub commander took the microphone and hit the switch, allowing his voice to broadcast all over the *Kilo*-class submarine.

"This is the captain. We have just received word that there is an enemy submarine in the area, possibly United States *Los Angeles* class. This submarine has already attacked and destroyed a civilian Russian freighter that had women and children on board. The president of the Russian Republic has ordered the Black Sea fleet to destroy it.

"We believe that this submarine is in our area, perhaps within ten miles of our current position.

"It is my intention, gentlemen, that the *Alrosa* shall be the submarine that will carry out our president's orders. We shall do so to avenge the death of innocent Russians. We shall do so to take control of the high seas and to show the Americans whose navy is superior, and we shall do so for the glory of Russia.

"Be prepared to go to battle stations. This is the captain. That is all."

The USS Honolulu
Black Sea depths

"Soup. Check this out." The Bloodhound handed his earphones to the sonar officer, Lieutenant Boers.

Boers had heard enough. He picked up the microphone for direct link to the control room. "Conn. Sonar. We have a possible submerged submarine! Bearing zero-one-five. Designate contact master two-nine!"

"Sonar. Conn. Aye. Man battle stations! Torpedo, rig for ultra quiet," cried the officer of the deck, Lieutenant McCaffity.

"Rig tubes one and three fully ready," Pete ordered.

"Rig tubes one and three. Aye, sir."

"Man battle stations!" All over the ship, red lights flashed. Crewmen sprinted and dashed to their positions. "Battle stations! Battle stations! All hands, man your battle stations!"

"XO, come with me. Mr. McCaffity, you have the conn."

"I have the conn. Aye, sir."

Pete rushed to the sonar room. Frank followed him.

The Bloodhound had both hands on the outside of his earphones. Intense concentration dominated his face. Lieutenant Boers was glued to the passive sonar screen.

"Okay, what do you got?" Frank asked.

"Sir, we have a possible submerged submarine," Boers said, "bearing zero-four-seven. Designate master two-nine. Best step for evasion, sir, is to dive deep. Recommend diving to eight-three-one feet, to avoid that sub."

"Very well." Pete picked up the microphone. "Lieutenant McCaffity, this is the captain. Increase your speed to standard. Come right to course two-seven-zero. Make your depth eight-three-one feet."

"Aye, aye, Captain," Lieutenant McCaffity said. "Chief of the Watch, all ahead standard. Dive. Make your depth eight-three-one feet."

"Aye, sir," the chief of the watch, who was also serving as the diving officer, acknowledged the order passed down from the captain. He stood just behind the helmsman, who pushed down on the steering wheel. This sent the submarine into a steep dive.

The *Honolulu* continued its dive as Pete and Frank returned to the control room.

The diving officer gave reports on the sub's descent. "Passing five-five-zero feet."

A message came in from the radio room. "Conn. Radio. Sir, we are out of VLF radio range. Full message capacity is cut off."

"Radio. Conn." Pete said. "Extend extremely low frequency antenna."

"Passing six hundred feet."

Back in the sonar room, a small red cylinder appeared on the passive sonar screen. Lieutenant Boers' eyes widened.

"Conn! Sonar! We have risk classification." Boers turned to one of the sonar technicians. "Mark that tape. Get the classification on your monitor."

Pete rushed into the sonar room. "What the heck is going on?"

"Sir," Boers said, "the master two-nine is classified as a Russian *Kilo*-class hunter killer. Bearing zero-one-zero, sir. He's close, but I don't think he's spotted us."

"Keep an eye on it," Pete said.

"Aye, sir."

Pete headed back to the control room.

"Passing eight hundred feet, sir."

"Continue to dive," Pete said. "Five degrees down bubble. Continue rigging for ultra quiet."

Pete picked up the microphone and switched to the 1MC. "Gentlemen, this is the captain. We have a Russian *Kilo*-class submarine out

there. We are rigging for ultra quiet. We've been set back on our time-
table because we rescued these orphans that we now have on board. But
we went back and got them, because it was the right thing to do."

He looked around the control room. All eyes were glued on him.

"Our plan is to dive deep and hope to avoid the enemy submarine.
But they're looking for us, as you know. Be ready. Be prepared. If that
sub comes around or even so much as opens up a tube door, we're going
to take her out." Pete exhaled. "This is the captain."

Pete hung the microphone back in its place. Dead silence was broken only by the diving officer's status report. Pete had decided to dive
even deeper.

"Passing nine hundred feet."

He checked the sonar sweep monitor in the control room. Nothing.
The oblong red image was gone.

"He's gone," Frank Pippen was looking over Pete's shoulder.

"The heck he is," Pete said. "He's up there." He looked up. "Somewhere."

"Nine-five-zero."

"Along with a dozen others just like him. Plus a whole fleet of aircraft and surface ships. All with torpedoes."

Depth dropped. Dropped more. 1100 ... 1200 ... 1250 ...

Pete was already deeper than he had intended to go. At 1475 feet,
the submarine would be at "crush depth" and in danger of imploding.
Enough was enough.

"Zero bubble."

"Zero bubble, aye, sir. Twelve hundred seventy-five feet, aye, sir."

The *Honolulu* was now headed in a westerly direction, toward the
coast of Romania, nearly 1300 feet below the surface.

In the sonar room, the Bloodhound detected movement. "Soup,
he's coming around," he called.

Lieutenant Boers picked up the microphone. "Conn! Sonar! The
Kilo's turning around, sir." A small red blip shot out from the larger,
oblong red cylinder. "Conn Sonar! Torpedo in the water! Bearing two-
four-one!"

A second red blip followed the first one. "Conn! Sonar! Second torpedo in the water! Bearing two-four-two!"

In the control room, sweat dripped off Pete's nose, splatting on the
floor. If either torp exploded anywhere near *Honolulu*, it was all over.

"All ahead flank! Right full rudder." The sub swung hard to the right.

"Conn! Sonar! Three thousand yards and closing, sir!"

"Sound the collision alarm!" Loud bells rung all over the ship.

"Torpedoes at twenty-five hundred yards, sir."

"Rig ship for impact!" Pete ordered. "Hang on to your seats, gentlemen!"

"Two thousand yards!" Lieutenant Boers' voice boomed on the 1MC, echoing in the ship's corridors.

"One thousand five hundred yards. Bearing zero-seven-zero. Zero-seven-five. One thousand two hundred yards." Men grabbed onto anything they could, as if that would somehow stop the flow of deathly freezing water that would flood the submarine from a direct hit.

"One thousand yards and closing fast," Boers' voice echoed. "Nine hundred fifty yards!"

"Launch the five-inch evasive device!" Pete shouted. "Launch countermeasures!"

"Countermeasures away, sir!"

Two metal canisters shot into the dark water from the hull of the submarine. The canisters, five-and-a-half inches in diameter at the base and propelled by small motors, gyrated and swirled through the water in a desperate attempt to deter the torpedoes from the submarine.

"Shift your rudder to left full!" Pete said. The helmsman complied. *Honolulu* swerved sharply through the dark water to the left, sliding coffee mugs, pencils, and anything else not buckled down in the opposite direction. The idea was to pull the ship away from the countermeasures, and pray that the torps fell for the bait.

"Three hundred yards and closing, sir." The sharp turn continued as Boers spoke.

"Sir, the first torpedo is going after the countermeasures! They missed! They missed!"

A massive underwater explosion rocked the *Honolulu*. The control room vibrated like the violent aftershock of a major earthquake. Men hung tightly to pipes, stationary cylinders, handles, anything they could find.

"We've got another torp out there!" Pete screamed. "Keep turning! Keep turning!"

Honolulu held her tight loop to the left.

"Conn! Sonar! Second torpedo incoming! It's going to be close!"

The second explosion rocked the submarine with a vengeance and sustained shaking unmatched by the first. *Honolulu* shook and rattled as if a giant jackhammer were pounding it from the inside out. The pounding continued. Men flopped to the steel decks and bounced about like ragdolls.

"Conn. Sonar! The Kilo's disappeared in the thermal, sir!" The shaking began to subside. Then it was over.

For now.

Alarms chimed throughout the submarine.

"All ahead standard," Pete ordered. "Rudder amidships!" The helmsman brought the steering wheel to a straightaway position.

Pete pulled himself off the deck. Alarm lights were blinking all throughout the control room. He went back on the 1MC. "All stations. Report damage. Report damage."

"Engine room reports number two ASW pump failed."

"Contol. Torpedo room. It's like someone's turned on the showers in here. We got two feet of water in the bilge and she's rising fast. Request a team of personnel to assist in flood containment."

"Chief of the Boat." Pete looked at Master Chief Sideman. "Grab a team and get to the torpedo room to isolate that flooding."

"Aye, Captain." Sideman rushed out of the control room.

"Sonar. Conn." Pete said. "Report hostile contact."

"Conn. Sonar. We lost him, sir."

"Keep your eyes open. He's not gone away."

"Aye, sir."

"Torpedo room, how's that flooding?"

"Still flooding, Captain. Two-and-a-half feet in the bilge, sir."

Pete wiped his forehead and uttered a quick, silent prayer. "Can you shut off the valves and isolate the water?"

"Negative so far, sir. But we're working on it."

"Let me know of any change in status, either positive or negative."

"Aye, sir."

"Sonar. Conn."

"Sonar, sir."

"Any sign of the Kilo yet?"

"Negative, Captain. He probably thinks he got us, sir."

"Let's pray to God he's wrong."

"Conn. Torpedo room." This was the voice of Master Chief Sideman.

"Go ahead, torpedo room."

"Good news, Captain. We've stopped the water for now. I think we should be okay, unless we take another hit. If we do, I don't think we can keep the water out, sir."

Pete exhaled. "Good work, Master Chief. Leave your team down there for a while in case that flooding starts again. But I need you back in the control room on the double."

"Aye, Captain."

"All right, gentlemen, let's get on with it. All ahead one-third." That was followed by two bells to the control room. "Steady as you go." Pete breathed out. "I'll be in the galley. XO, you have the conn."

"I have the conn, aye, sir," Frank Pippen parroted.

"Mr. Jamison, come with me."

"Aye, Captain."

Pete stepped out of the control room and headed for the galley. The master at arms guarding the passageway stepped aside and opened the door for his captain. Half the lights had gone out in the second explosion. The twelve orphans were huddled in one corner of the room. All were shaking and crying.

The woman, who had a large bruise on her left cheek, was wiping blood from a little girl's face. The young, scruffy-faced Russian sailor was tending to a little boy who had been badly bruised.

The woman—he had been told her name was Miss Katovich—looked up at him with tears in her eyes. *"Pazhalsta, Kapitán! Nam nada pamoach. Pazhalsta."*

"What's she saying, Mr. Jamison?"

"She's asking for help, sir."

"Tell her we will get someone down here as soon as we can."

"Yes, sir." Jamison relayed the message in Russian.

Pete picked up the microphone. "This is the captain. Get two corpsmen to the galley. Now."

He looked back down at the girl, whose fearful eyes were locked on him. "Ask her why they were on board the ship."

He waited for the translation.

"She says the orphans were to meet the presidents of Russia and Ukraine in Sevastopol, but the ship's captain tried to kill her."

Pete exchanged a startled glance with Lieutenant Jamison. "He what? Why would he want to do that?"

More Russian, then the translation. "She says the ship was carrying some kind of illegal cargo."

Pete raised his eyebrow. "Plutonium?"

"She doesn't know what the cargo was, Skipper. I asked. Claims she overheard a conversation on the bridge through the ship's loudspeaker system. Something about a rendezvous with an Egyptian freighter to transfer expensive cargo."

"Hmm," Pete mused. "The part about the expensive cargo sounds credible. The rest of it"—he scratched his chin—"I don't know."

A loud *ping* shot through the submarine. Then another. *Ping*. Then two more. *Ping. Ping*. The children looked up. Their eyes widened. Another round of fear washed across their faces.

"Galley. Conn. Skipper, are you still down there?" This was the XO, Frank Pippen.

"This is the captain," Pete said.

"Sir, I'm sure you can hear, but we're getting active sonar pings."

Ping, ping. Ping, ping.

"Yes, we hear 'em." Pete said. "They've probably dropped a thousand sonobuoys up there."

Pete looked at the faces of the children. He was prepared to die. His men were prepared to die.

But these innocent children?

This was not part of the bargain. He had no way of communicating with Washington. He briefly considered floating the radio buoy, but the transmission signal could be traced to the point of transmission by the Russians. Plus, if there were a hitch in unwinding the winch, that could be picked up on the enemy's passive sonar. Too risky, he thought. Floating the radio buoy was out of the question.

"Your orders, Captain?"

"Until further instructions, steady as she goes. I'll be in my stateroom."

"Aye, sir."

Odessa International Airport
Odessa, Ukraine

The presidents of Russia and Ukraine set up their war room in the VIP suite of the Odessa Intenational Airport. The heavily armed suite was quickly equipped with secure telephones, computers, and direct lines to Sevastopol. This allowed the presidents instant access to information coming from the Black Sea.

President Evtimov had hoped that his trip to Odessa would reso-lidify relations with Ukraine. But this was not what he had envisioned.

If the Americans were behind all this, and Evtimov suspected that they were, then Mack Williams had just delivered Ukraine back to Russia, all sealed and gift-wrapped in a surprise Christmas package.

Instead of working with President Butrin on some sort of useless humanitarian effort about beefing up orphanages, the president of the United States had united Ukraine and Russia in a common military goal — to seek out and destroy the submarine that had murdered Butrin's precious orphans.

Ukraine would fall back to the Russians even more swiftly than France had fallen to the Fascists. Evtimov thought of the photo of Hitler doing a jig when the Fascist Army captured Paris so easily in 1940. Evtimov might try the same thing in Kiev, but he needed to bridle his enthusiasm in front of Butrin.

Mustering a solemn face, the Russian gazed across the table at his Ukrainian counterpart. "Comrade President, I've just received word that one of our submarines, the *Alrosa*, has spotted what her computers classified as a *Los Angeles*–class submarine. The submarine was diving deep and heading south, on a projected course toward the Bosphorus."

Stunned silence.

"So it is true?" Butrin's eyes widened in disbelief.

Of course it was true. But Evtimov did not answer the question. Better to keep the Ukrainian guessing. "*Alrosa* fired two torpedoes. We believe we damaged it, but the sub got away. *Alrosa* tracked her for a few seconds heading west after the second explosion. Then she dropped off our sonar."

Evtimov studied Butrin's stunned face. The man was a self-proclaimed liberal who loved Western ideals. Now for America to prick all that idealism by murdering Butrin's precious orphans — it was worth the price of a billion rubles.

"What do you suggest we do, Vitaly?"

This was a good sign. The Ukrainian was using first names now.

"Joint cooperation between our great nations, Vlaçlav. We need each other now more than ever."

"*Dah*." Butrin nodded. "And what do you suggest?"

"May I suggest Ukraine take charge of search-and-rescue efforts? Perhaps some of these dear orphans got off the ship. I suggest that Russia oversee military aspects of this operation."

"*Dah*. Of course." Butrin nodded again. "And how are we to stop this submarine?"

"The Americans are not invincible. The depth charge is the oldest, most primitive antisubmarine weapon ever used. After World War II, most nations eliminated them. The Russian Navy, I am now happy to say, did not.

"I have ordered hundreds of them dropped all over the area near the engagement between *Alrosa* and the enemy submarine. This is the functional equivalent of carpet bombing the sea depths.

"We are also dropping hundreds of sonobuoys all over the area. Not a single whale or dolphin will swim an inch without us knowing about it.

"In addition to that, I am deploying the entire Black Sea fleet in a line just south of the spotting. The American submarine will never make it through alive."

The Ukrainian president did not respond.

"Vlaçlav, in the name of these twelve orphans, justice will be served. We will sink that sub, or force it to the surface."

CHAPTER 23

The USS Honolulu
Black Sea depths

The images of the orphans burned his conscious as if emblazoned there by a nuclear flash.

The bleeding.

The crying.

The shaking.

The sight had driven him into his stateroom—and driven him to his knees, where before he could even beseech the Almighty, his thoughts turned to Hannah and Coley.

Something wasn't right about all this. All Masha Katovich's talk about meetings with the presidents of Ukraine and Russia sounded bizarre. Was she credible? She spoke of valuable cargo on board the ship. Plutonium would qualify as that. What if the plutonium had been transferred to an Egyptian freighter?

Ping.

Ping.

His orders were clear. "Do not surrender under any circumstances." Orders or not, as a sub commander he was inclined to stand fast and fight—to fight his way beyond the thicket of ships and mines just to his south.

Ping.

Ping.

But the odds of surviving that scenario were not good. Maybe twenty percent if he were lucky. And if the information were correct—that the plutonium had been transferred to another freighter—then Washington needed that information—and fast.

He could float a communications buoy and try to get a signal off, but that would make the sub a guaranteed bull's-eye for ASW torpedoes. The best way to get that information into the right hands would be to surface the sub, and then somehow, some way try to get that message back to Washington.

Ping.

Ping.

If he disobeyed his direct orders and surfaced, he faced a court-martial and could start a war with Russia. But what about the children he now had on board?

If he were to stay and fight, would they die a terrifying death with cold seawater pouring into their undersea compartment, rising to their ankles, then their knees, then their necks?

Ping. Ping. Ping. Ping ...

Would they reach desperately for the last few inches of air near the ceiling before the sinking sub became a cold, watery grave? This was a death that he and his men were prepared to face. This was part of the bargain that all submariners understood may happen one day. The men on this mission especially understood.

Ping. Ping. Ping. Ping ...

An explosion rocked through the water. From its sound, Captain Miranda estimated it to be a mile away.

Another explosion. This one was closer.

Depth charges.

He opened the Bible that he had brought with him and read two verses from the book of James.

"If any of you lacks wisdom, then ask God who gives to everyone liberally ... and it will be given ... But ask in faith, not wavering. For those who waver are like a wave of the sea, driven with the wind and tossed."

Pete closed the Bible and spoke aloud.

"Eternal Father, strong to save, whose arm hath bound the restless wave, bestow wisdom to thy servant, for thou are the captain of my soul and I am the captain of this ship. Now, my responsibility as captain is not only for these men, but for these children and this woman as well."

Another underwater explosion shook the submarine.

He opened the Bible once more to a passage in James. "Religion that God our Father accepts as pure and faultless is this: to look after orphans and widows in their distress ..."

The sub shook from a fourth explosion. They were getting closer. Pete closed the book. His intercom sounded.

"Captain, sonar reports dozens of depth charges being dropped in the area. We're going to be in for quite a shaking, sir."

"Have the SEAL team leader report to the conn immediately."

"Aye, Captain."

"I'll be right there, Frank."

Ka-27 Chopper Number 3
Above the Black Sea

They crisscrossed the skies over the Black Sea like hovering dragonflies. They were Ka-27 helicopters from the 297th Russian helicopter squadron out of Sevastopol.

Junior Lieutenant Igor Pavalov, a chopper pilot just assigned to the 297th, looked out of his cockpit to the west, where other squadrons of Ka-27 and Ka-28 ASW helicopters buzzed over the water.

They flew over a two hundred mile line out west from Sevastopol. Long-range Bear bombers had already joined in the hunt, swarming the afternoon skies in a great aerial cage around the submarine's last reported position.

Pavalov had never participated in such a massive exercise. Nor had he released a live weapon in anger against a live target.

Hovering at fifty feet over the surface of the massive sea, he looked out in amazement at the sight before him. Thousands of parachutes filled the air, plopping sonobuoys into the water below.

Hundreds of depth charges were splashing into the water now.

Some would explode at one hundred to two hundred feet under the surface. Others would detonate at deeper depths. Eight hundred feet. One thousand feet.

If the depth charges did not destroy the enemy submarine, they would impose the ultimate weapon in psychological warfare.

And if the depth charges somehow missed the sub, the sonobuoys would find her and relay their signals to the dozens of Bear bombers circling the area with sonar-guided torpedoes ready to drop into the water.

A static-filled transmission burst into Pavalov's headset.

"Blue Light Leader to Blue Light Three."

"Blue Light Three."

"Release ordnance."

"Very well." Pavalov reached down to a simple switch in his cockpit and flipped it. "Releasing ordnance now."

The pilot looked down and saw a large metal canister splash down into the ocean and disappear under the water. This charge was designed to explode at a depth of one hundred feet.

Pavalov watched for a few moments.

A large, circular, white mushroom of water rose to the surface.

Whatever was down there stood no chance.

The USS Honolulu
Black Sea depths

The captain has the conn!" Frank Pippen announced as Pete reentered the control room.

"All ahead stop."

"All ahead stop, aye, Captain."

The *Honolulu*'s propeller disengaged, sending the sub in a forward drift. Disengaging the propeller eliminated the sound of churning water. The idea was to make the sub a harder target for passive sonar to detect.

A stocky, muscular officer entered the control room. Lieutenant John L. Smith wore a rubber wetsuit and diving shoes.

"You wanted to see me, Captain?"

"Lieutenant Smith. Good work by you and your men in getting those kids onboard."

"Our pleasure, sir," the sub's SEAL team leader said.

"What's your C-4 supply like?"

"We've got plenty of it, Skipper. A SEAL team without plastic explosives is like an airplane without wings."

"Good," Pete said, then turned to his OOD. "Mr. McCaffity, what's our distance to Sevastopol?"

"Just a little over one hundred miles, sir."

Pete did the math in his head. Assuming, for the sake of argument, that his sub were on the surface, being towed by a cruiser or ocean-going barge, and assuming further that the towing vessel was making

ten knots, and assuming that that process began two hours from now
… he checked his watch.

"Lieutenant Smith. Listen to me very carefully. I want you and your
men to rig explosives to every sensitive area of this ship. I want C-4
rigged in the internal compartments of fire control, launch computers,
navigational computers, all ship's data entries, everything in the control room. If there's a computer in a system anywhere, rig explosives to
blow it."

"Sir?" Smith said, as every eye in the control room locked onto
Pete. Another distant explosion shook the ship.

"Just listen. I want you to send a couple of divers outside and I want
C-4 rigged under the hull of the sub. I realize this will be a dangerous operation because of these depth charges they're dropping. But it's
necessary."

"Aye, sir."

"I want you to rig all explosives to detonate simultaneously in five
hours." Another explosion. "How fast can you have this done?"

The SEAL commander looked at his waterproof watch. "My men are
fast. Give us thirty minutes and we're there, sir."

Pete was not sure that they had thirty minutes. But he had no
choice. "Get to it. Now."

"Aye, sir." The SEAL commander left the control room.

"XO. On the 1MC."

"Aye, Captain." Frank Pippen handed the microphone to Pete.

"This is the captain speaking." He took a deep breath. "Gentlemen,
you can all hear the depth charges exploding in the water around us. We
all knew going into this mission the price that we may have to pay. We
have several options at this point.

"We can make a run south, try to find the *Volga River*, and hook up
with her. This submarine, gentlemen, is superior to anything the Russians have. You are the finest submarine crew ever assembled anywhere
in the world."

He hesitated as another distant depth charge vibrated the ship.

"But this is not a matter of quality. It is a matter of quantity. It's
a matter of overwhelming numbers against this ship. Right now, the
Russians are dropping everything they have in the water above us and
in a line south of us all the way across the northwest sector of the
Black Sea.

"We could make it, but in my judgment the odds are heavily against our survival.

"If it were just us, we would plow into the Russian's defensive line, do our best to break through, and die if we did not make it.

"But, gentlemen, this is not just us. We now have twelve orphans and a woman on board.

"In some cultures, and in some nations, that fact would not matter. Islamic terrorists have for years murdered and hidden behind children, using them as shields against bombs and killing them at random.

"But, gentlemen, this submarine, at this moment, is the sovereign territory of the United States of America.

"In America we do not kill women and children. We protect them. I cannot and will not take action that would cause these little ones to die.

"So here's what we're going to do. After our SEAL team completes a little assignment I have for them, we are going to initiate an emergency blow and we are going to surface the submarine."

That brought raised eyebrows in the control room.

"When we surface the boat, we are going to broadcast a surrender signal." The very sound of his words brought cramps to his stomach. "My guess is that we will be captured by the Russians. As your captain, I will step forward and accept sole responsibility for whatever we face, and I will request that you all be released. I cannot guarantee, however, that my request will be granted.

"If you are interrogated, and especially if you are interrogated about the plutonium, remember that you are to answer only in accordance with the Geneva Convention parameters. Name. Rank. Military identification number. I will handle the issue of the plutonium personally."

Ping. Ping. Ping. Ping.

"As for the Russians, they will think they have captured a *Los Angeles*–class nuclear submarine." *Ping. Ping. Ping. Ping.*

"They are in for a surprise."

Defense Ministry of the Russian Republic
Moscow, Russia

Olga Kominicha picked up the telephone on her desk and punched the button which would alert the man just inside the large oak office behind her desk that a very important member of the Russian military or the Russian government wished to speak with him.

In this case, Giorgy Alexeevich Popkov was being telephoned by Admiral Petrov Voynavich, commander of the Black Sea fleet. "Hurry," the admiral barked. "I have an urgent update for the defense minister from the Black Sea."

"Yes, Admiral. I buzzed him, but he did not answer." The defense minister was probably napping again from too large a spot of afternoon vodka. Or perhaps he was in his personal toilet accessible from inside the office. More likely sleeping off another vodka-induced buzz. "I will get him for you."

"Comrade Secretary." Still no answer on the intercom. The admiral's voice resonated with urgency. Olga had heard that the Navy was hunting an American submarine in the Black Sea. She was not supposed to know this, but rumors were impossible to contain sometimes within the Defense Ministry. Perhaps the call was related to this.

She stepped to the outside of her boss's closed door and knocked.

Nothing.

She opened the door.

Giorgy Alexeevich was sprawled out, lying back in the chair behind his desk. His eyes and mouth were frozen wide and open. Blood gushed from his mouth and the gash in his neck.

Olga screamed at the top of her lungs, then felt the room begin to spin. She hit the floor with a thud. And then, darkness.

The USS Honolulu
Black Sea depths

The depth charges shook like a jackhammer. *Pings* rang thorough the submarine every thirty seconds or so.

The Russian Navy was playing a giant game of Russian roulette. Pulling the trigger.

Firing blanks.

Thank God no live round had struck them. Yet. And despite all the pinging, there was no evidence yet that any of the sonobuoys had transmitted a contact to any of the Bear bombers overhead. At least no more torpedoes had been dropped into the water, nor had that *Kilo*-class sub come back around.

All that would change, Pete knew, if he tried running past the naval blockade that the Russians were stringing just south of him across the Black Sea.

All they could do at this point was sit in the water, and wait and pray.

Pete checked his watch. Twenty-five minutes had passed since he sent the SEALs into the water for the dangerous mission of attaching plastic explosives on the submarine's hull. Time was of the essence. There was little room for error. Any second, a depth charge could strike too close or a wave of torpedoes could close in on his isolated submarine.

Lieutenant Phil Jamison stepped into the control room.

"How are they, Phil?"

"Trembling and crying every time they hear a ping or the slightest shake from a depth charge."

"What did you tell 'em?"

"I told them not to worry, that we'd be safe soon. Didn't seem to do much good, sir."

"What about the woman?"

"Frankly, she seems to have nerves of steel. Said she was relieved to be aboard."

"Skipper," the OOD said. "The SEALs are finished. They're back in the sub now."

"Very well, Mr. McCaffity. Prepare for emergency surface maneuver."

"Aye, aye, sir."

Ka-27 Chopper Number 3
Above the Black Sea

Junior Lieutenant Igor Pavalov dropped his last depth charge into the sea, then waited several minutes for a visual confirmation that the bomb had exploded. Unlike his last two charges, which exploded at one hundred fifty feet, this baby would sink twice as deep, to three hundred feet, before sending a wave of explosive concussions and sound waves through the water.

Pavalov waited another minute or two. Another white mushroom rose to the surface of the water. Perhaps this one had struck the target. Perhaps he would get credit for sinking the American submarine. He would stand in Red Square before President Evtimov and receive the highest award bestowed on a Russian citizen.

He would be declared a "Hero of the Russian Federation." The honor had been bestowed to several military members fighting in Chechnya. So why not bestow it upon the Navy helicopter pilot who sunk an enemy submarine — an *American* submarine — which had somehow infiltrated the Black Sea?

He lingered a bit longer over the surface of the water, hoping to see debris from a submarine floating to the surface.

Nothing.

But he had expended ordnance and he was rapidly losing fuel. He would need to start heading back within the next fifteen minutes or be prepared for a long swim.

Pavalov rotated the chopper on a stationary, midair axis, pointing the nose on a course of ninety degrees — due east — then called his squadron leader and announced that he would be flying back to Sevastopol for refueling and reloading.

A large cylindrical nose burst through the sea like a whale leaping through the surface. The long, dark object shot above the water and then splashed down onto the surface.

This was no whale.

This was a submarine!

A *Los Angeles*–class submarine! It had broken the water perhaps a quarter of a mile just east of his position. And *his* depth charges had forced her to the surface!

If only he had a torpedo or more depth charges … he would go in for the kill right now.

"Light Blue Three to Light Blue Leader!"

"Go ahead, Light Blue Three."

"I have got it!"

"Got what?"

"The American submarine! My depth charges have forced her to surface!"

"What is your position?"

Pavalov gave the latitudinal and longitudinal coordinates.

"Maintain visual for as long as your fuel will allow. Your relief is on the way."

"Very well," Stavinskiy replied, fuming that someone else could get credit for the kill that he was responsible for.

"Maintaining visual," Pavalov said again over the radio. "Please allow the record to reflect that the submarine surfaced as a result of my depth charge."

He waited for an answer. No response. Pavalov inched the chopper forward, closing to within a hundred yards or so in front of the American submarine. He brought the chopper's altitude down to one hundred feet, so low that the prop blast was blowing a round circle on the water's surface.

The pilot brought his binoculars to his eyes for a better look. He studied the conning tower. Could the sub have surfaced to fire a missile? Of course not. It could have fired a missile from under the water. It had surfaced for one reason and one only.

The hatch on top of the sub swung open. Men stepped up onto the open bridge. They brought up an American flag. *The murderous pigs.* He thought for a moment of directing machine-gun fire at the men standing on the bridge.

But what glory was there in that? Shooting men standing on the top of a submarine would not make him a hero of the Russian Federation. The president wanted the sub sunk. This was his path to glory.

The men waved at him, like he was their best friend. *How odd, these Americans.* And then someone brought another flag to the bridge.

This was not an American flag.

This was a white flag! They waved it back and forth through the air! The Americans were surrendering!

His depth charges had forced the Americans to surrender! After he became a hero of the Russian Federation, there would be speeches and parades and parties in his honor.

Igor picked up the microphone again.

"Light Blue Three to Light Blue Leader! The American submarine is surrendering to me right now! Repeat, the American submarine is surrendering to me!"

CHAPTER 24

The USS Honolulu
The Black Sea

Pete stood on the open air bridge of his sub, his orange jacket flapping under the wind blasts from the five Russian ASW helicopters hovering in the late-afternoon sky. The choppers circled the *Honolulu.*

Two corvettes, naval vessels just smaller than a U.S. Navy destroyer, plowed through the water from the east.

Pete peered through his binoculars at the sharp, angular, grey ships churning toward his position. One had a hull number of 053 and the other was 071. "Well, well. More guests joining the party."

"Our taxi into Sevastopol?" Frank Pippen mused.

"Or wherever else they decide to take us," Pete said.

"Looks like they're making about fifteen knots, sir," Lieutenant Jamison said.

"Mr. Jamison, go check your registry of Russian naval vessels for hull numbers 053 and 071."

"Aye, sir."

A minute later, Jamison reappeared on the open air bridge. "053 is the *Povorino* and 071 is the *Suzdaltec*. Both are ASW corvettes."

Now a small craft was speeding toward the submarine from the *Suzdaltec*. Through the binoculars, Pete saw a boarding party which consisted of three officers and eight armed sailors.

"Chief of the Watch, prepare for boarding by our guests."

"Aye, Captain," the chief said. Within minutes, the portable floating ramp was deployed from the back of the submarine into the water. Pete,

Frank, and Jamison headed back toward the stern of the ship. The boat closed within a few yards of the stern. Its engines were idling.

A crew member from the boat held up a megaphone. "Ahoy the submarine." The crewmember spoke in broken English.

"Mr. Jamison, take the megaphone. Tell them that they may board, that our intentions are not hostile, and that we mean them no harm."

"Aye, Captain." Jamison complied.

"*Bashoya spaceeba.*" The reply came.

"He thanks us, Captain."

Lines were tossed back and forth between American and Russian sailors on the sub and on the boarding craft. A few minutes later the first Russian officer was making his way to the back of the submarine.

The Russian threw a salute at Pete, and Pete returned the salute.

"Tell him I am the commanding officer of the USS *Honolulu*, and tell him that he and his men are welcome aboard."

Jamison translated Pete's statement, then translated the Russian's reply. "He is the commanding officer of the Russian corvette *Suzdaltec*. He has orders to take this submarine and its crew into custody. He says that the helicopters surrounding the sub and the two ships out there are all armed with torpedoes which he will order to be launched at the sub if we do not peaceably surrender."

Pete pulled out a Montecristo, fired up a Bic lighter, and took a puff. "Ask him if he wants a cigar."

Jamison translated.

"*Nyet. Spaceeba.*"

"He says no thank you on the cigar. He wishes to know if we are going to voluntarily surrender."

Pete took another puff before answering. He looked up at the sun, now about to set over the water in the direction of Romania. "Tell the captain that I present to him the United States nuclear submarine, the USS *Honolulu*."

Russian corvette Suzdaltec
The Black Sea

The full moon hung low over the sea, painting a rich, luminescent carpet across the water and illuminating the silhouette of the *Honolulu*, which was in tow perhaps one hundred yards behind the *Suzdaltec.*

The orphans had been taken inside the Russian warship, but the American submarine crew was corralled on the fantail. Armed Russian sailors guarded Pete and his crew.

Pete stood in the middle of his crew, checking his watch. Standing next to him, Frank Pippen was doing the same thing.

Their eyes met. Neither spoke.

Thirty seconds passed. Two loud *booms* echoed across the water from the direction of the submarine. Two more *booms*. Pete caught the grin on Frank Pippen's face. The XO gave his skipper an unobtrusive thumbs-up.

Russian sailors scrambled to the fantail, waving their arms and yelling phrases that Pete could not understand. Flames burst in the open bridge area of the *Honolulu*. The submarine started sinking in the water.

Honolulu was taking on torrents of seawater, undoubtedly from the holes in her hull caused by the SEALs' handiwork with plastic explosives. She was going under, slowly, and her weight was pulling on the back of the *Suzdaltec*. Pete ordered his men to stay put.

Pete felt the *Suzdaltec*'s engines shift from ahead to neutral. This was to loosen the tension in the lines between the ship and the submarine. Even still, the fantail was listing, and water was starting to lap up over the stern.

Suzdaltec's commanding officer had come down from the bridge and was walking about the fantail, barking orders. Were they not going to cut the lines to the sinking sub? Would they let the waterlogged sub capsize and sink the corvette? Pete had heard about Russian inefficiency. He had surrendered his sub to save the orphans. But now, if the corvette went down, they could all wind up dying anyway.

"Mr. Jamison, what's going on?"

"The captain's talking about sending a boarding party back to the *Honolulu* to investigate."

"A boarding party? The idiot is going to wind up sinking his own ship."

"To be honest, sir, I think he and some of his officers were in the galley celebrating the capture of the *Honolulu* with a little too much vodka, sir."

"Great." The Russians would wind up getting them all drowned. "Lieutenant Jamison. Tell the Russian skipper that the sub is sinking, that it cannot be saved, and that he should cut the tow lines."

"Aye, Captain," Jamison said. He called out to the Russian skipper. *"Eezveneetzyah, Kapitán!"* Lieutenant Jamison got the Russian skipper's attention and translated the message as instructed.

The Russian captain walked over to the center of the listing fantail, waving his hands and frantically waving and yelling at Pete.

"What's he saying?" Pete asked.

"He's steamed that we sabotaged the sub, sir. Lots of cursing. Says we will be shot for it."

"Tell him he'll never live to see us shot if he doesn't cut those lines and cut them now!"

"Aye, sir."

Jamison relayed the message. More screaming from the Russian skipper. The ship's stern lapped lower into the sea. A moment later, however, Russian sailors cut the lines attaching *Suzdaltec* to the sinking *Honolulu*. The ship's stern rose back up to normal level.

Armed sailors broke through the perimeter and approached Pete. The barrels of their AK-47 assault rifles jabbed his neck and the back of his skull. They were yelling something in frantic Russian.

"What are they saying?"

"They want you to go with them, Skipper."

"Okay, I'll go."

The men pushed Pete at gunpoint into the ship's superstructure. Once inside, they forced him down a ladder, then into a windowless space somewhere below deck. They turned off the lights and locked the door.

The room was pitch dark, except for the faint light seeping under the passageway.

Pete kneeled in the dark and prayed for the safety of his crew.

The White House Situation Room
Emergency meeting of the National Security Council

Is it true?" President Mack Williams stood at the end of the long mahogany table, staring out over the members of his National Security Council. Most of them wore somber faces.

"Have the Russians really captured our submarine?"

Silence.

"Can no one answer my question?"

Mitchell Winstead, CIA director, spoke first. "No one can confirm seeing the *Honolulu*, at least not yet, Mr. President." The slim mathematician swiped sweat from his thinning hairline. "But we trust our sources on this one, sir. It doesn't look good."

The president buried his eyes in his left hand. "Secretary Lopez, where's our submarine? Does the Navy know?"

"Mr. President, we've not heard from them in six hours. Our last contact was an extremely low frequency signal indicating they had spotted the *Alexander Popovich*. We think that they attacked the freighter ... sunk it ... And then ... nothing, sir."

Mack stopped drinking years ago. He vowed to abstain while in public office. But now ... if he had a gin and tonic ... He dismissed that thought. "Director Winstead, what about this claim that the *Alexander Popovich* was carrying orphans?"

"Yes, sir," Winstead said. "We've tracked down those claims. They're true, Mr. President."

"It just keeps getting better and better."

"Mr. President," Secretary of Defense Lopez said.

"Secretary Lopez."

"Sir, the Russians have raised the alert levels of their nuclear forces to levels comparable to the Cuban Missile Crisis levels, sir. I recommend that we raise our level to DEFCON 2, sir."

Another knot twisted Mack's stomach.

"Mr. President," the secretary of state spoke up.

"Secretary Mauney."

"Rising to DEFCON 2 would be a mistake. Sir, that puts us on the precipice level for nuclear war."

"But, Mr. President," Secretary Lopez responded, "we must continue to show strength here. Remember, Russian forces in the Caucasus region threaten our Turkish allies. The Russians know only one word. Strength. They've raised their threat level. We must respond."

"But, sir," Secretary Mauney responded, "now is the time for calm and reason before all this blows up. I urge an open dialogue with the Russians before it's too late. Sir, I believe we should first have Secretary Lopez contact the Russian minister of defense to calm things down and assure them that our forces are not there to attack them. That would be followed up by you calling President Evtimov, sir."

The CIA director spoke up. "I'm afraid it won't be possible for Secretary Lopez to call Minister Popkov."

"What do you mean, Director Winstead?"

"Sir, our intelligence sources in Moscow say that Minister Popkov has been assassinated."

That news was a bucket of cold water on Mack's head.

"Not only that, sir, but we have satellite photos showing trucks fueling at least two dozen long-range intercontinental ballistic missiles in Siberia. These missiles had been drained of fuel as part of the Ballistic Missile Reduction Treaty negotiated by the previous administration."

"What's going on? Who's in charge of the military?"

"Sir, we hope that President Evtimov is still in charge. But the answer to the question is that we really don't know," Director Winstead said.

"Mr. President," the secretary of defense said. "All the more reason to raise the readiness status of our nuclear forces to DEFCON 2. We don't know who's running the show."

"Let's call President Evtimov," Secretary Mauney retorted. "Let's defuse this thing now. Please."

"Of course Evtimov will *claim* he's in charge." Secretary Lopez's voice was as tense as Mack had ever heard it. "But are we to believe that? Popkov is murdered. Then they raise their nuclear alert status to Cuban Missile Crisis levels? Sir, that means that they're targeting American cities again. Right now.

"The Russians know only strength. You'll get Evtimov's attention if we're at DEFCON 2. He'll know we mean business. And if someone other than Evtimov is running their military, whoever is in charge will know that we mean business too."

Mack stood, crossed his arms, and paced back and forth across the front of the ornate conference room. The secretary of defense was right. The Russians had for generations only understood and responded to strength. But the secretary of state was right too. This whole thing was spinning out of control. The thunder of war — of nuclear war — boomed in the distance.

The president stared at the red telephone on the table. In theory, he was supposed to pick up that phone, get the president of Russia on the line, and immediately defuse the specter of nuclear holocaust.

That was the theory anyway.

But there was theory, and then there was reality. Someone had murdered the man, who next to the Russian president himself, was directly in charge of Russia's deadly nuclear arsenal.

On top of that, nuclear warheads were being targeted at American cities again.

What to do? If rogue forces controlled the Russian military, failing to raise the level of United States forces could invite a preemptive strike. But raising the level of American forces could further provoke the Russians. A miscalculation either way could cost the lives of millions.

Lord, help me. We must remain so strong that no potential adversary will dare test our strength.

The words of Ronald Reagan rang in the back of his mind.

"Mr. Secretary." He looked at the secretary of defense. "Order United States nuclear forces to DEFCON 2."

CHAPTER 25

FSB Headquarters
Lubyanka Square, Moscow

The Russians had kept him in isolation for several hours, Pete assumed, first in a holding area onboard ship, and then at a holding facility in Odessa. But because they had taken his watch, and because he could not see outside, he could only estimate how much time had passed.

He saw sunlight again when they chained his arms and legs and led him out of an armored car across the tarmac to a plane at Odessa Airport. He was grateful for a few minutes of fresh air. He was also grateful that they had placed him in a seat by the window, which allowed him to at least enjoy the daylight, a welcome respite from the deadly silence of the armed guards accompanying him on the flight.

He had assumed they were taking him to Moscow, and his suspicions were confirmed when he spotted the spirals of the Kremlin through a break in the clouds.

A few minutes later, the plane touched down on a large, concrete runway.

At gunpoint, the guards rushed him to an armored jeep, and they sped away out of the airport with blaring sirens and whirling lights of police escorts both in front of and behind the armored jeep.

About thirty minutes later, the armored jeep sped down a large boulevard, heading straight up toward the multi-colored bulbed spirals towering into the overcast sky.

This world-famous sight looked more imposing in real life than it had in the pictures. But to be in an armed vehicle approaching St. Basil's Cathedral in the heart of Red Square, thousands of miles from home, Pete realized that he was about to be held accountable for his actions as commanding officer of the USS *Honolulu.*

A light rain fell as the jeep turned right just in front of the Kremlin. The driver swung around the perimeter of Red Square, turned right again, and headed into an underground parking deck of a large grey building with Stalinesque architecture.

Pete did not remember his geography of downtown Moscow all that well, but he assumed that this was Lubyanka Square, the former head-quarters for the old KGB, and now its successor, the FSB.

The jeep stopped near an underground freight elevator shaft, where half a dozen armed Russian soldiers were waiting.

One of them opened the door. A younger man, wearing a dark suit, spoke in perfect English. "I am Special Agent Vasily Borvich. I am a translator working for the Russian government. Come with me and these men, please."

A soldier pushed a button and the elevator doors swung open. All six soldiers stepped in, surrounding Pete with their guns. The translator stepped in and closed the doors, then pushed the button. The elevator started rising.

"Where's my crew?"

"It is not for you to ask questions."

The elevator stopped. The doors swung open into a large corridor with fluorescent lights and antiseptic-smelling tile floors.

"Step out of the elevator and follow me."

They stepped across the hallway from the elevator, their boots click-ing and echoing down the corridors. They walked through two ornate double doors.

The doors swung into a large, chandelier-filled courtroom. The courtroom was packed with people who turned and stared at Pete.

"Walk forward."

Pete stepped down the center aisle, through a wooden gate.

"Sit here." The translator pointed at a table to his left.

At the table to his right, a grim-faced Army officer stared him down with angry eyes.

Something was said in Russian. Three high-ranking military offi-cers, one each from the Russian Army, Navy, and Air Force, stepped through the door behind the big benches in front of Pete. All three looked to be in their fifties. With a solemn face, the Army officer in the middle nodded at a clerk.

A clerk began reading in English.

"This Russian Military Tribunal, convened to hear the charges of war crimes against this officer for attacking a civilian Russian ship with a civilian crew, is now in session. Please be seated."

The Army officer in the middle, a general, grunted something, and the translator spoke.

"Are you Commander Peter Miranda of the United States Navy?"

Pete stood. The Geneva Convention required him to provide his name, rank, and serial number.

"I am."

"Commander Miranda, you are charged with the following crimes, for which if you are convicted, could result in your being executed by firing squad or being sentenced to life in prison."

There was a pause, as the English translation was followed by more Russian.

"You are being charged with twenty-five counts of crimes against humanity, to wit, in that you commanded the United States submarine USS *Honolulu* on an illegal and secret military mission into the Black Sea, wherein you subsequently ordered your vessel to attack a civilian freighter, to wit, the Russian freighter *Alexander Popovich*, and that your actions have caused the untimely deaths of at least twenty-five known innocent civilians on board that ship."

More Russian. A murmuring rose from the courtroom. Pete looked around and caught the eyes of a young brunette woman sitting in the front row just behind him to his right. His eyes lingered on her for a moment, and then he recognized her as Masha Katovich, the young lady he had rescued.

"You are also being charged with conspiracy to destroy and destruction of property of the Russian Republic, to wit, in that after having surrendered the said USS *Honolulu* to the Navy of the Russian Republic, thus transferring ownership of said vessel to the Russian Republic, you did conspire to, and did in fact instruct certain subordinates to destroy said property by the use of explosive devices, which led to the sinking of such vessel in the Black Sea in waters west of the Crimean Peninsula."

More translation.

More astonishment from the crowd.

Pete looked around again. Masha Katovich was gone. He felt strange disappointment at her absence.

He'd sensed a sympathetic look on her face. Or so he thought. Then again, he had nearly killed her precious orphans. Perhaps his imagination had shifted into overdrive. She was probably the prosecution's star witness.

"You are also charged with violation of international law pertaining to transit of the high seas in that you broke various provisions of the Montreux Convention and the United Nations Convention on the Law of the Seas, to wit, in that you illegally and without justification brought your submarine in a submerged state through that international strait known as the Bosphorus, in violation of all semblances of international law prohibiting such submerged transit.

"To these charges, how do you plead?"

"I will plead to nothing until I know that my crew is safe and that they will be released."

"Silence!" the general shouted. "It is not for you to be concerned of the fate of war criminals."

"And I will not participate in this kangaroo court until I know my men are safe!"

"That is enough!" The admiral, just to the left of the general, snarled. "Your crew's fate will be tied to yours. If you are convicted, they will be convicted. If you are executed, they will be executed. And if you are acquitted, then they will be set free."

"That is not acceptable."

"Silence!" A banging gavel rapped from the one in the middle. "Perhaps the innocent children and crewmen of the freighter you sunk would say that a submarine against an unarmed freighter is not acceptable!"

"That freighter was being used by terrorists!"

"Ha!" The air marshal sitting to the right spoke up. "Typical American response justifying the unchecked use of military power against civilians. Everything is tied to terrorists!"

The general in the center spoke again. "How do you plead to these charges?"

"I do not understand these charges. Do I now have a right to counsel?"

"Aah. The brave commander, who is so brave as to attack an unarmed freighter, now wishes to hide behind an attorney?"

Mocking laughter arose at the translation.

"Very well! This is a military tribunal, Commander. And under our rules, you may have one Russian military attorney and one military attorney of your choosing from your country, should your host country agree to provide one. You will not be allowed a civilian attorney. Is this your wish, Commander?"

"Yes, sir. I wish to exercise my right to counsel."

"Very well!" the army general announced. "You will be removed to your cell, where you will communicate your desire for counsel to your translator. This court will reconvene in forty-eight hours."

Three more gavel bangs rang out. The generals and the admiral exited the courtroom.

Armed guards clamped cuffs on Pete's hands. They hustled him back behind the bench area, through a small door, into a narrow corridor. A moment later, they slammed the iron doors behind him in the cold cell.

The ornate Russian Orthodox Church was nestled in a grove of trees across from the large, rectangular brick compound that surrounded the United States Embassy. She remembered visiting this place last summer, shortly after Carol and Eugene Allison had left Ukraine.

Then she had taken a stroll through the summer heat to find a peaceful courtyard just outside the chapel, and to try something that the Allisons had taught her to do. Pray.

Today's short walk from Red Square through the blustery wind to the church was for the same purpose. The leaves were gone now, and the church seemed colder and greyer.

She had tried telling her Russian interrogators about the cargo transfer. But they responded as if she were the criminal.

"Do you realize that *Kapitán* Batsakov was a hero of the Soviet navy?" asked the scruffy one, with a burning cigarette dangling from his mouth. "And you seek to impugn his name?" He blew a cloud of stifling smoke. "The entire world is watching this, and impugning the reputation of a Soviet naval hero gives propaganda to the Americans."

The second interrogator, the fat, balding one, had been more accusatory. "I hope you are not attempting to blackmail the *kapitán's* estate or the Russian government for money, Miss Katovich. Do you know that blackmail is a felony under Russian law?"

She had to get the truth out.

The Russians had threatened to prosecute her if she talked, and they wanted to cover the matter for propaganda purposes. She had only one option.

The Americans.

The Allisons had claimed that prayer was talking to God.

Softly, she spoke into the biting wind. "God, show me what to do and let it be right. In Jesus' name."

She looked around. No one was there. At least she saw no one in the immediate vicinity. Only the wispy wind blew leaves in a circle.

The Russians had told her to be back at the courthouse in forty-eight hours. She was to report in every two hours. The bells in the church steeple chimed eleven times. She had one hour. Once she did not report, they would search for her — if they were not already looking for her.

She glanced across the wide boulevard, past the zooming cars at the opening in the tall brick wall.

Behind that wall was America. Through the Internet and through the Allisons, she in many ways felt that she knew America already. But could the Americans be trusted with this information? After all, she nearly died because of their attack. Dima nearly died. Oh, Dima!

On the other hand, if the Americans had not attacked, Batsakov and his crew would have murdered her. And the Americans did not let her children die. The Americans rescued them.

But what if they did not believe her? Suppose they did not give her a chance to talk, but kicked her back on the cold streets of Moscow? Would she be interrogated for going to the Americans first?

If her request for asylum was denied, then what?

"Help me, Jesus."

She pressed the *walk* button just in front of the embassy, bringing traffic to a halt. Quickly she stepped out onto the boulevard, walking across from the church to the compound. Better not to look around, she thought, so as to appear inconspicuous.

Her better judgment waned as she approached the middle of the boulevard. She looked back over her shoulder. Two stone-faced young men in black suits stepped rapidly into the crosswalk. They had to be Russian FSB.

She quickened her pace. The light changed as she reached the side of the road just in front of the U.S. embassy. Brakes squealed. A loud horn. The men were running for her in front of ongoing traffic!

She dashed toward the embassy, where several U.S. Marines were standing guard.

"Asylum! Please! I request asylum!"

The Marines grabbed her, twisting her arm behind her back. "Please, asylum."

"Sergeant, Corporal. Take her inside. Notify the political officer."

Masha looked over her shoulders as the Marines rushed her toward a guard shack.

The two young men in black suits were at the entrance to the compound. Other U.S. Marine guards stood at the entrance, blocking their way.

The White House

This is a travesty!" The president of the United States stood, pacing again. His Security Council had rushed into the Oval Office for yet another emergency session, and they were agape at images beamed from Moscow.

These were the images of an American submarine commander standing before a Russian military tribunal, then being hustled out of a Russian courtroom.

"They're calling it an attack against civilians, Mr. President," the secretary of state said. "They have no idea still that the freighter had plutonium on it. They still think the plutonium is somewhere in Chechnya."

Mack picked up the *Washington Post*, whose headlines read, "Russians Capture U.S. Sub Crew—War Fever Hot Among Superpowers." "This is just great." He tossed the paper back down on his desk.

"Why don't we approach the Russians about a prisoner swap?" the secretary of defense said. "We release the MiG pilot shot down over Georgia, and they release our crew."

"I don't think it'll work," the secretary of state said. "They've got the grand prize, and they want to make hay out of it with the international community."

"Why not try?" Secretary Lopez retorted. "In 1960 when the Soviets shot down our U-2 spy plane, they swapped the pilot, Gary Powers, for a KGB colonel, as I recall."

"But remember, Mr. Secretary," the secretary of state said, "the Soviets agreed to the prisoner swap *after* they first tried Powers on international television, convicted him of spying, and sentenced him to three years in prison and seven years hard labor. The Eisenhower Administration could do nothing about it."

"Well, if they insist on trying our sub crew, maybe we should try their pilot," the secretary of defense said.

"Mr. President," the secretary of state said, "we've gotten a request for individual military council this morning from the Russian embassy. Commander Miranda has requested that a JAG officer represent him."

The secretary of defense said, "Why should we go along with this kangaroo court idea?"

"Because we have a serviceman that needs help," the vice president said.

"Plus the Russians have offered it," the secretary of state added. "And taking them up on their offer shows at least we have some respect for their system, which might lead to meaningful negotiation out of this crisis. At least it's more than they offered in the Gary Powers spy trial back in 1960."

"Admiral Ayers, have you spoken with the judge advocate general about all this, and if so, does he have a recommendation?"

"Yes, Mr. President. Admiral Stumbaugh, the Navy JAG, highly recommends Lieutenant Commander Brewer for the job. He's the best we've got."

"Hmm." Mack let that thought resonate for a moment. He knew Zack Brewer personally. Zack had prosecuted three of the most famous courts-martial in U.S. Navy history. In perhaps the most famous, he prosecuted three Islamic U.S. Navy chaplains for treason, securing the death penalty against internationally acclaimed defense attorney Wellington Levinson in what the press called "the court-martial of the century."

"Okay, stay on it," the president said. "Personally I like the idea of Brewer too. I have total confidence in him in any international crisis. He's a proven commodity."

"Yes, sir, Mr. President."

"Okay." Mack eyed the secretary of state. "What's this about an asylum request?"

Secretary Mauney spoke up. "From a young woman claiming to be on board the *Alexander Popovich* when she sunk. The woman was the chaperone for these orphans. Claims she overheard a conversation between the captain and crew about transferring some illegal cargo at sea to an Egyptian freighter. Claims that there was actually a transfer of some small crates just a few hours before the sinking. Makes me wonder if it was the plutonium."

"I can't believe I'm hearing this!" The president stood and slammed his fist on the desk. "Don't tell me we've sunk a freighter full of orphans and lost the plutonium to boot!"

"We're checking it, sir," the CIA director said. "We've asked the Turks for a roster of Egyptian freighters going into and out of the Bosphorus the last couple of days. One freighter, the *Al Alamein*, never made it to any ports that we know of, and sailed back out of the Bosphorus within eighteen hours of entering."

"So where's this freighter now?"

"We think in the Mediterranean somewhere, Mr. President," the secretary of defense answered. "The Med's a big place. We're watching Gibraltar and the Suez Canal, which are the only ways out of there. Plus we've alerted the Brits, and they've agreed to let us know if they see anything pass by Gibraltar. Even if we find her, the plutonium may not be on board. I mean, we don't know how credible this lady is."

"All right, ladies and gentlemen," the president said. "I want the State Department to follow up with this Russian offer to have military counsel present for Commander Miranda. Meantime, the Statement Department will offer a prisoner exchange of their pilot for our crew. I don't think it'll work, but at least it's still talking. We will also propose a partial cease-fire, whereby Russians will pull back all divisions but one from Chechnya and we would pull out everybody except the 82nd from Turkey."

"The Turks won't like that, Mr. President," Lopez said.

"That's tough," Mack said. "The Turks aren't president. I am. Right now, we've got American and Russian nuclear forces on high alert. That's hair-trigger danger. Besides, we will maintain the overflights of Georgian airspace. That'll keep both the Georgians and the Turks happy."

"Meanwhile, Secretary Mauney, Admiral Ayers"—the president looked at his defense secretary and Joint Chiefs chairman—"find that Egyptian freighter. Is that clear?"

"Yes, sir, Mr. President," the responses came in unison.

"Very well. This meeting is adjourned. Be back in twelve hours."

The Al Alamein
Mediterranean Sea

There, *Kapitán*, that should keep you safe." Salman Dudayev snapped the last few buttons on the radioactive protection suit that would allow the commanding officer of the *Al Alamein* to inspect the top-secret engineering marvel that was being built in the bowels of his ship.

"We are working with raw, exposed plutonium which could expose us to lethal doses of radiation. There are a number of sharp objects in the lab. So we must be careful not to puncture our suits."

Captain Sadir nodded his head, and the men stepped into the sterile laboratory, lit by hanging fluorescent lights, where three other scientists in protective suits were working.

The bomb was being constructed on a long table, twenty feet in length. Metal cylinders were stretched out in a line along the table.

"Shall I explain the mechanics of all this, *Kapitán*?"

"Please," the captain said.

"Now that we have obtained the materials that we need, the mechanics of a hydrogen bomb are relatively simple. At the heart of a successful hydrogen bomb is a successful atomic bomb. Or actually several atomic bombs.

"You see these five metal cylinders on this table, *Kapitán*?"

"They look like large aluminum salad bowls welded together. These are bombs?"

"Yes. Actually each of these is a thermonuclear device. Within each cylinder are two half-spheres of the plutonium 239 taken from the Russian ship. We carefully molded the half-cylinders in each cylinder and left a small space between each half-cylinder. Dynamite will be placed outside each cylinder and detonated from a remote detonation switch.

"The dynamite ignites, slamming the half-cylinders of plutonium together, creating an atomic chain reaction!" Excitement overcame Salman as he thought of what would happen next. "This chain reaction ignites a hydrogen-fusion reaction, and in one great flash the *Al Alamein* becomes the most glorious ship in history!" Laughter poured from his mouth at the thought of all of it.

"More famous than the *Titanic*?"

"Oh, *Kapitán*, in one swoop we shall eclipse the single destructive power of the Pacific tsunamis, of Mount St. Helens, and of the greatest earthquakes ever to strike the earth." Hot and cold flashes shot through his body.

"What are all these strange-looking glass jars that I am seeing on the table?" the captain asked.

"Ah. Good question. Fusion is at the heart of the H-bomb process. Several A-bombs are detonated at the same time to create the extremely high temperatures necessary to fuse a substance called lithium deuteride into helium.

"In our case, *Kapitán*, we will be using five small atomic bombs, all laid out here on the table before you, which will create a massive temperature of one hundred million degrees Celsius. We will instantly become the sun floating upon the water. Such an extreme thermonuclear temperature is necessary to fuse lithium deuteride into helium.

"The glass jars that you see on the table will be filled with the lithium deuteride and will surround the five A-bombs in their casings. When the fusion begins in the A-bombs, and when one hundred million degrees is reached, then the lithium nucleus slams into the deuteride nucleus, and voila. This begins our hydrogen bomb detonation."

More hot and cold chills shot through Salman's body. An incomparably powerful weapon of mass destruction was now nearly complete. Aside from a few select weapons in the arsenals of the American and Russia militaries, this was the most powerful device in the entire world.

The captain asked a question. But Salman did not hear it. His mind was on the sublime. Allah had made him feel like a god. In a way, with such awesome destructive power at his fingertips, he *was* a god!

"My apologies, *Kapitán*. What was your question?"

"I asked, Salman, where is the detonation switch?"

"Ah, but perhaps this is the best news of all. I am rigging the detonation switch to the bridge. You and I, with your permission of course, will be topside, looking through the windows, out at the target. In fact, *Kapitán*, because you are the highest-ranking man on this great ship, I feel that is only appropriate that you yourself do the honors. I believe Allah would be pleased."

The captain paused, looking at the hydrogen bomb in the bowels of his ship. He looked at Salman. "We will throw the switch together, my boy. And together, we will watch Allah's glorious work from paradise."

CHAPTER 26

FSB headquarters
Moscow, Russia

You are making quite a few headlines in America and around the world, Commander." The FSB agent stood just outside the steel bars that barricaded Pete from the rest of the world. His English was perfect. "Your countrymen are not too happy with your cowardice in surrendering your crew and your submarine so quickly."

"Did you have a question?"

"Of course such allegations are unfair. You were only doing the chivalrous thing. To surrender a billion-dollar piece of machinery for a few children. Your press is so horrible and misrepresentative of the truth. Of course, they don't know that you sabatoged it and sunk it. They think we've got your submarine. And they say you and your crew have defected."

"I don't believe that."

"Ah. So you have confidence that your press always reports the right story, do you?"

"Our press isn't perfect, but I have more confidence in a free press than the propaganda that stems from this place."

The FSB agent laughed. "Perhaps if you help us understand the truth of what really happened we can set the record straight and quash all those unfounded rumors that you have become — what is the phrase they're using — a *communist*?" The agent unleashed a devious sneer. Pete wanted to jump through the bars and take his head off.

"You know," Pete said, "this type of interrogation is prevented by the Geneva Accords."

"Ah, the Geneva Accords." The FSB officer struck a cigarette. "I was under the impression that the Geneva Accords applied to prisoners of war — not to terrorists." A satisfying puff. "Your own government made this argument to justify its maltreatment of Arab citizens at prisoner facilities at Guantanamo Bay. And as far as I know, our governments are not at war yet. And because you are a terrorist, the Geneva Accords do not apply here."

"You can use that garbage to mistreat me all you want. Just don't mistreat my crew."

"My dear Commander Miranda. You will not be mistreated. You will have a fair trial!" A snicker and another puff. "Now if you are convicted, I cannot say what treatment you will receive." The agent dropped the cigarette on the floor and stamped it out. "Perhaps you will enjoy your extended stay in the Russian Republic. At least here you will not have to face young Coley Miranda, who was on the television last night crying because his father is a traitor to America."

"Liar!"

"Am I?"

Pete rushed at the bars, shaking them with all his might. "How do you know my son's name?"

Another sinister laugh. "Why, Commander, everyone who has seen the boy's tears over his father's cowardice knows the name of Coley Miranda." The agent blew an obnoxious cloud of smoke into Pete's cell. "Just as your daughter Hannah looks into the cameras and says that she hopes her traitorous father never comes home." The agent lit another cigarette. "What did she call you? Benedict Arnold?"

Pete pounded the bars with his fists. The words knifed his heart. "Cut the propaganda. You're a liar."

"Am I?" More putrid smoke blew from the agent's mouth. "You are of Chilean heritage, are you not? Your father was Chilean. Pinochet is dead. Michelle Bachelet, the first woman president of Chile, was a member of the East German communist party. Your actions are clear now to people in America. At least that is the way your press is portraying the reason you delivered an American submarine to a government with a rich communist heritage."

"That's a lie. My family supported Pinochet. Pinochet put an end to socialism in Chile, at least until the election of Bachelet."

The agent laughed. "Try telling that to your countrymen. Try convincing your children. You haven't seen your children in a year. You're a traitor to them. Why should they not believe that you are a traitor to your country?"

"Why don't you step behind these bars and tell me about my kids man to man?"

"Aahh ... a sensitive area? Hah. Just think what your children will think when their cowardly father is hanged for all the world to see." The agent threw the cigarette stub at Pete and walked away.

Office of the president of the Russian Republic
Staraya Square, Moscow

Iam not satisfied with the Army's inability to find the missing pluto-nium!" President Vitaly Evtimov thundered from behind his desk, boring his stare at General Anatoly Petrov, the Russian Army chief of staff. General Petrov had been called into the cabinet meeting to represent the Army in the place of former Defense Minister Giorgy Alexeevich Popkov.

"My apologies, Comrade President," the general said. "Unfortunately, Minister Popkov never developed our battle plan prior to his unfortunate death."

"Blaming your incompetence on a dead man, are you?"

"No, Comrade President. My apologies ..."

"... I was not referring to the Army's *battle plan*. I was referring to your plan for finding that plutonium that *your* subordinates lost, and your plan to find it before the rebels turn it into a thermonuclear device that could wipe out every troop we have in Chechnya!"

"Yes, sir. I understand, sir."

"Understand this. Someone ... I do not know who ... but *someone* was upset with Defense Minister Popkov for this whole plutonium affair. Now I have consolidated Popkov's power under my authority. You are second in command of the army. For your own protection, General, I expect this bumbling incompetence to end with Popkov's assassination. Do I make myself perfectly clear?"

"Perfectly, sir."

"Find that plutonium, and find it now!"

"Yes, sir."

Evtimov turned to his foreign minister, Alexander Alexeyvich Kotenkov. "Minister Kotenkov? You had something?"

"Yes, Comrade President, we have a communiqué from your old friend Mack Williams."

Evtimov folded his arms across his stomach and leaned back in his chair. "I suppose the cowboy president wants his submarine back?"

"He has not said that yet, Vitaly Sergeivich. He has, however, proposed a prisoner exchange."

"Ahh. And what sort of exchange does President Rambo have in mind?"

"Our fighter pilot for his submarine crew."

Evtimov unleashed a belly laugh, then tried containing his laughter by swigging down ice water. "Tell Williams that we will give them the lowest enlisted member of their sub crew when they return our pilot."

The foreign minister chuckled. "The Americans have also said that a Lieutenant Commander Brewer is available to defend their submarine commander."

"Brewer?" Evtimov was sure he had heard the name. "Is he the JAG officer that prosecuted the Muslim chaplains?"

"Yes, Comrade President."

Evtimov thought about that. "What do you think of this, Alexeyvich?"

"I believe we should allow this, Comrade President."

"Interesting. Why do you say this?"

"Public relations. Remember our purpose. We allow military counsel from an accused's home country because our system appears fair to the international community. Brewer's presence will not change the outcome, only call attention to what the Americans have done and make us look fair."

"Yes," Evtimov said.

"We let them bring their best counsel. Points for our side. Then he loses."

"Intriguing." Evtimov scratched his chin.

"Not only that, Comrade President, but I recommend that we move this trial from Moscow to St. Petersburg."

"St. Petersburg? What is wrong with Moscow?"

"Nothing is wrong with Moscow. But again, remember our overall strategic objective. The world will be watching this. Members of the international press will request to be present.

"St. Petersburg is our most beautiful city. We received rave reviews when we hosted the 2006 G-8 Summit there. Think of the symbolic power with the world media if we were to move this trial to St. Nicholas Naval Cathedral."

"Interesting," the president mused. "We prosecute this crew in the cathedral that has hallowed the loss of brave Russian sailors since the time of Peter the Great. Hmm. Perhaps we can erect a memorial there to the crew of the *Alexander Popovich*."

"A splendid idea, Comrade President. Plus if we try this case in Moscow, because the city is our capital, I fear that the trial will appear more political to the international community. It is not absolutely necessary that we move this trial, but in a public relations war, every small advantage helps. St. Nicholas Cathedral, a building that honors the brave dead lost at sea, would be the perfect backdrop for this war crimes trial. That is my recommendation."

The president thought about that for a moment. The foreign minister was correct about St. Petersburg. The city was Russia's most beautiful. And not only that, it was the home city of the president of the Russian Repubic.

"Very well. We shall move the trial to St. Petersburg. Meanwhile"— the president turned his attention to General Alexander Ivanov, military chief of the Russian Air Force—"I want the Americans to understand that we are not going to back down militarily. What is the status of our strategic bombers in Vladivostok?"

"We have thirty-nine Bear bombers operational and ready to fly, sir. In addition to that, we have another forty Backfire bombers at your disposal."

"Very well. Get the planes in the air. Send them north, and then east. I want them to buzz the coast of Alaska, just as far south along the coast as our fuel supplies will allow. Refuel them midair. Do whatever you need to do. But I want a show of strength against the Americans."

"Do you want them armed with nuclear warheads, Comrade President?"

Evtimov thought about that for a moment. "We have no assurances that the American planes flying near our border over Georgia have only conventional weapons, do we?"

"No, sir."

"Very well, arm the bombers with nuclear weapons."

Residence of Captain Bill Callahan
Canberra, Australia

Zack Brewer gripped the horseshoe, vicing it between his thumbs and fingers. He stepped forward with his left foot and pitched it underhand.

Clang.

Great. Another ringer.

He had gone from prosecuting the most high-profile court-martial in the history of the U.S. to tossing ringers in seclusion on the world's most remote continent as legal aide to the United States Naval Attaché. Despite all the typical "detailer talk" about how the billet would help his experience in international legal matters, Zack knew the reality of why he was here.

Death threats had been made against him, and Australia was the safest place for him. In other words, he'd been "put out to pasture" by the Navy for his own protection, but he was ready to get back to the fleet.

"Zack."

Oh no, not another offer of lemonade and cookies.

Shielding the sun with his right hand, he looked aross the lush grass to the back screen porch of the attaché's quarters.

"Right out here, Mrs. Callahan."

"Bill's on the phone, Zack. He says it's urgent."

Zack broke into a slight jog toward his hostess. She handed him the cordless phone.

"Yes, sir?"

"Pack your bags. Washington's got a high-profile assignment for you. I'll pick you up in one hour and brief you on the plane."

Zack's heart jumped. Finally, a ticket back into the action. Right now, anything sounded good. "Aye, aye, sir! I'll be ready!"

CHAPTER 27

British lookout post
The Rock of Gibraltar

Lieutenant Jeremy Tomlinson, Royal Navy of the British Empire, swung his telescope down into the broad channel separating the north wall of the Rock from the Spanish coastline.

The telescope swept the waterway. The bow of the long, low-lying freighter sailed into view.

The ship was churning from right to left. Tomlinson flicked the telescope just to the right to keep the ship in view.

The stern came into full view. From it fluttered a horizontally divided red-white-black flag with the so-called eagle of Saladin in the middle of the white stripe.

Tomlinson picked up the phone. "Gibraltar Lookout to HMS *Sabre*."

"HMS *Sabre*. Go ahead, Gibraltar."

"We've got an Egyptian freighter entering the channel. Can't make out the name on the stern. I'll leave that one to you, ole boy."

"Roger that, Gibraltar. We are on it."

HMS Sabre
The Straits of Gibraltar

Lieutenant Stephen Stacks, commanding officer of the HMS *Sabre*, scrambled his four-man crew. Within minutes, the patrol boat was cutting through the waters at Gibraltar Harbor.

Flash message traffic indicated that Britain's closest ally was on the hunt for an Egyptian freighter, the *Al Alamein*, and that such freighter might try escaping the Mediterranean either via the Suez Canal or the Straits of Gibraltar.

Stacks pushed down on the throttle, and the fifty-two-foot Royal Navy patrol boat planed out into the open water at more than thirty knots.

Sabre cleared the huge Rock's south side. A few minutes later, the freighter came into view, steaming west toward the Atlantic.

"Let's go have a look," Stacks announced. The British patrol boat sped out into the Straits, and then sliced a path across the rolling swells, straight for the slower-moving freighter.

Sabre closed to within one hundred yards, drawing a long blast from the freighter's horn. She veered to the right, shooting down the port side of the ship, then swung acoss her wake into the churning water behind her stern.

Stacks brought his binoculars to his eyes, aiming for the stern, just under the flapping red, white, and black horizontally striped Egyptian flag.

Al Alamein.

"We've found her."

The Al Alamein
Straits of Gibraltar

The British patrol boat is breaking off, *Kapitán*," one of the deckhands announced.

"The British are always pestering freighters, especially Arab freighters, around Gibraltar," the first officer said.

"Very well," Captain Hosni Sadir muttered, looking out the bridge at the open waters of the Atlantic Ocean. No other escort vessels were anywhere in sight. No aircraft were overhead.

His first officer was probably right. He'd seen it before himself. The Brits liked buzzing around the Straits in their speedboats like they owned the place—as if they were reminding the world that Lord Nelson had won the Battle of Trafalgar against the Spanish in these very waters hundreds of years ago.

Good.

Let them live in the past. They had no clue that his ship was now a floating hydrogen bomb.

Sadir looked over at Salman Dudayev, who was fiddling with some electric wires inside a black metal box over on the right side of the bridge.

"How is the detonator coming, Salman?"

"My work is nearly complete, *Kapitán*. Should you like, we could vaporize the Rock of Gibraltar from this very bridge."

Sadir smiled at that thought. If they ignited the bomb now, at least the British would no longer pester Arab freighters entering or exiting the Straits.

"Save the fireworks for our real target. Perhaps one day the Rock will bear a monument that we sailed past it on this day toward our glorious mission."

"Praise be to Allah," Salman Dudayev said.

"Radar officer, what do you see out there?"

"Nothing unusual, *Kapitán*. No one is paying us any attention. I predict smooth sailing all the way to our target."

"Very well," Sadir said. "All ahead full."

"All ahead full."

Al Alamein surged ahead in the water, planing slightly as she headed into the open waters of the Atlantic.

The USS Charlotte
Straits of Gibraltar

Alert one! Alert one! Incoming emergency action message! Alert One! Alert One! Incoming EAM!"

Commander Steve "Puck" Puckett, captain of the American nuclear submarine USS *Charlotte*, looked up at the loudspeaker blaring the announcement into the control room.

"XO, take the conn."

"Aye, Captain, I have the conn," Lieutenant Commander Todd Swanson said.

Puckett barreled through the narrow passageways, passing sailors who stood back and shouted, "Make way for the captain!"

Puck stepped into the radio room.

"Attention on deck!"

"What have you got?" Pete barked.

"The Brits have spotted the freighter. They're right on top of us, sir."

Puckett took the message from the radio officer's hands.

EMERGENCY ACTION MESSAGE

FROM: NATIONAL MILITARY COMMAND CENTER—WASHINGTON, D.C.

TO: USS *CHARLOTTE*

SUBJECT: ACTION MESSAGE

REMARKS:

British Patrol Boat HMS *Sabre* has spotted Egyptian freighter *Al Alamein* in Gibraltar Straits fifteen minutes ago, course bearing two-seven-zero degrees.

Sabre reports *Al Alamein* making run for open seas of Atlantic at fourteen knots.

Your orders are maintain surveillance of *Al Alamein* until ordered to break off by National Command Authority.

Be prepared to attack or board by SEAL team on orders of National Command Authority.

Commander Puckett rushed back to the bridge.

"Attention on deck!"

"I have the conn!" Puckett said. "Up scope!"

Puckett grabbed the periscope and swept the horizon. Within minutes the freighter came into view. She was cutting through the water about a mile to the submarine's east, making a run for the open sea.

"Down scope!" Puckett shouted, then picked up the microphone and dialed the sonar room. "Sonar, do you have a read on that freighter?"

"Aye, Captain, we've got her loud and clear. Single screw. Distinctive whine."

"Stay on it. Don't let her out of your ears."

"Aye, Captain."

"XO, get the navigational chart out for Gibraltar."

"Aye, sir." Lieutenant Commander Swanson complied, and the chart was rolled out on a small drafting table.

"Chief of the Boat, OOD, everyone gather around." Puckett called the officers in the control room around him. "All right, let's mark this for the log," Puckett said. "Here's our position." With a grease pencil, he marked the positon of the submarine. "Here's the position of the freighter. She's headed west." He marked the freighter's position.

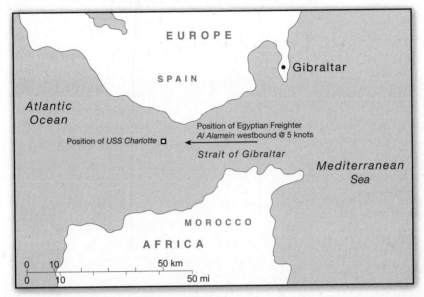

"We don't know where she's going, but Washington wants us to follow her and find out. If necessary, we're ordered to board her, or even sink her. So here's the plan. We'll let her pass over us, and then we'll maintain a depth of one hundred fifty feet, and we're going to follow in her wake. We'll use her noise to help camouflage our presence. Be ready and be alert." Puckett eyed his crew. "Any questions?"

There were none.

"Very well. Let's get on with it."

Pulkovo International Airport
St. Petersburg, Russia

In a brown leather bomber jacket and blue jeans, and carrying a small black briefcase, Zack Brewer stepped out of the British Airways 767 into the enclosed jetway.

Like the faces of the Russian passengers returning home, the jetway was cold. A wet fog blanketed the land.

Hustling through the jetway and into the antiseptic-smelling hallway, Zack got in the customs line on the left, the line reserved for non-Russians.

A stern-faced woman, wearing a green military suit, with a skirt cut at her knees, and clubbed, black leather laceup shoes, stepped out from behind the glass booth and walked down the line of foreigners waiting to come through.

"Commander Brewer!" the woman snapped in Slavic-accented English.

"*Dah meen yazavoot* Commander Brewer," Zack stepped out of line and responded in Russian.

The woman raised her eyebrows.

"You speak Russian, Commander?"

"*Neemeenoga*," Zack said.

"Your visa, your passport, and your military identification card, please."

Zack produced all three. The woman studied them for a moment. She took Zack's passport and visa, stamped them, and handed them back. "A car waits for you in front of the airport. Follow me."

They walked past the foreigners waiting in the customs line, and then stepped into the corridor of the airport. Two armed Russian soldiers joined them, trailing them all the way to the passenger pickup section at the front of the airport.

"Get into this car, please," the woman said. One of the Russian soldiers opened the back door of the black Mercedes. "U.S. embassy personnel are in the car."

Zack stepped into the car, sitting alone in the backseat. The car sped forward, sandwiched between two Russian military jeeps.

An officer turned to greet him from the front passenger seat. "Welcome to Russia, Commander."

"Thank you, ma'am."

"I'm Captain Ann Glover, the U.S. Naval Attaché to Russia."

"A pleasure, ma'am."

Zack looked out the window as the armed motorcade sped out past the blue and yellow buildings into the thick fog.

"You have to assume everything is bugged here, Zack. Even this car."

Zack thought about that. How would he communicate with his client if everything was bugged?

"You may wonder how you will represent your client under these circumstances."

"You're a mind reader, ma'am."

"I understand you've been briefed on the intelligence situation surrounding the capture of the crew?"

"Yes, ma'am."

"You'll have to prepare your defense primarily based on that."

Talk about being handcuffed.

"You have a problem with that, Zack?"

"If those are my orders, those are my orders."

They sped down a freeway, leaving the airport behind in the distance.

"So what do you know about St. Petersburg, Zack?"

"Let's see. The city was known as Leningrad during the Communist reign. When the USSR fell, they changed it back to St. Petersburg. Homeplace of Catherine the Great and President Evtimov. Supposedly Russia's most beautiful city."

"You know more than most Americans," Captain Glover said. "The city is on the eastern end of the Gulf of Finland. It is known as the Venice of the North because it literally sits on forty-four islands in the Delta of the Neva River."

The fog thickened, but the driver raced through it like he was Dale Earnhardt Jr. or something. This made Zack nervous. He did not want to be driving in such thick fog, let alone speeding through it at a hundred miles per hour.

"Why'd they change the trial from Moscow to St. Petersburg?" Zack tried distracting his mind from the specter of the Mercedes slamming into a concrete overpass.

"Symbolism, I think." Captain Gover shrugged her shoulders. "St. Petersburg is a Navy town. We've heard they want to move the trial to St. Nicholas Naval Cathedral. Maybe they got good vibes from the 2006 G-8 Summit."

Zack did not respond. He prayed silently for the task ahead and that the driver would slow down.

FSB federal detention facility
St. Petersburg, Russia

Two hours later

At least in Moscow, the cot was not so lumpy, nor was the cell so dark. Pete lay on his back, alone in the cell, wondering where they had taken him.

He had heard the phrase *"Saint Peeterborguyah"* bantered about, and assumed that they had transported him out of Moscow for whatever reason, perhaps to St. Petersburg.

But why?

To separate him from his crew?

For all Pete knew, the crew could be anywhere.

Perhaps the Russians moved him to foil a rescue attempt.

No.

That couldn't be it.

It would be one thing for Navy SEALs to rescue someone from a terrorist camp in the Gobi. But in the heart of Moscow? Or any industrialized city in Russia? That would be a tall order even for the renowned Navy SEALs.

Maybe they weren't interested in a rescue.

Maybe the FSB agent was right.

Perhaps America had turned against him. After all, he *had* surrendered his submarine. Wouldn't it make sense that he would have to be an international scapegoat if that was necessary to avert nuclear war?

What if the FSB agent was right? Were his own children disowning him? He'd not seen them in a year.

It was probably true. The agent had too much information to have made it all up.

What would he do now? How would he defend himself?

He would say nothing, let them torture him, and if necessary, let them kill him. After all, Jesus had not responded to the false charges against him. Why should he? All he could offer was silence.

Pete Miranda, the Chilean-American whiz kid of the U.S. naval submarine community, lay flat on his back, looking up at the dark ceiling. Tears ran down the corners of his eyes onto his cheeks.

The Al Alamein
The English Channel

From the bridge of his freighter, Captain Hosni Sadir looked out across the water at the magnificent White Cliffs of Dover rising high above the sea.

Why had Allah placed such magnificent natural displays in nations full of infidels?

The firing mechanism had now been armed. Perhaps he would teach Britain a lesson for its unholy alliance with the Americans against Muslim brothers in places like Afghanistan and Iraq.

He looked over at the switch, which Salman had labeled *Detonator*, and smiled.

What a waste to vaporize such beautiful cliffs that Allah had created for his glory.

Besides, London was not that far away. Just a hundred fifty miles or so.

Sadir could not suppress the grin crawling across his face.

CHAPTER 28

The White House

A ll right, what's the situation with this freighter?" President Williams demanded.

"She's entered the English Channel, sir," Admiral Ayers said. "Our concern is a threat to London."

"Let's see what you've got," the president said.

"Yes, sir." Ayers had an aide unravel a map showing the freighter's current position.

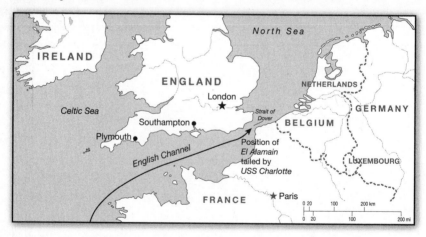

"We've got a problem if she turns left once she clears Dover. She's about seventy-five miles from the mouth of the Thames River, and from there, less than forty miles to London. If there's been a plutonium transfer to this freighter ... well, that could wipe out London, sir."

"Where's our submarine?"

"USS *Charlotte* is still on her tail, right in her wake. As far as we can tell, no one knows that we're there."

"All right, this freighter cannot threaten London. Notify the British of our concerns. Suggest that they have patrol boats prepared to intercept."

"Aye, Mr. President. But there may not be enough time for that."

"Notify them anyway. Have *Charlotte* ready to sink her if she turns back to the west once she clears Dover."

Admiral Ayers hesitated.

"Something wrong, Admiral?"

"I would remind you, Mr. President, that if we sink this freighter, and if it does contain that stolen plutonium, we lose the evidence we need to prove to the Russians that the *Honolulu* did not just sink an unarmed civilian freighter. We've already got Bear bombers buzzing our west coast. If word gets out that we've sunk another civilian freighter, we'll look like the Nazis did when their U-boats terrorized civilian shipping at the outbreak of World War II. Not to mention how we'd look in the Middle East by sinking an Egyptian ship. We can't afford to sink it, sir. We need that evidence to avert World War III."

Mack Williams thought about that. He was risking so much on the uncorroborated testimony of a Ukrainian woman who was almost killed by a U.S. sub. *Lord, stop me if I'm wrong.*

"And if they've got a bomb on that ship," Mack said, "and if that bomb incinerates London, we've got Armageddon anyway." Mack's eyes locked with the admiral's. "You've got your orders, Admiral. If that freighter turns slightly to the left, and if the British aren't there to stop her, then take her out."

"Yes, sir, Mr. President."

FSB federal detention facility
St. Petersburg, Russia

Pete awakened to the rattling of keys against iron.

"You have a visitor, Commander."

Bright fluorescent lights blurred Pete's vision. He sat up on the cot, squinting and rubbing his eyes to regain his vision.

The fuzziness faded into the image of a sharp-looking U.S. Naval officer, wearing a service dress blue uniform.

"Sir, I'm Lieutenant Commander Zack Brewer, United States Navy Judge Advocate General's Corps."

For a moment, Pete thought he was dreaming. Was he being supernaturally released from jail like the apostle Peter?

Pete felt joy, relief, and disappointment all wrapped together. He knew Zack Brewer's reputation. He knew the Navy had sent their best. Maybe they still cared. Or maybe they sent Brewer to find out if he was a traitor or not.

"Zack Brewer. Boy, am I glad to see you!" Pete extended his hand, and the Navy's most famous officer gripped firmly. "What's going on out there, Commander? What are they saying back home?"

Brewer looked over at the FSB agent.

"We don't have much time, Skipper. We're in court in thirty minutes. I've brought a set of service dress blues for you. Please change into them. I'll speak with you in the car on the way to the courthouse."

The White House

There's good news and there's bad news, Mr. President," Admiral John F. Ayers Jr. was saying.

"Let's hear the bad part first."

"Not only are we seeing Russian bombers off the coast of Alaska, but now they're moving Bear and Backfire bombers into Cuba."

The secretary of defense, who along with the secretary of state was in on this meeting, spoke up. "Sir, I see this as an intimidation tactic. If the Russians wanted to nuke us, they could easily launch a missile from a submarine sitting off the coast of North Carolina, and we'd never know they were there."

"I understand that, Mr. Secretary. But the American people won't understand it. They'll think we've got the second coming of the Cuban Missile Crisis fifty years later."

"Which is why we must give diplomacy a chance now, Mr. President," the secretary of state added.

"We've tried that, Mr. Secretary," the president responded. "Have the Russians responded to my cease-fire proposal that they pull back all divisions but one from Chechnya and we will pull out everybody except the 82nd Airborne from Turkey?"

Secretary Robert Mauney hesitated for a moment. "No, sir. Not yet. But we're still working on it."

"You put a reasonable proposal on the table, and they respond with moving Bear bombers full of atomic bombs into Cuba," Secretary of Defense Lopez said. "Not only that, but they're getting ready to put our submarine crew on trial for the world to see, claiming that we kill women and children. This is a public relations bonanza for them, sir. We must be firm. We cannot back down. And we cannot give ourselves away to that Egyptian freighter in the middle of the English Channel. "

"But, sir," Secretary Mauney jumped in. "We're playing Russian roulette with nuclear weapons. I know they haven't responded, sir. But please, forget the American pride thing. Call them again. Anything but this."

Images of Jesus in the Garden of Gethsemane rushed into Mack's mind. For a flash, he felt some of the heavy weight that the Savior had felt that night. Mack Williams was facing a possible nuclear confrontation, a confrontation that could desroy the world, and he did not know how to get out of it.

"Have we heard from Brewer?"

"Yes, sir," Admiral Ayers said. "He's in St. Petersburg. He'll do his best, I'm sure, but their system's rigged against him."

"What's the good news?" the president asked. Admiral Ayers and Secretary Lopez glanced at each other. Lopez nodded at Ayers.

"The good news, Mr. President—the freighter did not turn toward London."

"Where is it?"

Ayers unfurled the navigation map again.

"The tip of the arrow shows the position of the freighter. She's headed into the North Sea, Mr. President."

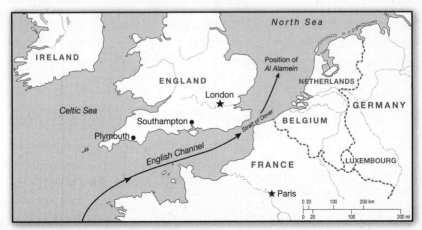

"The North Sea? What's up with that?"

"Don't know, sir. Britain's three naval bases, at Portsmouth, Devonport, and Clyde, are on the south and east sides of the island. Maybe they're going to disrupt North Sea oil supplies, or maybe they'll turn west when they clip the top of Scotland and head to the east coast of the United States."

"Okay," Mack said. "I want hourly updates on that freighter's position, and more often than that if she does something funky. I want fighter intercepts of any bomber flying off the U.S. coastline. Ride 'em like white on rice. If one of 'em turns inland at all, splash 'em. Also, Secretary Lopez, I'm ordering full mobilization of United States Armed Forces. Call up all reserves."

"But, Mr. President," Secretary Mauney pleaded.

Mack raised his palm. "Those are my orders."

St. Nicholas Naval Cathedral
St. Petersburg, Russia

At least they had removed his handcuffs and let him get into uniform, Pete thought as he rode in the back of the black Mercedes with Zack Brewer to the courthouse. Captain Ann Glover, the U.S. Naval Attaché, sat in the front seat, along with the driver, who was also a U.S. embassy employee.

Zack had warned him that everything was possibly bugged, including the car used by U.S. embassy personnel. Pete wondered how Zack would handle his case without a chance to prepare for whatever awaited.

The armed Russian military jeep swung to the right, and the Mercedes followed. The car stopped. An army of photographers, television cameras, and press types were waiting along the sidewalk.

"Just wait on the Russians," Captain Glover ordered. "They're supposed to provide an armed escort inside."

"And remember, sir," Zack added, "don't answer any press questions. If any answer is needed, I will handle it."

"Right, Commander." Pete looked out the window at the huge light blue baroque building with its white columns, a green roof, and golden spires reaching into the wintry sky. "That is an impressive courthouse."

"It's the courthouse for your case," Captain Glover said, "and it's also the St. Nicholas Naval Cathedral. It dates back to Peter the Great. It's the most hallowed naval site in all of Russia."

"So *this* is St. Nicholas," Zack said. "I've read quite a bit about it. Talk about media-orchestrated imagery."

"I don't follow," Pete said.

Captain Glover said, "St. Nicholas is a cathedral turned into a naval shrine. They have memorials to many Russian sailors lost at sea over the years. The locals call it the Sailor's Cathedral. One of their subs, the *Komsomolets*, went down off Norway in 1989, and there's a memorial to the forty-two dead sailors there. There's been talk in the last couple of days about erecting a memorial to the crew of the *Alexander Popovich* here."

"That's just great," Pete said. "Sounds like they're planning a fair and impartial trial."

The door opened. A Russian soldier motioned them to get out.

Pete stepped into the biting cold.

"Commander Miranda! Commander Brewer!" Members of the press shouted at them from both sides of the walkway leading into the building. "Is it true that you torpedoed a civilian ship carrying orphans?... What were your orders, sir?... Have you defected to Russia?"

"The commander has no comments at this time," Zack shouted over the barricade of Russian soldiers as they walked swiftly toward the doors of the building.

Soldiers opened the doors of the main entrance of the cathedral. Naval art commemorating the history of the Russian Navy adorned the walls under the ornate chandeliers, and spectators jammed the pews on both sides, as if they had come for an Easter Sunday service. Camera strobes popped like lightning in a summer thunderstorm. Spectators murmured at the presence of the American naval officers.

The soldiers nudged Pete and Zack down the aisle to the chancery, which had been transformed into a courtroom. They pointed the officers to an empty, ornate table to the right, which had several headsets plugged into a console panel.

A Russian naval officer, who looked to be in his thirties, walked up and spoke in English.

"I am Lieutenant Vaslov of the Baltic Sea Fleet. I will be sitting at counsel table to assist you with the intricacies of Russian military law should you desire. The headphones will give you a translation of the proceedings."

"Thank you, Lieutenant," Zack Brewer said.

"I know who you are, Commander Brewer. Let me make this clear. I did not volunteer for this assignment. I was ordered to take it."

"Thank you anyway," Zack said, then turned to Pete. "Let's have a seat, sir."

Zack sat on the left of the table, Pete in the center, and the angry Russian officer sat to the right. Pete turned around to scan the large crowd. He hoped to see Masha Katovich. Something about her seemed comforting.

Instead, he saw faces that looked pale and angry. His eyes caught a familiar face. His executive officer, Frank Pippen, was seated two rows behind counsel table. To Frank's right, Lieutenant Darwin McCaffity, and to his right, Lieutenant Walt Brown.

How had he missed them when he walked in? His entire crew sat in five rows behind the defense table, heavily guarded by Russian soldiers on each side. Pete and Frank exchanged subtle smiles and nods. Then he remembered what the angry admiral told him in Moscow.

Your crew's fate will be tied to yours. If you are convicted, they will be convicted. And if you are acquitted, then they will be set free.

Pete broke eye contact with his exec. He looked at the still-empty prosecution table. Just behind it, a young pair of innocent eyes reached out and froze him.

Dima. The orphan on my sub. And beside Dima, all the other orphans sat in the row. They had other chaperones now. Masha Katovich was nowhere in sight.

"Put on your headset, Commander," Zack Brewer said.

Pete complied.

"All rise!"

There was a shuffling in the pews of the cathedral. The three old officers he had faced in Moscow walked in. Two younger army officers carrying briefcases, probably military lawyers, stood behind the prosecution table.

"Everyone may sit except the accused, his attorneys, and the crew of the USS *Honolulu*." The general sitting in the middle banged his gavel, then looked over at the admiral.

"Now, Commander Miranda, when we last spoke, I asked you how you would plead to the charges against you and you said you wanted an attorney. I see now that you have not only one attorney—but two. An American naval officer, and a fine member of the Russian Navy to provide you assistance. So I ask you again ... how do you plead?"

"I am Lieutenant Commander Zack Brewer of the United States Navy. I represent Commander Peter Miranda in these proceedings. To the charges and specifications, my client pleads ... not guilty!"

CHAPTER 29

The White House

Mr. President, USS *Charlotte* reports that the Egyptian freighter is turning east—from the North Sea into the Baltic Sea," Admiral John Ayers announced.

"The Baltic Sea? Why there?"

"I don't know, Mr. President," Ayers said. "At least it's headed away from England."

"Something's not adding up. Let's see the navigational charts."

"Aye, aye, Mr. President."

Admiral Ayers pointed his fingers. His aide rolled out the latest navigational chart.

"He's headed straight to Copenhagen," Secretary of State Mauney observed.

"Why would terrorists want to blow up Copenhagen?" the secretary of defense asked.

"Why do they murder innocent women and children in civilian office towers?" the vice president asked.

"Maybe Copenhagen because it's a Western capital," Secretary Mauney said.

"I can see London," Secretary Lopez said. "But Copenhagen makes no sense to me."

"Or maybe he's going through the Danish Straits and into the Baltic," Cynthia Hewitt, national security advisor, said.

Secretary Lopez spoke up. "The question, Mr. President, is whether we can afford to let that freighter get so close to a major Western capital. I remind you, sir, that you were prepared to take her out if she turned

toward London, and now she will pass within a few miles of Copenhagen if she remains on this course."

Mack scratched his head. "Secretary Mauney, are you advocating that I take military action now? You've been the one member of this cabinet who's opposed military action from the very beginning."

"That's your decision, Mr. President. But this freighter's proximity to Copenhagen makes me uneasy."

"I share Secretary Mauney's concerns," Secretary Lopez said, "but let's face it. Copenhagen isn't London. Britain means more to America than any other ally except possibly Israel."

"Sure. They could light the fuse on Copenhagen, but that makes no sense. We should hold off until we can get more information on this Egyptian skipper," Secretary Lopez continued. "I'll bet he's going into the Baltic to make an anonymous cargo transfer to another freighter—maybe Swedish or Finnish. You know a Swedish or Finnish freighter could sail into New York harbor without batting an eye, whereas an Egyptian freighter will garner some second looks. I say we keep tailing her, and when she initiates a cargo transfer, we surface the sub and have the SEAL team on the *Charlotte* board her."

"That's a plausible theory," the CIA director said.

"Why not board it now, Mr. President?" Cynthia Hewitt asked.

She had a good point. And what if millions died in Copenhagen because he failed to act? Mack again prayed silently for guidance.

"Because we're already in trouble for the perception that we sink unarmed freighters and because the freighter has done nothing illegal on the high seas that we're aware of." Why didn't that explanation take the knot out of his stomach? He turned to his CIA director. "Mr. Director, where's the dossier on this Egyptian captain?"

"We're working on it, Mr. President."

"Speed it up. I want to know everything about him. I want to know who his mamma was, who his daddy is, where he was educated, what groups he's been a member of ... the whole works."

"Yes, sir, Mr. President."

St. Nicholas Naval Cathedral
St. Petersburg, Russia

In the case of the People of the Russian Republic versus Commander Peter Miranda, on the charges of crimes against humanity and destruction of—and conspiracy to destroy—property of the Russian Republic, we will now hear from the prosecution."

A slim officer wearing the green dress uniform of the Russian Army rose to his feet. He stared for a second at Pete, and then turned and faced the three crusty officers sitting at the tables in the chancery of the cathedral.

"Generals. Admiral. I am Major Konstantin Andropov of the Russian Army. We gather today, in this great cathedral, a building dedicated to the great men of the sea who gave their lives for the motherland ... to see that justice is done.

"Russia is a great nation. We are at peace. True, we have our internal conflicts such as Chechnya, as every nation has such conflicts. But we are at peace.

"The question in this trial is whether our great and peaceful nation will extend protection to our civilian ships on the high seas from acts of aggression and piracy.

"Today, I am sad to report that one of our own ships, the freighter *Alexander Popovich*, has been sunk and its crew murdered by the heinous war crimes committed by the defendant and his crew."

The major turned directly to Pete and pointed. "This, gentlemen, is Commander Peter Miranda. He is the captain of the American submarine *Honolulu*, and it is he who ordered the unjustified and indiscriminate attack on a civilian Russian freighter—a freighter which had no means of defending itself.

"This man is an international terrorist of the darkest order. He violated international laws and the law of the high seas by sailing his submarine through the Bosphorus submerged. He attacked a civilian ship, taking the lives of innocent Russians who were only doing their jobs on the sea to try and earn a living for their families."

Andropov turned back to the panel. "There are several people in this courtroom today that I would like to introduce. Ludmilla Batsakov, please stand."

Pete looked around. A stout, matronly lady with white hair and a severely wrinkled face stood in the row just behind the orphans. Andropov waved his hand grandly as he turned back to the panel. "This, gentlemen, is Ludmilla Batsakov—the mother of *Kapitán* Yuri Mikalvich Batsakov."

Wailing and crying erupted from the woman at the mention of her son's name. Two Russian soldiers rushed to her aid, offering tissues and water.

"And I remind you, gentlemen," Andropov said over the woman's dramatic wailing, "that *Kapitán* Batsakov was not the only innocent Russian to die. I present to you the family of the deceased crewmembers of the *Alexander Popovich*." They stood in the row just beside the Batsakov woman—an assortment of wives, mothers, and girlfriends—and children. More groaning and crying arose from the choir of the bereaved, as Andropov turned back to the panelists again.

"And finally, the most horrific part of all this: This terrorist tried to murder a group of innocent orphans on board the *Alexander Popovich*." He turned and surveyed the first row behind counsel table. "Stand, children."

Pete caught Dima's eyes as the orphans, some of whom were trembling at all the attention, rose sheepishly as a group just behind the prosecution's table. "As a result of this man's acts, these little ones were subject to smoke and fire, to water and oil, were thrown into the sea, where they were rescued by one heroic Russian sailor, Aleksey Anatolyvich. Please stand, Aleksey Anatolyvich." Aleksey stood there, looking down at his feet. "He single-handedly got them into lifeboats and saved them all.

"At that point this man" — Andropov pointed again at Pete — "came up with another sinister idea. Seeing that the orphans surviving could be a witness to what happened, he did what terrorists do as a matter of routine. He took these young orphans hostage. He surfaced, captured them all at gunpoint, then dove under the sea again, where he made a run south, trying to escape through the Bosphorus.

"Ah, but it was not to be." Andropov wagged his index finger back and forth like a windshield wiper in a rainstorm. "For you see, the Navy of the Russian Republic, the Black Sea Fleet, put a noose around the terrorist's neck and forced him to the surface. And only because of the heroism of our Navy do these children live today!"

Applause broke out in the courtroom. Andropov waited for the applause to subside, then continued.

"But today we can right the wrongs committed by the terrorist and his crew. That this ... this ... man committed these crimes is indisputable." Andropov turned around and shot Pete an evil glare. "The only real issue is what shall we do about him? *Hmm?*"

He turned back to the three senior officers. "Miranda must be convicted and he must be executed. Miranda's crewmen likewise must be executed. This must be done swiftly and efficiently.

"Thank you."

Pete had watched Zack Brewer on television during the Quasay court-martial. Zack had the reputation for being one of the best trial lawyers not only in the Navy, but in the world. But this was different. These rules were skewed. Surely even Zack was now in over his head.

Zack strode over to the podium, displaying a confident air, without a single note.

"General Prokofiev"—he looked at the officer in the middle of the tribunal—"distinguished officers of this court-martial, and the great citizens of the Russian Republic, I bring you greetings on behalf of the people of the United States of America.

"Although we stand here this day in disagreement over the facts surrounding the sinking of the *Alexander Popovich*, we choose to first embrace something that we do not disagree upon. We choose first, gentlemen, to embrace the common heritage of our peoples. It is a common heritage that came together in the twentieth century to suppress the most vicious threat to freedom ever imposed by man. The great and noble sacrifices of your armies on hallowed ground at places like Stalingrad—and our armies on the beaches of Normandy and in the terrible blizzard of Bastogne—was blood spilled, Russian and American blood. Our blood was spilled in a common and eternal effort to rid the world forever of the oppressive Nazi jackboot.

"We had our differences in the so-called Cold War—yes—but never was a shot fired. And in the end, we came together to fight yet another enemy."

Zack paused, looked at the prosecutor, and then resumed. "That common enemy ... was radical Islam." Zack paused once again, this time to sip a glass of water. "Muslim terrorists brought our buildings down in New York in 2001, and Muslim terrorists murdered 186 of your children in the Beslan Massacre in 2004.

"The airliners that crashed into the World Trade Center were registered as American airliners. They became weapons of mass destruction in the hands of Muslim terrorists, yet the American flag was painted on them all.

"And likewise, gentlemen, the *Alexander Popovich*, though flying under the great flag of this great nation, I am sad to say, had also become a weapon of mass destruction whose captain had sold out to Muslim terrorists for money."

A half second delay for the translation. Then murmuring arose in the courtroom. Then loud, angry voices. The woman identified as Ludmilla Batsakov, Captain Batsakov's mother, was standing, shaking her fists at Zack, and screaming something in Russian.

"Come to order." General Prokofiev, the chief judge sitting in the middle, whapped his gavel. "Sit down or you will be arrested and put on trial for public disorder!" Another *whap*. Russian soldiers moved towards pockets of standing protestors. "Commander Brewer, I warn you that in Russia, slander is a felony. You are a guest in this country at the invitation of the Russian government. But be forewarned that you may not violate our laws without running the risk of arrest and prosecution yourself. Do you understand?"

Zack Brewer looked squarely into the eye of the general. "I respect your laws, General Prokofiev. But we will prove what I have said is true. Our government believes that the freighter was carrying plutonium—weapons-grade plutonium that was illegally stolen from your Army by Islamic Chechen terrorists in the Caucasus Mountains. In the end, we are confident that Commander Miranda and his crew will be acquitted."

That translation brought another eruption in the courtroom, followed by more whapping from the general.

Zack turned and walked to the counsel table and sat. Pete did not know how Zack planned to proceed.

But this he did know.

Zack Brewer had nerves of steel.

Office of the president of the Russian Republic
Staraya Square, Moscow

Three hours later

President Vitaly Evtimov wanted to scream and yell. His problem at the moment, however, was that the man he wanted to choke, former Defense Minister Giorgy Alexeevich Popkov, was already dead.

"How do the Americans know about the missing plutonium?" President Evtimov slammed his fist on the large wooden desk. "We took every precaution against releasing this information! Now Brewer makes this announcement in the court-martial for the entire world to hear! Someone must have leaked. I demand to know who."

"Perhaps Brewer is bluffing!" the president's chief of staff noted.

"How could he bluff about such a thing?" the foreign minister asked. "He was right about the plutonium missing, he was right about who stole it, and he was right about where the theft took place."

The president sipped vodka. "But if he is right about what happened, could he be right also about the plutonium being on a ship?"

Foreign Minister Kotenkov addressed that. "We were assured by Giorgy Alexeevich that the plutonium had been taken to Chechnya."

"Giorgy Alexeevich!" Evtimov thundered. "He was useless as a defense minister. And he's useless as a dead man. He was useful only in delivering Aslambek Kadyrov the materials he needs to build a Chechen bomb."

"Perhaps the Americans are right," Kotenkov added, "perhaps the plutonium is at the bottom of the sea. If they are right, then we must know."

Evtimov turned to his chief of staff. "Contact Admiral Voynavich. Tell him I want the Black Sea Fleet to find this ship on the bottom of the sea, and then find out if it has plutonium on board."

"Yes, Comrade President."

"And issue a statement denying that any plutonium is missing."

The Al Alamein
100 miles south of Gotland Island
The Baltic Sea

Captain Sadir looked around the bridge at the men who had volunteered for this mission—the men who had eagerly volunteered for martyrdom. Sadir looked over at Salman Dudayev and nodded.

Dudayev nodded back.

It was time.

"Gentlemen, I bring you here today to the bridge of this great ship because each of you has volunteered to give your lives in what will be the greatest act of jihad in history."

He relished their fierce, piercing eyes. These were the eyes of true warriors.

"You all know that we sailed into the Black Sea and took valuable cargo from the Russian freighter. You all know what that cargo was, and you all know that there is a great weapon to be used to Allah's glory in the belly of this ship.

"What you do not know, at least not yet, is our final destination. I know that all kinds of rumors have floated around the crew. Some have hoped for New York. Some thought London. And believe me, when we sailed through the English Channel, I felt tempted to change our mission and pay back the British for being America's footstool in their satanic war against holy Islam."

Enthusiastic nodding from at least half his officers.

"But we have another mission. And until now, only Mr. Dudayev and I have known that mission. But now is the time for you to be brought into the fold.

"At this point, we are approximately two hundred fifty miles southwest of the Gulf of Finland." Their eyes glued to him. "When we get there, the *Al Alamein* will turn due east. We will sail past Estonia to our south and Finland to our north. We will sail until we reach Kotlin Island. This island is about twenty miles west of the main part of St. Petersburg. But we will not stop there.

"Igor, the map please."

"From Kotlin Island we will sail past the causeways and sail to the mouth of the Neva River, the prize jewel of the city. We will never dock, but instead, from this bridge, I will initiate the process that will turn our ship into the largest hydrogen bomb in the history of the world."

Applause, cheering, and fist shaking.

"Through us, Allah will repay the godless Russians a hundred thousand fold for the blood and carnage they have poured on our country.

The entire city of St. Petersburg shall be vaporized, and the radiation shall kill millions of Russians hundreds of miles away, all the way to Moscow!"

More cheering and shouting.

"Those who are left behind shall demand a permanent withdrawal of the Russians from Chechnya, and shall demand freedom for our country while we dance with a thousand maidens in paradise!"

"Glory to Allah for this privilege!" one of them shouted.

"And blessed be the prophet Mohammed, peace be upon him!" another said.

Sadir raised his hands. "Glory to Allah indeed. Now let us all return to our stations and finish the work we have begun."

CHAPTER 30

The White House

Mr. President," Admiral John Ayers spoke with an elevated urgency in his voice, "USS *Charlotte* reports that the *Al Alamein* is now turning east from the Baltic Sea into the Gulf of Finland."

"When?" Mack asked.

"Within the last hour, sir."

"Let's see the charts."

"Yes, sir."

The president, along with the vice president, the secretaries of defense and state, the White House chief of staff, the director of central intelligence, and the national security advisor looked on as Admiral Ayers spoke.

"Right now, the *Al Alamein* is about one hundred twenty-five miles southwest of Helsinki and some three hundred miles from St. Petersburg."

"What's going on here?" Mack wondered out loud.

"At least it's not London or New York," the secretary of defense muttered.

"Why would they want to threaten Helsinki?" Vice President Surber asked. "Sure, Finland is a member of NATO, but they had their shot at London, for goodness sakes."

"Maybe," Secretary Mauney said, "we're all off base and there's nothing on that freighter but freight."

"Surely they're not targeting St. Petersburg?" Vice President Surber said.

"That makes no sense," said Cynthia Hewitt. "Neither al-Qaeda nor the Council of Ishmael seems to care much about the Russians. They want to kill Westerners. I can't imagine them using a nuclear device—if that's what they have—on an insignificant target like that."

"Unless this is somehow all related to Chechnya," Vice President Surber noted.

"Possible but unlikely, Mr. Vice President," the CIA director noted.

"Do we have a dossier on the Egyptian skipper yet?" Mack asked.

"Not yet, but we're still working on it, sir," the CIA director responded.

"That's not good enough! I need info on this skipper," the president said. "And I need to find out what the target is! We need *something* that supports our suspicions that this freighter is carrying that nuclear fuel!" He eyed his CIA director. "Director Winstead, put the heat on your people for that dossier. That may give us a clue. Remember, time may be running out."

"Yes, sir."

St. Nicholas Naval Cathedral
St. Petersburg, Russia

Television lights, cameras, and media representatives from every major nation dotted the packed, ornate, cathedral-turned-courthouse.

The three Russian military judges had been gone an hour now, and Zack wondered if the enlongated recess was extended to prepare his arrest warrant for violation of the Russian slander laws.

Zack sipped the chlorine-heavy Russian water. He glanced over at Pete Miranda, who looked pale.

Zack could handle about anything the American judicial system could throw at him. In America, in the military justice system, he knew the rules.

But this?

This was an international sideshow designed to win over wavering nations back into Russia's camp by making America look bad, and everybody knew it.

If that's the way the Russians wanted to play, so be it.

"All persons stand," the translation came through the headphones, as the three grim-faced officers made their way from the side doors in the front of the cathedral, through a cascade of flashes, to their tables. Good. No arrest warrant for Zack.

"Is the prosecution ready to proceed?"

"We are," Major Peter Andropov announced.

"Very well. Call your first witness."

Now. Zack rose to his feet. "Excuse me, General Smirnov."

"What is it, Commander Brewer?"

"My apologies, Comrade General, but the defense has a motion, sir."

"What kind of a motion?"

"With greatest deference to the tribunal, the defense at this time makes a motion to dismiss."

After his statement was translated, angry shouts in Russian erupted all over the courtroom. Zack looked over his shoulder. They were standing—angry bearded men and women in frumpy dresses—yelling and shaking their fists in the air. Their eyes were ablaze.

He turned and looked back at the tribunal. General Smirnov's black eyes burned down upon him. The general rapped his gavel on the desk and yelled something in Russian at the tumultuous gallery. The crowd settled down.

"And what gives you the right to make such a motion at this time, Commander?"

"With all due respect, General, the Geneva Accords gives me that right."

"What do you mean?"

"General, Article 17 provides that no physical or mental torture, nor any other form of coercion, may be inflicted on prisoners of war to secure from them information of any kind whatever. Prisoners of war who refuse to answer may not be threatened, insulted, or exposed to unpleasant or disadvantageous treatment of any kind.

"This tribunal seeks, by this trial, to force information from my client that he is not required to give."

The general slammed his fist on that table. "But your client is no prisoner of war. There is no war between our countries, at least not yet. Plus he has not been tortured."

"I disagree with you, General. The Geneva Accords provide a broad definition of what constitutes a *prisoner of war*."

Zack raised his voice to speak over the uproar in the courtroom.

"In fact, Article 4 of the Third Geneva Convention protects captured military personnel, and even some civilians and guerrilla fighters. It applies from the moment a prisoner is captured until he is released or repatriated.

"One of the main provisions requires that a prisoner only give his name, date of birth, rank, and service number.

"This tribunal puts my client in the position of having to give more information than just his name, date of birth, rank, and service number in order to defend himself. And that, General, is a violation of international law and is a violation of the Geneva Accords. There-fore, this action should be dismissed and my client and his crew should be afforded full protection to which they are entitled pursuant to the Geneva Accords. I have a brief here, with copies in Russian, English, French, German, Italian, and Spanish, which outlines our position under the norms of international law." Zack waved copies of the briefs in the air for the international press to see.

The Russian translation rang throughout the courtroom. Another murmuring arose from the crowd. Journalists furiously scribbled notes, as the three flag officers conferred among themselves. General Prokofiev, in particular, was red-faced, and was banging his fists on the table in the front of the courtroom.

Zack did not expect them to grant his motion. He was hoping against hope. But raising the Geneva Accords, he hoped, would at least slow down the steamroller. Maybe, just maybe he could buy the U.S. Navy enough time to find this mysterious Egyptian freighter—if such a freighter really existed. All he could do was stall. And pray.

General Smirnov looked out at Zack and snarled, "Commander Brewer, you may approach with your brief. Bring us the copies in Russian, please."

"Yes, sir, General." Zack picked up three of the copies that had been translated into Russian and walked across the marble floors to the table, where the three officers sat.

They each met him with icy stares as he approached. He nodded at each, laid the briefs on the tables before them, then quickly pivoted around into the glare of television lights and returned to counsel table.

They flipped through the pages, shook their heads, and huddled again. Their below-the-breath comments appeared heated, almost as if they were arguing with one another.

Finally General Smirnov stood. "Commander Brewer, the panel has considered your motion and we find it to be without merit. However, out of our great respect for the Geneva Conventions, and because the Russian Federation is a party to those accords, we are going to take a recess to study the matter overnight and to confer with legal counsel."

"Thank you, General."

"But let me warn you, Commander, that we will tolerate no more frivolous motions."

Zack did not respond.

The panel rose and walked out of the room.

The White House

"At least Brewer bought us some time," the president remarked, "which is something we don't have much of."

"They're sensitive about being accused of violating the Geneva Conventions," Secretary Mauney said. "At least they want to give the *appearance* of considering the motion, even if they have already denied it. Great strategy by Brewer."

"Zack's our best," Secretary Lopez remarked. "That's why we sent him."

"That's the truth," Admiral Ayers added.

"Director Winstead, do you have that dossier yet?" the president asked, as CIA Director Mitch Winstead walked into the Oval Office with a briefcase in hand. He sat in a circle of chairs occupied by the usual group. Mack noticed that he was drawing anxious stares.

"Yes, sir, Mr. President. And I think I finally have some answers."

"Let's have it."

The CIA director extracted papers from his briefcase, made eye contact with the president, then looked down and began reading bullet points. "This is from sources inside the Egyptian Merchant Marine. Captain Hosni Sadir was born in Cairo. He served in the Egyptian Navy, where he commanded a destroyer homeported out of Alexandria. Our background shows that he is of Chechen origin and has ties there.

"His grandparents were deported by Stalin with other Islamic Chechens during World War II, and after that, Sadir's family emigrated to Egypt.

"Despite all that, the family has maintained very close ties to their relatives back in Chechnya. In 1997, when Maskhadov introduced Islamic law to Chechnya, Sadir filed paperwork to move back to Chechnya. But then, the Russians killed Maskhadov. Then many of Sadir's Chechen relatives were massacared in a Russian attack on a mosque in Grozny."

There was a brief pause.

"So Captain Sadir doesn't like the Russians," National Security Advisor Cynthia Hewitt said.

"That's an understatement, Miss Hewitt," Director Winstead replied. "It gets worse."

"Great," Mack said. "Let's hear it."

"We got a copy of the ship's passenger manifest. One of the passengers is a native Chechen named Salman Dudayev."

"Doesn't ring a bell," the secretary of state said.

"Dudayev is an American-trained physicist—he studied at MIT—who had close ties to Maskhadov. Although Chechnya has been considered as Russia's problem, we've maintained a file on this guy because his education and political affiliations puts him in a category of persons who could be very dangerous if weapons-grade uranium or plutonium ever fell into his hands."

"You are sure Dudayev is on that ship?" the president asked.

Winstead nodded his head. "Mr. President, we paid a ton of money to get that manifest. We have absolutely no reason to doubt its accuracy, sir."

"Dear Lord, help us." Mack rubbed his temples. "Is everybody here thinking what I'm thinking?"

"It's St. Petersburg," Secretary Lopez said.

"It's gotta be," Secretary Mauney nodded in rare agreement with the SECDEF. "This Masha Katovich girl is proving to be reliable."

"We've got a lot of people there," Vice President Surber said.

It came again—that feeling that someone had tossed an icepack on the back of Mack Williams' neck.

"Should we notify the Russians?" Cynthia Hewitt asked.

"Won't do any good," Mack said. "By the time we convince them that they're in danger, St. Petersburg and our crew would already be incinerated."

"And given our current political climate with them," Secretary Mauney added, "Moscow would blame a nuclear attack against St. Petersburg on us."

"Precisely," Vice President Surber added.

"Which means we can expect a nuclear retaliation against the United States," Defense Secretary Lopez said.

The secretary of state nodded his head in agreement. "We've got to sink this freighter, and we must do it now."

"And lose the evidence that we need to prove our case to the Russians that we did not sink an innocent civilian freighter?" the national security advisor asked. "We need that evidence for the world to see."

"Admiral Ayers," the president said, "can *Charlotte* stop this freighter and board it without sinking it?"

"Yes, sir. We have a contingency plan for that option."

"Let's hear it."

"We disarm our Mark-48 torps and fire into the ship's propeller. If we get a lucky shot, we disable the prop, leaving her dead in the water. We surface our SEAL team and board the ship."

"What happens if they blow the ship before our SEALs can take control?" Vice President Surber asked.

"That could happen," Admiral Ayers said, "but they may take a little time to figure out what happened. Hopefully, it's enough."

"How close are they to St. Petersburg, Admiral?"

"Close, sir. About thirty miles west of Kotlin Island. Put it this way; they're close enough that if they blew a nuclear device now, depending on the size of the device, it could devastate St. Petersburg. Depending on weather patterns, nuclear fallout could kill hundreds of thousands living along the Gulf of Finland. That includes the city of Helsinki, which is less than two hundred miles to the west, and beyond that, the city of Stockholm, another couple of hundred miles to the west and across the Baltic Sea. The weather will determine who dies, Mr. President. But unlike the Bikini Atoll tests or our tests in Nevada in the early sixties, this is a highly populated area. Hundreds of thousands will die, sir, and we have no control over the weather.

"We've got a narrow window, Mr. President," Ayers continued. "Whatever you order, sir, we've got to act fast or we simply won't have enough time."

"I say sink her, Mr. President," the vice president said. "We're looking at nuclear holocaust if that ship blows."

"And we might be looking at nuclear war if we don't produce that plutonium to convince the Russians we didn't sink one of their civilian ships," the secretary of defense said.

Mack thought about that. *Lord, make my decision the right one.*

"Secretary Lopez, send the orders. Have the *Charlotte* unarm the Mark-48s. Attack her propeller. Stop her in the water. SEAL team is ordered to board and secure the ship.

"That is all."

CHAPTER 31

The USS Charlotte
Gulf of Finland

"Skipper, radio reports emergency message from Washington!"

"Let's go, XO!" Puck shouted to Todd Swanson. "Follow me! Officer-of-the-deck, take the conn!"

"I have the conn, aye, sir."

Puck bounded out of the control room, with his executive officer in tow. In the radio room, his radio officer was waiting for him with message in hand. Puck ripped the message from the officer's hand and flattened it out in front of a high-wattage reading light.

EMERGENCY ACTION MESSAGE

FROM: NATIONAL MILITARY COMMAND CENTER — WASHINGTON, D.C.
TO: USS *CHARLOTTE*
SUBJECT: ACTION MESSAGE

REMARKS:

Intelligence assessments reports Egyptian freighter *Al Alamein* probably transporting weapons-grade plutonium stolen from Russian arsenal.

Intelligence further reports Chechen nuclear physicist may be onboard.

Al Alamein may be transporting active thermonuclear device and may be planning suicide nuclear attack on St. Petersburg, Russia.

USS *Charlotte* ordered to disable *Al Alamein* with unarmed torpedoes.

SEAL team ordered to seize control of vessel and any nuclear contraband potentially on board.

Proceed with extreme caution and stealth. In the event of large nuclear blast, the *Al Alamein* is now within range to destroy St. Petersburg.

Execute orders immediately.

Captain Puckett handed the message to Todd Swanson. "XO, sound the alarm. Man battle stations. Let's get moving!"

The Al Alamein
Gulf of Finland

From the bridge of his ship, Captain Hosni Sadir brought his binoculars to his eyes and scanned the eastern horizon, just out front of the bow of his ship. A gray haze hung low over the water in the distance.

Sadir dropped the binoculars and pointed out. "It's out there somewhere. Kotlin Island. We should be able to see it soon. It's actually part of St. Petersburg, you know."

"How far are we, *Kapitán*?" Salman asked.

"Less than twenty miles to Kotlin Island."

"I cannot contain my excitement," Salman said. "We could throw the switch now, and with the power of our bomb, we would destroy everything within a hundred miles. We could wipe out the city of St. Petersburg even now."

Hosni saw the fire in the young physicist's eyes. "You have done well, my friend."

"*We* have done well, *Kapitán*."

Hosni brought the binoculars back to his eyes. The haze was fading now. Still, no sign of the low-lying land mass that would mark the entrance to the waterways surrounding St. Petersburg. "Soon, my friend, 9/11 shall be but a footnote on the ash heap of history!" He handed the binoculars to Salman.

"We are going to kill millions of them, *Kapitán*." Salman peered through the binoculars. "Allah has brought us this far. We're so close and we can now accomplish our mission. Perhaps we should pull the switch now."

Hosni touched Salman's shoulders. "Patience, my young friend. Care for a cigarette?"

"Thank you," Salman said, as Hosni flicked a red Camel from his pack and handed it to Hosni.

"Light?"

"Thank you, *Kapitán*."

Hosni ignited his butane lighter and held the flame out. Salman sucked in. "We will burn them alive either way, Salman, whether we pull the switch now or tomorrow." He took a satisfying draw. The nicotine jump-started his adrenaline. "But let history show, Salman, that we sailed the *Al Alamein* right into the Neva River, brought her up to the very banks of St. Petersburg, and then pulled the switch. I want to see with my eyes all that we shall vaporize."

St. Nicholas Naval Cathedral
St. Petersburg, Russia

At the front right of the crowded courtroom, Pete Miranda sat between Zack Brewer and his detailed interpreter and Russian defense counsel, Lieutenant Vaslov of the Baltic Sea Fleet. Across the aisle, Major Peter Andropov, the Russian Army prosecutor, sat steely eyed writing notes on a pad.

"They should be back at any moment," Zack whispered over the slight roar coming from the back of the courtroom.

"What do you expect?" Pete asked.

"I expect they will rule on our motion or at least address it in some way. I don't expect them to dismiss the case."

"Some sort of face-saving position?"

"Exactly," Zack said.

Lieutenant Commander Zack Brewer was an amazing naval officer, Pete thought. The JAG officer carried a courageous air like Daniel from the Bible. And like Daniel, Zack marched into the lion's den, and with some fancy legal footwork about the Geneva Conventions, at least delayed an inevitable mauling.

Still, Pete resolved that a mauling was inevitable — that he was going to die. Something told him that his entire crew, and even his JAG officer defense counsel, were all in mortal danger. He was ready if that should happen, but the thought of never seeing Coley and Hannah again was a dagger in his soul.

"All rise!"

The three flag officers of the tribunal marched in bearing wrinkled and angry-looking faces.

"Be seated," General Igor Smirnov snapped. Wearing thick plastic black-rimmed glasses, he leaned forward at the defense table. "Commander Brewer, we have considered your motion concerning the Geneva Accords." Smirnov paused, almost as if expecting an answer from Brewer. "We shall delay a ruling pending further study and advice by Russian international law attorneys." A slight smile crept across Zack's face. Perhaps they had bought more time, Pete thought.

"However," Smirnov continued, "we cannot delay these proceedings. Therefore, we shall allow the prosecution to continue its case and rule upon Commander Brewer's motion at the end of the trial."

Zack rose. "Objection, General. It is this *process* that violates Articles 4 and 17 of the Geneva Accords." An explosion of flashes followed.

The red-faced Russian glared at Zack. "Sit down, Commander, or our guards will remove you from the courtroom and leave your client's defense to Lieutenant Vaslov. I remind you that you are a guest of this country, not a member of its bar."

"I will sit, but I will not withdraw my objection," Zack barked.

"You are in contempt, Commander."

"Hold me in contempt if you'd like," Zack snapped. "Proceeding under these circumstances is contemptuous to the Geneva Accords, and every established principle of international law."

"The guards will escort Commander Brewer to the temporary holding facility. This court shall stand in recess for one hour as we work to ensure that the commander receives a full briefing of the procedures and rules of Russian military courts."

"All rise."

Pete rose as Zack shucked off the hands of the Russian guards and walked with them voluntarily up into the chancel area, where he disappeared behind a door.

USS Charlotte
Gulf of Finland

What's our range to the target?" Commander Puckett asked.

"The freighter has now opened up a distance of four thousand two hundred yards. That gap is widening, sir."

"Good," Puckett said. "That gives us some firing room. Are the Mark-48s unarmed?"

"Aye, Captain. Torps one and three are unarmed and ready for firing."

"Very well," Puck said. "Fire torp one."

"Firing torp one."

A swoosh rushed through the boat, as the first Mark-48 torpedo, weighing 3400 pounds and nineteen feet long, popped out the forward torpedo tube and lunged into the water.

"Fire torp three."

"Firing torp three."

Another swooshing pulsation followed.

"XO, status of SEAL team?"

"Ready to go in the water at your command, sir," Lieutenant Commander Todd Swanson said.

"Very well," Puck said. "Torp one range to target."

"Torp one range to target thirty-eight hundred yards and closing."

"Torp three range to target."

"Torp three range to target thirty-nine hundred yards and closing."

The Al Alamein
Gulf of Finland

Kapitán, we are picking up FM radio from Kotlin Island and St. Petersburg!" the radio officer announced.

"Good." Dadir felt himself smile. "We are nearly at point-blank range."

Salman Dudayev burst onto the bridge, out of breath. His face was red and contorted.

"*Kapitán*, we may have a problem."

"What, Salman? Is something wrong with our bomb?"

"No, *Kapitán*. I have been monitoring Russian broadcasts on the radio," Salman said. "The Russians are trying an American submarine captain in St. Petersburg for sinking the freighter *Alexander Popovich* — the same freighter that we got the plutonium from."

"What? Are you sure?"

"Yes, *Kapitán*. Apparently the Americans sunk her with a submarine in the Black Sea."

Sadir thought for a second. "The Black Sea? That is impossible. There are no American submarines in the Black Sea."

"It is all over Russian radio and also the BBC, *Kapitán*. Somehow, they did it. Somehow, the Americans must have discovered that the plutonium was once aboard the Russian freighter."

Sadir thought about that. "Even if this is true, the Americans sank the *Alexander Popovich* in the Black Sea. We are now a long way from the Black Sea. It appears that the Americans have sunk the wrong ship."

A violent shaking rocked the stern of the freighter, as if the ship had been hit by a giant sledgehammer. Men on the bridge staggered from the vibration. That was followed by a second shaking.

"What was that?" Sadir demanded. "A collision with a ship? What is our depth here?"

"Depth one-three-zero fathoms, sir," the helmsman said. "We must have struck something that we missed on the radar."

"Bridge, engineering," the voice came over the bridge loudspeaker from the engine room.

"What is it?" Captain Sadir asked.

"Sir, we've lost propulsion."

"I will be right there." Sadir motioned to Dudayev. "Salman, come with me."

Captain Sadir stormed out of the bridge, headed for the engine room.

They moved swiftly through the icy Baltic water.

In black wetsuits and black fins, twelve United States Navy SEALs glided under the dark hull of the disabled freighter.

On their backs, they carried oxygen tanks and weapons. Some carried flotation devices to be deployed, while others carried lightweight harpoon guns with rigging line.

Lieutenant Michael W. Reel, United States Navy, was their leader.

Making handsignals illuminated by underwater flashlights, Reel directed his team members into a semicircle just below the aftsection of the stern.

It was time.

Reel pointed to his second in command, Lieutenant JG Leo Maloney, then pointed at his watch.

Reel gave Maloney a full five fingers, signaling to set stopwatches at five minutes. Maloney complied, then clicked the stem of his watch, setting off the five-minute countdown. Maloney mimicked his leader.

Reel followed with a thumbs-up, and the SEAL team parted—five SEALs following Reel to the waters off the starboard side of the ship, the other five following Maloney to the port side.

Captain Sadir rushed into the ship's engine room. The whine of turning gears and spinning shafts made it difficult to hear. Crew members were scurrying about, and the ship's chief engineer was turning a valve with a wrench. "What is the matter?" Sadir demanded.

"Something is wrong." The chief engineer laid down the wrench and raised his voice above the level of the noise.

Sadir nervously struck a cigarette. "Elaborate."

"Our engines are spinning," the engineer said, "but the screw is not pushing us through the water."

Salman Dudayev spoke up. "Could this all be related to the sinking of the *Alexander Popovich*? Have the Americans found us?"

"I have considered that," Sadir said. "But we are not sinking. If the Americans know about us and wanted to torpedo us, we would be at the bottom of the ocean now."

"I do not like the feel of it," Salman said.

Sadir turned to his engineer. "What are our options?"

The engineer cast a worried glance. "If this were a matter of repairing our engines, our options would be good, *Kapitán*. But the propeller is in the water. It is hard to access. We would need to send a diving party overboard to assess the problem. And even then, we may have to call for assistance. We are not prepared for major underwater repairs."

Sadir considered that. He could not afford to radio for help. That would attract too much attention. And if he drifted in the sea lanes for too long, he would attract attention like a sitting duck.

"Salman, what would be the effects on St. Petersburg if we blow the ship from here?"

The physicist's eyes lit. "*Kapitán*, we have constructed a five-megaton nuclear device in the bowels of your ship. When we detonate this device, within ten seconds, the fireball will be over three miles in diameter! Fifty seconds after the explosion, the blast wave will reach the shore of St. Petersburg, just thirty-six miles away.

"When it hits the shores of St. Petersburg, it will destroy or damage even the most heavily fortified concrete buildings and kill most of its inhabitants! And then there is the tremendous radioactive fallout, which will be intensified by the fact that we are blowing the bomb out on the water."

Perhaps Salman was right.

Perhaps they should blow the ship right now.

Sadir looked at his engineer. "Send a diving party overboard to examine the screw. I want your report back within the hour. If this job is irreparable, or if we have to request assistance, we will blow the ship from here."

"Yes, *Kapitán*."

Lieutenant Mike Reel popped out of the water, just beside the starboard hull. He looked up at the side of the ship as the heads of Petty Officers May, McCants, Williams, Manuel, and Felton popped up out of the water in a semicircle around him.

On the left side of the ship, Reel knew that another circle of Navy SEALs, the squadron headed by Lieutenant JG Leo Maloney, was bobbing in the water, waiting for the time to deliver a coordinated strike against the rogue freighter.

Reel gave a thumbs-up, which was reciprocated by his group. The SEALs were ready.

Reel checked his watch. Ten seconds. Nine seconds. Eight. Seven ...

Floating in the water on the left side of the crippled ship, Maloney watched the countdown on his watch.

Five. Four. Three. Two. One.

"Now."

Pow. Pow. Pow. Pow.

Lightweight harpoon guns shot steel hooks upward, stringing rope from the water up to the gunwales of the ship.

"All secure," announced Petty Officers Black, Doherty, Perkins, Jordan, and Worthy.

"Let's go," Maloney ordered.

The SEALs dropped their oxygen tanks in the water, then, like Batman and Robin, began pulling themselves up the rope, rising up the side of the ship.

Maloney was the first to reach the top. Already, Lieutenant Reel had scampered onto the deck, and his men, all in black wetsuits and carrying knives and rifles, were gathering just across the ship.

The SEALs had not been discovered. Not yet anyway.

That would change.

St. Nicholas Naval Cathedral
St. Petersburg, Russia

What's going on? Pete wondered, as he sat alone with his Russian-appointed counsel, Lieutenant Peter Vaslov, at the table in the front of the courtroom. Zack Brewer had not returned to counsel table, at least not yet, and Pete wondered if he would ever see Zack again.

Probably not.

Perhaps this was the beginning of the end. He looked out the windows of the great cathedral. The weather was turning uglier. Clouds darkened, threatening rain, or even hail.

Pete turned and glanced at his crew. They were all there, sitting on the rows between the stone-faced Russian guards. Frank, Walt, Darwin, the Bloodhound.

He'd seen their look before. Their eyes begged for leadership—for a command decision that would suddenly make all this go away. They were looking to him for answers, but he had no answers, other than to wait and die.

Pete could bear their faces no more. He looked away, only to find the stares of the orphans that had been on board the *Alexander Popovich* and then the *Honolulu*. Theirs were the looks of confusion—of fear. He felt a surging rage that the Russians would require them to be here for theater and political show. Then his eyes caught the face of the boy named Dima.

The boy's eyes—they looked almost crossed—were magnified by the gawky glasses on his face. These eyes he had seen before. They were the eyes of a son looking at a father figure. How strange—these longing eyes of the orphan. And then, it hit him. The orphan felt a bond with the man who had rescued him and Masha from the sea.

His son, Coley, had once looked at him this way.

Pete turned away, lest the international media spot the tears flooding his eyes.

The Al Alamein
Gulf of Finland

Salman Dudayev looked up. Captain Sadir was climbing the ladder from the engine room to the main deck of the ship. Salman was under him and had just stepped onto the ladder when he heard Sadir yelling, "Who are you? What are you doing on my ship?"

The physicist double-stepped up the ladder behind the captain, quickly reaching the open air of the main deck.

Waving a pistol in his hand, Captain Sadir turned toward the stern area of the ship, toward a group of ten wet, dripping frogmen who had appeared out of the sea.

"Get off of my ship!" Shots rang out from the pistol. The frogmen ducked under and behind boxes and crates on the stern area and fired back. Bullets whined and ricocheted off the ship's steel superstructure.

Suddenly the captain's head exploded like a burst watermelon. His body flopped to the deck, pumping a stream of blood from the head wound.

Salman crouched low, and then took off across the deck, towards the hatch and the interior ladder that led back up to the bridge.

"You! Freeze!" He recognized the English from his days at MIT. Salman ignored the command. He sprinted through the sounds of bullets ricocheting through the steel superstructure. Salman ducked into the passageway and headed up the ladder.

The thunder of stampeding feet rumbled in pursuit behind Salman's back. He was a scientist, not an athlete, and they were closing fast.

To the bridge. He had to get to the bridge. He had to reach the detonator.

Leo, take your men below," Lieutenant Mike Reel yelled at Lieutenant JG Leo Maloney. Maloney's men went down the hatch. Reel and his men sprinted after the man that got away.

"Stop! Halt!" Reel yelled. Reel was closing fast, but the man was not responding. From the rear, the man resembled the profile photographs of the Chechen physicist, Dudayev, that the SEALs had studied, but Reel couldn't be sure. The only thing Reel was sure of at the moment, as he scrambled across the deck, was this. The man wasn't stopping and he was heading in the direction of the bridge.

He was also sure that they were close enough to St. Petersburg that a nuclear fireball of sufficient magnitude would engulf or destroy the city. And the crew of a United States nuclear submarine was being held in that city.

"Stop!" Reel closed to within about ten feet of the man and squeezed the trigger of his Uzi. A burst of machinegun fire shot out over the sea. The man kept running, then bounded up a ladder headed directly for a section of the bridge.

Reel's mind raced like the speed of light.

Racing, racing, the thoughts flew like electricity lighting a power grid.

Only a maniac on some sort of suicide mission would fail to stop at this point. Reel knew it in his gut. The guy was going for the bomb. He knew it.

But what if he were wrong? What if the guy was only a sailor scared out of his wits by some guy in a wetsuit who had just killed his captain?

Reel was the deadliest of warriors. He was a Navy SEAL. But SEAL or no SEAL, Americans didn't kill civilians. Not without good reason.

This was happening so fast. Reel bounded up the ladder, grabbing at the man's boot. It was just out of reach.

He heard the thunder of the boots of his fellow SEALs crossing the deck below.

The man reached the catwalk at the top of the ladder and rushed into the bridge. Reel ran in behind him.

It all turned slow motion now, almost like suspended animation in an underwater ballet.

Four men stood around the perimeter of the bridge. One had a gun. He swung it to point it at Reel.

Reel opened fire, bringing three of the men down. The fourth held his hands in the air. The man Reel was chasing raced across a bridge and lunged for an electronic box with a handle.

A detonation device!

The man's hands reached the handle.

Reel pulled the trigger, spraying bullets into the man's back. Blood oozed and splattered from numerous bulletholes in the back of his shirt.

The man slumped forward, his hands and body pushing down on the detonator.

"Dear Jesus, please help us!"

Flashing lights lit the detonator, yellow lights dancing up and down it like lights on a Christmas tree.

Reel squeezed his trigger and fired a wall of bullets into the detonator, then held his breath.

Leo Maloney and his men stormed down the ladder leading to the decks below. Their mission—to search each and every compartment of the ship. If nukes were on board, they would find them, or die trying.

Maloney was the first to hit the deck at the bottom of the ladder. He motioned Petty Officer McCants and two men to the left. Two other SEALs turned to the right. They jogged a few feet to the intersection of another passageway to their left. Maloney spotted two armed guards standing in front of a door.

"Put down your weapons!" Maloney ordered. The guards opened fire. The SEALs fired back, mowing the guards down to the deck.

"Let's go!" Maloney ordered. His men hurdled over the bleeding sailors and shot open the door.

A device was spread out on a long, six-legged aluminum table. Five large, stainless steel cylinders, each the size of a beach ball, were lined in a row along it, all connected with wires.

In an instant, blinking red and yellow lights lit on the device and flashing gadgets danced around the cylinders.

"It's arming itself!"

Maloney's stomach dropped from his body. He squeezed the trigger on his Uzi, firing every bullet left in his magazine at the device.

"McCants, shoot the thing!"

"Aye, sir!" Petty Officer McCants, in a blasting fury, emptied his Uzi submachinegun into the metal cylinders as well.

Electrical impulses, like tiny lightning bolts, shot back and forth between the cylinders.

"Lord in heaven, please put this thing out!"

The electrical charges continued for a moment, and then ...

"Sir, I think it's dying!" McCants announced.

"Keep praying, sailor!"

Lights on the left side of the device went dark. The lights on the right side followed.

Then, silence.

Leo Maloney allowed himself a long exhale.

A familiar voice came through his headset. "Maloney. McCants. Report."

Maloney caught McCants' eyes. The rugged SEAL's forehead was beaded with large sweat drops, but a small smile crept across his face.

Maloney pushed the communications button on his headset. "I think we found the bomb, sir. Recommend we get our nuclear guys in here, ASAP, but I think we've disabled it."

"Roger that, Maloney. Bravo, Sierra. We've found the detonator on the bridge. Suffice it to say, the detonator is also disabled."

Maloney gave a thumbs-up and a smile to the other SEAL team members, which ignited an eruption of cheers.

"Great news, sir. Awaiting your orders."

"Very well, you and McCants secure the bomb, and have the other SEALs fan out and secure the rest of the ship. We've got control of the bridge, and I'm going to notify USS *Charlotte*—mission accomplished."

CHAPTER 32

The Al Alamein
Gulf of Finland

Twenty-four hours later

They appeared like dragonflies buzzing the eastern sky—two drab-green military helicopters billowing slight trails of black smoke in their wake.

They grew larger and their rotary sound increased.

A quartet of fighter planes accompanied the choppers. One jet flew out front. One flew at the three o'clock position. The third flew at nine o'clock, and the fourth flew in the rear.

The lead fighter flew directly over the ship, sporting a red star under each of its wings. Two other fighters, not part of the quartet that accompanied the helicopters, were orbiting the ship, keeping a watchful eye on the happenings on deck. These were American F/A-18s from the aircraft carrier *George W. Bush.*

Just under the circling jet fighters, one of the helicopters broke off to the right, circling around on a course from whence it came.

The second chopper, also with a red star and Cyrillic writing on the side, feathered down, gently onto the deck of the ship, landing not far from the H-3 Sea King helicopter that was already sitting on the deck.

The Sea King was also olive-green, and had the word *MARINES* painted in white on the side along with the phrase *UNITED STATES OF AMERICA.*

The chopper with the red star shut down its engines. The door opened. Military officers in green moved a ladder into place. Several army and navy officers of the Russian Federation stepped down, followed by a man dressed in a blue suit whose appearance was all too familiar to Mack Williams.

The man, slim and handsome, strode swiftly across the deck and extended his hand.

"You suggested a shipboard summit, Mr. President?" President Vitaly Evtimov spoke in crisp English but showed no signs of warmth in his face. Mack remembered that his Russian counterpart had mastered English as an intelligence officer in the old KGB-turned-FSB.

"Churchill and Roosevelt once met on a battleship for a summit in the Atlantic during World War Two," Mack said.

"Somehow, a freighter does not have the same majesty as a battleship," the Russian president said. "Besides, I am sure you did not call me here to discuss history." Evtimov pulled his hand away. "Especially not the history of the English-speaking people."

Mack nodded and shot the Russian a smile. "I asked you to come, sir, because I believe we have something that may belong to you."

"I thought that may be the case," Evtimov said.

"Did you bring your nuclear team?"

"I have done as you have asked."

"Thank you," Mack said, silently praying for a thawing in the man's heart. "If you are ready, sir, my men will lead you and your team below deck. I will remain topside to give you privacy."

"Very well," Evtimov said. He disappeared below deck with a contingent of U.S. Navy SEALs and Russian nuclear scientists.

Thirty minutes later, the first Navy SEAL came back up from below decks. He was followed by several of the Russian scientists and military officers, followed by the president of the Russian Republic.

Evtimov walked toward Mack, his black eyes locked onto the American president. "It appears this freighter was headed to St. Petersburg, and that detonation of that device even from here would have destroyed the city."

"Yes, Mr. President," Mack said. "We are convinced of that. They were about to detonate the hydrogen bomb stored below."

Evtimov looked away, then turned and looked toward the east, toward Russia's most storied and beautiful city. A moment later, the Russian president looked back at Mack.

Evtimov extended his hand. "The Russian Republic extends its thanks to the United States Navy for its assistance in helping to recover property that was stolen from the Russian Army."

Mack clasped Evtimov's hand. "We also have a pilot who belongs to you, Mr. President. We would like to send him home."

The Russian nodded. "And I believe we have a submarine crew that may wish to go home before the onset of the harsh Russian winter. I will have my staff work out the arrangements."

"Will you come to Washington? I'd like to take you to dinner."

Evtimov smiled. "If you will meet me in St. Petersburg. After all, I believe your Navy helped us save it."

"Do you believe in God, Mr. President?"

Evtimov paused. "I believe that the State is God."

Mack smiled. "I encourage you to rethink your position."

"Oh? How so?" Finally, a smile, although slight, from the Russian.

"It was not the state that saved millions of your people. It was not even the United States Navy or the Navy SEALs."

"No?" A curious look from the Russian. "Then I suppose God did all this?"

"Only the hand of God, Mr. President. Only the hand of God allowed our SEALs to board this vessel and shoot through the connection wires to that bomb—even as its creator was pushing the detonator. Less than a quarter of a second, Mr. President. Our bullets riddled the connection lines to that bomb less than a quarter of a second before the terrorist that built it pushed the detonator. That bomb blown this close to St. Petersburg would've made Hiroshima look like an amusement park. This was all stopped only by the hand of God Almighty."

The Russian's smile broke into a grin, then morphed back into the cold face that had arrived on board over an hour ago. "I will keep that in mind."

"I will pray that you do."

Embassy of the United States of America
Moscow, Russia

The oppressive feeling of horror had subsided, and for that, Masha was grateful. Because of the events of the last twenty-four hours, she had found favor with the Americans, who now believed everything she had told them. A visa was being prepared allowing her to visit the United States. For her, this was a dream come true! She would be sure to find her missionary friends, the Allisons, and their seven children, who lived somewhere in North Carolina.

After that, somehow, someway, she would return to Russia and find Dima. No matter how long it took, she would put her faith in God that she and Dima would be together again, and that she would find a way to get him to America.

Even still, she could not shake her concern for the American sub commander whose torpedoes, ironically, had saved her life. From the guest lounge of the embassy, she found herself checking with CNN at least every half hour for updates. She checked her watch, and unmuted the television, where the American newsman Tom Miller appeared on the screen, along with the translated text.

"This is Tom Miller in Washington.

"In a surprising turn of events, the White House and the Kremlin have each issued statements within the last hour announcing that the majority of all American and Russian military forces in the Chechen-Turkish theater are withdrawing from the area.

"The White House confirms that the majority of United States forces built up in Turkey will be returned, including the heralded 82nd Airborne Division, and NATO military overflights over Georgia will cease immediately.

"At the same time, the Kremlin announced that all its divisions would commence withdrawal from Chechnya, pulling back to a point north of Volvograd.

"The Kremlin also announced that Russia was dismissing all charges against Commander Pete Miranda and his crew. The U.S. Navy confirmed that Miranda, the crew, along with defense counsel Lieutenant Commander Zack Brewer would be flown to Oceana Naval Air Station later in the week.

"Neither the U.S. nor Russia have offered a full explanation for all this, other than to say that an understanding was worked out between Presidents Williams and Evtimov at an undisclosed location, believed to be somewhere in Europe.

"The White House confirmed that such a meeting did occur, and that the world should be grateful to God that much was accomplished between the old rivals to promote peace.

"The Vatican praised today's developments, with Pope Benedict issuing a statement quoting from Jesus' Sermon on the Mount. Said the Pope, 'Blessed are the peacemakers, for they will be called sons of God.'"

Oceana Naval Air Station
Virginia Beach, Virginia

The large Air Force transport circled low over the vast expanse of the Oceana Naval Air Station. From his window seat just in front of the left wing, Pete Miranda looked down, where a large crowd of civilians, military, and press were gathered near the tarmac. The plane swooped down toward the runway, and after the thump of the plane's rubber wheels against the concrete, the hangars and grounded F-18 jet aircraft of the Oceana Naval Air Station rushed by in a blur.

Captain Ann Glover, the U.S. Naval Attaché to Russia, stood at the front of the plane.

"Gentlemen, remember our protocol for debarkation. Lieutenant Commander Brewer will exit first, and then we will pause for a few minutes and bring Commander Miranda and the crew off."

The thought of home.

Would he see them? He prayed silently that they would be there for him.

Captain Glover motioned Zack and Pete to the front of the plane. They stood by the door, as flight attendants threw open the door just behind the cockpit.

The warm Virginia breeze and sunlight filled the cabin, and a large crowd of several thousand stood in a huge semicircle behind a large yellow ribbon. The crowd was holding a large, long, red, white, and blue sign that stretched about thirty feet from left to right.

Welcome Home Commander Miranda and Crew of USS Honolulu.

Tears welled in Pete's eyes.

"Remember, no comments to the press!" Captain Glover said. "Okay, Zack, get out of here."

From the top of the plane, Pete watched as his JAG officer, dressed sharply in his service dress blue uniform, made his way down the steps. Zack reached the tarmac and shot a salute to two admirals at the base of the plane.

Pete recognized one of the admirals as Vice Admiral Charles McClure, commander of U.S. submarine forces in the Atlantic Fleet. McClure caught Pete's eye with a nod and a smile.

"Ladies and gentlemen," a voice resonated from a loudspeaker. "Please give a big Navy welcome home to Commander Pete Miranda, and the crew of the USS *Honolulu!*"

The crowd broke into cheering and applause. The Navy band broke into a brassy rendition of "Anchors Aweigh."

"That's your cue, Commander!" Captain Glover said.

Pete waved as he descended the stairway. The crowd cheered even harder. He reached the bottom, directing a salute to Vice Admiral McClure.

McClure returned the salute. "The Navy is proud of you, Pete. You did the right thing."

"Thank you, Admiral." Pete waited for the admiral to drop his salute.

"There's someone else who's proud of you too."

"Sir?"

The admiral motioned to the right of the human horseshoe.

A boy and a girl stepped from the edge of the crowd, then sprinted with open arms across the tarmac.

"Hannah! Coley!" Pete fell to his knees. His children fell into his arms.

"We missed you, Daddy!" Hannah hugged him and kissed him over and over again on the cheeks. "We were so scared you would never come back!"

"Can you stay with us for a while?" Coley's eyes flooded with tears.

"Come here, you two!" Pete wrapped them both under his arms and kissed them both on the head. "I'll never leave you again."

"You promise, Daddy?" Hannah looked up at him. At thirteen, she was becoming a lovely young lady. How had he let the time slip away?

"I promise, Hannah, that I'll never miss another one of your dance recitals." He looked at his son. "And Coley, I'll be at all your soccer games from here on."

"But how will you be at my games if the Navy sends you out in your submarine again?"

Pete stood, running his hands through his kids' hair. "Because tomorrow, kids, I'm putting in my papers. I'm retiring from the Navy."

"Really?" they exclaimed in unison.

"Really. We'll be together forever, kids." He kissed them once more. "Forever."

The Navy Justice Series

Defiance

Don Brown

From a murder in Paris to a courtroom in California to a terrorist camp in the Gobi Desert, Don Brown's follow-up to *Treason* and *Hostage* plunges into a suspense-filled journey of danger, duty, and hope.

The Commander's bodyguard is Shannon McGilverry, a crack NCIS agent assigned to protect Navy JAG Officer Zack Brewer. Zack is being hunted by terrorists, stalked by a psychopath, and is working his way through a perilous, politically charged trial. When another Navy JAG officer is murdered, it's clear that Zack is in harm's way.

As his bodyguard, Shannon must do more than protect Zack. She also must set aside her growing feelings for the brilliant attorney and investigate rumors that the love of his life, Diane Colcerninan, may still be alive. Zack finds himself in need of his faith more than ever as Navy SEALS launch a daring rescue attempt that has the potential to trigger World War III.

Softcover: 978-0-310-27213-7

Pick up a copy today at your favorite bookstore!

ZONDERVAN®
.com

The Navy Justice Series

Hostage

Don Brown

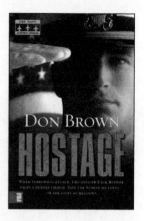

Zack Brewer faces a choice. It can prevent the next war. But it will cost the life of the person he loves the most.

JAG Officer Zack Brewer's prosecution of three terrorists posing as Navy chaplains was called the "court martial of the century" by the press. Now, with the limelight behind him, all Zack wants to do is forget. But the radical Islamic organization behind the chaplains has a long memory — and a thirst for revenge.

Now the Navy has a need for Zack that eclipses all else. When an unthinkable act of aggression brings Israel and its Arab neighbors to the brink of war, Zack and co-counsel Diane Colcernian are called to the case of a lifetime. As leading nations focus their gaze upon these two, other eyes are watching as well.

Zack and Diane are in harm's way.

A kidnapping, an ultimatum ... and suddenly, Zack faces an impossible choice. If he loses this case, the world could explode into war. If he wins, his partner — the woman he loves — will die.

And Zack himself may not survive to make the decision.

Softcover: 978-0-310-25934-3

Pick up a copy today at your favorite bookstore!

The Navy Justice Series

Treason

Don Brown

The stakes are high … and the entire world is waiting for the verdict.

The Navy has uncovered a group of radical Islamic clerics who have infiltrated the Navy Chaplain Corps, inciting sailors and marines to acts of terrorism. And Lieutenant Zack Brewer has been chosen to prosecute them for treason and murder.

Only three years out of law school, Zack has already made a name for himself, winning the coveted Navy Commendation medal. Just coming off a high-profile win, this case will challenge the very core of Zack's skills and his Christian beliefs — beliefs that could cost him the case and his career.

With Diane Colcernian, his staunchest rival, as assistant prosecutor, Zack takes on internationally acclaimed criminal defense lawyer Wells Levinson. And when Zack and Diane finally agree to put aside their animosity, it causes more problems than they realize.

Softcover: 978-0-310-25933-6

Pick up a copy today at your favorite bookstore!

Share Your Thoughts

With the Author: Your comments will be forwarded to
the author when you send them to *zauthor@zondervan.com*.

With Zondervan: Submit your review of this book
by writing to *zreview@zondervan.com*.

Free Online Resources at
www.zondervan.com/hello

 Zondervan AuthorTracker: Be notified whenever your
favorite authors publish new books, go on tour, or post
an update about what's happening in their lives.

 Daily Bible Verses and Devotions: Enrich your life
with daily Bible verses or devotions that help you start
every morning focused on God.

 Free Email Publications: Sign up for newsletters on
fiction, Christian living, church ministry, parenting, and
more.

 Zondervan Bible Search: Find and compare
Bible passages in a variety of translations at
www.zondervanbiblesearch.com.

 Other Benefits: Register yourself to receive online
benefits like coupons and special offers, or to participate
in research.